Also by Ana Huang

KINGS OF SIN SERIES

A series of interconnected standalones

King of Wrath

King of Pride

King of Greed

King of Sloth

TWISTED SERIES

A series of interconnected standalones

Twisted Love

Twisted Games

Twisted Hate

Twisted Lies

IF LOVE SERIES

If We Ever Meet Again (Duet Book 1)

If the Sun Never Sets (Duet Book 2)

If Love Had a Price (Standalone)

If We Were Perfect (Standalone)

KING OF WRATH

ANA HUANG

Bloom books

To fighting for who you love—including yourself

Cover design by Cat/TRC Designs
Cover images by Rashevskyi Viacheslav/Shutterstock, Dmitry Nesterov/Shutterstock, rabbit75/DepositPhotos, doozie/DepositPhotos, Masha Kotscur/DepositPhotos
Internal images © akvlv/iStockphoto; Babich Alexander/Shutterstock

Published by Bloom Books, an imprint of Sourcebooks
P.O. Box 4410, Naperville, Illinois 60567-4410
(630) 961-3900
sourcebooks.com

Originally self-published in 2022 by Ana Huang.

Cataloging-in-Publication data is on file with the Library of Congress.

Printed and bound in the United States of America.
LSC 21

Playlist

"Empire State of Mind"—Jay-Z feat. Alicia Keys

"Luxurious"—Gwen Stefani

"Red"—Taylor Swift

"Teeth"—5 Seconds of Summer

"Partition"—Beyoncé

"Pretty Boy"—Cavale

"All Mine"—PLAzA

"Can't Help Falling in Love"—Elvis Presley

"We Found Love"—Rihanna

"Counting Stars"—One Republic

"The Heart Wants What It Wants"—Selena Gomez

"Stay"—Rihanna

Content Warning

This story contains explicit sexual content, profanity, mild violence, and topics that may be sensitive to some readers.

CHAPTER 1

Vivian

"I CAN'T BELIEVE HE'S HERE. HE NEVER COMES TO these things unless it's hosted by a friend."

"Did you see he bumped Arno Reinhart down a spot on the *Forbes* billionaires list? Poor Arnie nearly had a meltdown in the middle of Jean-Georges when he found out."

The whispers started halfway through the Frederick Wildlife Trust's annual fundraiser for endangered animals.

This year, the small, sand-colored piping plover was the alleged star of the show, but none of the gala's two hundred guests were discussing the bird's welfare over their Veuve Clicquot and caviar cannoli.

"I heard his family's villa in Lake Como is undergoing a one-*hundred*-million dollar renovation. The place is centuries old, so I suppose it's time."

Each whisper grew in intensity, accompanied by furtive glances and the occasional dreamy sigh.

I didn't turn to see who had the normally cool-as-ice members of Manhattan high society in such a tizzy. I didn't really care. I was too focused on a certain department store heiress as she tottered toward the swag table in sky-high heels. She quickly glanced around before swiping one of the personalized gift bags and dropping it in her purse.

The minute she walked off, I spoke into my earpiece. "Shannon, Code Pink at the swag table. Find out whose bag she took and replace it."

Tonight's bags each contained over eight thousand dollars' worth of swag, but it was easier to fold the cost into the event budget than confront the Denman's heiress.

My assistant groaned over the line. "Tilly Denman *again*? Doesn't she have enough money to buy everything on that table *and* have millions left over?"

"Yes, but it's not about the money for her. It's the adrenaline rush," I said. "Go. I'll order banana pudding from Magnolia Bakery tomorrow to make up for the strenuous task of replacing the gift bag. And for God's sake, find out where Penelope is. She's supposed to be manning the gift station."

"Ha ha," Shannon said, obviously picking up on my sarcasm. "Fine. I'll check on the gift bags and Penelope, but I expect a *big* tub of banana pudding tomorrow."

I laughed and shook my head as the line cut off.

While she took care of the gift bag situation, I circled the room and kept an eye out for other fires, large or small.

When I first went into business, it felt weird working events I would otherwise be invited to as a guest. But I'd gotten used to it over the years, and the income allowed me a small degree of independence from my parents.

It wasn't part of my trust fund, nor was it my inheritance. It was money I'd earned, fair and square, as a luxury event planner in Manhattan.

I loved the challenge of creating beautiful events from scratch, and wealthy people loved beautiful things. It was a win-win.

I was double-checking the sound setup for the keynote speech later that night when Shannon rushed toward me. "Vivian! You didn't tell me he was here!" she hissed.

"Who?"

"*Dante Russo.*"

All thoughts of swag bags and sound checks flew out of my head.

I jerked my gaze to Shannon's, taking in her bright eyes and flushed cheeks.

"Dante Russo?" My heart thudded for no apparent reason. "But he didn't RSVP yes."

"Well, the rules of RSVPs don't apply to him." She practically vibrated with excitement. "I can't believe he showed up. People will be talking about this for *weeks*."

The earlier whispers suddenly made sense.

Dante Russo, the enigmatic CEO of the luxury goods conglomerate the Russo Group, rarely attended public events that weren't hosted by himself, one of his close friends, or one of his important business associates. The Frederick Wildlife Trust didn't fall under any of those categories.

He was also one of the wealthiest and therefore most watched men in New York.

Shannon was right. People would be buzzing about his attendance for weeks, if not months.

"Good," I said, trying to rein in my suddenly runaway heartbeat. "Maybe it'll bring more awareness to the piping plover issue."

She rolled her eyes. "Vivian, no one cares—" She stopped, looked around, and lowered her voice. "*No one actually cares* about the piping plovers. I mean, I'm sad they're endangered, but let's be honest. The people are here for the scene only."

Once again, she was right. Still, no matter their reason for attending, the guests were raising money for a good cause, and the events kept my business running.

"The real topic of the night," Shannon said, "is how good Dante looks. I've never seen a man fill out a tuxedo so well."

"You have a boyfriend, Shan."

"So? We're allowed to appreciate other people's beauty."

"Yes, well, I think you've *appreciated* enough. We're here to work, not ogle the guests." I gently pushed her toward the dessert table. "Can you bring out more Viennese tartlets? We're running low."

"Buzzkill," she grumbled, but she did as I said.

I tried to refocus on the sound setup, but I couldn't resist scanning the room for the surprise guest of the night. My gaze skimmed past the DJ and the 3D piping plover display and rested on the crowd by the entrance.

It was so thick I couldn't see beyond the outer edges, but I'd bet my entire bank account Dante was the center of their attention.

My suspicions were confirmed when the crowd shifted briefly to reveal a glimpse of dark hair and broad shoulders.

A rush of awareness ran the length of my spine.

Dante and I belonged to tangential social circles, but we'd never officially met. From what I'd heard of his reputation, I was happy keeping it that way.

Still, his presence was magnetic, and I felt the pull of it all the way across the room.

An insistent buzz against my hip washed away the tingles coating my skin and drew my attention away from Dante's fan club. My stomach sank when I fished my personal cell out of my purse and saw who was calling.

I shouldn't take personal calls in the middle of a work event, but one simply didn't ignore a summons from Francis Lau.

I double-checked to make sure there were no emergencies requiring my immediate attention before I slipped into the nearest restroom.

"Hello, Father." The formal greeting rolled off my tongue easily after almost twenty years of practice.

I used to call him Dad, but after Lau Jewels took off and we moved out of our cramped two-bedroom into a Beacon Hill mansion, he insisted on being called Father instead. Apparently, it sounded more "sophisticated" and "upper class."

"Where are you?" His deep voice rumbled over the line. "Why is it so echoey?"

"I'm at work. I snuck into a bathroom to take your call." I leaned my hip against the counter and felt compelled to add, "It's a fundraiser for the endangered piping plover."

I smiled at his heavy sigh. My father had little patience for the obscure causes people used as an excuse to party, though he attended the events and donated anyway. It was the proper thing to do.

"Every day, I learn about a new endangered animal," he grumbled. "Your mother is on a fundraising committee for some fish or other, like we don't eat seafood every week."

My mother, formerly an aesthetician, was now a professional socialite and charity committee member.

"Since you're at work, I'll keep this short," my father said. "We'd like you to join us for dinner on Friday night. We have important news."

Despite his wording, it wasn't a request.

My smile faded. "*This* Friday night?" It was Tuesday, and I lived in New York while my parents lived in Boston.

It was a last-minute request even by their standards.

"Yes." My father didn't elaborate. "Dinner is at seven sharp. Don't be late." He hung up.

My phone stayed frozen on my ear for an extra beat before I removed it. It slipped against my clammy palm and almost clattered to the floor before I shoved it back into my purse.

It was funny how one sentence could send me into an anxiety spiral.

We have important news.

Did something happen with the company? Was someone sick or dying? Were my parents selling their house and moving to New York like they'd once threatened to do?

My mind raced through a thousand questions and possibilities.

I didn't have an answer, but I knew one thing.

An emergency summons to the Lau manor never boded well.

CHAPTER 2

MY PARENTS' LIVING ROOM LOOKED LIKE SOMETHING out of an *Architectural Digest* spread. Tufted settees sat at right angles to carved wood tables; porcelain tea sets jostled for space next to priceless tchotchkes. Even the air smelled cold and impersonal, like generically expensive freshener.

Some people had homes; my parents had a showpiece.

"Your skin looks dull." My mother examined me with a critical eye. "Have you been keeping up with your monthly facials?"

She sat across from me, her own skin glowing with pearlescent luminosity.

"Yes, Mother." My cheeks ached from the forced politeness of my smile.

I'd stepped foot in my childhood home ten minutes ago, and I'd already been criticized for my hair (too messy), my nails (too long), and now, my complexion.

Just another night at the Lau manor.

"Good. Remember, you can't let yourself go," my mother said. "You're not married yet."

I held back a sigh. *Here we go again.*

Despite my thriving career in Manhattan, where the event planning market was more cutthroat than a designer sample sale, my parents were fixated on my lack of a boyfriend and, therefore, lack of marital prospects.

They tolerated my work because it was no longer fashionable for heiresses to do nothing, but they were *salivating* for a son-in-law, one who could increase their foothold in the circles of the old money elite.

We were rich, but we would never be old money. Not in this generation.

"I'm still young," I said patiently. "I have plenty of time to meet someone."

I was only twenty-eight, but my parents acted like I would shrivel into the Crypt Keeper the second midnight struck on my thirtieth birthday.

"You're almost thirty," my mother countered. "You're not getting any younger, and you *have* to start thinking about marriage and kids. The longer you wait, the smaller the dating pool becomes."

"I *am* thinking about it." *Thinking about the year of freedom I have left before I'm forced to marry a banker with a numeral after his last name.* "As for getting younger, that's what Botox and plastic surgery are for."

If my sister were here, she would've laughed. Since she wasn't, my joke fell flatter than a poorly baked soufflé.

My mother's lips thinned.

Beside her, my father's thick, gray-tipped brows formed a stern V over the bridge of his nose.

Sixty years old, spry, and fit, Francis Lau looked every inch the self-made CEO. He'd expanded Lau Jewels from a small, family-run shop to a multinational behemoth over three decades, and a silent stare from him was enough to make me shrink back against the couch cushions.

"Every time we bring up marriage, you make a joke." His tone seeped with disapproval. "Marriage is *not* a joke, Vivian. It's an important matter for our family. Look at your sister. Thanks to her, we're now connected to the royal family of Eldorra."

I bit my tongue so hard the taste of copper filled my mouth.

My sister had married an Eldorran earl who was a second cousin twice removed from the queen. Our "connection" to the small European kingdom's royal family was a stretch, but in my father's eyes, an aristocratic title was an aristocratic title.

"I know it's not a joke," I said, reaching for my tea. I needed something to do with my hands. "But it's also not something I need to think about *right now*. I'm dating. Exploring my prospects. There are plenty of single men in New York. I just have to find the right one."

I left out the caveat: there were plenty of single men in New York, but the pool of single, straight, non-douchey, non-flaky, non-disturbingly eccentric men was much smaller.

My last date tried to rope me into a séance to contact his dead mother so she could "meet me and give her approval." Needless to say, I never saw him again.

But my parents didn't need to know that. As far as they were concerned, I was dating handsome trust fund scions left and right.

"We've given you plenty of time to find a proper match these past two years." My father sounded unimpressed by my spiel. "You haven't had a single serious boyfriend since your last... *relationship*. It's clear you don't feel the same urgency we do, which is why I took matters into my own hands."

My tea froze halfway to my lips. "Meaning?"

I thought the important news he'd alluded to had to do with my sister or the company. But what if...

My blood iced.

No. It can't be.

"Meaning I've secured a suitable match for you." My father dropped the bombshell with little to no warning or visible emotion. "It took quite a bit of work on my end, but the arrangement has been finalized."

I've secured a suitable match for you.

The fragments from his declaration blasted through my chest and nearly cleaved my outward composure in half.

My teacup clattered back onto its plate, earning me a frown from my mother.

For once, I was too busy processing to worry about her disapproval.

Arranged marriages were common practice in our world of big business and power plays, where marriages weren't love matches; they were alliances. My parents married my sister off for a title, and I'd known my turn was coming. I just hadn't expected it to come so…so *soon*.

A bitter cocktail of shock, dread, and horror sluiced down my throat. I was expected to enter a lifetime contract after "quite a bit of work" on my father's end.

Just what every woman wants to hear.

"We've let you drag your feet too long, and this match will be enormously beneficial for us," my father continued. "I'm sure you'll agree once you meet him at dinner."

The cocktail turned into poison and ate away at my insides.

"Dinner? As in *tonight's* dinner?" My voice sounded distant and strange, as if I was hearing it in a bad dream. "Why didn't you tell me earlier?"

Being ambushed with news of an arranged marriage match was bad enough. Meeting my future fiancé with zero preparation was a hundred times worse.

No wonder my mother was being even more critical than normal. She was expecting her future son-in-law as a guest.

My stomach lurched, and the possibility of expelling its contents all over my mother's prized Persian rug inched closer to reality.

Everything was happening too fast. The dinner summons, the news of my engagement, the impending meeting—my mind whirled from trying to keep up.

"He didn't confirm until today due to...scheduling complications." My father smoothed a hand over his shirt. "You'll have to meet him eventually. It doesn't matter whether it's tonight, a week, or a month from now."

Actually, it does *matter. There's a difference between being mentally prepared to meet my fiancé and having him thrown in my face with no warning.*

My retort simmered on low, destined never to reach a full boil. Talking back was strictly verboten in the Lau household. I was beholden to its rules even as an adult, and disobedience was always met with swift punishment and sharp words.

"We want to move things along as quickly as possible," my mother jumped in. "It takes time to plan a proper wedding, and your fiancé is, er, particular about the details."

Funny how she was already calling him my fiancé when I hadn't met the man yet.

"*Mode de Vie* named him one of the world's most eligible bachelors under forty last year. Rich, handsome, powerful. Honestly, your father outdid himself." My mother patted my father's arm, her face glowing.

I hadn't seen her this animated since she scored a seat on the Boston Society wine auction's planning committee last year.

"That's...great." My smile wobbled from the effort of keeping itself intact.

At least my match probably had all his teeth. I wouldn't have put it past my parents to marry me off to some decrepit billionaire on his deathbed. Money and status came first; everything else came a distant second.

I took a deep breath and willed my mind not to spiral down *that* particular path.

Get it together, Viv.

As upset as I was at my parents for springing this on me, I could freak out later, *after* I got through the evening. It wasn't like I could say no to the match. If I did, my parents would disown me.

Plus, my future husband—my stomach lurched again—would be here any minute, and I couldn't make a scene.

I wiped a palm against my thigh. My head felt dizzy, but I clung to the mask I always wore at home. *Cool. Calm. Respectable.*

"So." I swallowed my bile and forced a light tone. "Does Mr. Perfect have a name, or is he known only by his net worth?"

I didn't remember everyone who'd been on *Mode de Vie*'s list, but the people I *did* remember didn't inspire much confidence. If he—

"Net worth by strangers. Name by select friends and family."

My spine stiffened at the deep, unexpected voice behind me. It was so close I could *feel* the rumble of words against my back. They slid over me like sun-warmed honey—rich and sensual, with a faint Italian accent that made every nerve ending tingle with pleasure.

Heat slipped beneath my skin.

"Ah, there you are." My father rose, a strangely triumphant gleam in his eyes. "Thank you for coming at such short notice."

"How could I pass up the opportunity to meet your lovely daughter?"

A hint of mockery tainted the word *lovely* and instantly washed away any budding attraction I had to a voice, of all things.

Ice doused the heat in my veins.

So much for Mr. Perfect.

I'd learned to trust my gut when it came to people, and my gut told me the owner of the voice was as thrilled about the dinner as I was.

"Vivian, say hello to our guest." If my mother beamed any harder, her face would split in half.

I half expected her to prop her cheek on her hand and sigh dreamily like a schoolgirl with a crush.

I pushed the disturbing image out of my mind before I lifted my chin.

Stood.

Turned.

And all the air whooshed out of my lungs.

Thick black hair. Olive skin. A slightly crooked nose that enhanced rather than detracted from his ruggedly masculine charm.

My future husband was devastation poured into a suit. Not handsome by conventional means, but so powerful and compelling his presence swallowed every molecule of oxygen in the room like a black hole consuming a newborn star.

There were generically good-looking men, and there was *him*.

And unlike his voice, his face was eminently recognizable.

My heart sank beneath the weight of my shock.

Impossible. There was no way he was my arranged fiancé. This had to be a joke.

"Vivian." My mother disguised her rebuke as my name.

Right. Dinner. Fiancé. Meeting.

I shook myself out of my stupor and summoned a strained but polite smile. "Vivian Lau. It's a pleasure to meet you."

I held out my hand.

A beat passed before he took it. Warm strength engulfed my palm and sent a jolt of electricity up my arm.

"So I gathered from the multiple times your mother said your name." The laziness of his drawl played off the observation as a joke; the hardness of his eyes told me it was anything but. "Dante Russo. The pleasure is all mine."

There was the mockery again, subtle but cutting.

Dante Russo.

CEO of the Russo Group, Fortune 500 legend, and the man who'd created such a buzz at the Frederick Wildlife Trust gala three nights ago. He wasn't just an eligible bachelor; he was *the* bachelor. The elusive billionaire every woman wanted and no one could get.

He was thirty-six years old, famously married to his work, and up until now showed no intention of giving up his bachelor lifestyle.

Why then would Dante Russo of all people agree to an arranged marriage?

"I would introduce myself by my net worth," he said. "But it would be impolite to categorize you as a stranger given the purpose of tonight's dinner."

His smile didn't contain an ounce of warmth.

My cheeks heated at the reminder he'd overheard my joke. It hadn't been malicious, but discussing other people's money was considered uncouth even though everyone secretly did it.

"That's very considerate of you." My cool reply masked my embarrassment. "Don't worry, Mr. Russo. If I wanted to know your net worth, I could google it. I'm sure the information is as readily available as the tales of your legendary charm."

A glint sparked in his eyes, but he didn't take my bait. Instead, our gazes held for a charged moment before he slid his palm out of mine and swept a clinical, detached gaze over my body.

My hand tingled with warmth, but everywhere else, coolness touched my skin like the indifference of a god faced with a mortal.

I stiffened again beneath Dante's scrutiny, suddenly hyper-aware of my Cecelia Lau–approved tweed skirt suit, pearl studs, and low-heeled pumps. I'd even swapped out my favorite red lipstick in favor of the neutral color she preferred. This was my standard uniform for visiting my parents, and judging by the way Dante's lips thinned, he was less than impressed.

A mix of unease and irritation twisted my stomach when those dark, unforgiving eyes found mine again.

We'd exchanged only a handful of words, yet I already knew two things with gut certainty.

One, Dante was going to be my fiancé.

Two, we might kill each other before we ever made it to the altar.

CHAPTER 3

Dante

"THE WEDDING WILL TAKE PLACE IN SIX MONTHS," Francis said. "That's enough time to plan a proper celebration without dragging things out too long. However, public announcements should go out right away." He smiled, showing no hint of the snake coiled beneath his genial tone and expression.

We'd adjourned to the dining room soon after my arrival, and the conversation had immediately veered into wedding planning territory.

Distaste curled through me. Of *course* he'd want the world to know his daughter was getting hitched to a Russo as soon as possible.

Men like Francis would do anything to increase their social standing, including finding the balls to blackmail me in *my* office two weeks ago, right on the heels of my grandfather's death.

Fury reignited in my chest. If I had my way, he wouldn't have left New York with his bones intact. Unfortunately, my hands were tied, metaphorically speaking, and until I found a way to *un*tie them, I had to play nice.

For the most part.

"No, it won't." I wrapped my fingers around the stem of my wineglass and imagined it was Francis's neck I was strangling instead. "No one will believe I'm marrying someone with such short notice unless something was wrong."

For example, your daughter is pregnant, and this is a shotgun wedding. The insinuation had everyone shifting in their seats while I kept my face blank and my voice bored.

Restraint didn't come naturally to me. If I didn't like someone, I made damn sure they knew it, but extraordinary circumstances called for extraordinary measures.

Francis's mouth thinned. "Then what would you suggest?"

"A year is a more reasonable time frame."

Never was better, but sadly, it wasn't an option. A year would do. It was short enough that Francis would agree to it and long enough for me to find and destroy the blackmail evidence. Hopefully.

"Announcements should also go out later," I said. "A month gives us time to craft a proper story, considering your daughter and I have never so much as been seen in public together before."

"We don't need a month to come up with a story," he snapped.

Although arranged marriages were common in high society, the involved parties went to great lengths to conceal the true reason behind the nuptials. Acknowledging one's family joined with another simply for status reasons was considered vulgar.

"Two weeks," he said. "We'll announce the weekend Vivian moves into your house."

My jaw tensed. Beside me, Vivian stiffened, clearly caught off guard by the revelation she'd have to move in before the wedding. It was one of Francis's stipulations for keeping his mouth shut, and I was already dreading it. I hated people invading my personal space.

"I'm sure your family would like the announcements to go out sooner rather than later as well," Francis continued, placing a soft emphasis on the word *family*. "Don't you agree?"

I held his stare until he shifted and looked away.

"Two weeks it is."

The announcement date didn't matter. I'd simply wanted to make the planning as difficult for him as possible.

What mattered was the wedding date.

One year.

One year to destroy the photos and break the engagement. It would be a huge scandal, but my reputation could take the hit. The Laus' couldn't.

For the first time that night, I smiled.

Francis shifted again and cleared his throat. "Excellent. We'll work together to draft—"

"I'll draft it. Next."

I ignored his glare and took another sip of merlot.

The conversation devolved into a mind-numbing rundown of guest invites, flowers, and a million other things I didn't give a shit about.

Restless anger churned beneath my skin as I tuned Francis and his wife out.

Instead of working on the Santeri deal or relaxing at the Valhalla Club, I was stuck entertaining their bullshit on a Friday night.

Beside me, Vivian ate quietly, appearing lost in thought.

After several minutes of strained silence, she finally spoke. "How was your flight?"

"Fine."

"I appreciate you taking the time to fly in when we could've met in New York. I know you must be busy."

I cut a piece of veal and brought it to my mouth.

Vivian's stare burned a hole in my cheek while I chewed leisurely.

"I also heard the more zeroes one has in their bank account, the fewer words they're capable of speaking." Her deceptively pleasant voice could've sliced through butter. "You're proving the rumor correct."

"I thought a society heiress like yourself would know better than to discuss money in polite company."

"The key word is polite."

A ghost of a smile flickered over my mouth.

Under normal circumstances, I might've liked Vivian. She was beautiful and surprisingly witty, with intelligent brown eyes and the type of naturally refined bone structure no amount of money could buy. But with her pearls and Chanel tweed, she looked like a carbon copy of her mother and every other uptight heiress who only cared about their social status.

Plus, she was Francis's daughter. It wasn't her fault she was born to the bastard, but I didn't give a damn. No degree of beauty could erase that stain on her record.

"It's not *polite* to speak to a guest that way," I mocked softly. I reached for the salt. My sleeve grazed her arm, and she visibly tensed. "What would your parents say?"

I'd already clocked Vivian's hang-ups less than an hour into our acquaintance. Perfectionism, nonconfrontation, a desperate need for her parents' approval.

Boring, boring, boring.

Her eyes narrowed. "They'd say *guests* should adhere to social niceties as much as the host, including making an effort to hold a polite conversation."

"Yeah? Do social niceties include dressing like you stepped out of a Fifth Avenue Stepford wives factory?" I flicked a gaze over her suit and pearls.

I didn't give a shit if people like Cecelia wore such an outfit, but Vivian looked as out of place in the dowdy clothing as a diamond in a burlap sack. It pissed me off for no good reason.

"No, but they certainly *don't* include ruining a nice dinner with discourtesy," Vivian said coolly. "You should buy a nice set of manners to match your suit, Mr. Russo. As a luxury goods CEO, you know better than anyone how one ugly accessory can ruin an outfit."

Another smile, still faint but more concrete.

Not so boring after all.

However, the embers of my amusement hissed into a smoky death when her mother inserted herself into our conversation.

"Dante, is it true all Russos get married at the family estate in Lake Como? I hear renovations will be finished by next summer before the wedding."

My smile vanished as my muscles tightened at the reminder.

I turned away from Vivian to face Cecelia's eager expression.

"Yes," I said, my tone clipped. "All Russo weddings have taken place at Villa Serafina since the eighteenth century."

My many-times great grandfather had built the villa and named it after his wife. My family could trace its roots to Sicily, but they later migrated to Venice and built a fortune trading luxury textiles. By the time the Venice trading boom ended, they'd diversified enough to hold on to their riches, which they used to acquire property throughout Europe.

Now, centuries later, my modern relatives were scattered across the world—New York, Rome, Switzerland, Paris—but Villa Serafina remained the most beloved of all the family estates. I would rather drown myself in the Mediterranean than tarnish it with a farce of a wedding.

My anger came roaring back.

"Wonderful!" Cecelia beamed. "Oh, I'm so thrilled you'll

be part of the family soon. You and Vivian are a *perfect* match. You know, she speaks six languages, plays the piano and violin, and—"

"Excuse me." I pushed my chair back, cutting Cecelia off midsentence. The legs scraped against the floor with a satisfyingly harsh screech. "Nature calls."

Silence thudded in the wake of my shocking rudeness.

I didn't wait for anyone to speak before I walked out and left a fuming Francis, flustered Cecelia, and red-faced Vivian in the dining room.

My anger remained a restless burn beneath my skin, but it cooled with each step farther away from them.

In the past, I'd exacted retribution on those who crossed me immediately. Fuck revenge being a dish best served cold; my motto had always been strike fast, strike hard, and strike true.

The world moved too quickly for me not to move along with it. I took care of the problem harshly enough to ensure there wouldn't be any future problems, and I moved on.

Resolving the Lau situation, on the other hand, required patience. It was a virtue I wasn't familiar with, and it stretched tight over me like an ill-fitting suit.

The echo of my footsteps faded as marble floors gave way to carpet. I'd visited enough mansions with similar layouts to guess where the restroom was, but I bypassed it in favor of the solid mahogany door at the end of the hall.

A twist of the knob revealed an office styled after an English library. Wood paneling, overstuffed leather furniture, forest-green accents.

Francis's inner sanctum.

At least it wasn't overly festooned with gold like the rest of the house. My eyes were starting to bleed from the eyesore.

I left the door open and walked to the desk, my pace unhurried.

If Francis had a problem with me snooping through his office, he was welcome to confront me.

He wasn't stupid enough to leave the photos lying around behind an unlocked door when he knew I'd be here tonight. Even if the photos *were* here, he'd have backups stashed elsewhere.

I settled into his chair, plucked a Cuban cigar from the box in his drawer, and lit it while I examined the room. My anger gave way to calculation.

The dark computer screen tempted me, but I left the hacking to Christian, who was already tracking down digital copies of the photos. I moved on to a framed picture of Francis and his family in the Hamptons. Research told me they had a summer house in Bridgehampton, and I'd bet my newly acquired Renoir he kept at least one set of evidence there.

Where else...

"What are you doing?"

The smoke from my cigar obscured Vivian's face, but her disapproval came through loud and clear.

That was fast. I'd expected at least five more minutes before her parents forced her to come after me.

"Enjoying a smoke break." I took another lazy drag.

I didn't touch cigarettes, but I indulged in the occasional Cohiba. At least Francis had good taste in tobacco.

"In my father's office?"

"Obviously." Dark satisfaction filled my chest when the smoke dissolved to reveal Vivian's frown.

Finally. Some visible emotion.

I'd started to think I was stuck with a robot for the remainder of our ridiculous engagement.

She crossed the room, plucked the cigar from my hand, and dropped it in the half-empty glass of water on the desk without taking her eyes off mine.

"I understand you're probably used to doing whatever you want, but it's exceedingly rude to sneak off during a dinner party and smoke in your host's office." Tension lined her elegant features. "Please rejoin us in the dining room. Your food is getting cold."

"That's my problem, not yours." I leaned back. "Why don't you join me for a break? I promise it'll be more enjoyable than your mother's hand wringing over floral arrangements."

"Based on our interactions so far, I doubt it," she snapped.

I watched, amused, as she took a deep breath and released it in one long, controlled exhale.

"I don't understand why you're here," Vivian said, her voice calmer. "You're clearly unhappy about the arrangement, you don't need the money or connection with my family, and you can have any woman you want."

"Can I?" I drawled. "What if I want you?"

Her fingers curled into loose fists. "You don't."

"You give yourself too little credit." I rose and circled the desk until I stood close enough to see the pulse fluttering in her neck. How much faster would it beat if I wrapped her hair around my fist and pulled her head back? If I kissed her until her mouth bruised and hiked up her skirt until she begged me to fuck her?

Heat ran to my groin. I wasn't interested in actually fucking her, but she was so prim and proper she begged for corruption.

The silence was deafening as I lifted my hand and grazed my thumb over her bottom lip. Vivian's breathing shallowed, but she didn't move away. She stared at me, eyes full of defiance as I took my time exploring the lush curve of her mouth. It was full, soft, and disturbingly tempting compared to the stiff formality of the rest of her appearance.

"You're a beautiful woman," I said lazily. "Perhaps I saw you at an event and was so enamored I asked your father for your hand in marriage."

"Somehow, I doubt that's what happened." Her breath drifted over my skin. "What kind of deal did you make with my father?"

The reminder of the deal killed the sensuality of the moment as quickly as it came.

My thumb paused on the center of her bottom lip before I dropped my hand with a silent curse. My skin tingled with heat from the memory of her softness.

I hated Francis for the blackmail, but I loathed Vivian for being his pawn. So what the fuck was I doing, toying with her in his office?

"You should ask your dear father that question." My smile cut across my face, cruel and devoid of humor as I regathered my composure. "The details don't matter. Just know that if I had any other choice, I damn well wouldn't be getting married. But business is business, and you..." I shrugged. "You're simply part of the deal."

Vivian didn't know about her father's manipulation. Francis had warned me not to tell her, not that I would've anyway. The fewer people who knew about the blackmail, the better.

He'd uncovered one of my few weak spots, and I'd be damned if I broadcast it to the world.

Vivian's eyes glowed with anger. "You're an asshole."

"Yes, I am. Better get used to it, *mia cara*, because I'm also your future husband. Now, if you'll excuse me." I straightened my jacket with deliberate care. "I have to return to dinner. As you said earlier, my food's getting cold."

I brushed past her, reveling in the delicious taste of her indignation.

One day, she'd get her unspoken wish and wake up to a broken engagement. Until then, I'd bide my time and play along because Francis's ultimatum had been clear.

Marry Vivian, or my brother dies.

CHAPTER 4

Dante

NEITHER FRANCIS NOR CECELIA SAID A WORD ABOUT my long absence from the dinner table Friday night. Vivian didn't mention our little chat in the office, and I returned to New York dissatisfied and on edge.

I could've burned the Lau mansion to the ground with one flick of my lighter.

Unfortunately, doing so would've brought the authorities straight to my doorstep. Arson was bad for business, and I'd never stooped to murder...yet. But certain people tempted me to cross the line every day, one of whom I happened to share blood with.

"What's the emergency?" Luca slouched in the chair opposite mine with a yawn. "I just got off the plane. Give a guy time to sleep."

"According to the society pages, you haven't slept for the past month."

Instead, he'd been partying it up around the world. Mykonos one day, Ibiza the next. His last stop had been Monaco, where he'd lost fifty grand at the poker table.

"Exactly." He yawned again. "That's why I need sleep."

My jaw hardened.

Luca was five years younger than me, yet he acted like he was twenty-one instead of thirty-one. If he weren't my brother, I would've cut him off without hesitation, *especially* given the shit show I found myself in thanks to him.

"Aren't you curious why I called you here?"

Luca shrugged, oblivious to the storm brewing beneath my calm. "You missed your baby bro?"

"Not quite." I retrieved a manila folder from my drawer and placed it on the desk between us. "Open it."

He gave me a strange look but obliged. I kept my gaze trained on his face as he flipped through the photos, slowly at first, then faster as the panic set in.

Grim satisfaction passed through me when he finally looked up, his face several shades paler than when he'd entered. At least he understood what was at stake.

"Do you know who the woman in those photos is?" I asked.

Luca's throat bobbed with a hard swallow.

"Maria Romano." I tapped the photo on the top of the pile. "Niece of Mafia don Gabriele Romano. Twenty-seven years old, widowed, and the apple of her uncle's eye. The name should ring a bell, considering you were fucking her before you left for Europe, as evidenced by these photos."

My brother's hands fisted. "How did you—"

"That's not the right question, Luca. The right question is what kind of casket you'd like at your funeral, because that's what I'll have to fucking plan if Romano *ever* finds out about this!"

The storm broke halfway through my sentence, fueled by weeks' worth of pent-up fury and frustration.

Luca shrank back in his chair as I shoved my chair back and stood, my body vibrating at his sheer *idiocy*.

"A Mafia princess? Are you fucking *kidding* me?" I swept the folder off the desk in one furious motion, taking a glass paperweight out with it. The glass shattered with a deafening crash while the photos fluttered out and onto the ground.

Luca flinched.

"You've done some stupid shit in your life, but this has to take the cake," I seethed. "Do you know what Romano would do to you if he found out? He'd gut you like a fish in the slowest, most painful way possible. No amount of money would save you. He'll hang your body from a goddamn highway overpass as a warning—*if* there's even a body left after he's done with you!"

The last guy who'd touched a woman in Romano's family without his permission ended up with his dick cut off and his brains blown out in his bedroom. The guy had merely kissed Romano's cousin on the cheek. Rumor had it the mafioso didn't even *like* his cousin.

If he found out Luca slept with his beloved niece? My brother would beg for death.

Luca's skin took on a sickly green tint. "You don't un—"

"What the *hell* were you thinking? How the fuck did you even meet her?"

The Romanos were famously insular. Gabriele kept a tight leash on his people, and they rarely ventured outside their family-controlled joints.

"We met at a bar. We didn't talk long, but we hit it off and exchanged numbers." Luca spoke fast, like he was afraid I would attack if he stopped. "She doesn't have as many eyes on her now that she's widowed, but I swear, I didn't know who she was until after we slept together. She told me her father was in construction."

A vein throbbed in my temple. "He *is* in construction."

Along with nightclubs, restaurants, and a dozen other fronts for his dirty business.

If it'd been anyone other than Romano, I would've undercut

Francis's threat by paying them off or striking a mutually beneficial deal. But unlike some businessmen who were short-sighted enough to entangle themselves in the underworld, I didn't fuck with the Mafia. Once you got in, the only way to get out was in a casket, and I would rather set myself on fire than willingly put myself in a position where I had to answer to someone else.

Francis wanted what my last name could bring him. Romano? He'd want every last dollar and drop of blood, even *after* he slit my brother's throat.

"I know it seems bad, but you don't understand," Luca said, his expression tortured. "I love her."

A terrible calm descended upon me. "You love her."

"Yes." His face softened. "She's incredible. Beautiful, smart—"

"You love her, yet you've been fucking everything that moves for the past *two weeks*."

"I *didn't*." Luca turned bright red. "It was an act to maintain my reputation, you know? I had to leave for a bit because her cousin ran away and her uncle was cracking down on the whole family, but we were careful."

I had never been closer to murdering a family member.

"Apparently, not careful *enough*," I snarled, earning myself another flinch. I took a deep breath and waited for the explosive rage to pass before I sat, slowly and deliberately, so I didn't reach across the desk and strangle my only brother. "Do you want to know how I got those photos, Luca?"

He opened his mouth, then closed it and shook his head.

"Francis Lau walked into my office two weeks ago and tossed them on my desk. Coincidentally, he'd been in town earlier and saw you with Maria. He recognized the both of you and had you tailed. Once he got what he needed, he came over to cut a deal." A thin smile touched my lips. "Care to guess what the terms of the deal are?"

Luca shook his head again.

"I marry his daughter, and he'll keep the evidence to himself. If I don't, he'll send the photos to Romano, and you'll die."

I had an excellent private security force. They were well-trained, professional, and morally flexible enough to deal with intruders in a way that dissuaded future intruders from crossing me. However, there was a difference between security and punishment and war with the fucking Mafia.

Luca's eyes widened.

"*Shit.*" He rubbed a hand over his face. "Dante, I—"

"Don't say another word. Here's what you *will* do." I pinned him with a hard stare. "You will cut off all contact with Maria, effective immediately. I don't give a shit if she's your one true soul mate and you never find love again after her. From this moment on, she doesn't exist to you. You will not see, speak, or otherwise communicate with her. If you do, I will freeze every damn account you have and blacklist any person who assists you financially."

Our grandfather had been aware of Luca's wild spending habits and left me full control of the company and family finances in his will. Being blacklisted by me meant being blacklisted by everyone in our social circle, and even Luca's idiot friends weren't stupid enough to risk that.

"I'm also cutting your monthly allowance in half until you prove you're capable of making better choices."

"What?" Luca exploded. "You can't—"

"Interrupt me again, and it'll be cut to zero," I said icily. He fell silent, his expression mutinous. "You will *earn* the remaining half of the money by taking a job at one of our stores, where you'll be treated like any other employee. No special perks, no drinking or fucking on the job, and no leaving for lunch and rolling back in two hours later. If you slack off, you will be cut off completely. Understand?"

After a long silence, he pressed his lips into a thin line and jerked out a short nod.

"Good. Now get the *fuck* out of my office."

If I had to look at him for another minute, I might do something I'd regret.

He must've sensed the impending danger because he got up and hightailed it to the exit without another word.

"And, Luca?" I stopped him before he opened the door. "If I find out you've violated my rules and contacted Maria again, I'll kill you myself."

My fist slammed into his stomach, hard and precise. My first hit of the night.

Adrenaline buzzed through me as Kai grunted at the impact. Anyone else would've stumbled and gotten the wind knocked out of them, but in true Kai fashion, he only paused for a few seconds before shaking it off.

"You seem upset," he said as he countered with a left hook. I sidestepped it with millimeters to spare. "Bad day at work?"

A hint of amusement shaded his question despite the direct hit he'd just taken.

"Something like that."

Sweat dripped down my forehead and coated my back as I worked out my frustrations in the ring. I'd come straight to the Valhalla Club after work. Most members preferred the on-site spa, restaurants, or upscale gentleman's club, which meant the boxing gym rarely saw any traffic except for me and Kai.

"Heard the Santeri deal is moving along, so it can't be that." Kai was barely out of breath despite the aggressiveness of our opening round. "Maybe it's not work. Maybe..." His expression turned speculative. "It has to do with your engagement to a certain jewelry heiress."

He let out another small grunt when I landed a hit on his lower ribs, but that didn't stop him from laughing at my scowl.

"You should know better than to try and keep something so big a secret," he said. "The whole office is buzzing about it."

"Your staff should spend more time working and less time gossiping. Perhaps then circulation wouldn't be down."

My engagement announcement wasn't scheduled to run in *Mode de Vie*'s coveted online style section until mid-September, but the luxury fashion and lifestyle outlet was the crown jewel of the Youngs' media empire. I'd be surprised if Kai *didn't* know about the engagement ahead of time.

"Never thought I'd see the day you get married." He ignored my dig. "To Vivian Lau, no less. How'd you manage to keep her a secret for so long?"

"We're not married yet." I blocked another attempted punch. "And I didn't keep her a secret. Our engagement is a business arrangement. I didn't fucking wine and dine her before we closed the deal."

The word *engagement* left a bitter taste in my mouth. The thought of shackling myself to someone for the rest of my life was as appealing as walking into the ocean with concrete blocks strapped to my feet.

I preferred work over people, many of whom didn't appreciate coming in second place to contracts and meetings. But business was lucrative, practical, and, for the most part, predictable. Relationships were not.

"That makes more sense," Kai said. "I should've known mergers and acquisitions would take over even your personal life."

"Funny."

His laugh faded when I hit him with an uppercut to the jaw, and he retaliated with a punch that knocked the air from my lungs. Our conversation tapered off, replaced by grunts and curses as we pummeled the hell out of each other.

Kai was the most mild-mannered person I knew, but he had a vicious competitive streak. We'd started boxing together last year, and he'd become my go-to partner for blowing off steam because he never held back. Who needed therapy when you could punch your friend in the face every week?

Hit, duck, dodge, hit. Over and over until we ended the night with a tie and significantly more bruises than when we'd entered.

But I'd finally worked off the edge of my anger, and when I met Kai in the locker room after my shower, I'd gained enough clarity not to lose my shit on my brother again. I'd been *this* close to cutting him off after our conversation that afternoon, promises and conditions be damned. It would serve him right, but I didn't have the energy to deal with his inevitable temper tantrum right now.

"Feel better?" Kai was already dressed when I entered. Button-down shirt, blazer, thin black wire frames. All traces of the lethal fighter from the ring had vanished, replaced with the epitome of scholarly sophistication.

"Marginally." I got dressed and rubbed a hand over my sore jaw. "You pack a mean punch."

"That's why you called. You'd hate it if I took it easy on you."

I snorted. "As much as you would hate losing."

We exited the gym and took the elevator up to the first floor. The Valhalla Club was an exclusive global society for those with a certain net worth, and it had chapters all over the world. However, its New York headquarters were the largest and most opulent, spanning four stories and an entire city block in upper Manhattan.

"I've met Vivian a few times," Kai said casually as the elevator doors dinged open. "She's beautiful, smart, charming. You could've done a lot worse."

Irritation flickered in my chest. "Perhaps you should marry her instead."

I didn't care if Vivian was a supermodel saint who saved puppies from burning buildings in her free time. She was simply someone I had to tolerate until I destroyed all the photos. Unfortunately, Christian's latest update confirmed Francis had stored the photos both digitally and physically. Christian could easily take care of the digital evidence, but destroying physical evidence was trickier when we didn't know how many backups Francis had. I couldn't risk making a move until we were one hundred percent certain we'd tracked down his entire stash.

"If I could, I would." The shadows in Kai's eyes disappeared as quickly as they'd surfaced.

As the heir to the Young fortune, his future was even more etched in stone than mine.

"All I'm saying is don't be an asshole." Kai nodded in greeting at a passing club member and waited until they were out of earshot before adding, "It's not her fault she's stuck with a brute like you."

If he only knew.

"Worry less about my personal life and more about yours." I raised an eyebrow at his cuff links. Gold lions with amethyst eyes—part of the Young family crest. "Leonora Young won't wait forever for a grandchild."

"Luckily for her, she already has two, courtesy of my sister. And don't try to deflect," Kai said as we crossed the gleaming black marble entryway to the exit. "I meant what I said about Vivian. Be nice."

My back teeth clenched.

Whether I liked her or not, Vivian was my fiancée, and I was getting damn tired of hearing her name leave his mouth.

"Don't worry," I said. "I'll treat her exactly the way she deserves."

CHAPTER 5

Vivian

"WHAT DO YOU MEAN, YOU HAVEN'T TALKED TO YOUR fiancé since your engagement?" Isabella crossed her arms and leveled me with a reproving stare. "What type of ridiculous relationship is that?"

"An arranged one." The bar tilted before righting itself. Perhaps I shouldn't have had two and a half mai tais in a row, but my weekly happy hour with Isabella and Sloane was the one time I could let loose.

No judging eyes, no need to be perfect and "proper."

So what if I was a little tipsy? The bar was called the Tipsy Goat. It was expected.

"It's better that we haven't spoken," I added. "He's not the most pleasant conversationalist."

Even now, the memory of my first and so far only meeting with Dante sent a rush of indignation down my spine. He'd shown no remorse over skipping out on half our introductory dinner to smoke a cigar in my father's office, and he'd left without so much as a thank you or good night.

Dante was a billionaire, but he had the manners of an ill-bred troll.

"Then why are you marrying him?" Sloane raised a perfectly groomed brow. "Tell your parents to find you a better match."

"That's the problem. There *is* no better match in their eyes. They think he's perfect."

"Dante Russo, perfect?" Her brow arched higher. "His security team once hospitalized someone who tried to break into his house. The guy wound up in a months-long coma with broken ribs and a shattered kneecap. It's impressive, but I wouldn't say he's perfect."

Only Sloane would think putting a guy in a coma was impressive.

"Trust me, I know. I'm not the one you have to convince," I muttered.

Not that Dante's notorious ruthlessness mattered to my family. He could shoot someone during rush hour in midtown Manhattan and they'd say the person deserved it.

"I don't understand why you agreed to *any* engagement at all." Sloane shook her head. "You don't need your parents' money. You can marry who you want, and there's not a thing they can do about it."

"It's not about the money." Even if my parents cut off my inheritance, I had plenty left over from my job, investments, and trust fund, which I came into when I was twenty-one. "It's about…" I searched for the right word. "Family."

Isabella and Sloane exchanged glances.

This wasn't the first time we'd discussed my engagement *or* my relationship with my parents, but I felt compelled to defend them each time.

"Arranged marriages are expected in my family," I said. "My sister did it, and so will I. I've known this was coming since I was a teenager."

"Yeah, but what are they going to do if you say no?" Isabella asked. "Disown you?"

My stomach plummeted. I forced a tight laugh. "Maybe." *Absolutely.*

They'd lauded my aunt for disowning my cousin after she turned down a scholarship to Princeton to open a food truck. Refusing to marry a Russo was a thousand times worse.

If I broke the engagement, my parents would never see or speak to me again. They weren't perfect, but the prospect of getting cut off from my family and being all alone made the mai tais slosh dangerously in my stomach.

Isabella wouldn't understand though. Culturally, we were similar, though she was Filipina Chinese instead of Hong Kong Chinese. But she came from a large, loving family who was okay with her moving across the country to bartend and pursue her writing dreams.

If I expressed similar desires to my parents, they'd either lock me in my room and perform an exorcism or toss me onto the streets with nothing except the clothes on my back, figuratively speaking.

"I don't want to disappoint them," I said. "They raised me, and they sacrificed a lot so I can have the life I have now. Marrying Dante would help *all* of us."

Familial relationships shouldn't be transactional, but I couldn't shake the sense I owed my parents a huge debt for everything—the opportunities, the education, the freedom to live and work where I wanted without worrying about money. They were luxuries most people didn't have, and I didn't take them for granted.

Parents took care of their children. When the children grew up, they took care of their parents. In our case, that meant said children married well and expanded the family's wealth and influence. It was just the way our world worked.

Isabella sighed. We'd been friends since we met at a yoga class when I was twenty-two. The yoga lessons hadn't lasted; our friendship had. She knew better than to argue with me about my family.

"Okay, but that doesn't change the fact that you haven't spoken to him when you're moving in with him *next week*."

I fidgeted with my sapphire bracelet. I would've pushed back on giving up my West Village apartment to move into Dante's Upper East Side penthouse, but what would be the point? I would just be wasting my breath arguing with my father. However, other than Dante's address, I didn't have any details for the move. No keys, no building requirements, nothing.

"You have to talk to the man eventually," Isabella added. "Don't be a wuss."

"I am *not* a wuss." I turned to Sloane. "Am I?"

She glanced up from her phone. Technically, none of us were allowed to check our phones during happy hour. Whoever broke the rule had to pick up the tab for the night.

In reality, Sloane had been bankrolling our happy hours for the past six months. She put the *work* in workaholic.

"Although I disagree with Isabella's advice seventy-eight percent of the time, she's right. You have to talk to him before you move in." An elegant shrug. "There's an art exhibition at Dante's house tonight. You should attend."

Dante owned a notoriously impressive art collection rumored to be worth hundreds of millions of dollars. His annual private exhibition showcasing his latest acquisitions was one of the most coveted invites in Manhattan.

We were technically engaged, and my lack of an invitation would've been embarrassing had I not been so relieved. After I moved in, I'd have to spend *every* night with him, so I was clinging to my freedom while it lasted. The prospect of sharing a room, a *bed* with Dante Russo was…unnerving.

An image rose in my mind of him sitting behind my father's desk, eyes dark and posture arrogant, with tendrils of smoke curling around that boldly charismatic face.

An unexpected heat ran between my legs.

The press of his thumb against my lip, the smoky glint in his eyes when he'd looked at me...there'd been a moment, just one, when I thought he would kiss me. Not to show affection but to dirty me up. To dominate and corrupt.

The warmth curled low until the heavy expectancy of my friends' gazes pulled me back to the present. I wasn't in my father's office. I was in a bar, and they were waiting for an answer.

The exhibition. Right.

A cold rush of reality doused the heat.

"I can't show up uninvited," I said, hoping they couldn't see me blush beneath my alcohol-induced redness. "It's rude."

"You're not a random party crasher. You're his *fiancée*, even if you don't have a ring yet," Isabella countered. "Plus, you're moving in soon anyway. Consider it a preview of your new home—which you can't move into unless you *talk* to him."

I sighed, wishing I could rewind time by a month so I could mentally prepare myself for what was coming.

"I hate it when you make sense."

Isabella's cheeks dimpled. "Most people do. I would go with you because I love a good party crash—er, house tour, but I have a shift tonight."

By day, she was an aspiring erotic thriller author. By night, she served overpriced drinks to overgrown frat boy types at a dive bar in the East Village. She hated the bar, its clientele, and its creepy manager and was actively looking for another job, but until she found one, she was stuck.

"Sloane?" I asked hopefully.

If I were to confront Dante tonight, I'd need backup.

"I can't. Asher Donovan crashed his Ferrari in London. He's fine," Sloane said when Isabella and I gasped. Neither of us cared about sports, but the famous soccer star was too pretty to die.

"But I have to put out the media fire. This is the second car he's crashed in as many months."

Sloane ran a boutique public relations firm with a small but high-powered client roster. She was *always* putting out fires.

She motioned our server for the check, paid the tab, and made me promise to call her if I needed anything before she disappeared out the door in a cloud of Jo Malone perfume and platinum-blond hair.

Isabella left soon after for her shift, but I lingered in the booth, debating what to do next.

If I were smart, I'd go home and finish packing for my move. Nothing good would come of crashing Dante's party, and I could call him tomorrow if I really wanted.

Pack, shower, and sleep, I decided.

That was my plan, and I was going to stick to it.

"I'm sorry, ma'am, but you're not on the list. It doesn't matter whether you're Mr. Russo's mother, sister, or *fiancée*." The hostess raised a brow at my bare ring finger. "I can't let you in without an invitation."

My smile didn't falter. "If you call Dante, he'll confirm my identity," I said, even though I wasn't sure he would. I'd deal with that bridge when we got there. "This is simply an oversight."

I'd gone home as planned after happy hour and lasted a total of twenty minutes before I caved to Isabella and Sloane's suggestion. They were right. I couldn't sit around waiting for Dante when my move-in date loomed so close. I had to suck it up and see him, no matter how much he annoyed or unnerved me.

Of course, in order to see him, I had to get *into* the party.

The hostess's face reddened. "I assure you, there was no oversight. We are meticulous in—"

"Vivian, there you are."

An aristocratic British accent cut smoothly through our standoff.

I turned, surprise coasting through me when I saw the handsome Asian man smiling at me. His flawlessly chiseled face and deep, dark eyes would've almost been *too* perfect were it not for the simple black frames lending him a touch of approachability.

"Dante just texted. He's looking for you, but you weren't answering your phone." He came up beside me and retrieved an elegant cream invitation from his jacket pocket. He handed it to the hostess. "Kai Young plus one. I can bring Ms. Lau in so we don't bother Dante on his big night."

She glared at me but offered Kai a tight smile.

"Of course, Mr. Young. Enjoy the party." She stepped aside, as did the pair of unsmiling, suited guards behind her.

Unlike nightclubs or bars, exclusive events like this rarely asked for IDs. The staff was expected to memorize and pair the guests' faces with their names on sight.

I waited until we were out of earshot before I turned to Kai with a grateful smile. "Thank you. You didn't have to do that."

Kai and I weren't close friends, but we often attended the same parties and chatted whenever we crossed paths. His thoughtful, reserved demeanor was a breath of fresh air in the narcissistic jungle of Manhattan high society.

"You're welcome." His formal tone made me smile.

Born in Hong Kong, raised in London, and educated at Oxford and Cambridge, Kai's mannerisms were a clear reflection of his upbringing.

"I'm sure your absence on the list was an oversight on Dante's part." He whisked two glasses of champagne off a passing server's tray and handed one to me. "Speaking of which, congratulations on your engagement. Or should I say condolences?"

My smile blossomed into a laugh. "The jury is still out."

From what I'd heard, Kai and Dante were friends. I wasn't sure what Dante told him about our engagement, but I was erring on the side of caution. As far as the public was concerned, we were a happy, loving couple who couldn't be more thrilled to be engaged.

"Smart. Most people treat Dante like he walks on water." Kai's eyes sparkled. "He needs someone to remind him he's mortal just like the rest of us."

"Oh, trust me," I said. "I don't think he's a god."

More like the devil sent to work on my last nerve.

Kai laughed. We made small talk for another few minutes before he excused himself to talk to an old college friend.

Why couldn't I have ended up with someone like him? He was polite, charming, and rich enough to meet my parents' standards. Instead, I was stuck with a brooding Italian who wouldn't know good manners if they slapped him in the face.

I sighed and set my empty glass on a nearby tray before I wandered through the penthouse, taking in the gorgeous architecture and decor.

Dante had eschewed the modern minimalism so popular with his bachelor brethren in favor of handcrafted furniture and rich jewel tones. Turkish and Persian silk rugs covered the gleaming floors, and lush velvet drapes framed floor-to-ceiling windows boasting panoramic views of Central Park and the city's iconic skyline.

I passed two sitting rooms, four powder rooms, one screening room, and one gaming lounge before I entered the long, skylit gallery where the actual exhibition took place.

I hadn't spotted Dante yet, but he was most likely...

My steps slowed when a familiar head of glossy black hair came into view.

Dante stood at the other end of the hall, talking to a beautiful redhead and an Asian man with cheekbones sharp enough to cut ice. He smiled at something they said, his expression warm.

So he was capable of normal human emotion after all. *Good to know.*

My blood burned a little hotter, either from the alcohol or from the sight of his real smile. I chose to believe it was the former.

Dante must've felt the weight of my stare because he stopped talking and looked up. Our eyes locked, and the warmth disappeared from his face like the sun beneath the horizon.

My heartbeats crashed against each other. A double-length hallway's worth of space separated us, but his displeasure was so potent it seeped through the air and into my body like a deadly poison.

Dante excused himself from his guests and stalked toward me, his powerful, muscled frame slicing through the crowd with the single-minded surety of a predator locked on to its prey. Tingles of alarm cascaded down my spine, but I forced myself to hold my ground even as every self-preservation instinct screamed at me to *run*.

It's fine. He won't kill you in public. Probably. Maybe.

"Lovely party. I'm afraid my invitation got lost in the mail, but I made it," I said when he neared. I plucked a glass off a nearby tray and held it out. "Champagne?"

"Your invitation isn't what's lost, *mia cara.*" The velvety endearment would've been swoon-worthy had it not been for the darkness seething beneath the surface. He didn't touch the offered drink. "What are you doing here?"

"Enjoying the food and artwork." I brought the glass to my lips and took a sip. Nothing tasted quite as sweet as liquid courage. "You have exquisite taste, though your manners could use improvement."

A hard smile slashed across his mouth. "How ironic you're always lecturing me on manners when you're the one who showed up uninvited to a private event."

"We're engaged." I stopped beating around the bush and cut straight to the heart of the matter. The faster I got this out of the way, the faster I could leave. "We haven't exchanged a single word since the dinner even though I'm supposed to move in *next week*. I don't expect love declarations and flowers every day"—*though that'd be nice*—"but I do expect basic courtesy and communication skills. Since you appear incapable of taking the initiative, I did it myself." I finished my drink and set it down. "Oh, and don't consider this me showing up uninvited. Consider it me accepting your invitation early. After all, you did agree to me moving in, did you not? I simply wanted a look at my new home before I committed to it."

My pulse raced with nerves, but I kept an even tone. I couldn't set a precedent of backing down whenever Dante was upset. If he sensed any weakness, he'd pounce.

Dante's smile didn't reach his eyes.

"That was quite a speech. You certainly didn't have this much to say at dinner the other night." The cold steel of his voice melted into rough silk as his gaze swept over me, gathering heat the farther it traveled. "I almost don't recognize you."

The intimacy of his double meaning throbbed in my veins and dropped between my legs.

My tweed and pearls were safely tucked in the back of my closet now that I'd returned to New York. Instead, I wore a classic black cocktail dress, heels, and my favorite red lipstick. Diamonds glittered around my neck and on my ears. It wasn't anything groundbreaking, but it was the best I could do when rushing to get ready.

However, the intensity of Dante's scrutiny made me feel like I'd showed up to a church reunion in a string bikini.

My stomach tightened when his gaze trailed from my face down over my chest to where my dress hugged my hips. It skimmed over the bare length of my legs, the perusal almost obscene in its laziness and erotic in its thoroughness, like the caress of a lover determined to map every inch of my body with his attention.

My throat dried. A flame ignited low in my stomach, and I suddenly wished I'd worn a conservative suit again tonight. It was safer. Less capable of fogging my mind with rough drawls and electric attraction.

What were we talking about?

"Different occasions require different approaches." I grasped for words and hoped they made sense.

I cocked an eyebrow, praying Dante couldn't hear how fast my heart was beating. I knew it was physically impossible, but I couldn't shake the eerie sense he could see straight through me like I was made of nothing more than a thousand pieces of broken, transparent glass.

"You might want to try that strategy sometime," I added, determined to keep the conversation going so I didn't sink into the mind-numbing heat of his stare again. "People might like you better."

"I would if I cared about others' opinions." He dragged his eyes back up to mine, the picture of mocking cruelty once more. "Unlike some of my esteemed guests, I don't derive my self-worth from what people think of me."

The insinuation hit me in the gut, and my skin went from overly hot to ice cold in the blink of an eye. Nobody flipped a switch from tolerable to asshole faster than Dante Russo. It took every ounce of willpower not to toss the nearest drink in his face.

He had some nerve, but the worst part was, he wasn't wrong. The insults with a grain of truth always cut the deepest.

"Good. Because I assure you, their opinion of you is quite low," I snapped.

Do not slap him. Do not make a scene.

I took a deep breath and wrapped it up before I went against my own advice.

"As delightful as I find our conversation, I have to excuse myself as I have other places to be. However, I expect all logistical information related to my move in my inbox by tomorrow at noon. I would hate to have to show up in front of your building and reveal your incompetence to your neighbors." I touched the diamond pendant at my throat. "Imagine how embarrassing it would be if people found out the great Dante Russo couldn't coordinate something as simple as his fiancée's move-in."

Dante's glare could've melted the gold frames hanging on the walls.

"You might not care what others personally think of you, but reputation is everything in business. If you can't handle your home life, how could you possibly handle your office dealings?" I took a business card out of my clutch and tucked it into the jacket pocket of his suit. "I assume you already have my contact information, but in case you don't, here's my card. I look forward to your email."

I walked away before he could respond.

The heat of his anger lashed at my back, but I'd detected a tiny flash of something else in his eyes before I left.

Respect.

I kept walking, my heart in my throat and my feet moving faster and faster until I reached the nearest guest bathroom. Only when the door closed behind me did I slump against the wall and cover my face with my hands.

Breathe.

My surge of adrenaline was already fading, leaving me drained and anxious.

I'd stood off against Dante and won…for now. But I wasn't naive enough to think that was the end of it. Even if standing up to him had garnered me grudging points in his eyes, he wouldn't let an uneven score against him stand.

Somehow, I'd entered into a cold war with my fiancé, and tonight was just the opening battle.

CHAPTER 6

Dante

I SENT VIVIAN THE INFORMATION SHE NEEDED FOR HER move at precisely noon on Sunday. Not out of fear she'd cause a scene in front of my building but out of reluctant admiration for the stunt she'd pulled at my exhibition.

It turned out the delicate little rose had some steel in her spine after all.

The following weekend, Vivian showed up at my house again, this time with an army of movers in tow. Greta, my housekeeper, and Edward, my butler, took charge of guiding the movers through the apartment while I led Vivian to her room. Neither of us spoke, and the silence expanded with each step until it became a living, breathing entity between us.

Annoyance wormed its way into my chest. Vivian had been perfectly friendly to Greta, Edward, and the rest of my staff, whom she'd greeted with warm smiles and fucking cookies from Levain. But when she got to me, she'd shut down like *I* was the one moving into *her* house and disrupting her carefully planned life. Like I was the one who'd showed up uninvited at her party wearing an outfit that could send a man to his fucking knees. A week later, the image of that black dress clinging to her curves was still ingrained in my mind, as was the fire in her eyes when she'd laid into me.

There was none of that fire now. Vivian was the picture of cool elegance walking next to me, and it pissed me off for no explicable reason. Or maybe my ire had something to do with the fact that, even in a casual blouse and skirt, her presence awoke an unwanted heat in my gut. My body had never reacted so viscerally to anyone before, and I didn't even fucking like her.

We stopped in front of a carved wood door.

"This is your room." I'd set her up in the farthest suite from mine, and it was still too close. "Greta will unpack for you later."

My voice sounded abnormally loud after the oppressive quiet.

One of her brows rose. "Separate rooms until marriage. I didn't realize you were such a traditionalist."

"I didn't realize you were so eager to share a bed with me."

A small smirk curved my mouth when Vivian's cheeks pinked. It was her first loss of composure all morning.

"I didn't say I wanted to share a bed with you," she said coolly. "I simply pointed out the outdatedness of your thinking. Sleeping in separate rooms is for married couples who are fighting, not newly engaged couples who are supposed to be in love. Word will get out. People will talk."

"It won't, and they won't." My household staff had been with me for years and prided themselves on their discretion. "If they do, I'll take care of it. But since we're on the subject of public image, we should establish the boundaries of our relationship."

"Ah, communication. I do believe you're finally graduating from the Neanderthal stage of your life."

I ignored her wry insult and continued, "In public, we'll play the part of a loving couple. We'll attend events together, smile for the cameras, and pretend we like each other. You'll also have full access to the Russo Group portfolio of brands. If you want anything from any of our collections, call my assistant Helena and she'll take care of it. On your nightstand, you'll find her number, a black Amex, and your engagement ring. Wear it."

The engagement announcement ran that morning. Vivian and I were officially tied together, which meant my reputation was also at stake.

I didn't care whether people personally liked me, but public perception was important in my line of work. Obvious discord would raise too many questions, and the last thing I needed was nosy society columnists sniffing around.

"A ring on my bedside table. How romantic." Vivian touched the sapphire bracelet on her wrist. "You truly know how to make a woman feel special."

"I'm not here to make you feel special." I dipped my head toward hers. The sweet, slightly tart scent of apples stole into my lungs as I enunciated my next words with crisp precision. "I'm here because I made a deal with your father."

Vivian didn't back away, but surprise and a hint of uncertainty surfaced in her eyes when I ran a leisurely knuckle over the gold chain around her neck.

Even at this close a distance, her skin was flawless, like cream poured over silk. Long dark lashes framed deep brown eyes, and a tiny beauty mark, so small one would have to be as close as I was to see it, dotted the area above her lush lips.

My eyes dipped to her mouth. The heat from my gut spread to my stomach. She wore the same lipstick from the exhibition. Bold, red, and seductive, like a siren's call amid a sea of tranquil calm.

I wanted to rub my thumb across her bottom lip and smear her perfect lipstick until she was nothing more than a beautiful mess. To peel back the composed mask and see the ugliness underneath.

Vivian may be wrapped in a pretty package, but a Lau was a Lau. They were all cut from the same mold.

"Don't expect dinner dates or sweet nothings at home, *mia cara*," I said, my words as soft and lazy as my touch. "You won't get either."

Instead of touching her mouth, I skimmed the back of my hand across her collarbone, over the curve of her shoulder, and down her arm until it reached the frantic beat at her wrist.

"Get rid of any romantic notions you may have of us falling in love and living happily ever after. It won't happen." I pressed a thumb against her pulse, hard, and smiled when she jerked at the sudden, rough movement. "This is a business arrangement. Nothing more. Are we clear?"

Vivian pressed her lips into a stubborn line.

The air was alive with the crackle of electricity and animosity. It sizzled against my skin, drawing my muscles tight and fanning the strange, hungry fire in my stomach.

When she remained mutinously silent, I reached up and closed my hand around her throat. Lightly, just enough to feel the shallowness of her breaths.

My voice dropped to a dangerous warning. "Are. We. Clear?"

Vivian's eyes flashed. "Crystal." The promise of retribution lurked beneath her even reply.

"Good." I released her and stepped back with a mocking smile. "Welcome home, sweetheart."

I left without waiting for a response.

The warmth of Vivian's skin lingered on my palm until I closed my hand around my lighter and let the cold metal chase away the remnants of her touch.

"Don't start," I said when I passed a frowning Greta. She was dusting in the sitting room, close enough to hear at least part of my conversation with Vivian.

The movers must've already left.

"You were too harsh," she admonished, confirming my earlier suspicion.

Greta was over seventy, but her hearing gave bats a run for their money.

"Not harsh. Honest." I checked my watch. I had a lunch meeting with a visiting CEO in two hours, and I needed to prep before I left. "Would you rather I lead her on? Indulge her childhood fantasies about Prince Charming coming in and sweeping her off her feet?"

"How do you know she has those fantasies?" Greta swept her duster over the fireplace mantel with more force than necessary. "She seems like the practical sort."

"You met her half an hour ago."

I couldn't believe I was arguing with my housekeeper over my fiancée. It must be those goddamned cookies Vivian bribed her with. Greta had a sweet tooth and a special fondness for chocolate chip.

"I have good instincts when it comes to people. Otherwise..." Another aggressive sweep over the mantel. "I would've written you off as an overbearing clone of your grandfather years ago."

My face shut down.

"Remember who you work for," I warned, my tone dark.

"*Non osare farmi una ramanzina quando sono stata io a pulirti il culo da piccolo.*" *Don't lecture someone who changed your diapers.* "If you want to fire me, fire me. But I know there's a heart in there somewhere, *ragazzo mio*. Use it and treat your future wife with respect."

"I gave her a black Amex and a diamond ring." Every woman would kill for those things, and they were more than Vivian deserved, considering who her father was.

Greta stared at me for a full minute before she shook her head and muttered furiously in Italian under her breath. I couldn't hear what she was saying, but I imagined it was none too complimentary.

I stopped next to Greta and placed a hand on the duster, forcing her to still.

"You're a valued member of my household, but there are only so many liberties I'll allow," I said coolly. "If you'd like a vacation to clear your head, let me know and it can be arranged."

The threat hung in the air as an offer.

Her eyes narrowed. "No vacation needed."

"Good."

Greta had worked for my family since I was a baby. She'd helped raise me and Luca since my parents were shit at the job, and she'd run my grandfather's household until I convinced her to work for me four years ago. Instead of being upset, my grandfather had gifted me a bottle of ten-thousand-dollar wine for successfully undercutting him.

While I had a soft spot for Greta and considered her the grandmother I never had—both of my biological grandmothers died before I was born—I would not tolerate blatant disrespect. If she were anyone else, I would've fired and blacklisted her the second the word *harsh* left her mouth.

A polite cough pulled my attention toward the doorway where Edward stood with a neutral expression.

"Sir, the movers have officially vacated the premises," he said. "Would you like me to give Ms. Lau the full tour?"

I'd taken Vivian directly to her room without showing her the rest of the house. Hell, she'd already seen half of it at last week's exhibition.

"Please do." She should know the apartment's full layout. I didn't want her accidentally wandering into my room or office.

He inclined his head and disappeared down the hall. Greta marched past me and disappeared into another corner of the penthouse without a word, but her disapproval lingered like the scent of her favorite lemon-scented cleaner.

I pinched the bridge of my nose.

Less than an hour after moving in, Vivian was already causing chaos. Discord with my staff was only the start. She would move things around. Disrupt the environment I'd carefully cultivated. I would come home not knowing what to see or expect.

Aggravation rose in my chest. I stalked out of the living room and into my office, where I attempted to review the materials for my meeting. But even though I'd closed the door and was sequestered on the opposite side of the house from Vivian's room, I still smelled the faint, maddening scent of apples.

CHAPTER 7

Vivian

I WAS A LAW-ABIDING CITIZEN, BUT IF ANYONE COULD drive me to mariticide, it was my future husband.

I hated his arrogance, his rudeness, and the mocking way he called me *mia cara*. I hated the way my pulse kicked at the rough span of his hand around my neck. And I hated how he always seemed larger than life, like the molecules of any space he entered had to fold in on themselves to accommodate him.

Are. We. Clear? His maddening voice echoed in my head.

It was clear, all right. It was clear Dante Russo was Satan in a nice suit.

I forced my lungs to expand past my anger. *In, one, two, three. Out, one, two, three.*

Only when my blood pressure returned to normal levels did I open the door to my new room instead of hunting down the sharpest knife I could find.

As promised, a business card with Dante's assistant's number and a black Amex waited on the nightstand next to a distinctive red ring box. When I popped open the lid, a colorless diamond winked back at me.

I brushed my fingers over the dazzling gem. Six carats, a rare Asscher cut, with smaller baguette diamonds adorning each shoulder.

I should've been thrilled. The ring was stunning and, judging by the diamond's color and clarity, worth at least a hundred thousand dollars. It was the type of ring most women would kill to have. But when I plucked it from the box and slid it onto my finger, I felt…nothing.

Nothing except the cool brush of platinum and a heavy weight that felt more like a prison than a promise.

Most engagement rings were symbols of love and commitment. Mine was the equivalent of a signature on a merger contract.

A strange tightness gripped my throat. I shouldn't have expected anything more than what Dante gave me. Some arranged marriages, like my sister's, turned into real love, but the overall odds weren't great.

I sank onto the bed. The tightness spread from my throat to my chest. It was stupid to feel sad. So what if Dante had proposed in the most impersonal way possible? I'd known since our first meeting we wouldn't mesh. At least he'd been honest about his intentions and boundaries. Still, a part of me had hoped our previous interactions were flukes and we would gradually warm up to each other, but no. My future husband was simply a jerk.

The buzz of a new text interrupted my wallowing.

I picked up my phone, expecting another congratulatory message or a reminder from Isabella to invite her over once I settled in.

Instead, I saw a text from the last person I'd expected to hear from.

Heath: Happy Pumpkin Hot Chocolate Day :)

I stared at the words, waiting for them to disappear like I'd accidentally conjured them. They didn't.

My stomach twisted.

Of all the days he could've texted out of the blue, it had to be today, right after I moved into Dante's house. The universe possessed a sick sense of humor.

There were a million things I wanted to say, but I stuck with something safe and neutral.

Me: Do they have those in California?
Heath: Pumpkin hot chocolate? Nah
Heath: You're only allowed to drink smoothies and green juices here or you'll get voted off the island

My small smile faded as quickly as it appeared. We shouldn't be talking, but I couldn't bring myself to block him.

Heath: I've been emailing Bonnie Sue's every day asking them to open shop in SF, but no dice so far

A pang hit me at the mention of Bonnie Sue's. It was a popular café near Columbia, where Heath and I had attended undergrad. It was famous for its seasonal pumpkin hot chocolate, and even though I didn't like pumpkin and he didn't like hot chocolate, we'd showed up every year for its annual return in mid-September. Forget the fall equinox; the real first day of fall was the day the drink reappeared on Bonnie Sue's menu.

Me: It'll happen. Persistence always wins

Guilt ballooned in my chest as Heath and I exchanged more small talk. He asked about my job and the city; I asked about his dog and the weather in San Francisco.

It was our longest conversation in years. Normally, we only

texted each other on holidays and birthdays, and we never talked on the phone. It was easier to pretend we were casual acquaintances that way even though we were anything but.

Heath Arnett.

My college best friend. My ex-boyfriend. And my first love.

Once upon a time, I thought we'd get married. I'd convinced myself we would overcome my parents' objections and live happily ever after, but our breakup two years ago proved my hopes had been just that—hopes. Flimsy and insubstantial in the face of my parents' wrath.

I shook off memories of *that* day and tried to refocus.

Me: How's your company doing?

After our breakup, Heath moved to California and expanded his cloud storage app into the powerhouse it was today. The last time I checked, it was one of the top fifteen most downloaded apps in the United States.

Heath: Pretty amazing. We're going public at the end of this year
Heath: We're expecting a big IPO. Perhaps...

The three dots that indicated he was typing popped up, disappeared, then popped up again.

Heath: We can revisit things after it does

My guilt hardened into dread.

He didn't know about the engagement. I hadn't posted about it online, we didn't have mutual friends anymore, and Heath didn't follow the society pages, which meant I had to tell him. I couldn't lie by omission and let him think there was a chance of us getting back together.

Heath: If you want to, of course

I could practically see him pushing his hand through his hair the way he always did when he was nervous.

My teeth dug into my bottom lip. I knew part of the reason he'd worked so hard on the startup was to prove my parents wrong. They'd been furious when they found out I'd kept our relationship from them for years and even more furious when they discovered Heath didn't come from an "appropriate" background.

At the time, he'd made a good living as a software engineer who'd worked on his app on the side, but he wasn't a Russo or a Young. My father had threatened to disown me if I didn't end things with Heath, and in the end, I'd chosen family over love.

Heath probably thought my parents would change their minds after his company went public and he became a millionaire. I didn't have the heart to tell him they wouldn't.

My family had plenty of money, but we were nouveau riche. No matter how much we donated to charity or how many zeroes we had in our bank accounts, certain parts of society would always remain closed to us...*unless* we married into old money.

Heath would never be old money, which meant my parents would never approve of him as a love match.

Just tell him.

I eased a deep breath into my lungs before I bit the bullet.

Me: I'm engaged

It wasn't the smoothest transition, but it was short, clear, and direct.

I resisted falling back into my childhood habit of biting my nails while I waited for a reply.

It never came.

Me: It happened a few weeks ago. My parents set it up.

Me: I meant to tell you earlier

I should have stopped, but I couldn't hold back my text version of word vomit.

Me: The wedding is in a year.

Crickets.

Five minutes passed, but my phone remained dark and silent.

I let out a small groan and tossed it to the side.

I *shouldn't* feel guilty. Heath and I broke up a long time ago, and honestly, I was surprised he wanted a second chance. I would've thought—

A soft knock interrupted the chaos of my thoughts.

I sucked in another lungful of air and smoothed my expression into one of polite neutrality before I answered. "Come in."

The door opened, revealing distinguished silver hair and a perfectly pressed black suit.

Edward, Dante's butler.

"Ms. Vivian, Mr. Dante requested I take you on a full tour of the house," he said, his British accent as crisp as his clothes. "Is now a good time, or would you like me to return at an hour of your choosing?"

I glanced at my phone, then at the cold, beautiful room around me. This was now my home. I could lock myself in my suite, throw a pity party, and agonize over the past, or I could try and make the most of my situation.

I stood and summoned a smile that felt only mildly forced. "Now is perfect."

That night, Dante and I ate our first meal together as a couple.

I meant that in the loosest sense of the word.

I wore his ring, and we lived under the same roof, but the chasm between us made the Grand Canyon look like an ordinary hole in the ground.

I made a valiant attempt to close it. "I love your art collection," I said. "The paintings are beautiful." *Except for the one that looks like cat vomit.* The piece, titled *Magda*, was so out of place in his gallery I did a double take when I saw it. "Do you have a favorite piece?"

It wasn't the most inspired topic, but I was grasping at straws. So far, I'd pulled six words out of Dante, three of which had been *pass the salt*. He was basically two devolutions away from being a nicely dressed mime.

"I don't play favorites." He cut into his steak.

My teeth clenched, but I swallowed my irritation. Since our less-than-stellar interaction during my move-in, I'd moved past the shock and anger stages of our engagement into resignation. I was stuck with Dante, whether I liked it or not. I had to make the most of it. If we didn't...

Images of cold days, lonely nights, and fake smiles filled my head.

My stomach tightened with unease before I took a sip of water and tried again. "What are your expectations in private?"

His knife and fork paused over his plate. "Excuse me?"

A noticeable reaction. *Progress.*

"Earlier, you said we'll play the part of a loving couple in public and warned me to, quote, unquote, *get rid of any romantic notions I may have of us falling in love*. But we never discussed what our private lives would look like beyond separate bedrooms," I said. "Do we eat dinner together every night? Discuss our work problems? Go grocery shopping and argue over which brand of wine to buy?"

"No, no, and no," he said flatly. "I don't grocery shop."

Of course you don't.

"We'll live our lives separately. I'm not your friend, therapist, or confidante, Vivian. Tonight's dinner is simply because it's your first night, and I happen to be home." His knife and fork moved again. "Speaking of which, I have a business trip in Europe coming up. I leave in two days. I'll be gone for a month."

He might as well have slapped me in the face.

I stared at him and waited for him to tell me it was a joke. When he didn't, a surge of indignation washed away my attempts to play nice.

"A month? What type of business trip requires you to be gone for a *month*?"

"The type that makes me money."

The indignation fanned into anger. He wasn't even *trying*. Maybe the business trip was legitimate, but I move in, and he leaves for a month? The timing was too convenient to ignore.

"You have plenty of money already," I snapped, too annoyed to mince words. "But you clearly *don't* have an interest in even being civil, so why are you here?"

Dante cocked an eyebrow. "This is my house, Vivian."

"I mean *here*. This engagement." I gestured between us. "You avoided my question the first time, but I'm asking again. What could you possibly get out of our match that you couldn't get on your own?"

Lau Jewels was a big company, but the Russo Group eclipsed it tenfold. It didn't make sense. My father told me it had something to do with market access in Asia, which was admittedly Lau Jewels' strong point and the Russo Group's weak one, but was that important enough for Dante to upend his personal life for?

His expression stiffened. "It doesn't matter."

"Considering it's the reason we're together, I think it does."

"No, it doesn't. Why do you care about the reason we're together?" His voice turned cold, mocking. "You'll marry me either way. The dutiful daughter who does everything her daddy says. I could be gone for the next year until our wedding, and you'd *still* go through with it. Wouldn't you?"

An icy claw of shock snatched the breath from my lungs. I didn't know how the conversation had escalated so quickly, but somehow, without trying, Dante had hit me right in the ugliest, most undesirable part of myself. The part I loathed but couldn't shake.

"Now I understand." I fought for calm, but a tremble of anger bled through. "An arranged marriage is the *only* way you could get someone to marry you. You are so...so..." I struggled to find the right word. "*Horrible.*"

Not my best work, but it'd do.

Dark amusement slid through his eyes. "If I'm so horrible, then tell your family the wedding's off." He nodded at my phone. "Call them right now. We'll move you back into your apartment like this never happened."

It was equal parts challenge and seduction. He didn't think I would do it, but his voice was so rich and coaxing it almost compelled me to obey.

My fingers curled around my fork. The metal dug into my skin, cold and unforgiving.

I didn't touch my phone. I wanted to even more than I wanted to toss my wine in Dante's smug face, but I *couldn't.*

My father's anger. My mother's criticism. The failure if I didn't go through with the wedding...

I couldn't do it.

Dante's amusement disappeared into the tense atmosphere. Something sparked in his eyes. Disappointment? Disapproval? It was impossible to tell.

"Exactly," he said softly.

The finality of that word cut deeper than a freshly honed knife.

We finished dinner in silence, but my steak had lost its flavor. I washed it down with more wine and let the warmth eat away at my shame.

CHAPTER 8

Dante

DESPITE WHAT VIVIAN THOUGHT, I'D SCHEDULED MY Europe trip before she moved in. A majority of Russo Group brands were headquartered on the continent, and I blocked off a month every year to hold in-person meetings with the heads of our European subsidiaries.

This year's timing just happened to be extremely convenient.

However, I made sure to keep tabs on Luca and Vivian while I was gone. I'd assigned Luca a sales role at one of our jewelry subsidiaries' retail stores. He was a people person, and putting him in a back office somewhere would only spell disaster for him and the store in question. According to the store manager, he had a rough start—my brother had never been punctual—but by the time I returned to New York, he seemed to have settled, albeit begrudgingly, into his new role.

Vivian, on the other hand, had taken to her new surroundings like a duck to water. Greta and Edward gushed about her in every report, and I came home to find a new painting in the gallery, towels monogrammed with *D&V* in the bathrooms, and fucking flowers everywhere.

"Dante, relax your expression," Winona said. "Give me a smile…that's it! Perfect."

The camera shutter clicked in rapid succession.

Vivian and I had spent the morning taking engagement photos in Central Park. It was as excruciating as I'd imagined, filled with fake smiles and faker embraces as Winona guided us into poses designed to show off how in "love" we were.

"Vivian, put your arms around his neck and move closer."

I stiffened when Vivian obliged and took a tentative step toward me.

"Closer. I can practically drive a tractor between you right now," Winona joked.

"Do as she says so we can get this over with," I ground out. The sooner I put more distance between us, the better.

"You grow more charming every day." Vivian's voice was so sweet I could've drizzled it over pancakes. "Europe truly did wonders for your personality."

"Closer," Winona encouraged. If she picked up on our hostility, she didn't acknowledge it. "One more step…"

Vivian's breasts grazed my chest when she closed the remaining gap between us.

My muscles went rigid.

"Dante, put your arms around Vivian."

For fuck's sake.

Since I just wanted to get the torture over with, I set my jaw and placed my hands on Vivian's hips. Heat seared through the silk of her dress, and her damned apple scent crawled into my lungs again. Neither of us moved, afraid the slightest shift would inadvertently bring us even closer.

"I received an interesting call from my accountant when I was in Paris," I said in an effort to distract myself from our disturbing proximity. "One hundred thousand dollars charged to my Amex in one day, including ten grand on flowers. Care to explain?"

"You gave me a black Amex. I used it," Vivian said with an elegant shrug. "What can I say? I like flowers. And shoes."

Translation: You were an asshole before you left, and I took it out on your bank account.

A subtle but petty act of revenge. Good for her.

There was no one more irritating than someone who didn't stand up for herself.

"Clearly," I said, trying not to breathe too deep so her scent didn't envelop me completely. "And the towels?"

"They were a gift from my mother."

Of course they were.

"Let me know in advance the next time you leave for a month," she said. "I want time to plan a party, redecorate the living room, maybe come up with a robust shopping list. It's amazing how much you can do with no spending limit."

I narrowed my eyes. I didn't care about the credit card usage. Luca once spent a million dollars on a ridiculous twenty-four-karat solid gold bathtub for a pajama party. A hundred grand was nothing.

What pissed me off was the way Vivian rearranged everything while I was gone. The towels and flowers were just the tip of the iceberg. There was new art on the walls, aromatherapy piping through hidden diffusers, and a massage room where the gift-wrapping room used to be.

I left for a month and came back to find my home transformed into a fucking Club Med.

"You had a good time while I was gone, did you?" A dangerous current twined around my words.

"I had a *wonderful* time." Vivian threaded her fingers through my hair and tugged hard enough to hurt. She smiled. "The house has been so pleasant without all the scowls and grunts."

"Here I thought you'd miss me." I tsked. "I'm hurt."

"I would apologize, but catering to your feelings isn't part of our arrangement. It's *just* a business deal. Remember?"

A reluctant smile touched my mouth.

Touché.

"Look at you two. So sweet." Winona sighed. "Dante, why don't you give her a kiss on the lips? It'll be the perfect photo to wrap up the shoot."

My smile disappeared.

Vivian went stiff in my arms. "That's not necessary," she said quickly. "We don't...we don't like PDA."

"There's no one here except us," Winona pointed out.

I'd pulled some strings and reserved swaths of the park for the photo shoot. I hated public crowds. Too loud, too unpredictable, too *there.*

"Yes, but..." Vivian faltered. She looked like a rabbit caught in headlights.

Annoyance flared at her horrified expression. I didn't *want* to kiss her, but I didn't appreciate how she acted like kissing me was the equivalent of getting bitten by a poisonous snake.

"We really don't feel comfortable kissing in front of *any* third party," Vivian finally finished.

She tried to step back, but my hold on her hips prevented her from doing so.

My annoyance deepened. We'd agreed to play the part of a loving couple in public, but she wasn't acting particularly loving.

"If you don't want to, that's fine, but it's not an engagement shoot without a kiss." Winona looked puzzled by our hesitation. "I promise I won't be scandalized."

"Right." Vivian scraped her teeth across her bottom lip.

Christ. If she waffled any harder, she'd have a prime spot on Sarabeth's brunch menu, syrup and all.

Instead of waiting for her to make a decision sometime in the next century, I dipped my head and brushed my mouth over hers. Softly, just long enough to hear the camera shutter click again.

Vivian's body morphed from stiff to rigid. Her lips parted on a sharp inhale, and I tasted something sweet flavored with a hint of spices.

My blood thrummed. It was just supposed to be a quick kiss for the camera. I should pull back, but her mouth was so warm and soft I couldn't resist another taste. And another.

Before I knew it, my hand slid up of its own accord. My fingers sank into her hair and evoked an overwhelming urge to deepen the kiss. To wrap my fist around all that silk and tug until her mouth opened fully for me, letting me explore and plunder at my will.

My blood thrummed louder. I blamed my senseless actions on the month apart. Absence made the heart grow fonder and all that crap. It was the only plausible reason why kissing Francis Lau's daughter didn't make me want to scrub bleach all over myself.

Vivian tilted her chin up a fraction, giving me better access. My—

"We got the shot!" Winona's voice yanked us apart as suddenly and violently as if someone had fired a gun.

One second, we were kissing. The next, my hands were gone from Vivian's hip and hair, her arms had dropped from around my neck, and my heart was racing like I'd just completed an Ironman Triathlon.

Vivian and I stared at each other for a frozen second before quickly looking away. The kiss had lasted less than a minute, but my mouth turned with the imprint of her lips. Heaviness settled on my skin like a cashmere blanket as Winona rose from her crouching position.

"You two might be the most photogenic couple I've ever

worked with." She grinned. "I can't wait for you to see the final photos."

"Thank you," Vivian said, her face pink. "I'm sure they'll be great."

"Are we done?" I removed my jacket and ignored her reproving look. We'd done the damn shoot. What more did she want?

And why was it so fucking hot in the middle of October?

"Yes, I'll email you a link to the gallery in two weeks," Winona said, unfazed by my curt reply. "Congratulations again on your engagement."

Vivian thanked her again while I brushed past her toward the stairs leading away from Bethesda Terrace. I needed to put more distance between us immediately.

Unfortunately, Vivian soon fell into step with me again, and we walked in silence toward one of the park exits while I cursed myself for my lapse of judgment. Not just the kiss but the photo shoot altogether. I should've hired someone to photoshop us into the park. That way, I wouldn't have to deal with...*this*.

The restless buzz beneath my skin. The tightening of my muscles when her scent wafted into my nose. The memory of her mouth on mine.

It wasn't about the kiss, which we'd had to do if we didn't want to arouse Winona's suspicion. It was about the fact that I'd lingered.

Vivian finally spoke when we passed through the exit onto Seventy-Ninth and Fifth. "About the kiss back there—"

"It was for the photo." I didn't look at her.

"I know, but—"

"Are you hungry?" I nodded at the food cart on the corner of the street. I would rather bathe in acid than discuss what happened.

Vivian sighed but dropped the subject. "I could use some

food," she admitted. Her eyebrows winged up when I stopped in front of the food cart. "What are you doing?"

"Buying breakfast." I pulled a crisp twenty out of my wallet. "Two coffees and signature bagels. Keep the change. Thanks, Omar."

While I wanted to get away from Vivian as soon as possible, I was damn hungry. We'd woken up too early for breakfast, and I couldn't buy food without getting some for her too.

I was an asshole, not a boor.

I turned to find her staring at me like I'd sprouted horns and feathers in the middle of Fifth Avenue.

"What?"

"You're on a first-name basis with the owner."

"Obviously." I slid my wallet back into my pocket. "I run here in the mornings when I have time, and I've tried all the breakfast carts around the park. Omar's the best."

"Here I thought you only ate caviar and human hearts."

"Don't be ridiculous. Caviar tastes awful with human hearts."

Vivian's laugh evoked a strange sensation in my chest. *Heartburn? Investigate later.*

I took the food and handed one of the paper cups and wrapped bagels to her. "I pay for quality, not price. Expensive doesn't always equal good, especially when it comes to food."

"For once, we agree." She followed me to a nearby bench and tucked her dress beneath her thighs before sitting. "We should check the temperature in hell."

The corner of my mouth kicked up, but I flattened it before she noticed.

"One of my favorite restaurants before it closed was this tiny little place in Boston's Chinatown," Vivian said hesitantly, like she was deciding whether or not to share the information with me even as the words left her mouth. "If you weren't looking for it, you'd miss it. The decor looked like something out of the early nineties and the floors were suspiciously sticky, but they had the best dumplings I'd ever tasted."

Curiosity got the better of me. "Why did it close?"

"The owner died, and his son didn't want to take it over. He sold it to someone who turned it into an electronics repair shop." A wistful note entered her voice. "My family and I ate there every week, but I guess we would've stopped going even if it'd stayed open. They only go to Michelin-starred places now. If they saw me eating from a food truck, they'd have a coronary."

I took a slow sip of coffee as I processed what she said. I'd assumed Vivian was fully under her parents' thumb, but judging by her tone, all was not perfect in the Lau family.

"My brother and I used to go to this place in Midtown when we were kids," I said. "Moondust Diner. The neighborhood was a tourist trap, but the diner had the best milkshakes in the city. Two dollars, glasses almost as big as our heads. We went there every week after school until our grandfather found out. He was furious. Said Russos don't frequent cheap diners and assigned someone to walk us home straight after school. We never went back after that."

I'd never told anyone about the diner, but since she shared about the dumpling shop, I felt compelled to reciprocate.

The kiss really *had* fucked with my head.

"Two-dollar milkshakes? I would've been a dentist's nightmare," Vivian joked.

"Mine wasn't my biggest fan either."

The Moondust Diner still existed, but I wasn't a kid anymore. My sweet tooth had faded, and I didn't have time for trips down nostalgia lane.

We ate quietly for another minute before I said, "Things must have changed quite a bit after your father's business took off."

I could always use more intel on the Laus, and if anyone knew Francis well, it was his daughter. At least that was the reason I gave myself for not leaving even though I'd finished my food.

"That's an understatement." Vivian traced the rim of her coffee cup with her finger. "When I was fourteen, my mother sat me down for the talk. It wasn't about sex; it was about expectations for who I should and could date. I was free to be with anyone I wanted *as long as* they met certain criteria. That was also the day I found out I was expected to have an arranged marriage if I didn't find anyone 'suitable' within a certain time."

I'd suspected as much. New money families like the Laus typically tried to enhance their social status through marriage. Old money families did it too, but they were more subtle about it.

"I take it your parents weren't fans of your exes." If they were, Vivian and I wouldn't be engaged.

"No." A shadow passed over her face. "What about you? Any exes you thought about marrying?"

"I wasn't interested in marriage."

"Hmm. I'm not surprised."

I slanted a glance at her. "Meaning?"

"Meaning you're a control freak. You probably hated—and *still* hate—the idea of someone coming in and upending your life. The more people in the household, the harder it is to control your surroundings."

My shock must've been evident because Vivian laughed and gave me a half-teasing, half-smug smile.

"It's pretty obvious in the way you run your household," she said. "Plus, during meals, you're anal about your foods not touching. You put the meat on the upper left side of your plate, vegetables on the upper right, and carbs and grains on the bottom. You did it at my parents' house and on my first night at your place, before you left for Europe." She sipped her coffee, managing to look regal even while drinking from a paper cup. "Control freak," she summarized.

Reluctant admiration swept through me. "Impressive."

I'd been particular about my foods touching since I was a child. I didn't know why; the sight and texture of mixed foods just made my skin crawl.

"It comes with the job," Vivian said. "Event planning requires strong attention to detail, especially when you're dealing with the types of clients I have."

Rich. Entitled. Needy.

She didn't need to say it for me to know what she meant.

"Why event planning instead of the family business?" I was genuinely curious.

Vivian shrugged. "I like jewelry as a consumer, but I have no interest in the corporate side of the business," she said. "Running Lau Jewels wouldn't be a creative endeavor. It would be about stockholders, financial reports, and a thousand other things I don't care about. I hate numbers, and I'm not good at them. My sister, Agnes, is the one who likes that stuff. She's the company's head of sales and marketing, and when my father retires, she'll take over as CEO."

There won't be a company left to take over after I'm done.

A small twist of unease tugged at my gut before I dismissed it. Her father deserved what was coming to him. Vivian and her sister didn't, but ruin and collateral damage went hand in hand. It was the cost of doing business.

"What about you? Did you ever want to do something else?" Vivian asked.

"No."

I'd spent my entire life preparing to take over the Russo Group. Pursuing another career path had never even crossed my mind.

"My father refused to take over the company, so it was up

to me to carry on the Russo tradition," I said. "Abnegating was never an option."

"Your father could but you couldn't? Seems unfair."

"There's no such thing as fairness in the business world. Besides, my father would've been shit as CEO. He's the type of guy who cares more about being liked than getting the job done. He would've run the company into the ground within years, and my grandfather knew it. That was why he didn't push him into taking an executive role."

The words came out of their own accord.

I wasn't sure why I was telling Vivian about my family. An hour ago, I would've rather jumped off the Empire State Building than spend another minute playing nice with her. Maybe the kiss had short-circuited my brain, or maybe it was because this was my first moment of almost peace since my grandfather died.

The past few months had been headache after headache. Funeral arrangements, Francis's blackmail, Luca's bullshit, the engagement and Europe trip and regular business and social obligations I had to keep up with.

It was nice to sit and breathe for a minute.

"Speaking of my parents, they'd like to meet you," I said. Introducing Vivian to them was a headache I'd hoped to avoid, though I'd known the chances of fending them off for a year or however long it took to break the engagement were slim. "We're spending Thanksgiving with them."

According to Christian's report, the Laus weren't big on Thanksgiving, so Vivian shouldn't be too upset about missing the holiday with her family.

Not that I cared if she was.

"Okay." She paused, obviously waiting for more information. When I didn't provide any, she asked, "Do your parents live in New York?"

"A little farther." I tossed my empty coffee cup in a nearby trash can. "Bali."

For now. My parents hadn't spent more than three consecutive months in one place in decades.

Vivian's mouth parted. "You want us to fly to *Bali* to meet your parents for Thanksgiving?"

"We'll be there for a week. We leave the Sunday prior and come back the following Monday."

"Dante." She sounded like she was struggling to keep calm. "I can't just go to Bali for a week with less than two months' notice. I have a job, plans—"

"It's a holiday weekend," I said impatiently. "What are you planning? The Macy's Thanksgiving Day Parade?"

She crumpled her bagel wrapper with a white-knuckled hand. "I have to be back that Monday morning for a client meeting. I'll be tired, jet-lagged—"

"Then we'll leave Saturday instead." My parents were the ones who'd insisted we stay a week. Vivian's work gave me a good excuse to cut out early. "We're taking my jet, and we'll be staying at my parents' villa. It's not a big deal. We're going to Bali, for fuck's sake. Everyone wants to go to Bali."

"That's not the point. We should be consulting each other on this type of stuff. You're my fiancé, not my boss. You can't just tell me to jump and expect me to jump."

God, this was tedious. "Considering I'm the one who paid for your shoes and flowers, I think I can do exactly that."

I knew it was the wrong thing to say the second the words left my mouth, but it was too late to take them back.

Vivian stood abruptly. A breeze blew her skirt around her thighs, and a passing jogger gawked at her until I chased him off with a glare.

"Thank God you showed your true colors again," she said,

her cheeks flushed. "I was beginning to think you were human." She threw out her cup and wrapper. "Thank you for breakfast. Let's never do this again."

She walked away, her shoulders stiff.

Behind his cart, Omar shook his head and frowned at me.

I ignored him. Who cared if that'd been an asshole thing to say? I'd already let my guard down more than I should've that morning. Vivian was the daughter of the enemy, and I would do well to remember that.

I stayed on the bench for a while longer, trying to recapture the magic from earlier, but the peace was gone.

When I returned home, I found a check waiting on my bedside table for exactly one hundred thousand dollars.

CHAPTER 9

Vivian

THE FLEA MARKET WAS ALIVE WITH THE SOUNDS OF haggling and the faint honks of cabs from the neighboring streets. The scent of churros swirled through the air, and everywhere I looked, I saw an explosion of different colors, textures, and fabrics.

I'd been visiting the same market every Saturday for years. It was a treasure trove of inspiration and one-of-a-kind items I couldn't find in the carefully curated luxury stores, and it never failed to pull me out of a creative rut. It was also my favorite place to visit when I needed to clear my head.

Today, however, it did neither of those things.

No matter how hard I tried, I couldn't shake the memory of Dante's mouth on mine. The firmness of his lips. The heat of his body. The subtle, expensive scent of his cologne and the self-assured weight of his hands on my hips. Days later, I could still *feel* the vividness of the moment as clearly as if it'd just happened.

It was infuriating. Almost as infuriating as how I'd opened up to him over breakfast, only for him to revert to asshole status after a brief, shocking display of humanity.

There'd been a moment when I'd *liked* Dante, though that

might've been my loneliness talking. Contrary to what I'd told him at the photo shoot, there was something unsettling about coming home every day to a silent, spotless house. Our month apart had eased the sting of his words before he left for Europe, and I hadn't realized how much Dante's presence electrified the space until he was gone.

"We've been to this stall already," Isabella said.

"Hmm?" I toyed with the fringe on a purple patterned scarf.

"This stall. We've been here already," she repeated. "You bought the pashmina?"

I blinked as the rest of the stall's contents came into sharp focus. She was right. It was one of the first vendors we'd visited when we arrived.

"Sorry." I released the scarf with a sigh. "I'm a bit out of it today."

I'm too busy thinking about my jerk fiancé.

"Really? I couldn't tell." Isabella's teasing smile faded when I didn't return it. "What's wrong? You normally blitz through this place like hellhounds are chasing us."

Isabella loved thrifting and joined my Saturday excursions whenever she could. I'd tried to convince Sloane to come once, but the chances of her stepping foot in a flea market were slimmer than a Jimmy Choo stiletto heel.

"I just have a lot on my mind."

I wanted to tell Isabella about the photo shoot, but there was nothing *to* tell. Dante and I had touched lips for thirty seconds for a photo. Anything beyond that was hormones and my dry spell talking.

Besides, I wasn't lying. Between my job, my fraught relationship with Dante, my new social obligations as the future Mrs. Russo, and my miles-long to-do list for the wedding, I was running on fumes.

"We're almost done," I added. "I just need to find a gold mirror for Buffy Darlington's granddaughter's sweet sixteen."

"I can't believe we live in a world where there are people named Buffy Darlington." Isabella shuddered. "Her parents must've hated her."

"Buffy Darlington the Third, to be exact. It's a family name."

"That's even worse."

I laughed. "Well, name aside, Buffy is the grande dame of New York society *and* the head of the Legacy Ball committee. I have to impress her, or I can kiss my business goodbye."

The Legacy Ball was the most exclusive event on the international circuit. It rotated locations every year, and the upcoming ball in May happened to take place right here in New York. Hosting it was considered a huge honor. I'd hoped for a shot at the position, but it'd gone to the wife of a hedge fund tycoon instead.

"Speaking of high society, how's your new job?" I asked.

Isabella quit the dive bar last week after landing a highly coveted job at the Valhalla Club, a members-only society for the world's wealthiest and most powerful. My father had been trying to gain admission for years, but the Boston chapter was closed to new applicants, and our family wasn't connected enough to slip through the back door.

Isabella's face lit up. "It's *amazing*. Higher pay, better benefits, *and* fewer hours than anything else I'd find in the city. It beats bartending with Creepy Colin breathing all over me by a mile. Maybe I'll actually have time to finish my book…" She trailed off as she stared over my shoulder. "Um, Viv?"

"Hmm?" I spotted a gold mirror on a nearby table. Buffy's granddaughter's party was *Beauty and the Beast* themed, and while I'd finalized the decor already, I wanted a unique piece to tie everything together.

"You might want to look behind you." A strange note dampened her voice.

Curiosity kindled as I turned to see what Isabella was staring at. Not much rattled her.

At first, all I saw were passersby holding churros and vendors hawking their wares. Then I noticed the person standing behind us.

Sandy-blond hair. Blue eyes. A once lanky frame that'd filled out with muscle over the years.

My shopping bags thudded to the ground as shock displaced the air in my lungs.

Heath.

"I'm sorry for ambushing you. I was passing by, and I remembered you loved coming here every Saturday." Heath let out a small laugh. "I guess you still do."

I returned his smile with a wary one of my own. "Old habits die hard."

After I'd gotten over my shock and Isabella had excused herself to "nap and write," Heath and I had left the market to grab coffee at a tiny outdoor café down the street. There were no other customers, so it was just us talking over cappuccinos like two years hadn't passed since we last saw each other.

It was surreal.

"Are you here on vacation?" I asked.

Heath had randomly sent me a photo of the pumpkin hot chocolate at Bonnie Sue's the other day, so I knew he was in town. It was the first text he'd sent since I told him I was engaged.

He hadn't mentioned the engagement, and I hadn't made plans to see him.

"Work. I have a meeting with investors on Monday and

figured I'd fly in early to enjoy the city. It's been a while." He rubbed a hand over the back of his neck. "I would've called you but..."

"You don't have to explain."

Today was an anomaly. We normally didn't tell each other when we were in town or catch up over drinks. We didn't have that type of relationship anymore.

"Right." Heath cleared his throat. "You look good, Viv. Really good."

My face softened. "So do you."

The Heath I'd dated had been a poster boy for New England prep. The one sitting in front of me looked like he belonged on the poster for a California surfer movie. Tanner, healthier, more muscled.

I'd often wondered what would happen if I ran into Heath again. I'd expected to feel sadness, regret, and maybe longing. We'd been friends and dated for years; feelings didn't disappear just because people parted ways. They did, however, dull with time, because all I felt right now was the cold breeze on my skin and a strange unease in the pit of my stomach.

"How's the IPO prep going?" I asked for lack of anything better to say.

We used to talk about everything under the sun. Now, we were more hesitant than strangers forced to share a table at an overly crowded restaurant.

"It's great. Stressful, but we're making good progress." Company IPOs, or initial public offerings, required extensive preparation, so Heath was probably getting only a few hours of sleep a night until his was done. "How's, uh, event planning?"

"Good. I hired someone to run our social media a few months ago, so we're up to a team of four."

"Good."

We had to stop using the word *good.*

The uncomfortable silence expanded. Heath and I stared awkwardly at each other for another minute before his gaze dropped to my engagement ring. A storm of emotions clouded his eyes, and I resisted the urge to pull my hand off the table and into my lap.

"You weren't joking about the engagement."

A pang hit my chest at his first direct acknowledgment of my new relationship status.

"I wouldn't joke about something like that," I said softly.

"I know. I just thought..." He tipped his head back and blew out a long breath. "When's the wedding?"

"Next year. Early August." I rubbed a nervous thumb over my ring. It was cold and hard to the touch.

"At the Russos' estate in Lake Como?"

He must've looked up the news after I told him.

"Yes."

"You and Dante Russo. Your parents must be thrilled." Heath met my eyes again with a sardonic smile. "What's he worth? Like a billion dollars?"

Two.

"Something like that."

"How'd you two meet?"

"At an event," I replied vaguely. I didn't want to lie to Heath, but I didn't want to tell him it was an arranged marriage either. My parents' approval was a sore subject for both of us. Unfortunately, he knew me well enough to pick up on the nuances of my nonanswer.

His eyes narrowed. The unease in my stomach swirled faster as realization dawned slow and horrified across his face.

"Wait. Are you marrying him because you want to or because your *parents* want you to?"

I shifted in my seat, suddenly wishing I'd skipped the market today.

I didn't answer, but my silence told him all he needed to know.

"Dammit, Viv." Frustration seeped into his voice. "I *knew* you'd never willingly choose someone like Dante. I looked him up after your text. All those rumors about him and what he's like... no amount of money in the world is worth it. What the hell were your parents thinking? Besides the fact that he's a billionaire." An uncharacteristically bitter edge poisoned his words.

"He's not *that* bad," I said, strangely defensive of Dante even though he'd been a jerk during ninety percent of our interactions.

But...the kiss. The breakfast. The story of the Moondust Diner. They were small things in the grand scheme of our relationship, but they gave me hope.

Dante Russo had a human side. He just didn't show it often.

"That's what he wants you to think. Even if he isn't as bad as the rumors say, do you want to be married to someone who's already married to his work?"

My mind flashed to Dante's month-long trip to Europe. I rubbed my ring again, my insides twisted with frustration. I felt like a bird trapped in a cage of circumstances beyond my control, unable to do anything except sing and look pretty.

Heath leaned forward, his expression intense. "You don't *have* to marry him, Viv."

"Heath—"

"I mean it." The fierceness of his tone startled me. "You've always done what your parents told you to do, but this isn't about a job or where you go to college. This is about the rest of your life. You're not a teenager anymore, and you have your own money. You can push back."

We'd had this conversation before, and it ended the same way every time.

"It's not about pushing back," I said. "They're my *family*, Heath. I can't turn my back on them."

His laugh lacked humor. "I should've known you were going to say that." He leaned back, his gaze heavy on mine. "I haven't dated anyone since we broke up, you know. Not seriously. My longest relationship after you lasted a month."

Another pang worked its way through my chest at his low confession.

"Neither have I," I said quietly. "But I'm engaged now, and this conversation is inappropriate."

I didn't like Dante, but I would never cheat on him or disrespect the implicit promise I'd made when I accepted his ring.

Heath painted a tempting picture of a world where I was free to do as I pleased, but that was all it was, a picture. Fantasy, not reality. In the real world, I had duties and obligations to fulfill. No matter how rude or overbearing Dante was, I had to make my engagement work, one way or another. There was no other option.

"You should go," I said. "I'm sure you have a lot to do before your Monday meeting."

Heath stared at me for a second before he shook his head.

"Right." He pushed his chair back and stood. His bitter expression returned, but his voice was soft as he left. "It was good seeing you, Viv. If you ever change your mind, you know where to find me."

I watched him walk away, my heart heavy and my thoughts running in a dozen different directions. So much had happened in the past week, it felt like a fever dream.

Dante returning from Europe.

Our kiss and first real conversation together.

Heath showing up out of the blue and asking me to break my engagement.

Dante and I hadn't discussed our dating history, but what would he say if he found out what happened with Heath today? No matter his feelings toward me, he didn't strike me as the type of man who'd respond well to other people interfering in his relationships.

His security team once hospitalized someone who tried to break into his house. The guy wound up in a months-long coma with broken ribs and a shattered kneecap.

Sloane's voice echoed in my head, followed by an image of coal-dark eyes and calloused hands.

A shiver skated down my spine. I was suddenly glad Dante didn't take any interest in my comings and goings. If he did…I had a strong feeling Heath might not make it to see his company's IPO.

CHAPTER 10

Dante

"ANOTHER ONE BITES THE DUST. SOMETHING MUST BE in the water, with the way everyone around me is suddenly getting hitched," Christian drawled. "How *are* things with your blushing bride? Blissful, I hope."

"Cut the crap, Harper, or I'll throw you out myself," I growled. My engagement party was insufferable enough without dealing with him. I was still unsettled from my kiss with Vivian last week, and now I had to make small talk with a bunch of people I didn't particularly care for.

A wicked smile slashed across Christian's face. "Not blissful, then."

In the fourteen years I'd known Christian Harper, not a single one had passed without him inciting me to near murder. It was almost impressive on his part.

Instead of strangling him like I wanted, I smoothed a casual hand over my tie. "Compared to your pining? It's fucking paradise."

His eyes narrowed. "I don't pine."

"No. You simply slash the rent for everyone who wants to live in your building for no good reason."

He wasn't the only one who kept tabs on the people in his circle.

As a computer genius, owner of a luxury building in DC, and the CEO of Harper Security, an elite private security firm, Christian had eyes and ears everywhere. He knew about Francis's blackmail. Hell, he was the one I'd tasked with tracking down and destroying the evidence. He was also an asshole who got off on seeing how far he could push people. Some pushed back. Most didn't. Unfortunately for him, I was one of the few who called him out on his bullshit without hesitation.

"I'm not here to discuss my business decisions with you," he said coldly. If anything could rile up the normally composed Christian, it was the mention, however indirect, of a certain tenant in his building. "I'm here to celebrate this *exciting* new chapter of your life." He lifted his glass. "A toast to you and Vivian. May you have a long, happy life together."

"Fuck off."

The bastard laughed in response, but the mention of Vivian unwittingly brought my eyes to where she stood chatting with an elegant older couple. She'd been the consummate hostess all day, mingling and charming the guests until I couldn't take two steps without someone gushing to me about how lovely she was.

It was galling.

My eyes lingered on the sweep of hair cascading over her shoulder and the swirl of silk around her knees. Her parents were here, but she wasn't wearing tweed, thank God. Instead, she wore an ivory dress that flowed over her curves and made my pulse pound. Short sleeves, modest neck, elegant cut. The dress wasn't racy by any means, but the way she glowed in it—the way her skin looked smoother than the silk and the way the skirt ruffled in the breeze—made my blood burn a little hotter.

Vivian laughed at something the couple said. Her whole face lit up, and I realized I'd never seen her genuine, unguarded smile before. No sarcasm or prim facade, just sparkling eyes, rosy cheeks, and an airy lightness that transformed her from beautiful to stunning.

Awareness kindled in my chest, hot and unwanted.

"Should I come back after you've finished ogling her?" Christian swirled the ice in his glass. "I don't want to intrude on a private moment."

"I'm not ogling her." I dragged my eyes away from Vivian, but her presence remained a tangible heat on my skin. I tried to shake it off to no avail. "Enough bullshit. Give me an update on the project."

He sobered. "Business operations are going as planned. The other situation is progressing, but not as quickly as we'd hoped."

The pieces were falling in place for Francis's business takedown, but we were still stalled on the evidence front.

Dammit.

"Just get it done before the wedding. Keep me updated."

"I always do." The amused glint in Christian's eyes returned when he looked over my shoulder. "Incoming."

I sensed her before I saw her. The sound of her heels, the smell of her perfume, the soft rustle of fabric against skin. I drained my drink in one long pull as Vivian came up beside me.

"Apologies for interrupting." She touched my arm and smiled at Christian, playing the role of apologetic fiancée perfectly.

My skin tingled beneath her hand, and I almost shook her off before I remembered where we were. *Engagement party. Loving couple. Pretend.*

"I need to steal Dante for a moment. *Mode de Vie* would like a photo for their wedding feature."

"Of course," Christian drawled. "Have fun."

One day, I'd pay him back for all the crap he gave me about Vivian.

I followed her to the photo setup, where Francis waited with Cecelia, Vivian's sister, Agnes, and Agnes's husband. My brother stood off to the side, his eyes glued to his phone while the photographer fiddled with his camera.

Something dangerous uncoiled in my chest. I'd avoided Francis all day. He didn't deserve my attention in public, which would only elevate his status, and I didn't need more temptation to commit murder. Apparently, my run had come to an end.

"You didn't tell me this was a family photo." The word *family* came out with an acerbic bite.

"I didn't realize it mattered." Vivian slid a sideways glance at me. "I asked *Mode de Vie* to wait until everyone was together, but they specifically wanted a photo from the party. However, they agreed to take another one with your parents whenever they're stateside."

I almost laughed at the insinuation I was upset over my parents' absence. I couldn't remember the last time Giovanni and Janis Russo showed up for one of their kids' milestones.

"I'll survive without a photo of our big, happy family," I said, my tone dry.

I took my place in front of the camera as far away from Francis as possible. When the photographer gave us the go-ahead, I wrapped my arm around Vivian's waist and forced a tight smile.

God, I hated photo shoots. Luckily, this one didn't require a kiss, and we got the shot in less than five minutes. Vivian's friends pulled her away after for some reason or other while Luca turned to me.

"Hey, uh, I just wanted to say...congratulations? On the engagement."

My glare could've set the room on fire.

He held up his hands. "Whoa, I'm trying to play nice, okay? I'm..." He lowered his hands and glanced around the room before facing me again. Guilt slashed across his expression. "I'm sorry this fell on you."

His voice was barely audible over the other guests' chatter, but it cut straight into my chest.

"It is what it is." I was used to cleaning up after my brother. Hell, considering some of his past choices, I should be glad he hadn't *joined* the Mafia.

Things were shit, but they could always be worse.

Luca wiped a hand over his face. "I know, but I…fuck. I know you never wanted to get married. This is a big deal, Dante, and I know you're working on finding—"

"Luca." His name was a warning. "Not now."

Christian was discreet; my brother wasn't. I didn't want anyone overhearing us at my own damn party.

"Right. Well, I just wanted to congratulate—I mean, apologize. And thank you." His expression turned embarrassed. "I know I don't say this often, but you're a good brother. You always have been."

Tightness crowded my chest before I acknowledged his statement with a curt nod.

"Go enjoy the party. I'll see you at dinner next week."

I wanted to see how things were going at Lohman & Sons and make sure he was staying away from Maria. Despite his seeming remorse, I didn't trust him enough to go long periods without checking in on him.

After Luca left, I made my way to the bar only to get stopped by Francis, who'd been busy talking to Kai until now.

"Excellent turnout," he said as Kai shot me an indecipherable glance before slipping away. "It looks like the entire East Coast Valhalla membership is here." A pause, then, "You have quite a presence in the club, don't you?"

I regarded him coolly, the tightness from my conversation

with Luca sinking beneath a well of distaste. My great-grandfather had been one of the club's twelve founding members. If I nominated someone for admission, they were guaranteed a spot, provided they met the basic eligibility criteria.

"Not any more or less than other members," I said.

"Right." Francis's smile came alive like a shark sensing blood in the water. "I hear there'll be an opening in the Boston chapter soon. Some nasty business with Peltzer's bankruptcy."

Ironic he should sound so gleeful about it when he would be in the same boat as Peltzer soon.

I couldn't fucking wait. Until then...

"So I heard." I tilted my head. "You were denied the last time you applied, no? Perhaps you'll have better luck this time."

Francis's face darkened before relaxing into another smile. "I'm sure I will with your support. We're practically family now, and family helps each other out. Don't they?" He cast a meaningful look in Luca's direction.

Rage clamped my jaw tight at his obvious threat.

Legacy Valhalla members were granted five nominations in their lifetime. I'd already used two—one for Christian, one for Dominic. I would rather cut off my dick than waste a third on Francis.

"I don't have much insight into the Boston chapter." It was only half a lie. I had connections there, but each chapter acted fairly independently in accordance with the local culture, politics, and traditions. "Valhalla's membership committee is diligent in its selection process. If someone is worthy of being admitted, they'll be admitted."

Red splashed across Francis's cheeks at my subtle dig.

"While I'm all for helping family..." My smile hardened into a warning. "They should know better than to push too hard. It never turns out well for the parties involved."

Francis had enough balls to blackmail me but not enough to pretend he owned me. He was testing my breaking point to see how far he could take things. Little did he know, he'd crossed it the minute he walked into my office and put those photos on my desk.

Before he could respond, Vivian returned, her cheeks noticeably more flushed than before. I wondered how many drinks she'd had with her friends.

"What did I miss?" she asked.

"Your father and I were just discussing wedding logistics." I didn't take my eyes off Francis. "Isn't that right?"

Resentment filled his eyes, but he didn't dispute my account. "Right."

Vivian's eyes roved between us. She must've picked up on the underlying hostility because she quickly nudged her father toward *Mode de Vie*'s lifestyle columnist before pulling me aside.

"I don't know what you were really talking about, but you shouldn't provoke my father," she said. "It's like provoking a wounded tiger."

A wisp of amusement cooled my anger. "I'm not scared of your father, *mia cara*. If he doesn't like what I say, he can take it up with me himself."

"Don't call me that. *Mia cara*," she clarified. "It's insulting."

I notched an eyebrow. "How so?"

"You don't mean it."

"People say things they don't mean all the time." I nodded at a silver-haired guest standing by the bar. "For example, your riveting conversation with Thomas Dreyer earlier. Don't tell me you were actually interested in the minutiae of tax write-offs."

"How did you hear...never mind. It doesn't matter." Vivian shook her head. "Look, I know this is business to you. You're not high on my dream list of people to marry either, but it doesn't change the fact that we have to live with each other. We should at least *try* and make the most of the situation."

What the fuck?

A rush of irritation ran down my spine. "Who exactly *is* on your dream list of people to marry?"

"Seriously?" Exasperation bled into her voice. "*That's* your takeaway from what I just said?"

"How long is the list?"

It didn't matter that I was forced into the engagement. My fiancée shouldn't have a list of other men she'd rather marry. Period.

"It doesn't matter."

"It sure as hell does."

"I don't—" Vivian's sentence cut off when a drunken guest passed by and accidentally knocked into her.

She stumbled, and my hand instinctively shot out before she crashed into a nearby table of champagne. We both froze, our eyes locked on where our bodies touched.

The surrounding noise dulled into a muted roar, overpowered by the heavy thuds of my heartbeat and the sudden hum of electricity in the air.

Even in heels, Vivian stood a full six inches shorter than me, and I could see the downward sweep of her lashes as her gaze homed in on where my fingers encircled her wrist. It was so delicate I could've snapped it without trying.

Her pulse quickened, tempting me to prolong my hold before I came to my senses and dropped her hand like it was a hot coal. The spell splintered at the loss of contact, and the sounds from the rest of the party burst through the cracks until it shattered into nothing.

Vivian pulled back and rubbed her wrist, her cheeks pink.

"What I was trying to say before we got off track is we should attempt to get along," she said breathlessly. "Get to know each other. Maybe go on a date or two."

Some of the earlier tension dissipated.

"Are you asking me out, *mia cara*?" A smile touched my lips at her glare.

"I told you to stop calling me that."

"Yes, you did."

I was going to call her *mia cara* every chance I got.

Vivian closed her eyes and looked like she was praying for patience before she opened them again a few seconds later.

"Fine, let's compromise. You can call me *mia cara*, *sparingly*, if you agree to the truce."

"I wasn't aware we were at war," I drawled.

I rubbed a thumb over my bottom lip, contemplating her offer. Originally, I'd planned on ignoring Vivian until I ended the engagement. Out of sight, out of mind. But her little flashes of defiance intrigued me, as did the insights she inadvertently shared about her family.

Perhaps keeping her at arm's length was the wrong strategy.

Keep your friends close and your enemies closer.

I made my final decision in a split second.

"It's a deal." I held out my hand.

Vivian eyed it with a flicker of surprise, then wariness, before she took it.

Her breath escaped in a small gasp when I grasped her tighter and pulled her to me.

"Have to keep up appearances," I murmured. I inclined my head to our right, where at least a dozen guests were sneaking peeks at us.

My inbox had exploded after news of my engagement broke. No one believed I was engaged until they saw it with their own eyes, and I bet dozens of candid shots of me and Vivian would hit the internet later that night, if they hadn't already.

I trailed my free hand up her spine and curled it around the back of her neck before I lowered my mouth to her ear. "Welcome to the truce, *mia cara*."

My breath fanned across her cheek.

She stiffened, her own breaths taking on an uneven rhythm.

I smiled.

This was going to be fun.

CHAPTER 11

Vivian

I COULDN'T SLEEP.

I'd collapsed into bed three hours ago, my body exhausted but my mind racing like I'd injected it with a dozen shots of espresso. I'd tried counting sheep, fantasizing about Asher Donovan, and listening to my alarm clock's built-in white noise feature, but none of it worked.

Every time I closed my eyes, images from the engagement party played on a broken loop.

Dante's hand around my wrist.

The graze of his fingers along my spine.

The low rumble of his voice in my ear.

Welcome to the truce, mia cara.

Tingles erupted over every inch of my body.

I groaned and turned on my side, hoping the change in position would shake the persistent memory of Dante's touch and rough velvet voice. It didn't.

Honestly, I was surprised he'd agreed so readily to the truce. We hadn't exchanged more than a dozen words since I left him on the sidewalk bench after our engagement shoot, but actively ignoring him was more draining than I'd expected.

The penthouse was massive, yet we somehow ran into each other multiple times a day—him coming out of his bedroom while I walked to mine, me catching a breath of fresh air while he took a call on the balcony, both of us sneaking into the screening room for a late-night movie at the same time. One of us always left when we saw the other, but I couldn't turn the corner without my heart rate jumping in anticipation of colliding with Dante.

The truce was the best option for my sanity and blood pressure.

Plus, the one unguarded conversation we'd had so far had been...nice. Unexpected, but nice. There was a heart somewhere beneath Dante's grumpy, scowling exterior. It may be black and shriveled, but it was there.

The numbers on my clock flipped from 12:02 a.m. to 12:03 a.m. My stomach emitted an angry growl at the same time. After subsisting on nothing except a handful of hors d'oeuvres and champagne all day, it was finally rebelling.

I groaned again. It was technically too late to eat, but...

What the hell. I couldn't sleep anyway.

After a moment's hesitation, I tossed my covers off and tiptoed out of my room and down the hall. I hadn't had a midnight snack in years, but I was suddenly craving an old favorite food combo.

I flipped on the kitchen lights, opened the fridge, and scanned the contents until I located a jar of sliced pickles and a bowl of chocolate pudding on the bottom shelf.

Aha!

I set my bounty on the kitchen island before I hunted for the last ingredient.

Dried pasta, condiments, cookies, seaweed crisps... I opened and closed the endless row of cabinets, searching for a distinctive cardboard tube. The cabinets were so high I had to stand on tiptoes to see into the back, and my arms and thighs were starting to ache. Why did Dante have so much storage space? Who needed an entire cabinet of *cooking oils*?

If I didn't—

"What are you doing?"

I jumped and stifled a scream at the unexpected voice. My hip banged against the counter when I whipped around, sparking a jolt of pain whose reverberations matched the suddenly frantic beats of my heart.

Dante stood in the doorway, his gaze bemused as it traveled between me and the open cabinet.

For once, he wasn't wearing a suit and tie. Instead, a white T-shirt stretched across his shoulders, emphasizing the sculpted planes of his muscles and the deep bronze of his skin. Black sweatpants hung just low enough to elicit dirty thoughts before I quashed them.

"You scared me." My voice came out breathier than intended. "What are you doing up?"

It was a stupid question. Obviously, he was up for the same reason I was, but I couldn't think straight through the fog of adrenaline.

"Couldn't sleep." The rough drawl drifted toward me and settled low between my legs. "Guess I'm not the only one."

His eyes held mine for a brief moment before they flicked over me.

A sense of déjà vu spilled down the length of my spine, but unlike at our first meeting, I detected a crack in Dante's indifference. It was tiny, just a shadow of a flame, but it was enough to fill my stomach with flutters.

His perusal paused at my midsection. The shadow expanded, darkening his eyes from rich brown to near obsidian.

I looked down, and my heart stumbled when I saw what caught his attention.

I slept hot, so I usually wore some variation of a silk camisole and boy shorts to bed. It was fine for the privacy of my bedroom but completely inappropriate when faced with company. The shorts stopped an inch above midthigh, and my top had ridden up sometime during my cabinet foraging, revealing a generous expanse of bare skin.

When I looked up again, Dante's gaze had returned to my face.

I held still, afraid to breathe as he moved toward me with the languid, powerful grace of a predator stalking its prey. Every soft footfall was another lit flame in the space between us.

He stopped when his body heat enveloped mine. Inches away, so close I could count the individual stubble shadowing his jaw.

"What are you looking for?" His casual tone clashed with the tension brewing in the air, but I simply said the first thing that came to mind.

"Pringles. Classic."

There was no answer like the truth.

I discreetly tugged my top down while Dante reached into the cabinet above my head. The tiny breeze from his movement brushed my skin. Goose bumps pebbled, and something hot coiled in my stomach.

He retrieved an unopened can of chips and handed it to me without a word.

"Thank you." I clutched the tube, unsure what to do next. Part of me wanted to escape to the safety of my room. The other part wanted to stay and see how long I could play with fire without getting burned.

"Pringles, pickles, and pudding." Dante saved me from a decision. "Interesting combination."

Relief loosened the knot in my chest. My breath came out easier now that I had something to focus on other than my body's unwilling reaction to his.

"They taste good together. Don't knock it till you've tried it." I took control of my limbs again and sidestepped him on my way to the island.

The touch of his gaze followed me, an insistent pressure on the small of my back.

I opened the can of Pringles. *Don't turn around.*

"Apologies. Far be it from me to question your snack choices." A trace of dry amusement ran through his voice.

I heard the fridge open behind me, followed by the clink of silverware and the *click* of a shutting cabinet door.

A minute later, Dante slid onto the stool beside me.

My mouth parted when he began assembling his snack.

"You make fun of me for my food choices but you're pouring *soy sauce* over ice cream?"

The earlier tension retreated in the face of my shock. Forget the way his muscles flexed with each movement or the way his shirt hugged his torso. He was committing a crime against humanity right before my eyes.

"Drizzling, not pouring. And don't knock it till you've tried it," Dante mocked, throwing my earlier words back at me. "I bet it tastes better than the abomination you put together."

His brow hitched at the chip in my hand, which I'd dipped in pudding and topped with a pickle.

My eyes narrowed at the silent challenge.

"I doubt it." I lifted his hand and dropped my lovingly assembled snack in his open palm. He stared at it like it was a piece of old gum stuck to his shoe. "Let's swap and see who's wrong and who's right."

I pulled his bowl toward me with a small grimace. I loved ice cream and I loved soy sauce...*separately*. Some things weren't meant to mix, but I was willing to choke it down to make my point.

Namely, I was right, and he was wrong.

"I'm always right," Dante said. He eyed me and then my snack with a hint of intrigue. "Fine. I'll bite. On the count of three."

I almost asked if the pun was on purpose before I remembered his sense of humor was more underdeveloped than a toddler's vocabulary.

"One," I said.

"Two." His grimace matched mine.

"Three."

I spooned a serving of ice cream into my mouth at the same time as he bit into my chip.

Silence filled the room, interrupted only by the crunch of food and the hum of the fridge.

I'd braced myself for a wave of revulsion, but the combination of French vanilla and soy sauce was...

That can't be right. Maybe my taste buds were broken.

I helped myself to another scoop just to make sure.

Dante's mouth curled into a knowing grin. "Going back for seconds already?"

"Don't act so smug. It's not *that* good," I lied.

"In that case, I'll take the ice cream back—"

"No!" I pulled the bowl closer to my chest. "I've already eaten from it. It's...unhygienic to share food. Get your own bowl."

Dante's grin widened.

I let out a sigh. "Fine. It tastes good. Are you happy?" I shot a pointed look at the island top. "I'm not the only one who was wrong. You've finished half the chips in the past five minutes."

"That's an exaggeration." He dipped another pickle and chip combo in the pudding. "But this isn't as terrible as I thought."

"See? I'll never steer you wrong when it comes to food." I dug my spoon into a fresh scoop of vanilla and relaxed into the unfamiliar but not unpleasant ease between us. Maybe the truce had been a good idea after all. "How did you come up with this combo anyway?"

I couldn't imagine Dante sampling different food pairings in his free time until he found a winner like I had. From what I saw, he barely had time to eat.

He was silent for a long moment before he said, "Luca and I hung out in the kitchen a lot as kids. We had a game room, pool, all the latest toys...pretty much everything anyone under the age of twelve could want. But sometimes, we wanted company other than each other, and the chef was one of the few people in the household who treated us like actual people. He let us play around in there when he wasn't cooking." Dante shrugged. "We were kids. We experimented."

My insides warmed at the mental image of little Dante running around the kitchen with his brother.

"You two must be close."

I'd met Luca at the engagement party. He'd been polite enough, though I got the sense he wasn't thrilled about my marriage to his brother. We'd only talked for a few minutes before he abruptly excused himself.

Dante's face shuttered. "Not as close as we used to be."

I paused at the strange note in his voice. For some reason, his brother was a sore subject.

"Does he work for the company?" I ventured when he didn't offer any more information.

I didn't want to push Dante too hard and have him shut down when we were finally making progress, but I couldn't contain my curiosity. I didn't know much about him beyond what was public knowledge.

He came from a very old, very wealthy family that made its fortune in textiles before his grandfather founded the Russo Group and expanded the family empire into what it was today.

He'd graduated top of his class from Harvard Business School and increased his company's market value fivefold since taking over as CEO. He eliminated his competition with shocking effectiveness, either by crushing or acquiring them, and the ruthlessness of his security team had catapulted him to mythical status.

I may have read up on Dante while he was in Europe.

"He does now." Dante's tone suggested the change had not been Luca's choice. "He interned at the company in college. It was a disaster, so our grandfather allowed him to 'pursue his passions' instead of taking on a corporate role. He already had me as an heir; he didn't need Luca. But giving my brother too much freedom was a mistake. Luca bounced around from job to job for a decade. He was a DJ one day, an actor the next. He sank half his trust fund into a nightclub that folded within eight months of opening. He needs stability and structure, not more time and money to burn."

It was the most words I'd heard come out of Dante's mouth since we met.

"So you gave him a job," I surmised. "What does he do now?"

"Salesman." The corner of Dante's mouth kicked up when I gave him a skeptical look. "He doesn't get special treatment because he's my brother. When I started at the Russo Group, I worked as a stock clerk. It was one of the greatest lessons my grandfather taught me. In order to lead a company, you have to *know* the company. Every facet, every position, every detail. Leaders who are out of touch are leaders who fail."

Somehow, Dante managed to surprise me every time we talked. I'd expected him to run his company from the top down with no care for his employees and blatant abuse of nepotism the way many of his peers did, but his philosophy made sense.

Since I couldn't say that without offending him, I stuck to the topic of his brother.

"I get the sense Luca doesn't like me," I admitted. "Every time I tried to talk to him at the party, he made an excuse and left."

Dante paused. Tension dampened the air for a second before his shoulders relaxed and the clouds disappeared.

"Don't take it personally. He gets moody at those types of things." He smoothly switched subjects. "Speaking of the party, you never told me who's on your dream husband list."

Oh, for God's sake.

I'd mentioned the list as a joke. I didn't know why he was so fixated on it. But since he *was*...I might as well have some fun.

"I'll tell you if you promise not to get an inferiority complex," I said sweetly. I ticked off the names of my favorite celebrities. "Nate Reynolds, Asher Donovan, Rafael Pessoa..."

Dante looked unimpressed. "I didn't realize you were such a big soccer fan."

Asher Donovan and Rafael Pessoa both played for Holchester United in the UK.

"I'm a soccer player fan," I corrected. "There's a difference."

I'd watched a total of three sports games in my life. I'd only mentioned Asher and Rafael because I saw them in an ad campaign yesterday and they were fresh on my mind.

"Reynolds is married, and Donovan and Pessoa live in Europe," Dante said silkily. "I'm afraid you're out of luck, *mia cara*."

"True." I heaved a long-suffering sigh. "In that case, I guess you'll have to do."

A laugh bubbled in my throat when he narrowed his eyes. "You're baiting me."

"Just a little."

My laugh finally spilled out at his scowl. I could practically see the bruises forming on his ego.

I didn't have any romantic notions about him being interested in the list because he liked me. He probably hated the idea of not being number one on *anyone's* list.

We didn't talk much after that, but the silence between us was less jagged than those from the early days of our engagement.

I snuck a glance at Dante as he methodically spread a layer of pudding on the last chip, his brow wrinkled in concentration. It was strangely adorable. I almost laughed again when I pictured how he'd react if he found out anyone described him as *adorable*.

I hid my smile as I swirled my spoon through my melting ice cream.

I was suddenly glad I couldn't sleep earlier.

CHAPTER 12

Vivian

"MAYBE YOU GUYS WILL FINALLY FUCK TONIGHT." Isabella's voice crackled through my phone, which I'd propped against the wall so I could see her while I got ready. "It's not a truce without an orgasm to close the deal."

"*Isa.*"

"What? It's true. You deserve some fun after working your butt off these past few weeks." Her keyboard clicks paused, and a distracted expression crossed her face. "Speaking of fun, what do you think my character's signature murder method should be? Poison, strangulation, or good ol' hacking with a butcher's knife?"

"Poison." It was the only one that didn't turn my stomach when I pictured it.

"Hacking it is. Thanks, Viv. You're the best."

I sighed.

Isabella sat in her room, her pet snake Monty draped over her shoulders while she typed furiously on her laptop. Behind her, a mountain of clothes covered her bed and half obscured the oil portrait of Monty that Sloane and I had commissioned as a joke for her birthday last year. Most writers preferred silence and solitude, but Isabella worked best surrounded by chaos. She said growing up with four older brothers had conditioned her to thrive in mayhem.

"Anyway," she said after several minutes of hacking her poor characters to pieces on the page. "Back to the topic at hand. You need to take the sex for a test drive before you commit. You don't want to be stuck with someone bad in bed. Not that I think Dante would have that problem," she added. "I bet he fucks like—"

"Stop." I held up a hand. "We are *not* discussing my fiancé's sexual prowess over the phone. Or ever."

"There's nothing *to* discuss. You haven't had sex yet." Isabella's cheeks dimpled while Monty forked his tongue as if in agreement. "You'll have to do it eventually. If not before the wedding, then on the wedding night and honeymoon...unless you both plan on being celibate for the rest of your lives." She wrinkled her nose.

I put on my earrings in silence, but a flutter of nerves cascaded through my stomach. She made a good point. I'd been so focused on planning the actual wedding I hadn't given much thought to what would happen *after*.

The marriage bed. The honeymoon. The heat of Dante's naked torso against mine and his mouth—

My throat dried, and I banished the X-rated mental image to the darkest recesses of my mind before it took root.

"We'll cross that bridge when we get there," I said in a hopefully convincing tone. "We barely know each other."

My truce with Dante had held up surprisingly well since our late-night snack rendezvous last week, but despite the occasional conversation when we were both home—a rare occurrence given our busy schedules—my future husband remained an enigma.

"No better night to get to know each other than tonight." Isabella leaned back and stretched her arms over her head. A mischievous glint lit her eyes. "There are plenty of sexy nooks and crannies at the club."

"Don't tell me you've taken advantage of those already. It's only been..." I mentally calculated how long she'd been working at Valhalla. "Three weeks."

"Of course not." She dropped her arms. "It's against the rules to fraternize with members. I'm all for rule breaking, but this is the best job I've had in years. I'm not losing it so I can be a notch in some rich guy's bedpost, no matter how hot he is." Her expression flickered before it brightened again. "Fucking or no fucking, I can't wait for you to see the place. It's absolutely bonkers. The entry hall floor is inlaid with solid twenty-four-karat gold, and there's a rooftop helipad with a helicopter rental service that'll fly you anywhere within the tristate area for lunch..."

She continued describing Valhalla's amenities in detail.

I smiled at Isabella's enthusiasm even as nerves invaded my stomach. Tonight was my official society debut as Dante Russo's fiancée.

Our engagement party didn't count; that had been a private affair attended by friends and family. The annual fall costume gala at the Valhalla Club, on the other hand, was a different matter.

I'd attended dozens of high-society events before, but I'd never been invited to Valhalla since my family weren't members. I was more on edge than I cared to admit, but at least Isabella would be there. She was working the second half of the gala, which meant one guaranteed friendly face.

I stayed on the phone with her for another few minutes until she left for her shift. After I hung up, I took a deep breath, double-checked my reflection, and applied a second coat of red lipstick for extra confidence before I exited my room.

The faint sounds of Greta's favorite Italian game show drifted from the kitchen as I walked to the foyer. She liked watching TV while cooking and said Dante had installed the kitchen's small flat-screen for her when she started working for him. He'd threatened to remove it if any of her meals weren't up to par, but no one took his threats seriously. He was ruthless with outsiders, but he treated his staff like family, albeit one he kept at an arm's length and had extremely high expectations of.

My stomach dipped when he came into view.

Dante waited in the foyer, his head bent over his phone. He'd adhered to the gala's 1920s theme with his trademark precision: sleek three-piece charcoal tweed suit, matching newsboy cap, signature frown.

"If you keep scowling, your face will freeze that way." I attempted a light tone, but it came out embarrassingly breathy.

His eyes flicked up. "Very f—" The abrupt break in his sentence charged the air, as sudden and devastating as a lightning strike.

My steps faltered, then halted altogether. Every nerve ending sparked with awareness, sending goose bumps down my spine and oxygen out of my lungs as our gazes met.

Dante didn't take his eyes off mine, but his attention somehow touched every inch of my body until it came alive, like a black-and-white film thrown into Technicolor.

"You look..." He paused, an unidentifiable emotion passing over his face. "Nice."

The dark, velvety pitch of the word *nice* sent a thrill through my veins.

The mirror next to him reflected what he saw—an ivory beaded lace gown that bared my back and shoulders and fell to my thighs in a graceful line. Intricate, thickly woven patterns over strategic areas saved the dress from being completely see-through, but it would've still bordered on scandalous had it not been for the elegant cut. The outfit bared miles of skin and made me look almost naked from a distance, but one didn't dress to blend into the surroundings at Valhalla. They dressed to stand out.

"Thank you." I swallowed my hoarseness and tried again. "So do you. The twenties suit you."

The corner of his mouth tipped up. "Thank you."

He held out his arm. After a brief hesitation, I took it.

Silence wrapped around us as we took the elevator to the lobby and slid into the back seat of the waiting Rolls-Royce. I smoothed a hand over my skirt, unsure what else to do.

"How's work?" I asked when the silence stretched into uncomfortable territory. "I've barely seen you all week."

"Missed me?" Amusement lengthened his drawl.

"As much as a sailor misses scurvy."

Surprise burst through me at his laugh. Not a chuckle, not a scoff, but an honest-to-God laugh. The rich sound filled the car and seeped beneath my skin, where it transformed into a bloom of pleasure.

"You truly come up with the most flattering comparisons." His dry tone contrasted with the sparkle in his eyes.

My stomach swooped like I'd just plunged down the slope of a roller coaster. The sight of a laughing, unguarded Dante was utterly catastrophic for my ovaries.

"It's a talent I honed growing up." I tried to focus past my body's unwilling and, frankly, annoying reaction to a simple laugh. "During boring social events, my sister and I played a game where we had to come up with a good animal comparison for each guest. Alice Fong was a rabbit because she only ate salads and was constantly twitching her nose. Bryce Collins was a donkey because, well, he was a stubborn ass. So on and so forth." My cheeks heated. "It sounds silly, but it helped us pass the time."

"I don't doubt it." Dante leaned back, the picture of casual insouciance. "What would you liken me to?"

A dragon.

Glorious in his power, terrifying in his anger, and magnificent even in repose.

"If you'd asked me before our truce, I would've said an ill-mannered boar," I said instead. "Since we're being nice, I'll upgrade you to a honey badger."

"The most fearless animal in the world. I'll take it."

I blinked at how well he took it. Most people would not appreciate being compared to a honey badger.

"To answer your earlier question, work has been...aggravating." Dante's cuff links glinted in the light from a passing streetlamp. Silver, elegant, stamped with the letter *V*. "The deal I'm working on is a pain in the ass, but I'm flying to California on Tuesday to hopefully close it."

"The Santeri deal?" I'd read about it in the news.

One eyebrow rose. "Yes."

"You'll get it done. You've never lost out on an acquisition before."

His answering smile could've melted butter. "I appreciate your faith in me, *mia cara*."

Warmth spread through me like wildfire. Dante's voice and use of the term *mia cara* should be outlawed. They were too lethal to unleash on an unsuspecting female population.

"How was Tippy Darlington's birthday?" he asked casually. "Buffy happy?"

Another tendril of surprise snaked through my chest. I'd mentioned the party to him in passing only once, weeks ago. I couldn't believe he remembered.

"It went well. Buffy is thrilled."

"Good."

I suppressed a smile as I turned and stared out the window. The question about the Darlingtons made me oddly happy.

Friday night Manhattan traffic was a nightmare, but eventually, we broke through the gridlock and pulled up to a pair of giant black iron gates flanked by stone guardhouses. Dante flashed his chip-embedded invitation and membership card at one of the stoic-faced guards. The guard typed something on his computer, and a full thirty seconds passed before the gates slid open with a smooth electronic whir.

"Car and biometric scans," Dante said in reply to my questioning stare. "Every person or vehicle that wants access to the property is registered in the club's in-house system, including staff and contractors. If someone attempts to enter without proper authorization once, they'll be turned away with a stern warning. If they attempt twice…" An elegant shrug. "There won't be a third time."

I chose not to ask what he meant. Sometimes, ignorance was bliss.

We drove down a winding road lit by hundreds of glowing lanterns in the trees. I felt like we were at a country estate instead of upper Manhattan. How could such a place exist in the middle of the city? Whoever built it must have sunk a fortune into buying all the land and permits necessary to create a veritable private oasis on some of the most coveted real estate in the country.

I grew up surrounded by wealth, but this was on another level.

"Don't be nervous." Dante's gruff voice interrupted my musings. "It's just a party."

"I'm not nervous."

"Your knuckles are white."

I looked down at where I clutched my knee in a death grip. My knuckles were, indeed, white. I relaxed them, only for my knee to bounce with anticipation instead.

Dante closed his hand over mine and pressed it against my thigh, forcing me to still. A rush of awareness shot through me and narrowed in on the sight of his hand swallowing mine. His grip was firm but surprisingly gentle, and after a moment of frozen surprise, I chanced a peek at him.

Dante stared straight ahead, his profile like granite. He looked bored, almost distracted, but the reassuring strength of his touch melted the edges of my rising anxiety. My heartbeats gradually slowed as the trees cleared and the Valhalla Club itself came into view. My breath whooshed out in one soft gasp.

Wow.

I shouldn't have expected any less, but Valhalla was an absolute masterpiece of architecture. The elegant, neoclassical main building stretched over four stories and an entire city block. Soft floodlights illuminated its grand white exterior, and an opulent crimson carpet covered the stairs leading up to the double-height entrance.

A line of luxury cars snaked down the drive, the subject of eagle-eyed scrutiny from the expressionless guards on duty. Ours stopped behind an armored Mercedes.

Dante and I exited the car and walked to the entrance, where a steady stream of guests in bespoke suits and exquisite dresses ascended the stairs.

Despite the literal red carpet and buzz of excitement in the air, there were no photographers present. People didn't attend a Valhalla event to flaunt for the public; they were here to flaunt for each other.

Dante placed a hand on the small of my back and guided me into the entry hall, where I immediately spotted what Isabella was talking about—a magnificent gold *V* inlaid into the floor, its three points touching the surrounding circle and glowing bright against an expanse of gleaming black marble.

The gala took place in the club's ballroom, but we couldn't move two feet without someone stopping us to greet Dante.

"How long have you been a member?" I asked after we

extricated ourselves from yet another conversation about the stock market. "You seem to know everyone. Or everyone seems to know you."

"Since I was twenty-one. It's the minimum age for members." A wry smile flickered over Dante's mouth. "Didn't stop my grandfather from trying to back-channel his way into a membership for me when I was eighteen, but there are things even Enzo Russo couldn't do."

It was only the second time he'd mentioned his grandfather, the first being after our engagement shoot. Enzo Russo, the legendary businessman and founder of the Russo Group, had died over the summer from a heart attack. His death had dominated headlines for well over a month.

Dante had taken over as CEO years before Enzo's death, but his grandfather had stayed on as president and chairman of the board. Now, Dante held all three positions.

"Do you miss him?" I asked softly.

"*Miss* isn't the right word." We passed through the foyer and down a long hallway toward what I assumed was the ballroom. Dante's voice was devoid of emotion. "He raised me and taught me everything I know about business and the world. I respected him, but we'd never been close. Not the way grandfathers and grandsons are supposed to be close."

"What about your parents?" I didn't know much about Giovanni and Janis Russo other than Giovanni had passed on running the company.

"They're doing what they always do," Dante said cryptically. "You'll see."

Right. We were spending Thanksgiving with them in Bali.

We passed through another security check near the ballroom before the doors opened and instantly transported me into a world of glittering 1920s decadence.

An art deco bar spanned the full length of the eastern wall, its black lacquer and gold accents shining with as much luster as the bottles of top-shelf liquor behind it. For those who didn't want to wait at the bar, impeccably dressed servers circulated with gin and tonics, martini carts, and champagne trolleys brimming with bubbly.

Lively music from the jazz band danced over the soft clink of glasses and elegant laughter, and intimate spaces were scattered throughout the room like oases of rich velvets and plush seating. In one corner, dealers lorded over half a dozen poker tables; in another, a silent film played via an old-school projector reel.

The ballroom itself soared four stories toward a glass dome, where a breathtaking projection of the night sky painted it with constellations so vivid I almost believed I could see Orion and Cassiopeia from Manhattan.

"Live up to your expectations?" Dante's hand lingered on my lower back.

I nodded, too distracted by the surrounding opulence and hint of possessiveness in his touch to come up with a witty answer.

Dante and I spent the first hour mingling with other club members. Unlike at our engagement party, we were perfectly in sync, stepping in when the other didn't answer and excusing ourselves when the conversation had run its course.

Toward the end of the hour, Dominic Davenport, whom I remembered from our party, pulled him away to discuss business. I took the opportunity for a quick bathroom break with Dominic's wife, Alessandra.

"I love your dress," she said as we retouched our makeup. "Is it Lilah Amiri?"

"Yes," I said, impressed. Lilah was a talented but up-and-coming designer; not many people recognized her work on sight.

"I saw it at New York Fashion Week and thought it would be perfect for tonight."

"You were right. Dante can't take his eyes off you." Alessandra smiled, a trace of sadness crossing her face. "You're very lucky to have such an attentive partner."

With her thick, caramel-brown hair and blue-gray eyes, she was extraordinarily beautiful, but she also seemed deeply unhappy. Our exchange about the dress had been the most animated I'd seen her all night.

"It's not all sunshine and roses. Dante and I have our differences. Trust me."

"Differences are better than nothing," she murmured. We exited the bathroom, but she stopped at the entrance to the ballroom. "I'm sorry. I've come down with a terrible headache. Can you please tell Dominic I've gone home?"

A frown touched my brow. "Of course, but wouldn't you rather tell him yourself? I'm sure he'll want to know if you're not feeling well."

"No. Once he gets into business mode, it's impossible to pry him away." A tiny, bitter smile flashed across Alessandra's face. "I'll leave him to his work. It was nice meeting you, Vivian."

"You too. I hope you feel better soon."

I waited until she disappeared around the corner before I approached Dominic and Dante.

Dominic's gaze flicked to the empty space next to me.

"Alessandra said to tell you she has a headache and had to go home," I explained.

Unidentifiable emotion flashed through his eyes before it vanished beneath pools of inscrutable blue. "Thank you for letting me know."

I paused, waiting for more of a reaction. None came.

Men. They were clueless half the time and callous the other half.

Dante and Dominic weren't done talking shop, so I excused myself again and wound my way to the bar. Discussing the ups and downs of the S&P 500 was not my idea of a fun Friday night.

A smile broke out on my face when I spotted a familiar glint of purple-black hair behind the counter.

"What does a girl have to do to get a drink around here?" I quipped, taking the stool closest to her.

Isabella looked up from the drink she was making. "Finally, the VIP deigns to drop by." She garnished the glass with a wedge of lime and slid it toward me. "Gin and tonic, just the way you like it."

"Perfect timing." I took a sip. "Have I mentioned how amazing you are?"

"Yes, but I don't mind hearing it again." Her eyes sparkled. "I saw you coming from a mile away. I guess people aren't interested in seeking out drinks when they can have the drinks brought to them." The bar was empty save for a couple sitting at the far end, but the themed alcohol carts were a huge hit. "I get paid the full amount no matter how many drinks I serve, so it's no skin off my back." Isabella patted her pocket. "I do, however, have a gift for you. Say the word, and it's yours."

I sighed, already knowing where the conversation was headed. Once she latched onto an idea, she was relentless. "Save your breath. I'm not having sex with him."

"Why? He's hot. You're hot. The sex is guaranteed to be hot," she argued. "Come on, Viv. Let me live vicariously through you. My life is so boring these days."

Despite her naturally flirtatious personality and propensity for writing about sex and murder, Isabella hadn't dated anyone in over a year. I didn't blame her after what happened. If I were her, I'd swear off guys for the foreseeable future too.

"You can live vicariously through books too. Stick to those, because sex with Dante tonight? Not happening."

No matter how good he looked or how my body responded to the idea.

Isabella's lips pursed in disappointment. "Fine, but if you change your mind, I have strawberry-flavored condoms. Magnum size, ribbed for your—"

A light cough interrupted her.

Isabella's smile dropped like a concrete kite, and I turned to see Kai watching us with bemusement.

"Apologies for interrupting, but I'd like to order another drink." He set his empty glass on the counter. "I can't get through another conversation about the latest society scandal without more alcohol, I'm afraid."

Wryness touched his last sentence.

"Of course." Isabella regained her composure with admirable speed. "What can I get for you?"

"Gin and tonic. Strawberry flavored."

I almost choked on my drink while Isabella's face turned an alarming shade of red. She stared at Kai, obviously trying to figure out if he was mocking her.

He stared back, his face the picture of polite impassiveness.

"One strawberry gin and tonic, coming right up," she said. She busied herself with the drink, her embarrassment a tangible weight in the air.

"Should I be worried she'll spit in my drink?" Kai took the stool next to mine, looking like he'd just stepped off the set of a *Great Gatsby* revival.

Between him and Dante, I was convinced a twenties-style outfit increased a man's attractiveness tenfold.

"She's not that vindictive...most of the time. And if she does, you'll see her." I hesitated, then asked, "How much of our conversation did you hear?"

"I don't know what you're talking about," he said mildly.

Relief settled in my chest. I didn't think Kai was the gossiping type, but it was nice to have confirmation.

"Kai Young, you deserve all the goodness in the world."

He laughed. "I'll keep that in mind for days when I'm feeling low." He accepted his drink from Isabella, who gave him a tight smile before double-speeding it to the other end of the bar.

His amused gaze lingered on her for a fraction of a beat before he shifted his attention back to me.

"How's living with Dante? Has he driven you mad with his insistence on spacing all his candles exactly six inches apart yet?"

"Don't get me started." Dante's control freak tendencies extended past his food quirks and into every area of the household. Sometimes, it was oddly charming. Other times, it made me want to drive a steak knife through his thigh. "The other day, our housekeeper Greta moved the candles in the living room..."

Kai and I chatted for a while, our conversation winding from Dante to the gala to our upcoming holiday plans until he received an urgent email and excused himself to answer it.

While he typed on his phone, I scanned the room, breathless from alcohol and the electric buzz in the air. My distracted survey stopped on a pair of cool, dark eyes, and the breath stalled in my lungs.

Dante watched me, his face unreadable, but heat flickered beneath his stony stare. He appeared to be completely ignoring Dominic.

The seconds stretched into a long thrum of tension. Tiny sparks ignited all over my body, and my heart fluttered with a wild rhythm I was sure couldn't be healthy.

A muscle ticked in Dante's jaw when he slid his gaze to Kai for a brief second before bringing it back to me.

"Apologies." Kai's calm voice shattered the tension and chased away the sparks. "News doesn't stop even for a Valhalla event." He placed his phone on the counter next to his glass.

Dominic said something that turned Dante's head, and I pulled my eyes away from him with considerable effort.

"No worries." I mustered a smile over the frantic beats of my heart. I felt like I'd run a marathon while sitting for the past minute. "The world is still spinning, I hope."

"It depends on who you ask..."

I made it a point not to look at Dante again as I listened to Kai discuss the latest breaking news. If he wanted to talk to me, he knew where I was. But no matter how hard I tried, I couldn't shake the warmth of Dante's attention or cage the butterflies it'd set free.

CHAPTER 13

Dante

"ASIAN SHARE MARKETS HAVE RISEN, AND DOW futures are up, but the risk appetite..."

I tuned Dominic out.

He was a markets savant who'd turned his fledgling company into a Wall Street powerhouse in less than two decades. I respected him, and I listened to anything he had to say regarding stocks, money, and finance.

Except for tonight.

My jaw tightened when another silvery peal of laughter floated over from the bar. Vivian had been talking to Kai for the past seven minutes. Not just talking—she was smiling and laughing like he was an award-winning comedian when I knew for a fact he wasn't that damn funny.

Irritation pierced my chest when she leaned closer to show him her phone. He said something, and she laughed again.

She'd never laughed that much with me, and I was her goddamned fiancé.

"Let's finish this over lunch." I cut Dominic off before he could go into detail about the impact of the Federal Reserve's latest announcement. "I have to talk to Vivian."

He took the interruption in stride. "I'll have my assistant set something up."

I was already halfway across the room before the last word left his mouth.

"Sorry that took so long." I rested my hand on Vivian's bare back and pinned Kai with a hard stare. "Thank you for keeping my fiancée company while I spoke with Dom, but I'm afraid I have to steal her away." I placed a small emphasis on the word *fiancée*. "I haven't had a chance to give her a proper tour of the club yet."

"Of course." Kai stood, the picture of British politeness. A whisper of mirth lurked at the corners of his mouth. "Vivian, it was a pleasure, as always. Dante, I'll see you around, I'm sure."

As always? What did he mean, *as always?*

"Next time you want to mark your territory, you might as well urinate in a circle around me," Vivian said after Kai left. "It'll be more subtle."

"I was not marking my territory." The idea was absurd. I wasn't a fucking dog. "I was saving you from Kai. Be careful around him. He's not as gentlemanly as he appears."

"Compared to you, who bulldozed into the middle of our conversation like a bull in a china shop?"

"Subtlety is overrated."

"For you? Definitely." Vivian rose, her dress shimmering like stars painted on her curves.

My entire body tightened.

That fucking dress. The sight of her appearing in the foyer, all red lips, smooth skin, and nude lace, was forever ingrained in my memory, and I hated her for it.

"I believe you offered a tour of the club?" She raised one elegant dark brow. "That's why you sent Kai away, is it not?"

I offered a thin smile in response and held out my arm. She took it.

"What were you and Kai talking about?" I ignored the guests trying to catch my attention on our way out the door. I'd reached my small talk quota for the night.

"Andromeda. The constellation," Vivian clarified. She gestured at the hyperrealistic projection splashed across the glass dome. Different constellations twinkled down at us, including Andromeda.

The projection was scientifically inaccurate since many of the constellations depicted wouldn't appear together in the same place, but fantasy trumped reality at Valhalla.

"Kai's a fan of Greek mythology, and our discussion about Andromeda the myth turned into one about astronomy."

"Kai pretends to like Greek mythology to pick up women," I said stiffly. I led her out of the ballroom and toward the main staircase. "Don't be fooled."

I didn't know if it was true, but it *could* be true. I wouldn't be doing my due diligence if I didn't share the possibility with Vivian, would I?

"Good to know." Vivian looked like she was holding back a laugh. "There's no bigger turn-on for a woman than the story of another woman being chained to a rock as a sacrifice."

The echo of her sarcasm faded into silence as we took the stairs to the second floor. I pointed out the Parisian-style lounge, the billiards room, and the beauty room, but my attention was split between the tour and the woman beside me. I'd walked the halls of Valhalla countless times, but every interaction with Vivian was like our first. I noticed something new about her every day—the tiny beauty mark above her upper lip, the way she slid her pendant along its chain when she was uncomfortable, and the mildly crooked slant of her smile when she was genuinely amused.

It was infuriating. I didn't *want* to notice these things

about her, yet I inadvertently hoarded them the way dragons hoarded jewels.

"Our last stop of the night." I halted in front of a pair of huge wooden doors.

They opened without a sound, but Vivian's sharp inhale was audible.

Every chapter of the Valhalla Club possessed a unique element that set it apart. Cape Town was known for its wraparound aquarium, Tokyo for its three-hundred-sixty-degree views from atop one of the city's highest buildings. New York had its helipad and secret underground tunnel system. But the library was the heart and soul of almost every branch. It was where deals were brokered, confidences shared, and alliances forged or broken.

Tonight, for once, it was empty.

"Wow." Vivian's reverent whisper drifted through the still air as we stepped inside.

I closed the doors behind us, cocooning us in hushed silence.

Thousands of books stretched up and across three walls toward the cathedral ceiling like a leather-bound forest complete with rolling ladders and wooden handrails. Five larger-than-life stained-glass windows stood sentry over assorted seating areas and desks lit with vintage brass and emerald lamps. The ceiling itself was carved with the house crests of the club's founding families, including the distinctive twin Russo dragons.

"This place is incredible." Vivian brushed her fingers over an antique globe.

A small smile touched my mouth.

Vivian grew up in a world of wealth and fancy galas similar to tonight's. Most people in her position would rather eat glass than express visible awe over something as common as a nice library, but she was never afraid to show how much she enjoyed something, whether it was one of Greta's home-cooked meals or a globe from the nineteenth century.

It was one of my favorite things about her, even though I shouldn't have a favorite *any*thing about her. She was still the daughter of the enemy. But in that moment, I found it hard to care.

"There's an entire astronomy section on the second level." I leaned my shoulder against the wall and tucked a hand in my pocket, watching her examine an oil painting of Venice. "Coincidentally, it's right next to the mythology section."

"Yes," she murmured, sounding distracted. "Kai mentioned it."

Annoyance flared, sudden and incomprehensible, in my chest. "Did he? What else did you talk about?"

"Not this again." She dropped her hand from a bronze statuette of Athena and faced me, exasperation scrawled all over her features. "We talked about normal things. Work, the weather, the news. Why are you so hung up on our conversation?"

"I'm not *hung up*," I said. "I'm simply curious as to what he said that was so funny. The last time I checked, neither work, the weather, nor the news is particularly hilarious."

Vivian examined me for a moment before the soft glow of amusement filled her eyes. "Dante Russo, are you…jealous?"

A soft growl rumbled through my chest. "That's the most ridiculous thing I've ever heard."

"Maybe." She tilted her head, her hair fanning over her shoulders in a cloud of raven silk. "I wouldn't blame you if you were. Nothing is going on between me and Kai, but he's quite handsome. And that *accent*. There's something about a British accent that just does it for me. I blame it on…"

Vivian faltered when I pushed off the wall and walked toward her, my steps slow and methodical.

"My obsession with…"

She inched back, the teasing glint in her eyes replaced with equal parts trepidation and anticipation.

"*Pride and Prejudice* when I was younger," she finished breathlessly.

Her back hit one of the bookshelves.

I stopped a hair's breadth away from her, so close the beads of her dress grazed the front of my suit.

"Are you baiting me, *mia cara*?" A dangerous edge ran beneath the soft inquiry.

I hated the sound of Kai's name on her tongue. I hated the way she laughed so easily in his presence. And I hated how much I cared about either of those things.

Vivian's throat rippled with a swallow. "Simply making an observation."

The library's hushed silence buckled beneath the weight of the gathering tension. It hissed and sparked like crackles of electricity, barreling down my spine and lighting up my blood.

I tucked a stray strand of hair behind her ear, the movement gentle, almost tender before my hand skimmed down the side of her neck and curled around the back.

"You forget." I pressed my fingers against her nape, forcing her to look up at me. "You're *my* fiancée. Not Kai's. Not anyone else's. I don't give a fuck how *handsome* they are or what type of accent they have. You're mine, and no one"—I dipped my head, my lips brushing hers with each word—"touches what's mine."

Vivian's breathing shallowed, but a hint of fire returned to her voice when she spoke again. "I'm *not* yours. Our engagement is, as you've told me many times, just business. Or are you the one who's forgotten?"

"I haven't forgotten anything." I grazed my knuckles up her bare thigh, inch by inch, until I hit the hem of her dress.

Her body drew taut, its heat a wild temptation that sank into my bones and urged me to close the remaining, infinitesimal space between us. To crush my mouth to hers and smear her perfect lipstick so thoroughly no one would doubt for a fucking second who she belonged to.

"If you want me to stop, just say the word." I pushed my leg between her knees, nudging them apart.

Vivian opened her mouth, then closed it when my thumb traced a small circle over her soft skin. The flush on her cheeks spread to her neck and chest.

"Say it." I trailed my fingers up her inner thigh in a lazy caress. My cock strained against my zipper, begging for attention, but I ignored it. "You can't, can you?" I mocked.

Her teeth sank into her bottom lip. Lust and defiance battled for dominance in her eyes. "You're an asshole."

My fingers brushed against drenched silk.

She grasped my shoulders, her nails digging into my back when I slid her underwear aside and rubbed my thumb over her swollen clit. Her body jerked. Small trembles ran through her as her teeth dug deeper into her lip.

"I'm an asshole, yet you're dripping all over my hand." I kept my thumb on her clit while I slipped a finger inside her. "What does that say about you?"

I slid a second finger inside, filling her. Stretching her. Stroking and curling until I hit her most sensitive spot.

The trembles gave way to a full-body shudder. Sweat beaded on her forehead, but she remained stubbornly silent.

"Answer me." Command hardened my voice into steel.

Vivian shook her head.

"If you won't say it, I will." I slowly withdrew both fingers, then thrust them inside her again. "It says you're mine. *Puoi negarlo quanto vuoi, ma è la verità.*"

"You don't even like me," she panted.

"*Like* has nothing to do with this."

I pressed the heel of my palm against her clit until a gasping moan broke free. She bucked against my hand, forcing me deeper.

"That's it." My velvety murmur glided between us. "Give in to it, sweetheart. Let me feel you come all over my hand."

"Fuck you."

I let out a soft laugh. "That's the idea."

Vivian put up a good fight, but her resistance gradually melted and she clutched my shoulders harder, grinding shamelessly against my hand while I increased my pace. Her little moans and pants mingled with the slick sounds of my fingers fucking her pussy, and soon, my fingers were soaked with her juices.

I didn't touch my cock even though it was so fucking hard it ached. I was too enraptured by the sight of Vivian's arousal—flushed cheeks, parted lips, heavy-lidded eyes.

It was the most beautiful thing I'd ever seen.

My rhythm continued. In and out, faster and deeper, until she finally split apart with a sharp cry.

I kept my fingers inside her and pressed my thumb against her clit again, letting her ride out the waves of her orgasm until her trembles subsided. Only then did I withdraw my hand while she slumped against the bookcase, her chest heaving.

"Make no mistake, *mia cara*." I grasped her chin and tilted it up. I pulled her bottom lip down with my thumb, letting her taste her own arousal. "This *is* business. And if there's one thing I take seriously, it's my investments."

CHAPTER 14

Vivian

I DREAMED OF DANTE THREE NIGHTS IN A ROW.

I couldn't recall what happened in the dreams, but I woke up each morning with the phantom touch of his hands between my thighs and a tight ball of need in my stomach. Cold showers only helped temporarily, and Dante's absence while he was in California was both a blessing and a curse.

A blessing because I didn't have to face him with amorphous memories of sex dreams running through my head. A curse because without new interactions to distract me, all I could think about was our night in Valhalla's library.

His grip on my neck. His fingers filling me as I shamelessly rode his hand to orgasm. The desire in his eyes as he watched me come apart in his arms, so hot and potent it'd almost driven me to the peak again.

A shiver that had nothing to do with the weather rolled over my body. The day had dawned gray and drizzly, and while I usually only liked the rain when I was tucked snug and warm in my bed, I relished the chill today. It cleared my thoughts—as much as they could be cleared anyway.

I checked my watch as I wound past the puddles gathering on the sidewalk, umbrella in hand. I'd finished lunch in record time since I wanted to browse Lohman & Sons before my next meeting at two. It was the Russo Group's largest jewelry subsidiary. Up until now, I mostly wore my family's brand of jewels, my engagement ring notwithstanding, but since I was marrying a Russo, it made sense to add more of their products to my collection.

Rain and retail therapy. Two things guaranteed to take my mind off Dante.

The ring of my phone dragged me out of my thoughts before they took me down an unwanted path. An unknown caller on my work phone. Unusual but not unheard of.

"This is Vivian." I slipped into my professional voice and stopped in front of the Lohman & Sons entrance. An elegant older woman passed by with an immaculately groomed white poodle. Both wore matching quilted Chanel jackets.

Only on the Upper East Side.

"Vivian, dear, how are you?" Buffy's throaty voice oozed over the phone. "This is Buffy Darlington."

My heart skipped a beat. I hadn't talked to Buffy since her granddaughter's birthday two weeks ago. The payments were settled, the contracts fulfilled. The Darlingtons seemed happy with the event, but then why would Buffy be calling me on a random Tuesday afternoon? We were both active on the Manhattan social scene, but we ran in very different circles. We didn't call each other just to chitchat.

"I'm well, thank you. How are you?"

"Wonderful. I heard you were at the Valhalla Club's gala over the weekend. I was quite upset about missing it, but poor Balenciaga was having stomach issues and we had to rush him to the vet."

Balenciaga was one of Buffy's five prized Malteses, along with

Prada, Givenchy, Chanel, and Dior. Each dog only wore clothing by the designer corresponding to their name. There'd been a whole spread about them in *Mode de Vie* two years ago.

"I'm sorry to hear that," I said politely. "I hope Balenciaga's feeling better."

"Thank you. He's doing much better now." I heard the clatter of china in the background before Buffy spoke again. "While I can discuss my precious babies all day, I must admit, I have an ulterior motive for calling."

I'd figured as much. People like Buffy didn't contact you out of the blue unless you could do something for them.

"As you may know, I'm the chairwoman of the Legacy Ball committee this year. I'm in charge of the overall production, including choosing the host or hostess and guiding them through the planning process."

My pulse spiked at the mention of the ball.

"Arabella Creighton *was* the hostess," Buffy said. "But unfortunately, she had to resign from her position due to unforeseen circumstances."

Unforeseen circumstances was an understatement. Arabella's husband had been charged with embezzlement and corporate fraud over the weekend. Photos of the FBI marching him out of his Park Avenue town house in his pajamas had been splashed across all the front pages since Saturday.

Three days.

Buffy and the committee worked fast. The last thing they wanted was for any whiff of a scandal to taint the ball on their watch.

"As you can imagine, we've been frantic, considering the ball is only six months away. The event planning process requires *extensive* preparation, and we have to start from scratch again since Arabella's work is...no longer tenable."

Translation: they were going to pretend Arabella was never attached to the event because it looked bad for them.

"The ladies and I discussed possibilities as a new hostess, and I presented you as an option since you did such a wonderful job with Tippy's party."

"Thank you." My pulse was in overdrive now.

I didn't want to get my hopes up, but hosting the Legacy Ball would be a game changer. It was the ultimate stamp of social approval.

"Some of the other members were resistant at first, since the Legacy Ball has traditionally been hosted by those who come from…a certain lineage."

A.k.a. two or more generations of wealth. My smile dimmed.

"However, you *are* engaged to Dante Russo. We have great respect for the Russo family, both present and future members, and after much deliberation, we'd like to formally invite you to be the new host of the Legacy Ball."

A wisp of unease tugged at my stomach, but I pushed it aside. Hosting the ball was hosting the ball, regardless of the reasons behind it.

"I'd be honored and delighted to accept. Thank you for thinking of me."

"Wonderful! I'll send you the details later this afternoon. I'm looking forward to working with you again, Vivian. Oh, and please do say hi to Dante for me."

Buffy hung up.

I closed my umbrella and entered Lohman & Sons, my skin buzzing with anticipation. Decor, catering, entertainment...there were so many possibilities given how big the ball's budget was.

I'd planned on taking my two o'clock call at home, but I should head back to the office—

"Vivian?"

Surprise crept through me at the familiar brown eyes staring at me from behind the counter.

"Luca? What are you..." My question tapered off when a piece of an earlier conversation with Dante rose to the forefront of my mind.

What does he do now?

Salesman.

Of course. It made sense Luca was working at one of the Russo Group's subsidiary stores, but it was still a shock to see him working at the very shop I dropped in on.

"Working hard." A hint of dryness surfaced before it smoothed into a generic sales smile. "How can I help you?"

It felt odd being waited on by my future brother-in-law, but I didn't want to make it weird by treating him differently.

"I'm looking for two new pieces," I said. "A statement piece and something versatile I can wear every day."

For the next forty-five minutes, Luca walked me through the store's finest offerings. He was actually an excellent salesperson—knowledgeable about the products and persuasive without being pushy.

"This is one of our newest pieces." He retrieved a dazzling ruby and diamond dragon bracelet from the display case. "It consists of forty round and pear-shaped rubies weighing approximately four point five carats and thirty marquise, round, and pear-shaped diamonds weighing approximately four carats. It's part of our Exclusive collection, which means there are only ten in existence. Queen Bridget of Eldorra owns the sapphire version."

My breath caught. I'd grown up around jewels my entire life, and I recognized a standout piece when I saw it. The rubies were a pure, vibrant red with no orange or purple overtones, and the bracelet's overall craftsmanship was exquisite.

"I'll take it."

Luca's smile warmed a fraction of a degree. "Excellent."

The cost of the bracelet and the discreet emerald earrings I'd chosen as an everyday piece totaled two hundred thousand, five hundred dollars.

I handed over my black Amex.

"You should come over for dinner soon," I said as Luca processed the payment. "Dante and I would love to see you."

A long pause, followed by a vague, "I'll see you at Thanksgiving."

Frustration needled at me. I hadn't seen or talked to Luca since the engagement party. I couldn't shake the sense he disliked me for some reason, and his cool reply confirmed it.

"Have I offended you in some way?" I had half an hour before my meeting and no time to beat around the bush. "I get the sense you don't like me very much."

Luca slid the sales receipt across the counter. I signed it and waited for an answer.

His work wasn't the best place to have this conversation, but the rest of the customers had left, and the other staff members were out of earshot. This was the best chance I had of getting a straight answer. I'd bet my new jewels he would go out of his way to avoid me if we weren't forced to talk one on one.

"I don't dislike you," he finally said. "But I'm protective of my brother. It's always been the two of us, even when our grandfather was alive." Luca's voice dropped. "I know Dante. He never wanted marriage. Then, one day, out of the blue, he announces he's engaged? It's not like him."

A strange current ran beneath his words, like they were a mere cover for what he really wanted to say. It made sense though, even if I was startled by how readily he'd answered. I'd expected him to deflect.

"And yes, I'm aware of the business side of the arrangement," he said. "But your family gets much more out of the deal than ours, does it not?"

Heat crawled down the back of my neck. Everyone knew Dante was "marrying down," but no one dared say it to my face.

Except his brother.

"I understand your concerns," I said calmly. If Luca was trying to get a rise out of me, he wouldn't succeed. "I'm not here to disrupt your relationship with Dante. He'll always be, first and foremost, your brother. But I'll also be your sister-in-law soon, and I hope we can at least establish a civil rapport, for both ours and Dante's sakes. We'll see each other plenty at family functions in the future, *including* Thanksgiving, and I would hate for animosity to ruin a good meal."

Luca stared at me, his surprise tangible. After a long, drawn-out moment, his face softened into a small but somewhat genuine smile.

"Dante got lucky," he muttered. "It could've been a lot worse."

My brows pulled together at the odd response. Before I could question him on it, an explosion of noise yanked my attention to the entrance.

My blood iced.

Three masked men stood by the door, two of them holding assault rifles and one holding a hammer and a duffel bag. One security guard lay unconscious on the floor next to them; the other faced down the barrel of a gun with his hands in the air.

"Everybody get on the fucking ground!" One of the men waved his gun while his accomplice smashed the glass of the nearest display. "Get down!"

Luca and the other two employees complied, their faces leached of color.

"Vivian," Luca hissed. "*Get down.*"

I wanted to. Every instinct screamed at me to crawl into a

corner and curl up until the danger was over, but my muscles refused to obey my brain's commands. I'd lived in New York for years, but I'd never experienced a mugging or assault. Sometimes, I'd watch the news and wonder how I'd react if I were caught in such a situation.

Now I knew.

Not well.

One second, I was signing receipts and talking to Luca. The next, the sight of the masked men had pressed Pause on the tape of my life, and all I could do was watch, numb, as the one who'd shouted instructions caught sight of me still standing.

Anger lit his eyes.

Fear ricocheted through my body as he stalked toward me, yet my feet remained rooted to the floor. No matter how hard I fought the creeping paralysis, I couldn't move. Everything felt surreal. The store, the robbers, *me*. It was like I'd floated out of my body and was watching the scene play out as an invisible third party.

The masked man neared.

Closer.

Closer.

Closer.

My pulse reached deafening levels and drowned out everything except the heavy, ominous thud of his boots.

I should be focused on how to escape my current situation, but time flipped back with every footfall. My first camping trip with my family. Walking across the graduation stage at Columbia. Meeting Dante. Life events, big and small, that'd shaped me into who and where I was today.

How many more of those did I have left, if any?

Pressure squeezed the oxygen from my lungs.

Get down. But I couldn't.

Thud. Thud. Thud.

He was here.

The last thud finally kicked my fight or flight into high gear. My body jerked, a gasp of life in the face of death, but it was too late. The cold metal of a gun pressed against the underside of my chin.

"Did you not hear me the first time?" The man's hot, wet breath fanned across my face. My stomach turned. "I said *get on the fucking floor*, bitch."

His dark eyes gleamed with malice.

Some criminals were all bravado. They just wanted to snatch the goods and leave without actually killing anyone. But the man in front of me? He wouldn't hesitate to murder someone in cold blood. He looked like he was itching for it.

The drumming of my heart reached a fever pitch. Less than an hour ago, I'd been agonizing over Dante and over the moon about hosting the Legacy Ball.

Now...

There was a possibility I might not make it to the next morning, much less the ball or my wedding.

CHAPTER 15

Dante

"THIS BETTER BE IMPORTANT." I PUT MY PHONE ON speaker and shrugged off my jacket. "This is the first damn break I've had since I landed."

My trip to San Francisco had been a whirlwind of meetings, photo ops, and dealing with people whose heads were so far up their asses they'd require surgery to see daylight. I'd barely slept in the past forty-eight hours, but we were finally closing the deal with Franco Santeri in two hours.

Until then, I wanted to shower, eat, and, if I was lucky, grab some shut-eye for five minutes.

"It is. There was an attempted robbery at the Lohman & Sons flagship store in New York." Giulio, my head of corporate security in North America, cut straight to the chase. He was one of Christian's men, but he'd worked for me for so long he answered directly to me instead of Christian. "We apprehended the perpetrators before they escaped. They're currently in our custody."

"Was anyone hurt?"

"One of the security guards was knocked unconscious and has a concussion. Other than that, no, sir."

"Good. Take care of it the way we usually do. Make it clean."

There hadn't been an attempted robbery of a Russo Group property in two years, but fools were born every day.

I kept to the right side of the law when it came to finances and boardroom dealings. But when it came to people who tried to steal from me? I had no qualms about making an example out of them. Shattered bones and blood. They were a universally understood language.

"Of course," Giulio said. "But, ah, that's not all."

I checked the time, my patience running thin after a three-hour bullshit meeting on projections that could've been an email. "Get to the point, Giulio."

There was a short pause before he said, "Your fiancée was in the store at the time of the attempted robbery."

My hand stilled on the clasp of my watch. "Vivian was in the store?"

"Yes, sir. She was shopping and happened to be in the wrong place at the wrong time."

Blood roared in my ears, and a sick feeling formed in the pit of my stomach. "How is she?"

"She's shaken up. One of the robbers held her at gunpoint when she was too slow getting on the ground, but our men neutralized the situation before she was hurt." Giulio coughed. "Your brother was there as well. He was on shift today, and he was the one who secretly called for backup."

All our employees at high-risk locations like jewelry stores wore custom watches with disguised panic buttons. It had been Christian's idea. Criminals expected panic buttons under a desk or near the register; they didn't expect it on a watch, which was both discreet and easier to access.

But I wasn't thinking about the effectiveness of our security protocol right now.

One of the robbers held her at gunpoint.

Blackness snuffed out my vision. When it returned a split second later, rage drenched the room in crimson.

"Where are they now?" My voice was tight. Controlled. At complete odds with the bloody images of retribution playing out in my mind.

"Ms. Vivian is at the penthouse, and Mr. Luca is at his home in Greenwich Village."

My jaw ticked. My brother was like Teflon when it came to life-and-death situations. He once got mugged in LA, took a nap, and spent the same night partying it up with half of young Hollywood.

Vivian, on the other hand…

The sick feeling spread, clawing at my insides like it was seeking escape.

"I'll have the full report in your inbox within the next hour," Giulio said. "Is there anything else you need from me at this time?"

"The one who held Vivian at gunpoint? Leave him for me."

Another pause. "Of course."

I hung up, my earlier exhaustion and hunger hardening into a ball of restless energy. I really fucking wished there was a boxing ring at the hotel. If I didn't release the anger choking me, I would implode.

An image of Vivian's face surfaced in my mind. Pale skin. Dark eyes wide with fear. Bright-red blood staining her clothes.

If backup hadn't arrived on time…

My gut twisted into a painful knot.

She was safe. Giulio wouldn't lie about that. But until I saw her myself…

I paced the room and scrubbed a hand over my face. I'd spent the past year putting the Santeri deal together. I couldn't fuck it up. Plus, I was flying home tomorrow morning anyway. Half a day wouldn't make a difference.

Vivian was at home. She was *fine*.

My pacing continued. The clock ticked toward the quarter of the hour.

Dammit.

A string of curses flew past my lips as I grabbed my jacket with one hand and dialed my assistant with the other on my way out the door.

"There's an emergency in New York. Call the Santeri team and have them meet me in the hotel conference room in thirty minutes. Tell them the rest of their stay is on the Russo Group, and send Franco the limited-edition Lohman & Sons watch as an apology. The one that's not coming out until next year."

The CEO of Santeri Wines was a notorious horophile who collected forty-thousand-dollar timepieces the way kids collected baseball cards.

Helena didn't miss a beat. "Consider it done."

Franco had an ego bigger than his Napa Valley ranch. He was pissed about the last-minute summons, as expected, but the apology gifts mollified him enough for him to sign the acquisition deal without much complaint.

Santeri Wines, one of the most valuable wine brands on the market, was officially a Russo Group subsidiary.

Instead of celebrating, I said my goodbyes and cut a straight path from the conference room to the car waiting outside.

"Where to, sir?" the driver asked.

"SFO." San Francisco Airport. I'd left without my luggage, but Helena would take care of that for me. "I need to return to New York immediately."

Vivian

I couldn't stop shivering.

I stepped out of the bathroom, my skin ice cold despite my bathrobe, the heated floors, and the hot bath I'd soaked in for the past hour. It was late evening, hours after the attempted Lohman & Sons robbery, but I was still stuck on the showroom floor with a gun under my chin and evil staring back at me.

The entire incident had lasted less than ten minutes before backup security arrived and neutralized the situation. No one got hurt, but I couldn't stop thinking about what-ifs.

What if backup had arrived a minute too late?

What if the robber had shot first and asked questions later?

What if I'd died? What would I have to show for it except a closet full of nice clothes and a life spent doing the "right thing"?

I would've died without visiting the Atacama Desert for stargazing or falling in love more than once. Things I'd always thought I would have time to do because I was only in my late twenties, dammit, and I was supposed to be invincible at this age.

The faint slam of the front door saved me from my thoughts, but my heart skittered with trepidation. Who was here? Dante wouldn't be home until tomorrow, and the staff was already indoors. Even if they weren't, they wouldn't slam the door like that.

My trepidation heightened when the sound of footsteps grew louder and the door to my bedroom was flung open. I grabbed a vase off my dresser, ready to throw it at the intruder until I registered the dark hair and hard, unforgiving face.

"Dante?" My heart gradually slowed as I set the vase down. "You're not supposed to be back until tomorrow. What are..."

I didn't get the chance to finish my sentence before he crossed the room in two long strides and gripped my arms.

"Are you hurt?" he demanded. He scanned me from head to toe, his expression tight.

What...*the robbery*. Of course. He was the CEO. Someone must've told him what happened.

"I'm fine. A little shaken but fine." I forced a smile. "You're supposed to be in California until tomorrow. What are you doing home early?"

"There was an attempted robbery at one of my flagship stores, Vivian." A muscle worked in his jaw. "Of course I came back right away."

"But the Santeri deal..."

"Is closed." His iron grip remained on my arms, strong yet gentle.

"Oh." I couldn't think of anything else to say.

The day had been surreal, made all the more surreal by Dante's sudden appearance.

It was only then that I noticed his rumpled shirt and tousled hair, like he'd been running his fingers through it. For some reason, the visual made my eyes blur with tears. It was too human, too *normal* for a day like today.

Dante's fingers tightened around me. "Be honest, Vivian," he said, the words somehow both comforting and commanding. "Are you okay?"

Not *are you hurt?* but *are you okay?* Two different questions.

Pressure built inside me, but I nodded.

His eyes were a dark storm, his face etched with lines of anger and panic. At my response, skepticism joined the mix, soft but visible.

"He held you at gunpoint," he said, his voice lower. Tauter. Promising retribution.

The pressure pushed against my eardrums, an invisible force dragging me deep beneath a turbulent ocean.

My smile wobbled. "Yes. Not the..." I eased a deep breath past my tightening lungs. *Don't cry.* "Not the highlight of my week, I must admit."

Dante's body vibrated with tension. It lined his jaw and coiled beneath his skin, like a viper waiting to strike.

"Did he do anything else?"

I shook my head. Oxygen thinned by the second, making each word difficult, but I pushed forward. "Security got there before anyone was hurt. I'm okay. Really." The last word pitched higher than the rest.

The muscle in his jaw ticked again. "You're shaking."

Was I? I checked. Yes, I was.

Tiny trembles rippled through my body. My knees quaked; goose bumps peppered my arms. If it weren't for the warmth and strength of Dante's hold, I might've collapsed on the floor.

I noted these things with detachment, like I was watching myself in a film I wasn't particularly invested in.

"It's the cold," I said. I didn't know who turned on the air-conditioning in November, but my room was a meat locker.

Dante stroked my skin with his thumb. Concern pooled in his eyes. "The heat is on, *mia cara*," he said softly.

The pressure expanded to my throat.

"Well, then, it must be broken." I rambled on, my string of useless words the only thread holding me together. "You should get it fixed. I'm sure you could get someone here soon. You're..." Something wet trickled down my cheeks. "You're Dante Russo. You can..." I couldn't breathe properly. *Air. I need air.* "You can do anything."

My voice cracked.

One crack. That was all it took.

The thread snapped, and I broke down, sobs racking my body as the emotion and trauma of the day overwhelmed me.

The high of the Legacy Ball news followed by the terror of the robbery.

The thud of heavy boots against the marble floors in that cold, stark room.

The metal against my skin and the unshakeable sense that if I died today, I'd do so without ever having lived. Not as Vivian Lau. Not as *me*.

Dante's arms wrapped around me. He didn't speak, but his embrace was so strong and reassuring it erased any self-consciousness I might've had.

The turbulent waters closed overhead, drowning out the light. They tossed me back and forth until my body shook from the force of my cries. My stomach hurt, my eyes ached, and my throat was so raw it hurt to breathe.

And still, Dante held me.

I pressed my face against his chest, my shoulders heaving while he rubbed a hand over my back. He murmured something in Italian, but I couldn't decipher what he said. All I knew was, in the icy aftermath of the robbery, his voice and embrace were the only things keeping me warm.

CHAPTER 16

Dante

"YOU GOT BLOOD ON MY SHIRT, BRAX." I ROLLED UP MY sleeves, hiding the bloodstain in question. "That's the third strike."

He glared at me, his expression mutinous beneath the blood and bruises. He was tied to a chair, his arms and legs bound with rope. He was the only one of his accomplices still conscious. The other two slumped in their seats, their heads lolling and their blood hitting the floor in a steady *drip, drip, drip*. Several of their limbs bent at unnatural angles.

"You talk too much." Brax spat out a mouthful of dark red liquid.

Brax Miller. Ex-con with a mile-long rap sheet, balls of steel, and a brain the size of a walnut.

I smiled, then hit him again.

His head snapped back, and a pained groan filled the air.

My bruised knuckles stung. The room jokingly dubbed the Holding Cell in my private security headquarters smelled like copper, sweat, and the thick, cloying scent of fear.

It was two days after the attempted robbery at Lohman & Sons, longer than we'd ever held someone. My police contacts turned a blind eye to my activities because I saved them time and manpower, and I knew when to draw the line. I'd never killed someone.

Yet.

But I was really fucking tempted right now.

"The first hour was for trying to rob one of my stores. The second…" I held out my hand. Giulio placed something cold and heavy in my palm, his face impassive. "Is for threatening my wife."

My fist closed around the weapon.

I normally let my team handle these unpleasantries. Robbery, vandalism, *disrespect*. They were unacceptable but impersonal. Nothing more than crimes to be punished and examples to be set in the most brutal and therefore effective manner possible. They didn't require my personal attention.

But this? What Brax did to Vivian?

This was fucking personal.

A fresh tsunami of rage rolled through me when I pictured the piece of shit in front of me pointing a gun at her. She wasn't my wife yet, but she was mine.

No one threatened what was mine.

"So she's your wife." Brax coughed, his bravado dented but intact. "I understand why you're upset. She's beautiful, though she would've been much more beautiful with blood painting that pretty skin of hers."

His grin was made of mockery and crimson, too stupid to realize his mistake. Like I said, a brain the size of a walnut.

I put on my brass knuckles, walked over, and yanked his pathetic head back. "I'm not the one who talks too much."

A second later, a howl of agony ripped through the air.

It did nothing to ease the wrath inside me, and I didn't stop until the howls stopped altogether.

I left my men to clean up the mess in the Holding Cell.

I'd come close to killing Brax, but the bastard lived, barely. Tomorrow, he and his accomplices would turn themselves in to the police. It was a much more appealing alternative than staying with my team.

The apartment smelled like soup and roasted chicken when I returned home. Greta had been fussing over Vivian since the robbery, which in her world meant plying Vivian with enough food to feed all of midtown Manhattan during lunch hour.

I barely noticed the stinging hot water as I showered off the blood and sweat.

Vivian insisted she was fine, but few people recovered from having a gun pressed to their head that quickly. According to Greta, she was currently taking a nap, and she never napped this late in the day. Or ever, now that I thought about it.

I turned off the water, my thoughts as clouded as the steamed-up mirror.

I'd done my part. I'd punished the perpetrators, personally attended to Brax, and checked on Luca during my ride home from security HQ. He'd bounced back as quickly as I'd expected; the man sailed through life like a Teflon ship. But he wasn't the one who'd had a gun in his face.

Dammit.

With a low growl of annoyance, I toweled off, changed into fresh clothes, and headed into the kitchen, where I convinced Greta to part with a bowl of her precious soup.

"You'll spoil dinner," she warned.

"It's not for me."

A frown pinched her lips before realization dawned, and her disapproval relaxed into a downright delighted smile.

"Ah. In that case, take as much soup as you need! Here."

She shoved a plate of sourdough bread and butter at me. "Take this too."

"What happened to spoiling dinner?" I grumbled, but I took the damn bread.

I made it to Vivian's door before I second-guessed my decision. Should I wake her up from her nap? Greta said she'd worked from home today and hadn't eaten lunch, but maybe she needed the rest. *Or* she could've already woken up and was counting her diamonds or whatever the hell jewelry heiresses did in their free time.

Should I knock or leave and come back?

I didn't get a chance to decide before Vivian decided for me.

The door swung open, revealing sleepy dark eyes that widened in panic when she saw me. She screamed, causing me to startle and nearly drop the soup.

"Fuck!" I caught myself in the nick of time, but a few drops of hot liquid splashed over the side of the bowl and onto my arm.

"*Dante*. God." Vivian pressed a palm over her heaving chest. "You scared me."

"I was just about to knock," I half lied.

Her attention drifted to the food in my hands. She looked adorably sleep-rumpled with her tousled hair and a pillow crease on her cheek. Even with no makeup, her skin was flawless, and the faintest scent of apples turned the edges of my mind hazy.

"You brought me food?" Her face softened in a way that worsened the haze.

"No. Yes," I said, unable to decide whether to admit to checking up on her. I could tell her it was Greta's idea. Bringing her chicken soup of my own accord seemed dangerously intimate, like something a real fiancé would do.

Vivian gave me a strange look.

Christ, Russo, get it together.

An hour ago, I was beating the hell out of a six-foot-two criminal. Now, I was incoherent over fucking soup and bread.

"Greta said you didn't eat lunch. Figured you might be hungry." I went for the vaguest answer possible.

"Thank you. That's so thoughtful," Vivian said, still with that soft expression doing strange things to my mind.

Her fingers brushed mine when she took the bowl and plate. A tiny current of electricity sizzled over my skin. My body tightened with the effort of containing a physical reaction—a surprised jolt, a more deliberate brush of our hands.

Vivian paused like she felt it too before hurriedly continuing, "It's perfect timing, because I was going to grab a snack. My call with the Legacy Ball committee ran over, and I forgot to eat lunch. "

She'd told me earlier she was hosting this year's ball. It was a big deal, and I couldn't stop a glimmer of pride from sparking in my chest.

"That's going well then."

"As well as anything with a three-hundred-page handbook can go," she joked.

Silence fell. I should leave now that I'd given her her food and confirmed she was functioning just fine, but a strange tug at my chest prevented me from leaving.

I blamed the cursed haze in my mind for what I said next. "If you want company, I was planning to grab a snack too. Not hungry enough for a full dinner."

Surprise slid across Vivian's face, followed by a hint of pleasure. "Sure. East sitting room in five?"

I gave a curt nod.

Luckily, Greta wasn't in the kitchen when I returned. I grabbed another bowl of soup and joined Vivian in the east sitting room.

The chicken broth was rich and hearty enough to comprise

a full meal on its own. We ate in silence for a while until Vivian spoke again.

"How's Luca? After...you know."

"He's fine. He's been through worse." Though I should check on him again just in case. "He once got mugged by a monkey in Bali. Almost died trying to get his phone back."

Vivian spluttered out a laugh. "Excuse me?"

"It's true." My mouth curved, both at the memory of my brother's indignation over the crime and at her smile. "Obviously, he got out okay, but some of those temple monkeys are ruthless."

"I'll keep that in mind for our trip."

We were leaving for Bali in three weeks to see my parents for Thanksgiving. I was already dreading it, but I pushed that aside for now.

"And you?" I dropped all pretense and fixed my gaze on Vivian. "How are you doing?"

Vivian's amusement disappeared in the wake of my question. The air shifted and condensed, squeezing out the earlier lightheartedness.

"I'm okay," she said quietly. "I'm having some trouble sleeping, hence the naps, but it's more shock than anything. I wasn't hurt. I'll get over it."

Maybe she was right. She was much calmer now than the first night, but a niggling thread of concern still unraveled in my stomach.

"If you want to talk to someone, the company has people on hand," I said gruffly. Our contracted therapists were some of the top practitioners in the city. "Just let me know."

"Thank you." Her smile returned, softer this time. "For the other night and for this." She nodded at the half-empty bowls between us.

"You're welcome," I said stiffly, unsure how to handle

whatever the hell was happening here. I had no frame of reference for the strange fog clouding my brain or the twinge in my chest when I looked at her.

It wasn't wrath, like with Brax.

It wasn't hatred, like with Francis.

It wasn't lust or dislike or any of the other emotions that had shaped my previous interactions with Vivian.

I didn't know what it was, but it unsettled the hell out of me.

CHAPTER 17

Dante

VIVIAN DID END UP SPEAKING TO ONE OF OUR THERA-pists after the Lohman & Sons incident. She never discussed her sessions, but by the time we arrived in Bali, her sleep had improved and she was mostly back to her normal witty, sarcastic self.

I told myself my relief had nothing to do with her *personally* and that I was simply glad she was in the right headspace to meet my parents.

"Are you sure your parents live here?" Vivian stared at the villa in front of us.

Hand-hewn sculptures dotted the lawn in a riot of primary colors, and an overabundance of wind chimes tinkled by the front door. Giant sunflowers sprouted up the walls in splashes of yellow and green paint.

It looked like a cross between a luxury villa and a day care center.

"Yes." The place had Janis Russo written all over it. The front door flew open, revealing a mass of curly brown hair and a floor-length caftan. "Prepare yourself."

"*Darling*!" my mother cried. "Oh, it's so wonderful to see

you! My baby boy!" She rushed toward us and embraced me in a cloud of patchouli. "Have you lost weight? Are you eating enough? Sleeping enough? Having sex enough?"

Vivian disguised her laugh with a delicate cough.

I grimaced as my mother pulled back and examined me with a critical eye. "Hello, Mother."

"Stop. I told you to call me Janis. You're always so formal. I blame Enzo," she told Vivian. "His grandfather was a real stickler for the rules. You know he kicked someone out of a dinner party once for using the wrong fork? Started a whole international incident because the guest was the son of a UN ambassador. Though to be fair, you'd expect the son of a UN ambassador to know which fork is used for salads and which is used for entrées. Isn't that right?"

Vivian blinked, seemingly stunned by the whirlwind of energy before her.

"Now, let me take a look at you." My mother released me and placed her hands on Vivian's shoulders. "Oh, you're *beautiful*. Isn't she beautiful, Dante? Tell me, darling, what *do* you use for your skin? It's positively glowing. Argan oil? Snail mucin? La Mer..."

Vivian caught my eye over my mother's head. *Help me*, her gaze begged.

My mouth tugged up in a reluctant smile.

For all my mother's over-the-top effusiveness, she was right. Vivian *was* beautiful. Even after a twelve-hour flight, she glowed in a way that had nothing to do with her physical appearance.

A strange sensation coasted through my chest.

"Yes," I said. "She is."

Vivian's eyes widened a fraction while my mother beamed harder.

We held each other's stares for a suspended moment until my father's voice boomed across the lawn.

"Dante!" He strode through the front door, lean and tanned

in a linen shirt and shorts. "Good to see you, Son." He clapped a hand on my back before engulfing Vivian in a bear hug. "And you, my daughter-in-law! I can't believe it! Tell me, has Dante ever taken you scuba diving?"

"Uh, no—"

"*No*?" His voice boomed louder. "Why the hell not? I've been telling him to take you diving since you got engaged! You know, we conceived Luca after—"

I cut in before my parents could embarrass themselves, and me, further.

"Leave her alone, Father. As fascinating"—*scarring*—"as the story of Luca's conception is, we'd like to freshen up. It's been a long flight."

"Of course." My mother fluttered around us like a jeweled hummingbird. "Come, come. We have your room all ready for you. Luca doesn't arrive until tonight, so you have the second floor to yourselves for now."

"So that's your family," Vivian said as we followed my parents into the villa. "They're...not what I expected."

"Don't let their hippie facade fool you," I said. "My father is still a Russo, and my mother used to be a management consultant. Ask them to give up their credit cards and *really* rough it and see how mellow they are."

The airy, two-story villa was filled with natural woods, cream crochet, and bright local art adorning the walls. The backyard boasted an infinity pool and open-air yoga studio, and the four bedrooms were split half and half between the ground floor, where my parents stayed, and the upper floor.

"This is your room." My mother flung open the door with a flourish. "We spruced it up just for you."

Vivian's mouth parted in shock while a migraine bloomed at the base of my skull. "*Mother*."

"What?" she said innocently. "It's not every day my son and future daughter-in-law visit for Thanksgiving! I figured you'd like a more romantic atmosphere for your stay."

The migraine spread up my neck and behind my eyes with alarming speed.

My mother's idea of *romantic* was my idea of a nightmare. Red rose petals blanketed the floor. A bucket of chilled champagne sat on the nightstand next to two crystal flutes while a box of chocolates, condoms, and towels folded into the shape of swans rested at the base of the canopy bed. A fucking *couple portrait* of me and Vivian hung on the wall opposite the bed beneath a glittery banner that read, *Congratulations on your engagement!*

It looked like a goddamn honeymoon suite, except it was infinitely more horrifying because my own mother set it up.

"How the hell did you get the portrait?" I demanded.

"I used a photo from your engagement party as inspiration." Pride gleamed in my mother's eyes. "How do you like it? It's not my *best* work, but I'm in a bit of a creative rut."

I was going to murder someone before the end of the trip. There was no way around it. Whether it was my mother, father, or brother, it was going to happen.

"It's lovely," Vivian said with a gracious smile. "You captured the moment perfectly."

I pinched the bridge of my nose while my mother blushed. "Oh, you're too sweet. I *knew* I liked you." She patted Vivian's arm. "Anyway, I'll leave you two to get settled in. If you need more condoms, let me know." She winked at us before darting out the door. My father followed, too busy on his phone to pay attention to what was happening.

Silence descended, thick and heavy. Vivian's smile disappeared after my mother left. We stared at the portrait, then at each other, then at the bed.

It suddenly hit me that this would be our first time sharing a room. Sharing a *bed*.

Six days and five nights of sleeping next to her. Of seeing her in those ridiculously tiny outfits she called pajamas and listening to the water run while she bathed.

Six days and five nights of fucking torture.

I rubbed a hand over my face.

It was going to be a long week.

Vivian

Dante's parents were the opposite of their son—free-spirited, effervescent, and gregarious, with quick smiles and somewhat inappropriate senses of humor.

After Dante and I settled in, they insisted on taking us to lunch at their favorite restaurant, where they peppered us with more questions.

"I want to know everything. How you met, how he proposed." Janis rested her chin in her hands. Despite her bohemian clothing and attitude, she possessed the sheen of a New England socialite—high cheekbones, perfect skin, and the type of rich, glossy hair that took copious amounts of time and money to maintain. "Don't skimp on any details."

"I know her father," Dante said before I could answer. "We met at a dinner party at her parents' house in Boston and hit it off. We dated, and I proposed a few months later."

Technically true.

"Ah." Janis frowned, looking disappointed by Dante's unromantic summary of our courtship before she brightened again. "And the proposal?"

I was tempted to tell her he left the ring on my bedside table just to see how she'd react, but I didn't have the heart to crush her hopes.

Time to brush off my acting skills. I hadn't played Eliza Doolittle in my high school's production of *Pygmalion* for nothing.

"It happened in Central Park," I said smoothly. "It was a gorgeous morning, and I thought we were simply going for a walk..."

Janis and Gianni, as he insisted on being called, listened, their expressions enraptured, as I spun a dramatic story featuring flowers, tears, and swans. Dante appeared less charmed. His frown deepened with each word out of my mouth, and when I reached the part about him wrestling the swan who'd tried to run off with my brand-new engagement ring, he gave me a look so dark it could've snuffed out the sun.

"Swan wrestling, eh?" Gianni laughed. "Dante, *non manchi mai di sorprendermi.*"

"*Anche io non finisco mai di sorprendermi,*" Dante muttered.

I stifled a smile.

"What a unique proposal! I can see why you went to the trouble to get the ring back. It's stunning." Janis lifted my hand and examined the obscenely large diamond. It was so heavy that lifting my arm qualified as a workout. "Dante's always had a good eye, though I'd expected..."

Dante tensed.

Janis cleared her throat and dropped my hand. "Anyway, like I said, it's a beautiful ring."

Curiosity kindled in my chest when she and Gianni exchanged glances. What had she been about to say?

"We're sorry we couldn't make it to the engagement party," Gianni added, cutting through the sudden tension. "We would've loved to be there, but there was a festival featuring a local artist who hadn't attended a public event in *ten years* that same weekend."

"He's so talented," Janis piped up. "We simply *couldn't* miss the opportunity to see him."

I paused, waiting for the punchline. It never came.

Horror crawled through me. *That* was why they'd missed their son's engagement party? To meet some artist they didn't even know?

Next to me, Dante sipped his drink, his expression like granite. He appeared neither surprised nor perturbed by the revelation.

An unexpected pang hit my chest. How many times had his parents chosen their selfish desires over him for him to be so blasé about them missing his engagement? I knew they weren't close, considering Gianni and Janis left him with his grandfather, but still. They could've at least made up a decent excuse for why they weren't there.

I brought a salt-cured prawn to my mouth, but the formerly delicious seafood suddenly tasted like cardboard.

After lunch, Gianni and Janis encouraged us to "take a nice stroll" along the beach behind the restaurant while they finished their "post-lunch meditation," whatever that meant.

"Your parents seem nice," I ventured as we walked along the shore.

"As people, maybe. As parents? Not so much."

I slid a sideways glance at him, surprised by his candor.

Dante's linen shirt and pants lent him a more casual air than usual, but his features remained strikingly bold, his body powerful, and his jaw hard, as he walked beside me. He looked invincible, but that was the thing about humans. *No one* was invincible. They were all vulnerable to the same hurts and insecurities as everyone else.

Some people just hid it better.

Another pang rippled through my chest when I remembered how cavalier his parents had been about missing the engagement party.

"Your grandfather raised you and Luca, right?" I knew this, but I couldn't think of a better way to ease into the subject.

Dante responded with a curt nod. "My parents took off around the world soon after Luca was born. They couldn't bring two children on their travels, given how much they moved around, so they left us in our grandfather's care. They said it was for the best."

"Did they visit often?"

"Once a year at most. They sent postcards on Christmas and our birthdays." He spoke in a dry, detached tone. "Luca kept his in a special box. I threw mine out."

"I'm sorry," I said, my throat tight. "You must've missed them very much."

Dante had been a kid at the time, barely old enough to comprehend why his parents were suddenly there one day and gone the next.

Mine weren't perfect, but I couldn't imagine them dumping me at a relative's house so they could cavort around the world.

"Don't be. My parents were right. It was for the best." We stopped at the edge of the beach. "Don't be fooled by their hospitality, Vivian. They fuss over me whenever they see me because they *don't* see me often, and it makes them feel like they're doing their job as parents. They'll take us out to eat, buy us nice things, and ask about our lives, but if you ask them to stick around during the hard times, they're gone."

"What about your brother? What's his relationship with them?"

"Luca was an accident. I was planned because they needed an heir. My grandfather demanded it. But when my brother came along...taking care of two children was too much for my parents, and they bailed."

"So your grandfather took over instead."

"He was thrilled." Dante's dry tone returned. "My father disappointed him on the business front, but he could mold me into his perfect successor from a young age."

And he had. Dante was one of the most successful CEOs in the Fortune 500. He'd tripled the company's profits since taking over, but at what cost?

"Let me guess. He took you to boardroom playdates and gave you cartoon explainers on the stock market?" I quipped, hoping to ease the tension lining his shoulders.

The empathetic part of me wanted to shift to a lighter topic; the selfish part wanted to dig deeper. This was the most insight I'd gotten into Dante's background, and I worried one wrong word would cause him to shut down again.

Faint amusement ghosted through his eyes.

"Close. My grandfather ran his household the way he ran his business. He was the first, last, and only word on any subject. Everything operated by a strict set of rules, from our playtime hours to what hobbies Luca and I were allowed to pursue. I was seven when I took my first factory tour, ten when I started learning about contracts and negotiations."

In other words, he'd lost his childhood to his grandfather's ambitions.

A deep ache unfurled behind my ribs.

"Don't feel sorry for me," Dante said, correctly assessing my expression. "The Russo Group wouldn't be where it is now if it weren't for him and what he taught me."

"There's more to life than money and business," I said softly.

"Not in our world." A gentle breeze swept by, ruffling his hair. "People can join as many charities as they want, donate as much money as they want, but at the end of the day, it's about the bottom line. Look at Tim and Arabella Creighton. They were once superstars in Manhattan society. Now Tim's facing trial, and no one will touch Arabella with a ten-foot pole. All her supposed friends dropped her." Dante's mouth twisted. "If you think any of the people who kiss my ass now would stick around if the company folded tomorrow, you're sorely mistaken. The only languages they understand are money, power, and strength. Those that have it will do anything to keep it. Those who don't will do anything to get it."

"That's a terrible way to go through life," I said, even though I'd witnessed those scenarios play out enough times to know he was right.

"Some things make it better."

My heart faltered, then picked up speed again. Dante and I stood on a secluded stretch of beach, close enough to see the restaurant but far enough that its sounds and crowds didn't touch us.

A fissure cleaved his stony mask, revealing a trace of weariness that tugged at my soul. CEO Dante was all stern frowns and hard commands. This Dante was more vulnerable. More human. I'd spotted glimpses of him before, but this was the first time I'd been in his presence for so long. It felt like sinking into a warm bath after a long day in the rain.

"This wasn't how I'd planned to spend our first day in Bali," he said. "I promise family history lessons aren't the norm here."

"There's nothing wrong with a history lesson. *But...*" I switched to a more playful tone. "I want to learn more about this diving your father was talking about. I've never been to Bali before. What else is there to do?"

Dante's shoulders relaxed. "Don't bring up diving in front of my father, or he'll talk your ear off," he said as we started our walk back to the restaurant. We'd been gone for almost an hour; his parents must be wondering what happened to us. "To be fair, the island is one of the top diving destinations in the world. There are also some beautiful temples and a great art scene in Ubud..."

I half listened as he ran through the top activities in Bali. I was too distracted by his voice to pay attention to his words—deep and velvety, with a faint Italian accent that did unspeakable things to my insides. I'd teased him about loving Kai's British accent at Valhalla, but it was his I couldn't get enough of. Not just the voice but the intelligence, loyalty, vulnerability, and humor that lurked deep, *deep* beneath his grumpy surface.

Somewhere along the way, Dante Russo had morphed from a caricature of a rich, arrogant CEO into an actual human. One I *liked*, for the most part.

It was awful. No matter what happened at Valhalla or how much Dante shared about himself, I couldn't delude myself into thinking our relationship was anything more than what it was. That was a surefire way to a broken heart, and I already had enough broken things in my life.

Dante stepped closer to me to let another couple pass. Our fingers brushed, and my traitorous heart leaped into my throat.

This is just business, I reminded myself.

If I said it enough times, maybe I'd believe it.

CHAPTER 18

Vivian

OVER THE NEXT THREE DAYS, DANTE AND HIS PARENTS took me on a crash tour of Bali. We scuba dived in Nusa Penida, trekked to waterfalls in Munduk, and visited temples in Gianyar. The Russos had a private driver and boat, which made traversing the island easier.

By the time Thanksgiving night rolled around, I'd tanned into a golden brown and forgotten all about the pile of work waiting for me in New York. Even Dante frowned less.

I was glad I'd taken him up on his offer to see one of his company's therapists. Though I could've probably moved past the robbery without therapy over time, talking with Dr. Cho helped me process it in a way I couldn't have on my own. Our sessions would continue after Thanksgiving, but for now, they were enough to ensure my trip wasn't marred by sleepless nights and flashbacks to the press of metal against my chin.

"Luca, get off your phone," Janis admonished during dinner. "It's rude to text at the table."

"Sorry." He continued texting, his plate of food untouched.

Luca had arrived Monday night and spent the majority of his

time texting, sleeping, and lounging by the pool. It was like being on vacation with a teenager, except he was in his thirties and not his teens.

Janis pursed her lips, Gianni shook his head, and I quietly ate my potatoes while tension gathered over the table.

"Put your phone down." Dante didn't look up from his plate, but everyone, including his parents, flinched at the cutting steel in his voice.

After a drawn-out second, Luca straightened, set his phone to the side, and picked up his knife and fork.

Just like that, the tension dissipated and conversation resumed.

"If you ever tire of the corporate world, you should become a babysitter," I whispered to Dante while Gianni waxed nostalgic about his last trip to Indonesia five years ago. "I think you'd do great."

"I'm already a babysitter." Dante slid the words from the corner of his mouth. "Thirty-one years with no promotion. I'm ready to resign."

He grimaced at a speck of stuffing on one of his green beans and shoved the offending vegetable to the side.

A laugh bubbled up my throat. "Perhaps you should. I think your charge is all grown up."

"Do you really?" Dante cut me a skeptical glance.

"Well…" I flicked my gaze at Luca, who was shoveling food in his mouth and sneaking peeks at his phone when he thought his brother wasn't looking. "To an extent. But you're his brother, not his father. It's not your job to babysit him."

Dante assuming a caretaker role was a natural consequence of his parents' abandonment, but it was a heavy burden for one person to bear. Especially when the cared for was a grown man who seemed content to let his brother do all the heavy lifting.

The tiniest flicker passed through Dante's eyes. "It's always been my job. If I don't do it, no one else will."

"Then no one does it. You can support someone without fixing everything for them. They have to learn from their own mistakes."

"You seem very passionate about this topic." A hint of amusement laced his words.

"I don't want you to burn out. But if you take on too much for too long, you will." My voice gentled. "It's not healthy, physically *or* mentally."

Dante was thirty-six, working a high-stress job with a high-stress family. He had little to no downtime. If he kept this up...

My stomach tightened. The thought of anything happening to him bothered me more than it should've, and not just because he was my fiancé.

The flicker in his eyes returned, hotter and brighter. His expression softened. "Enjoy the meal, *mia cara*. Don't let my family bullshit ruin it."

A velvety flutter brushed my heart. "Don't worry. I can enjoy good food under any conditions."

It wasn't true, but it made Dante smile.

I shifted, and our legs grazed beneath the table. It was a whisper of a touch, but my body reacted like he'd slipped his hand beneath my skirt and caressed my thigh. The conversation from the rest of the table fell away as the mental image of his touch entered my bloodstream in an intoxicating rush.

There must be an invisible thread connecting my fantasies to his mind, because black bled into the edges of his eyes like he knew exactly what I was picturing.

My pulse drummed.

"*So*." Luca's voice snapped the thread with brutal efficiency.

Our heads jerked toward him in unison, and my pulse pounded for an entirely different reason when I noticed the speculative gleam in his eyes. The table was too large and our voices too low for him to have heard us talking about him, but he was clearly up to something.

"How's the wedding planning going?" Luca asked.

"Fine," Dante said before I could answer. The softness was gone, replaced with his usual curt tone.

"Glad to hear." The younger Russo took a bite of turkey, chewed, and swallowed before saying, "You and Vivian seem to be getting along *great*."

Dante's jaw hardened.

"Of *course* they're getting along great," Janis said. "They're in love! Honestly, Luca, what a silly thing to say."

I pushed my food around my plate, suddenly uneasy.

"You're right. Sorry," Luca said a tad too innocently. "Just never thought I'd see the day when Dante fell in love."

"Enough." Dante's tone was sharp. "This isn't a roundtable on my love life."

Luca's grin widened, but he heeded his brother's warning and didn't say any more after that.

After dinner, Dante, Luca, and Gianni cleaned the dining room and took out the garbage while Janis and I did the dishes.

"I like the way Dante is around you," she said. "He's less..."

"Uptight?" Normally, I would've never been so blunt to the man's mother, of all people, but wine and days of sun had loosened my tongue.

"Yes." Janis laughed. "He likes things done a certain way, and he's not afraid to tell you if they don't meet his standards. When he was a toddler, we tried feeding him broccoli with a bit of mashed potatoes on it. He threw the plate on the floor. Three-hundred-dollar Wedgwood. Can you believe it?" She shook her head.

I didn't ask why she'd been serving a toddler food on Wedgwood china. Instead, I broached a more sensitive topic, one that'd been weighing on my mind since my beach conversation with Dante.

"Was it hard saying goodbye to him and Luca?"

Her movements stilled for a split second. "I see he's been talking to you about us."

My bravado retreated in the face of possible confrontation. "Not that much."

At the end of the day, Janis was Dante's mother. I didn't want to antagonize her.

"It's okay, darling. I know he's not my biggest fan. Truth be told, I'm not a great mother, and Gianni is not a great father," she said matter-of-factly. "It's why we left the boys in their grandfather's care. He gave them the stability and discipline we couldn't." She paused before continuing in a softer voice, "We tried. Gianni and I quit traveling and settled in Italy after I found out I was pregnant with Dante. We stayed there for six years until after Luca was born." She ran a dirty dish under the water, her expression far off. "It sounds bad, but those six years made me realize I wasn't cut out for domestic life. I hated staying in one place, and I couldn't do anything right when it came to the boys. Gianni felt the same way, so we came to an agreement with Dante's grandfather. He became their legal guardian and moved them to New York. Gianni and I sold our farmhouse and...well." She gestured around the kitchen.

I remained silent. It wasn't my place to judge other people's parenting, but all I could think about was how Dante must've felt having his parents give up on him because taking care of him was too hard.

Then again, perhaps it really was for the best. Nothing good came from forcing someone to do something they didn't want to do.

"You must think we're terribly selfish," Janis said. "Perhaps we are. There have been many times when I wished I was the kind of mother they needed, but I'm not. Pretending otherwise would've hurt the boys more than it helped."

"Maybe, but they're both adults now," I said carefully. "I

think they would like to see their parents more often, even if it's only for milestones like birthdays." *And engagement parties.*

"Luca, maybe. Dante..." She clucked her tongue. "We had to twist his arm to get him to Bali. If it weren't for you, he would've brushed us off with another excuse about being too busy with work."

I wasn't surprised. Dante gave me the impression of someone who held a grudge for decades.

"I'm glad he has you now." Janis's smile returned, a tad more wistful than before. "He could use a partner. He takes too much care of other people, and he doesn't take enough care of himself."

Three months ago, I would've laughed at the idea of anyone describing Dante as caring. He was moody, hot-tempered, and dead set on getting his way. But now...

My mind flashed to our conversation on the beach, our snack night in the kitchen, and the thousands of little moments that revealed little glimpses of the man beneath the armor.

"I'll be honest, I was skeptical about the engagement at first." Janis handed me the freshly scrubbed plate, which I wiped and placed in the drying rack. "Knowing Dante, I wouldn't put it past him to marry someone strictly for business purposes."

A concrete block formed in my chest.

"Our families work in similar fields," I murmured. "So there is a business element to it."

"Yes, but I've seen the way he looks at you." She ran the last dirty dish under the water. "It's not about business."

She was wrong, but that didn't stop my pulse from spiking with anticipation. "How does he look at me?"

Janis smiled. "Like he never wants to look away."

CHAPTER 19

Dante

"A THANKSGIVING DAY CALL FROM DANTE RUSSO." Christian's drawl rolled over the phone. "I'm honored."

"You're the one who emailed me first on a federal holiday, Harper."

I'd retired to my room after cleaning up. My parents and Luca were downstairs, but I wasn't in the mood to play late-night UNO or whatever the hell they were doing. My parents would continue to be inappropriate, and my brother would bug me about Vivian. No fucking thank you.

"Ah, yes." Christian's voice sobered, a sign he was entering business mode. "We found another set of photos in a safety deposit box registered to an alias. Total count is now five."

Francis was a paranoid bastard.

"Do you think there's more?" I glanced at the en suite bathroom. The sound of running water leaked under the closed door like erotic white noise.

Vivian was in there. Wet. *Naked.*

Heat and annoyance rushed through me in equal measure. I turned my back to the door and waited for Christian's response.

"There could always be more," he said. "That's the game we're playing until we can confirm exactly how many backups Francis has."

Basically, I was playing chicken with my brother's life. I could call Francis's bluff, but…

I rubbed an aggravated hand over my jaw. It was too damn risky.

"My team will continue looking until you tell us to stop." Christian paused. "I have to say, I'm surprised you haven't checked in since October. I thought the issue held more urgency for you."

"I've been busy."

"Hmm." The sound resonated with knowing. "Or perhaps you're warming up to your bride-to-be? I heard you two disappeared for quite a while at Valhalla's New York gala."

My teeth clenched. Why was everyone so obsessed with my feelings toward her? "What we do in our private time is none of your business."

"Considering I'm actively surveilling her father on *your* request, it's partly my business." Ice clinked in the background. "Be careful, Dante. You can either have Vivian or you can have her father's head on a platter—figuratively speaking, of course. You can't have both."

The shower stopped running, followed by a beat of silence and the opening creak of the bathroom door.

"I'm well aware. Keep looking." I hung up right as Vivian stepped out in a cloud of steam and sweet-smelling fragrance.

Every muscle tensed.

Objectively, there was nothing indecent about her silk shorts and top. It was the same outfit she'd worn in the kitchen during our snack night, only in black instead of pink.

*Un*objectively, it should be outlawed. All that exposed skin couldn't be good for her. Never mind the fact that we were in tropical Bali; the outfit was a hypothermia case waiting to happen.

"Who were you talking to?" Vivian loosened her hair from its bun and ran her fingers through the dark strands. They cascaded down her back, begging me to wrap my fist around them and see if they were as soft as they looked.

My jaw muscles flexed. "Business associate."

I'd stayed up late the past three nights so I wouldn't have to share the room with Vivian while we were both awake. She was always asleep when I came in, and I was always gone when she woke up.

We didn't have that option tonight.

Apparently, Vivian wasn't in the mood for card games with my family either, so we were stuck in the same room. Awake. Half-dressed. *Together.*

Fuck my life.

"On Thanksgiving?" Vivian smoothed body lotion over her arms, oblivious to my torture.

I should've stayed in the damn living room.

"Money doesn't rest." I turned my back to her and pulled my shirt over my head. The air-conditioning was on full blast, but I was burning up.

I tossed the shirt over the arm of a nearby chair and faced her again only to find her staring at me with wide eyes.

"What are you doing?"

"Getting ready for bed." I cocked an eyebrow at her visible horror. "I sleep hot, *mia cara*. You wouldn't want me to roast to death overnight, would you?"

"Don't be dramatic," she muttered, setting her lotion back on the dresser. "You're a grown man. One night of sleeping with your clothes on won't kill you."

Vivian's eyes dropped to my bare torso before she quickly looked away, her cheeks red.

A knowing smirk worked its way onto my mouth, but it quickly faded when we turned off the lights and climbed into bed, making sure to stay as far apart as possible. It wasn't enough.

The California king was large enough to host a small orgy, but Vivian was still too close. Hell, I could be sleeping in the bathtub with the door closed and she'd *still* be too close.

Her scent stole into my lungs, blurring the usually crisp edges of my logic and reasoning, and her presence burned into my side like an open flame. The murmurs of our breaths overlapped in a heavy, hypnotic rhythm.

It was half past eleven. I could reasonably wake up at five. *Six and a half hours.* I could do this.

I stared at the ceiling, my jaw tight, while Vivian turned and tossed. Every dip of the mattress reminded me she was *there*. Half-naked, close enough to touch, and smelling like an apple orchard after a morning rainstorm.

I didn't even *like* apples.

"Stop it," I ground out. "Neither of us will get any sleep if you insist on moving around like that all night."

"I can't help it. My brain is..." She blew out a breath. "I can't sleep."

"Try." The sooner she fell asleep, the sooner I could relax. Relatively speaking.

"What great advice," she said. "I can't believe I didn't think of that. You should start a Dear Dante column in the local newspaper."

"Were you born with a smart mouth, or did your parents buy it for you after their first million?"

Vivian let out a sardonic breath. "If my parents had their way, I wouldn't say anything except *yes*, *of course*, and *I understand*."

A twinge of regret softened my aggravation.

"Most parents want obedient children." *Except mine, who didn't want children at all.*

"Hmm."

It struck me that Vivian knew more about my family dynamics than I did hers, which was ironic considering she was the more open one in our relationship. I rarely discussed my parents, both because the gossip mills churned overtime and because my relationship with them was nobody's business, but there was something about Vivian that pulled reluctant admissions and long-buried secrets out of me.

"Are your parents upset we're not celebrating Thanksgiving with them?" I asked.

"No. We're not big on the holiday."

Of course. I knew that.

More silence.

Moonlight spilled through the curtains and splashed liquid silver across our sheets. The AC hummed in the corner, a quiet companion to the thunder rumbling in the distance. The sense of an impending rainstorm snuck past the windows and soaked the air. It was the type of night that lulled people into drowsy disclosures and deep sleeps.

For me, it had the opposite effect. Energy buzzed like a live wire under my skin, heightening all my senses and setting me on edge.

"How much did your family change after your father's business took off?"

We'd touched on the topic after our engagement shoot, but she hadn't gone in depth about it beyond the arranged marriage expectations. Since neither of us could sleep, I might as well try to get some intel out of Vivian. Plus, the conversation kept my mind off other, more impure thoughts.

"A lot," she said. "One day, Agnes and I were attending public schools and eating school lunch. The next, we were at a fancy private academy with gourmet chefs and students showing up in chauffeured limos. Everything changed—our clothes, our house, our friends. Our *family*. At first, I loved it because what child *wouldn't* love dressing up and having new toys? But…" She drew in a deep breath. "The older I got, the more I realized how much money changed us. Not just materially but spiritually, for lack of a better word. We were new money, but my parents were desperate to prove we were just as good as Boston's old-money elite. There's a difference, you know."

I knew. Hierarchies existed even—*especially*—in the world of the rich and powerful.

"The desire for validation consumed them, especially my father," Vivian said. "I can't pinpoint the exact turning point, but I woke up one morning and the funny, caring man who'd carried me on his shoulders when I was a little girl and helped me build sandcastles on the beach was gone. In his place was someone who would do anything to reach the top of the social ladder."

If she only knew.

"I'm not complaining," she continued. "I know how lucky I am to have been raised with the money we had. But sometimes…" Another, more wistful breath. "I wonder if we would've been happier had Lau Jewels stayed a tiny shop on a side street in Boston."

Jesus. An unfamiliar ache settled in my chest. She and Francis shared the same blood. How could they be so damn different?

"Sorry for rambling." She sounded embarrassed. "I didn't mean to talk your ear off about my family."

"You don't have to apologize." Her words were sad, but her voice was so sweet I could listen to it forever. "This beats counting sheep."

Her laugh carried into the night like a soft melody. "Are you saying I'm putting you to sleep?"

Our legs brushed, and my muscles tensed at the brief contact. I hadn't realized how close we'd gotten. Against my better judgment, I turned my head to find her doing the same. Our gazes met, and the rhythm of our breaths splintered into something more jagged.

"Trust me," I said quietly. "Of all the things you do to me, putting me to sleep isn't one of them."

Moonlight kissed the curves of Vivian's face, accentuating the hollows of her cheekbones and the sensual fullness of her lips. Her eyes shone dark and luminous, like precious stones gleaming in the night. Surprise glinted in their depths at my words, along with a smoky wisp of desire that made heat curl in my groin.

I hadn't touched her since our tryst in Valhalla's library, but all I wanted in that moment was to see those eyes darken with pleasure again. To feel the softness of her body pressed against mine and hear her breathy little cries when she climaxed against me.

My blood pounded in my ears. The breeze from the vents grew hotter, the air thicker. The electricity from dinner returned and stretched the moment into one long, perfect thread of tension.

"We should go to sleep," Vivian breathed. There was a slight shake in her voice. "It's late."

"Agreed."

For a suspended moment, neither of us moved. Then another boom of thunder crashed in the distance, and the tension exploded with the force of a lit match in a barrel of gasoline.

My mouth crashed down on hers, and her arms wrapped around my neck, pulling me flush against her. A low moan vibrated against my mouth when I rolled on top of her and pinned her hips between my thighs. Raw desire took over, eradicating thoughts of anything except Vivian.

No Francis. No Luca. No blackmail. Just her.

I stroked my tongue against the seam of her lips, tasting her, demanding entry. They parted, and the heady, intoxicating taste of her coated my tongue.

I cupped the back of her neck and angled her head so I could deepen the kiss. Her hands sank into my hair. My palm swept beneath her top and over her stomach.

We kissed like we were drowning and the other person was our only source of oxygen. Wild. Frantic. Desperate.

And it still wasn't enough.

I needed more of it. More of *her*.

"Dante." Her soft cry when I cupped her breast almost undid me.

"Keep screaming my name, sweetheart." I kissed my way down her neck and chest, eager to map every inch of her body with my mouth. I closed my mouth around a clothed, peaked nipple and pinched the other between my thumb and forefinger, eliciting another moan of my name. Approval rumbled in my chest. "That's a good girl."

I made my way down her stomach to her thighs, my journey languid despite the need raging through me.

I smelled Vivian's arousal before I tugged her shorts and underwear down, but the sight of her pussy, so wet and ready and fucking *perfect*, hit me like a shot of pure heroin.

"Please." She panted, her grip strangling my hair when I nipped the soft skin of her inner thigh.

My cock pulsed so hard it ached, but I didn't touch it, too focused on the glistening temptation in front of me.

"Please what?"

I received only a whimper in response.

"Please eat out this pretty little cunt of yours?" I taunted, my voice soft but the words rough. "Tongue fuck you until you beg me to let you come? You have such a smart mouth, *mia cara*. Use it."

"*Yes*." The word was half plea, half demand. "I need your mouth on me. Dante, *please*."

This time, the sound of her voice, moaning my name in that way, *did* unravel me.

I pushed her legs farther apart and delved in like a man starved. I focused on her swollen clit, licking and sucking until her cries of pleasure crescendoed to the edge of pain.

Vivian writhed and bucked, begging me to stop one minute and keep going the next. She was dripping all over my face, and I couldn't get enough. I was addicted to the taste of her, to the way she sounded when I buried my tongue inside her and the way her back arched off the bed when she finally came with a full-body shudder.

I waited for her trembles to die down before I touched my tongue to her sensitized clit again and gave it a slow, leisurely lick.

"*Hai un sapore divino*," I murmured.

"No more," she pleaded. "I can't...*oh God*." Her protest split into another moan when I slid two fingers inside her up to the first knuckle. I kept my mouth on her clit and slowly worked my way up to the second knuckle before I pulled my fingers out and pushed them back in.

In and out, faster and faster, my mouth still exploring her clit until she drenched my face and her sharp cries filled the room again.

My cock throbbed in time with my pulse as I pushed myself onto my knees.

Vivian stared up at me, her cheeks flushed and her chest heaving from the aftermath of her orgasm. A light sheen of sweat misted her skin, and her face was so full of trust and satiated pleasure it made my gut twist.

No one had ever looked at me like that before.

Just like that, a cold trickle of reality pierced my fog of lust. It suddenly hit me who we were and what I'd done.

We weren't a normal engaged couple. She was the daughter of the enemy, and I'd been *forced* into this engagement, even if she didn't know it. I wasn't supposed to like her, much less desire her.

Vivian wrapped her arms around my neck and pressed her hips up against mine, the message clear.

Fuck me.

I wanted to. My body screamed for it. My cock ached for it. It would be so easy to sink into her softness and let it carry us away for the night.

But if I did, there would be no going back. Not for her, and not for me.

My hands fisted on the mattress as indecision warred.

You can either have Vivian or you can have her father's head on a platter—figuratively speaking, of course. You can't have both.

Ice water doused the remaining heat in my veins. Of all the voices I wanted to hear in bed, Christian's ranked in the bottom five, but the bastard had a point.

Vivian didn't have a perfect relationship with her family, but she still cared about them. One day soon, she'd find out the truth about our engagement and her father's deception, and she'd be devastated. Adding sex to the mix would only complicate things further.

"Dante?" Tentativeness crept into her voice at my hesitation.

Goddammit.

I unwound her arms from my neck and straightened, trying to ignore the hurt and confusion on her face.

"Get some rest," I said roughly. "It's been a long day."

I didn't wait for an answer before I got off the bed, headed into the bathroom, and locked the door. I turned the shower as cold as it would go, letting the icy water blast some fucking sense into me.

Self-loathing formed a concrete block in my chest. What the *hell* was I doing?

Kissing Vivian. Letting my guard down. Almost having *sex* with her in my parents' villa, for Christ's sake.

I'd intended to stay away from her until I took care of her father and ended our farce of an engagement. Now here I was, taking a cold shower at midnight so I didn't fuck up my plans any more than I already had.

I'd spent my life honing my control. Enzo Russo had drilled its importance into me since I was a child. Even when I occasionally lost my temper, I never lost sight of the bigger goal.

But I'd also never met anyone like Vivian. Of all the people in my life, she was the only one who could make me lose control.

CHAPTER 20

Dante

KAI'S PUNCH SNAPPED MY HEAD BACK WITH SUCH force my teeth rattled. The taste of copper filled my mouth, and when my vision finally cleared, his frown came into focus like a photograph in a developing tray.

"That was an easy dodge. Where's your head at today?"

"It was one hit. Don't get cocky."

"Three." He grunted when my uppercut caught him beneath the chin. "And that doesn't answer my question."

I blamed the next words out of my mouth on the residual impact of his strike.

"I kissed Vivian over Thanksgiving." *Willingly.* Of my own accord.

We'd done more than that, but I sure as fuck wasn't discussing our sex life with Kai.

The engagement photo shoot kiss had been forced. Bali had been...hell, I didn't know what Bali had been other than a mind fuck.

Vivian had been asleep or pretending to be asleep after I got out of the shower, and we'd avoided discussing what happened in the week since. She probably thought I'd rejected her for whatever reason, and I was too disconcerted to correct her.

Kai gave me a strange look. "You kissed your fiancée. So what?"

Fuck. The kiss had screwed me up so much I'd forgotten he didn't know I despised her family.

To him, our engagement was business, but most arranged marriages still involved physical intimacy before the wedding. If not sex, then at least something as simple as a kiss.

"It was different this time."

I shouldn't have done it. The kiss, opening up about my family, all of it. Yet I did it anyway.

Somehow, someway, Vivian Lau had burrowed under my skin, and I didn't know how to get her out without losing a piece of myself in the process.

A knowing glint passed through Kai's eyes. "Mixing business with pleasure. It's about time."

"Look who's talking." Kai's idea of fun was translating academic texts into Latin for no reason other than he was a show-off and bored as hell.

"What can I say? I prefer the company of words to people. Except for you, of course."

"Of course." He was so full of bullshit.

He laughed. "Cheer up, Russo. Liking your fiancée isn't the worst thing in the world."

Maybe not in his world. But it was in mine.

My efforts to avoid Vivian disintegrated when I returned home and promptly ran into her in the foyer.

"Oh my God. What happened?" Her horrified expression confirmed what I already knew—I looked like a mess.

And if I had any lingering doubts, the mirror hanging opposite the front door smashed them into smithereens.

Bruised jaw. Blackening eye. A cut over my brow.

Thank fuck I didn't have a board meeting in the next two weeks.

"Kai." I removed my coat and hung it on the brass tree. My tone was indifferent, but an unsettling warmth unfurled behind my ribs at her concern.

Vivian's brows pulled together. "Kai hit you? He doesn't seem like the type. He's usually so calm and…nice."

Just like that, the warmth turned into annoyance.

"I told you, he's not as nice as he seems," I said in a clipped voice. "But to clarify, we sometimes blow off steam by boxing. He happened to land more hits today since I was…distracted."

Thinking about you.

"You box for fun." Vivian set the vase of flowers in her arms on the marble side table. "That makes so much sense."

"What's that supposed to mean?"

"It means you have a temper." She straightened the stems, oblivious to my scowl. "I'm sure boxing helps, but have you ever thought about anger management classes?" A teasing note ran beneath her voice.

"I don't need anger management classes," I growled. First, she was the reason Kai got the upper hand in the ring. Now, she was insulting me? "I'm in full control of—" I broke off at her laugh. Realization dawned. "You're teasing me."

"It's too easy." Vivian's smile faded when she faced me again. Her eyes swept over my face, lingering on the nasty cut above my eye. "You should ice your bruises and clean that cut, or it'll get infected."

"I'll be fine." They weren't my first or worst injuries from the ring.

"Ice and disinfectant," she said firmly. "Now."

"Or what?" I shouldn't be indulging her, but she was so endearing when she tried to boss me around that I couldn't resist.

Her eyes narrowed. "Or I'll place every candlestick in this house at uneven intervals and make sure your foods touch every. Single. Meal. Greta will help me. She likes me more than you."

I took back what I said about her being endearing. She was fucking evil.

"Meet me in the guest bathroom. I'm getting the ice."

I didn't take well to people telling me what to do, but a reluctant wisp of admiration curled in my chest as I headed to the bathroom. I leaned against the counter and checked my watch. I had a mountain of paperwork to review, and God knew I should stay the hell away from Vivian until I sorted out my aggravating feelings toward her. Yet here I was, waiting for a goddamn ice pack.

My injuries didn't even hurt. Much.

The door opened, and Vivian entered carrying two small ice packs.

"I told you I'm fine," I grumbled, but a spark of pleasure lit in my chest when she brushed gentle fingers over my jaw.

"Dante, your skin is purple."

"Purple black." A smile tugged on my lips at her cutting look. "Precision is important, *mia cara.*"

"Are you trying to get a matching injury on the other side of your jaw?" she asked pointedly, pressing one of the packs against my face. "If so, I can help with that."

"It's not very sporting of you to threaten bodily harm while patching me up. Some might even say it's hypocritical."

"I don't like sports, and I'm an excellent multitasker."

"Yet Asher Donovan and Rafael Pessoa, two sports stars, are on your dream husband list."

I used to be a fan of both. Not anymore.

"First of all, you *have* to let that list go. Second of all—hold this over your eye." Vivian pushed the second ice pack into my hand while she dampened a washcloth. "Second of all, don't deflect from the main issue here, which is your utter refusal to ask for help."

"I can handle a few injuries. I've been through worse." Still, I didn't resist when she dabbed the cloth on my wound.

"Do I want to ask what you mean by *worse*?"

"I broke my nose the first time when I was fourteen. Some asshole was bullying Luca, so I hit him. He hit me back. It got ugly enough I had to go to the ER."

Vivian winced. "How old was the other kid?"

"Sixteen." Fletcher Alcott had been a real piece of work.

"A *sixteen-year-old* was picking on a nine-year-old?"

"Cowards always pick on people who can't fight back."

"Sadly true." She retrieved a bandage from the medicine cabinet. "You said that was the first time you broke your nose. What happened the second time?"

My mouth curled into a grin. "Got drunk in college and fell on the sidewalk."

Vivian's laugh washed through me like a cool breeze on a hot summer day. "I can't imagine you as a typical drunk college student."

"I did my best to erase any incriminating evidence, but the memories are there."

"I'm sure you did." She placed the Band-Aid over the cut and stepped back with a satisfied expression. "There. Much better."

"You're forgetting one thing." I tapped my jaw.

I didn't know why I was dragging this out when I didn't want to be here in the first place, but I couldn't remember the last time someone fussed over me. It felt...nice. Disturbingly so.

Vivian's brow wrinkled. "What?"

"My kiss."

Pink crept over her cheeks. "Now you're the one teasing me."

"I would never tease about such a serious matter," I said solemnly. "One kiss for each of my injuries. That's it. Would you deny a dying man his last wish?"

Her sparkling gaze held a touch of exasperation. "Don't be dramatic. You're the one who said you were, quote, unquote, *fine*. But since you insist on being such a baby about it..." She moved closer again. My pulse beat in my throat when she brushed her lips over my brow, then my jaw. "Better?"

"Much."

"You're incorrigible." Laughter bubbled beneath her voice.

"It's not the worst thing someone's called me."

"I believe it."

She turned her head a fraction, and our eyes held.

The bathroom smelled like lemon cleaner and ointment, two of the unsexiest scents known to mankind. That didn't stop heat from sparking in my blood or the memory of her taste from flooding my mind.

"About Bali." Her breath brushed my skin, warm and tentative.

My groin tightened. "Yeah?"

"You were right to stop things when you did. Our...what we did was a mistake."

Something that felt suspiciously like disappointment snaked through my chest.

"I know we're getting married, so we'll have to...eventually." Vivian skipped over the specifics. "But it's too soon. I had too much wine at Thanksgiving and got caught up in the moment. It was a..." She faltered when my hands rested on her hips. "A mistake. Right?"

Her skin branded my palm through the layer of cashmere.

A hard smile flickered over my mouth. "Right."

My touch lingered for a beat before I moved her to the side and headed to the exit.

I should've stopped in Bali, and what happened before I stopped was a mistake.

We were both right.

But it didn't mean I had to like it.

CHAPTER 21

Vivian

AFTER THANKSGIVING, THE YEAR PASSED IN THE BLINK of an eye. I'd like to say my first holiday season as an engaged woman was special or memorable, but it was more stressful than anything else.

The weeks between Black Friday and New Year's Eve were packed with work, social obligations, and endless questions about my upcoming wedding. Dante and I stayed overnight at my parents' house for Christmas, and it was just as awkward as I'd feared.

"If Mom fusses any more over him, people will think *she's* the one marrying him," my sister, Agnes, whispered as our mother plied Dante with another drink.

We only called her Mom to each other and never to her face.

"Imagine Father negotiating *that* arrangement," I whispered back.

We burst into giggles.

We were in the living room after our Christmas Eve dinner—my mother and Dante by the fireplace, my sister and me on the couch, and my father and Gunnar, Agnes's husband, on the other couch by the bar.

I didn't see Agnes much now that she lived in Eldorra, but whenever we were together, we reverted to being teenagers again.

"Girls, want to share what's so funny?" our father asked pointedly, looking up from his conversation with Gunnar.

Tall, blond, and blue-eyed, Gunnar was my sister's polar opposite looks-wise, but they shared a similar sense of humor and easygoing manner. He watched, his expression amused, as my sister and I sobered.

"Nothing's funny," we said in unison.

My father shook his head with an exasperated expression. "Vivian, put your jacket back on," he said. "It's freezing. You'll get sick."

"It's not *that* cold," I protested. "The fireplace is on."

But I put the jacket on anyway.

Besides marriage, my parents were forever fussing at me about wearing enough layers and drinking enough soup. It was one of the few holdovers from our pre-wealth days.

When I looked over at Dante, I found him watching us with narrowed eyes. I raised an eyebrow, and he gave a small shake of his head. I had no clue what that meant, but my curiosity over his reaction melted in the whirlwind of Christmas morning (where Gunnar announced he bought Agnes another pony for their country manor) and the Legacy Ball and wedding planning that dominated the weeks *after* New Year's.

Before I knew it, it was mid-January, and my anxiety had peaked to an all-time high.

T-minus four months until the ball.

T-minus seven months until the wedding.

God help me.

"You need a spa retreat," Isabella said. "Nothing restores the body like a weekend in the desert filled with deep-tissue massages and yoga."

"You hate yoga, and you once left a retreat early because it was too 'boring and woo-woo.'"

"For *me*. Not for you." Isabella lay stomach down on my office couch, her feet kicked up in the air as she scribbled in her notebook. Occasionally, a.k.a. every two minutes, she'd stop to sip her soda or nibble on a piece of dark chocolate. It was lunchtime, but she said she wasn't that hungry, and I hadn't had a chance to order takeout. "You should take Dante with you. It'll be a couples' getaway."

I looked up from the Legacy Ball seating chart. "Aren't you supposed to be writing the next great thriller instead of providing unsolicited advice on my love life?"

Sometimes, Isabella used my office as her office because the silence in her apartment was "too loud," which I was fine with as long as she didn't distract me while I was working.

"I'm drawing inspiration from real life. Perhaps I can write about an arranged marriage gone terribly wrong. The wife murders her husband after having a kinky affair with her sexy doorman… or not," she added hastily when I glared at her. "But you have to admit, sex and murder go hand in hand."

"Only to you." I moved the sticky notes with Dominic and Alessandra Davenport's names to the table with Kai. *Much better*. The last setup had Dominic sitting next to his biggest rival. "Should I worry about your exes?"

"Only the ones who pissed me off."

"That's all of them."

"Is it?" Isabella was the picture of innocence. "Oops."

A smile pulled on my lips. Her dating history was a string of red flags encompassing race car drivers, photographers, models, and, in one truly spectacular lapse of judgment, an aspiring poet with a Shakespeare tattoo and a penchant for spouting lines from *Romeo and Juliet* during sex.

The past year had been her longest break from men since I met her. She deserved it. Dealing with men was exhausting.

Case in point: my relationship with Dante. Trying to figure out where we stood was like trying to find my footing on a slab of particleboard in the middle of the ocean.

Isabella and I lapsed into silence again, but my mind kept straying toward a certain dark-haired Italian. We'd kissed, and Dante had given me not one but *two* mind-blowing orgasms, only to shut down immediately after.

Nothing beat the humiliation of asking him for sex only for him to leave me high and dry. At least I'd successfully (I hoped) played the entire night off as a mistake.

A knock interrupted my inner turmoil.

"Come in."

Shannon entered holding an extravagant bouquet of red roses. There must've been at least two dozen of them slotted into a slim crystal vase, and their scent instantly blanketed the room with cloying sweetness.

Isabella sat up, her eyes gleaming like a Page Six reporter who'd stumbled on a juicy society secret.

"These just came for you," Shannon said with a knowing smile. "Where do you want me to put them?"

My heart leapt in my throat. "My desk is fine. Thank you."

"Oh my God." Isabella beelined to my desk the second the door closed. "These roses must've cost hundreds of dollars. What's the occasion?"

"I have no idea," I admitted. Surprise and pleasure warred for dominance in my chest.

Dante had never sent me flowers before. Our relationship had smoothed into one of civil cohabitation and the occasional shared late-night snack since Bali, but we still weren't a "normal" couple by any means.

I couldn't imagine why he'd be sending me roses now. It wasn't a holiday, anniversary, or anyone's birthday.

"*Just because* flowers. The best kind." Isabella skimmed her fingers over a velvety petal. "Who knew Dante Russo was such a romantic?"

The pleasure edged out the surprise.

I searched the extravagant blooms until I found a tiny card with my name written on the front. I flipped it over, and my stomach plummeted.

"It's not from Dante."

"Then who's it…*oh*." Isabella's eyes widened when I showed her the note.

Vivian,

Happy belated new year. I thought of you at midnight but didn't have the guts to send you this until now. Hope you're doing well.

Love, Heath

PS. I'm here if you ever change your mind.

A cocktail of disappointment, unease, and confusion brewed in my stomach. Save for a *Merry Christmas* text, I hadn't talked to Heath since the flea market. His sending me flowers made even less sense than Dante sending them.

"*Love*, Heath." Isabella wrinkled her nose. "First, he shows up in New York and *coincidentally* runs into you. Now this. Man needs to move on. You've been broken up for years, and you—"

"Who's Heath?" The black-velvet voice wrenched my gaze to the entrance.

Charcoal suit. Broad shoulders. Expression as dark as his voice.

My pulse skittered into overdrive.

Dante stood in the doorway, brown paper bag in hand, his eyes glinting like shards of volcanic glass against the soft roses. His body held dangerously still, like the calm before a storm.

"Um…" I slid a panicked look at Isabella, who hopped off the desk and scooped her bag up from the floor.

"Well, this was fun, but I gotta go," she chirped in an overly bright voice. "Monty gets cranky if I don't feed him on time."

Traitor, my glare screamed.

Sorry, she mouthed. *Good luck.*

I was never letting her work in my office again.

She brushed past Dante with an awkward pat on his arm, and I watched, stomach twisting, as he walked toward me and set the paper bag next to the bouquet. He flipped the note and read it wordlessly, his jaw ticking in rhythm with each passing second.

"It's a New Year's gift," I said when the silence became too oppressive to bear. "Like the champagne glasses my mom bought us."

Tick. Tick. Tick.

I hadn't cheated on Dante or purposely sought out Heath myself. I had nothing to feel guilty about. Still, my nerves rattled like wind chimes in a tornado.

"These aren't champagne glasses, *mia cara*." Dante dropped the note the way one would a diseased carcass. "Nor are they from your mother, which brings me back to my question. Who is Heath?"

I inhaled a soft breath for courage. "My ex-boyfriend."

Dante's eyes sparked. "Your ex-boyfriend."

"Yes." I didn't want to lie, and Dante could probably find out who Heath was with the snap of a finger anyway.

"Why is your ex-boyfriend sending you roses and love notes?"

The velvety tone didn't change, but the undercurrent of danger rippled closer to the surface.

"It's not a love note."

"It damn well looks like one to me." If Dante ground his teeth any harder, they'd crumble into dust. "What does he mean by change your mind?"

"I told him about our engagement a few months ago." If I was telling the truth, I might as well tell the whole truth. "He showed up in New York and implied he'd be open to giving our relationship another shot. I declined. He left. The end."

Dante's eyes were nearly black now. "Obviously not the end, given this *lovely* bouquet he sent you."

"It's just flowers." I understood why he was upset, but he was making it into something bigger than it was. "They're harmless."

"Some fucker is sending you flowers, and you want to tell me it's harmless?" He picked up the card again. "*Thought of you at midnight. Hope you're doing well. Love, Heath.*" Sarcasm weighed heavy on the recitation. "It doesn't take a genius to know what he was doing while he was thinking of you at midnight."

Frustration overrode my misplaced guilt. "I can't control what other people do or say. I told him I wasn't interested in getting back together, and I'll tell him again if he persists. What do you want me to do? Get a restraining order against him?"

"Now that's an excellent idea."

"That's a *ridiculous* idea."

"Do you still love him?"

The question came from so out of left field I could only gape at him until I rustled up the only word I could find. "What?"

"Do you still *love* him?" The ticking jaw returned with vengeance.

"We broke up years ago."

"That doesn't answer my question."

I shifted beneath Dante's heavy stare. Did I still love Heath? I cared for him, and I missed the easy rapport we had. Our breakup had devastated me.

But I wasn't the same person I'd been when we were dating, and time had dulled my heartbreak into a distant echo of what it once was. When I thought of Heath, I thought of the comfort of being loved. I didn't necessarily think of *him*.

But if I didn't *have* to marry Dante and I could go back to Heath without alienating my parents, would I do it?

My head pounded with indecision.

"It doesn't matter," I finally said. "I'm engaged to you, and I'm not getting back together with Heath."

My answer only stoked the fire in Dante's eyes. "I won't have my fiancée pining away after another man before, during, or after the wedding."

"Why does it matter?" My frustration bubbled over into a rush of words. "You'll get your market access and business deal either way. Stop pretending like this is a normal engagement. It's not. We may have kissed and…and gotten more intimate, but we are *not* a love match. You've told me that time and again. You have me. But you don't get to dictate how I feel or who I think about. That is *not* part of the agreement."

Silence reigned in the aftermath of my rant, so thick I tasted it in the back of my throat.

Dante and I stared at each other, the air crackling like a frayed electric wire between us. One wrong move, and it'd burn me alive.

I braced myself for an explosion or yelling or some kind of veiled threat. Instead, after seconds that felt like hours, he turned and walked out without a word.

The door shut behind him, and I slumped against my desk, suddenly exhausted. I pressed the heels of my hands against my eyes, my throat tight.

Every time we made progress, we took two steps back. One minute, I thought Dante might be developing feelings for me. The next, he shut me out like an unwanted stepchild in the cold.

The caveman in Geico's old commercials communicated better than him.

What had he been doing here anyway? Dante's office was a few blocks from mine, but he'd never visited me at work before.

My eyes snagged on the paper bag he'd left behind. After a moment's hesitation, I opened it, and my stomach dipped in the strangest way.

Sitting at the bottom of the bag, nestled between paper-wrapped cutlery and a plethora of sauces, were two takeout boxes from my favorite sushi restaurant.

CHAPTER 22

Vivian

"PAY ATTENTION, *MICETTA*, OR YOU'LL CHOP YOUR finger off." Greta clucked in disapproval. "No one wants human parts in their dinner."

"Sorry," I murmured. I tried to rein in my wandering thoughts and refocus on the task at hand.

If my mother could see me now, mincing garlic in an old cashmere sweater and jeans, she'd have a coronary. Laus did not "toil away" in the kitchen or wear last season's clothes, but I enjoyed the mindless comfort of cooking. I'd invited Isabella and Sloane over for dinner, and we'd decided a girls' cooking night would be more fun than a formal sit-down.

We were right.

The kitchen smelled like the back of a rustic Tuscan restaurant. Tomato sauce bubbled on the stove, bowls of herbs and seasoning lined the counters, and the sparkling tartness of fresh lemons added an extra zing to the mouthwatering aromas.

At the other end of the kitchen, Isabella trimmed green beans while Sloane fixed us her signature martinis. Greta, who refused to leave us unsupervised, fluttered around the room, checking on a dozen different things and scolding us when we didn't prep the food properly.

It felt cozy and normal, like a real home.

So why did I feel so off-kilter?

Maybe because you and Dante are still on the outs, a voice in my head taunted.

We'd attended obligatory social events, celebrated Valentine's Day at Per Se, and attended a Lunar New Year performance at the Lincoln Center, but our relationship at home had been cold and distant since Dante's office visit.

I shouldn't be surprised. Dante withdrew any time things didn't go his way, and I was too annoyed by his overreaction to the flowers to seek him out. So here we were, back in a stalemate.

I chopped the garlic with more force than necessary.

"Here." Sloane appeared next to me and slid an apple martini onto the counter. "For when you're done with the knives. You look like you need it."

I mustered a small smile. "Thanks."

Sloane's platinum hair was twisted in its signature bun, but she'd removed her jacket and unglued her phone from her hand. In her world, she might as well be dancing barefoot on a bar top in Ibiza.

"Where's your dashing husband-to-be?" Isabella asked. "Still sulking about the flowers?"

She was determined to prove Dante and I would turn into a true love match by the wedding and brought him up every chance she got. I suspected she had a bet going with Sloane to see who would be right, since Sloane's opinion of love hovered somewhere between her appreciation for New York subway rats and people who wore sandals with socks.

"He's not sulking," I said, well aware of Greta's eagle-eyed presence. "He's busy."

He'd *been* busy for three weeks. If there was one thing Dante excelled at, it was avoiding hard conversations.

"He's sulking," Isabella, Greta, and Sloane said in unison.

"Trust me. I raised Dante since he was in diapers." Greta checked on the sauce. "You'll never meet a more stubborn, hardheaded man."

Don't I believe it.

"But..." She stirred the pot with a wooden spoon. "He also has a big heart, even if he doesn't show it. He is not...good with words. His grandfather, may he rest in peace, was a good businessman but not a good communicator. He passed those traits down to the boys."

A lump formed in my throat. That was exactly why I hadn't given up on Dante yet. He was a terrible communicator, and his hot and cold attitude made me want to tear my hair out, but underneath it all, there was someone worth waiting for.

"Are you talking him up because he installed a TV in the kitchen for you?" I asked lightly.

Greta's eyes gleamed. "When someone offers you bribery, it's rude not to take it."

Laughter floated through the kitchen, but it died a quick death when Dante and Kai appeared in the doorway.

I straightened, my pulse beating in my throat. Isabella stopped trimming her green beans while Sloane sipped her drink, her cool gaze taking in the newcomers like they were the ones entering *her* house.

"Dante, I didn't know you would be home for dinner." Greta wiped her hands on a dish towel. "The food's almost ready. I'll add two more plates to the table."

"No need. We only stopped by to pick up some documents. We'll be dining at Valhalla tonight." Dante's attention didn't stray from Greta. "I'm also flying to DC for business tomorrow. I'll be gone for a week."

"I see." Greta glanced at me.

I refocused on my garlic.

Dante's announcement was clearly for my benefit, but if he wasn't mature enough to address me directly like an adult, I wouldn't give him the satisfaction of my acknowledgment.

Next to him, Kai's gaze skimmed over me and Sloane to Isabella, who perched on the stool closest to the entrance. Her leather skirt, dangly earrings, and stiletto boots were the polar opposite of his suit, glasses, and silk handkerchief tucked in his breast pocket. She arched an eyebrow at his scrutiny before plucking a cherry tomato from the bowl next to her and popping it in her mouth. She didn't look away from him, making the otherwise innocent movement almost sexual.

Kai watched her show with the bland expression of someone waiting in line at the post office. Next to him, Dante remained in the doorway, silent and unmoving.

The clock ticked toward the half hour. Sauces bubbled and hissed on the stove, and my knife chopped a steady rhythm against the cutting board. The tension was almost as thick as Greta's signature fettuccine.

Greta cleared her throat. "Well, have a safe flight to DC. Bring back a souvenir or two, hmm? I'm sure people in the household will appreciate it."

She slid another glance in my direction.

Smooth, Greta.

"I'll keep that in mind," Dante said stiffly. "Enjoy dinner."

He left without sparing a glance at me.

"Ladies." Kai dipped his head before following him.

Their exit severed the tension holding us hostage.

I dropped my knife, and Greta muttered something under her breath while she removed the meat from the oven.

"I need some water." Isabella slid off her stool and headed to the fridge, her cheeks pink.

I stared at the cutting board, trying to sort through my mess of emotions. I should've been used to Dante's business trips by now, but the news of his upcoming travel stung more than it should've. Even if we didn't talk, his presence was a warm reassurance in the apartment. It was always a little colder when he wasn't home.

CHAPTER 23

Dante

I DIDN'T NEED TO VISIT DC.

I could've conducted my business there virtually, but I welcomed the break from the strained atmosphere at home. I also took the opportunity to check in on Christian, whom I'd tasked with a new project on top of the Francis situation.

He lounged on the couch opposite me, his eyes cool. We were in the library of his downtown penthouse, and we'd spent the past hour discussing Valhalla, business, and security. But judging by his expression, he was still pissed about what happened in the lobby earlier.

I'd merely kissed the hand of one of his neighbors—one whom he seemed to have a special interest in.

It wasn't every day I saw Christian Harper agonize over a woman, and I'd be damned if I let it slide without fucking with him. He'd get over it. They weren't even dating.

"Heath Arnett. CEO of a cloud storage startup that's going public at the end of this year," Christian said now. He lifted an eyebrow. "Since when do you care about cloud storage?"

The mention of Heath's name wiped away my amusement at Christian's response to a simple hand kiss.

I thought about you at midnight. Love, Heath.

Something dark and unwanted snaked through my chest.

"Don't play dumb." I tossed back the rest of my drink and set the crystal tumbler on a nearby side table. "Did you find anything good?"

I'd asked Christian to look into Heath's background. It'd taken him no time to figure out Heath's full name as well as everything about the man's work, family, and hobbies. Standard middle-class American upbringing. Undergrad at Columbia, where Heath met Vivian. A rising career as a software developer before he founded a startup that was currently going gangbusters.

But that was the shiny, top-level stuff. I wanted the seedy underbelly.

Christian smiled. Few things animated him more than ripping the skeletons out of someone's closet. "There's a chance he may have been involved in questionable activities leading to the growth of his company. Not criminal, but questionable. Enough that it could severely impact the performance of their IPO."

"Good. Take care of it before they go public."

I reached for the water next to my empty scotch, but it did nothing to soothe the burn in my blood.

"Of course." Christian watched me, an amused gleam creeping into his amber eyes. "You never answered my earlier question. Why do you care so much about this Heath? It can't possibly be because he's Vivian's ex-boyfriend. The man she was madly in love with until her parents made her break up with him because he didn't come from Russo-level money." Christian swirled his drink in his glass. "Heard he sent her roses after New Year's. Nice ones."

The burn intensified.

"He knows Vivian is my fiancée, and he sent her flowers anyway. It's disrespectful."

I hadn't told Christian about the Valhalla Club, Bali, or any of the changes in my relationship with Vivian. Handing him that information would be like handing dynamite to a destruction-minded toddler. Unfortunately, the bastard possessed an eerily accurate radar when it came to other people's weaknesses.

Not that Vivian was my weakness.

"Hmm." A knowing smile played on Christian's mouth. "That's one reason. Another reason, one I'm more inclined to believe, is that you're starting to develop feelings for your lovely future wife."

"Lay off the whiskey, Harper. It's clouding your judgment," I said coldly. "Vivian is more tolerable than I originally anticipated, but nothing's changed. I have no intention of marrying her *or* tying myself to the Laus."

For some reason, the sentiment tasted less sweet than it had six months ago. Bitterness edged the words like they'd been tainted by deceit, though I'd meant what I said.

I was attracted to Vivian. I'd accepted that much about myself. I even liked her, but not enough to take her father's blackmail lying down.

It didn't matter anyway. Once I demolished her father's empire, she wouldn't want anything to do with me. She was too loyal to her family. Such was the cost of business.

The back of my neck itched. I pushed my sleeves up, wishing it weren't so damn hot in here. Christian must have his heater on full blast.

"If you say so," he drawled. "Don't worry. We're close. Soon, you'll be rid of their entire family, and you can have your house to yourself again."

An odd ache gripped my chest.

"Looking forward to it," I said curtly. I poured myself another glass of Glenlivet, but an incoming call interrupted before I could take a sip.

Edward.

He never called unless there was an emergency. Did something happen to Vivian?

Ice crept through my veins. I quickly excused myself and stepped into the hall.

"What is it?" I demanded once Christian was out of earshot. "Is Vivian okay?"

"Ms. Vivian is fine," Edward assured me. "However, there's been a…" He let out a small cough. "Development I thought you should be aware of. She has a visitor."

I waited impatiently for him to finish. Vivian received visitors all the time. None of them warranted a phone call, unless…

"From what I gathered, it's a former paramour. I believe his name is Heath."

It took a beat for the implications to sink in. Once they did, fury slipped beneath my skin like a slow, creeping poison.

What the *fuck* was Heath doing in my house? He was supposed to be in fucking California.

I was going to murder Christian. He must've known Heath was in New York, and he hadn't said a damn thing about it.

"Normally, I wouldn't bother you with such a matter, but he was quite insistent on seeing Ms. Vivian. She agreed to let him in, but…" Another delicate cough. "Given his *unexpected* arrival, I wanted to alert you."

Blood drummed in my ears, distorting Edward's voice.

I was in DC.

Vivian was in New York with her ex.

I made up my mind in two seconds.

"Keep an eye on them, and don't let him leave until I'm home," I ordered. "I'm flying back tonight."

It was an eighty-minute commercial flight between the cities. My jet could make it in fifty.

"Yes, sir."

I hung up and reentered the library. Part of me wanted to strangle Christian for purposely withholding information from me, but I had a more pressing issue at hand.

"I have to go back to New York." I grabbed my jacket off the back of the couch. "There's a...personal matter I need to deal with."

Christian looked up from his phone and slid it into his pocket. "Sorry to hear that," he said mildly. "I'll walk you out."

Pinpricks of anger and something else vibrated beneath my skin on our way to the foyer.

Fear.

What the fuck was I afraid of? Heath wanted a second chance with Vivian; he wouldn't physically hurt her. I trusted Edward to manage the situation; one call from him, and my home security team would have Heath wishing he'd never stepped foot east of the Rockies.

But what if Vivian *wanted* to see him? Our relationship hadn't been the warmest since our office argument. She could've called Heath over while I was away. Heath could be convincing her to give him another chance right this minute.

It shouldn't matter, considering our match was doomed from the start. But for some unknown reason, it did.

Christian and I reached the front door.

"This personal matter..." he said as I exited into the hall. "Wouldn't happen to be Vivian's ex-boyfriend showing up at your house, would it?"

Surprise halted my steps, followed by a cold blast of fury. I turned, my glare lasering in on Christian. "What the *fuck* did you do, Harper?"

"I merely facilitated a reunion between your fiancée and an old friend," he said casually. "Since you enjoyed fucking with me so much, I figured I'd return the favor. Oh, and, Dante?" His smile lacked any hint of humor. "Touch Stella again, and you'll no longer *have* a fiancée."

The door slammed in my face.

Red dotted my vision until it coated the walls and floor with crimson.

That *fucker*.

Under normal circumstances, I wouldn't let his threat slide, but I didn't have time for his bullshit. I'd deal with Christian later.

It took ten minutes to reach my jet, fifty to land in New York, and another thirty to arrive at my apartment. Plenty of time for my fury to reach a full boil.

I should've handled the Heath situation myself instead of delegating to Christian. He was good at his job, but he weaponized any and all information at his disposal.

Then there was fucking Heath. I hadn't received any urgent updates from Edward, but the thought of him being in such close proximity to Vivian for almost two hours set my teeth on edge.

When I reached my apartment, Edward greeted me at the door, his face carefully blank. "Good evening, sir."

"Where are they?"

He didn't blink an eye at my curt response. "The living room."

I was gone before the last word fully left his mouth.

What could Heath and Vivian have been doing all this time? What were they talking about? Had they been in contact since he sent her those roses?

I stopped in the living room doorway. My eyes immediately found Vivian, who was backed against the wall next to the fireplace. Heath towered over her, his body partially obscuring her from view.

Fire ignited low in my gut. I walked toward them, my steps silent against the thick carpet, my muscles coiling with each stride.

"I told you, I didn't text you." Vivian's soft exasperation drifted into my ears when I neared. Neither of them noticed my arrival. "I don't know what happened, but the message isn't from me."

"You don't have to lie to me." Heath's voice needled my skin like tiny, annoying wasps. I wanted to reach down his throat and yank his tongue out. "You don't want to marry Dante. We both know that. You're only with him because of your parents. Look, just...just wait until my IPO, okay? Postpone the wedding."

"I can't do that." Exasperation edged into weariness. "I care about you, Heath. I always will. You were my first love. But I'm not...I can't do that to Dante or my family."

"Were?" The needling voice tightened.

"Heath..."

"I still love you. You know that. I've always loved you. If it weren't for your parents..." His head lowered. "Dammit, Viv. It was supposed to be us."

"I know." The thickness of her voice made my gut twist. "But it's not."

"Do you love him?"

My gut twisted further at Vivian's long pause.

"You don't," Heath said. "If you did, you wouldn't hesitate."

"It's not that simple."

I'd heard enough.

"Next time you try to steal a man's fiancée," I said, my voice deadly calm despite the rage tunneling through me, "don't be stupid enough to do it in his house."

Heath whipped around. Surprise flashed through his eyes, but he didn't get a chance to react before I hauled my arm back and slammed my fist into his face.

Vivian

A sickening crunch ripped the air, followed by a pained howl. Blood spurted from Heath's nose, and the scent of copper drenched my surroundings, seeping beneath my skin and rendering me immobile. I could only watch, horrified, as Dante hauled a spluttering Heath up by the collar and pinned him against the wall.

Anger carved harsh lines across Dante's face, hardening his jaw and turning his cheekbones into slashes of tension against the firelight. His eyes simmered with slow-burning fury, the type that snuck up and annihilated you before you knew it'd even arrived.

He'd always been intimidating, but in that moment, he looked larger than life, like the devil himself had left hell to exact his retribution.

"I don't give a fuck how long you and Vivian have known each other or how long ago you dated." Dante's soft snarl sent ice skittering down my spine. "You don't touch her. You don't talk to her. You don't even fucking think about her. If you do, I'll break every fucking bone in your body until your own mother won't recognize you. Understand?"

Beads of crimson dripped from Heath's chin down his shirt.

"You're out of your mind," he spat. Despite his bravado, his pupils were the size of quarters. Fear leaked from him, almost as potent as the smell of blood. "I'll sue you for assault."

Dante's smile was terrifying in its calmness. "You can try." He tightened his grip on Heath's shirt, his knuckles already bruised from the force of his punch.

The air sharpened with fresh, impending violence, enough that it finally yanked me out of my frozen stupor.

"*Stop.*" I found my voice right as Dante drew his arm back for another punch. "Let him go."

He didn't move.

"*Now.*"

A heavy beat passed before he released Heath, who slumped on the floor, coughing and clutching his nose. Judging by the crack earlier, it had to be broken, but I found it hard to summon sympathy after dealing with him for the past two hours.

"This is not a school playground," I said. "You're both grown men. *Act* like it."

My day had been shitty enough. First, someone spilled coffee all over my brand-new, *white* Theory dress during my morning latte run. Then, I found out a pipe had burst at the Legacy Ball's original venue. The place was flooded and would take months to repair, which meant I had three months to find and move all gala preparations to a new venue that would be available on such short notice, fit within my budget, and have the space and grandeur necessary to host five hundred extremely discerning, extremely judgmental guests.

I came home hoping to relax, only to have Heath show up at the door rambling about a text I supposedly sent him, telling him I wanted to reconcile.

Now, my fiancé and ex-boyfriend were at each other's throats, and there was blood dripping everywhere. Needless to say, my sympathy reserves were at an all-time low.

"Heath, you should go and get your nose looked at." Every second he and Dante stayed in the same room was another opportunity for more trouble. I'd go with him to the hospital, but considering Dante's current mood, offering to leave with him would hurt more than it helped.

Heath looked at me, his eyes tortured. "Viv..."

A rumble of warning emanated from Dante's chest.

"Go," I said. "Please."

He opened his mouth as if to say something else, but Dante's death glare had him scrambling up and out of the room without another word.

I waited until I heard the front door slam before I whirled on the other infuriating, migraine-inducing man in my life.

"What is *wrong* with you? You can't just go around punching people! You probably broke his nose!"

"I can do whatever I want," Dante said, the picture of remorselessness. "He deserved it."

A headache gathered behind my temples.

"No, you *can't*. News flash, having money doesn't absolve you from consequences. There's a…a proper way of doing things that doesn't include violence. You're lucky if he *doesn't* sue you for assault."

"*I'm* lucky?" Dante growled. "*He's* lucky I didn't break more than his nose for coming into my house and trying to wreck our engagement."

"I'm not saying he's right. I'm saying there was a better way to handle the situation than opening yourself up to an assault charge!"

Dante had enough lawyers and money to shake such a charge off like it was nothing, but that wasn't the point. It was the principle of the matter.

"He was touching you." Dante's eyes darkened to midnight. "Did you *want* him to touch you?"

Oh, for God's sake.

"You don't get to do that," I said through gritted teeth. "You don't get to storm in and act like a jealous fiancé when you've been ignoring me for *weeks*. I tried to talk to you about Heath after the flowers. You refused and ran off to DC."

His lips thinned. "I haven't been ignoring you, and I did not *run off* to DC."

"You gave me the cold shoulder, avoided eye and verbal

contact, and communicated in caveman grunts or via a third party at most. That's the textbook definition of ignoring."

Dante stared at me, his face like granite.

Frustration bubbled in my chest and rose up my throat.

"You open up, then you shut down. You kiss me, then you leave. We've been doing this back-and-forth dance for months, and I'm *sick* of it." I lifted my chin, my heart wavering beneath an onslaught of nerves. "I just want to know, once and for all. Is this still only business, or is it more?"

A muscle flexed in Dante's jaw. "It doesn't matter. We're getting married either way."

"It *does* matter. I'm not playing this game with you anymore." My frustration morphed into anger, turning my words into blades. "If this is business, we'll treat it as such. We'll produce an heir, smile for the cameras in public, and live our lives separately in private. That's it."

It wasn't the life I would've chosen, but I was in too deep to back out now. At least then, I'd know where we stood and adjust my expectations accordingly. No more overanalyzing every crumb of intimacy, searching for something that wasn't there. No more hanging on to the hopes Dante would change and I'd be one of the lucky ones whose arranged marriage turned into love.

"Live our lives separately in private?" Dante's voice dropped to a dangerous decibel. "What the fuck does that mean?"

"It means exactly what it sounds like. We do what we want, discreetly, and we don't question the other about it as long as it doesn't affect our...public image."

My words faltered at the storm gathering in his eyes.

"Are you talking about an affair, Vivian?"

Goose bumps erupted in alarm over my chest and shoulders.

"*No*, and that's not the point. Answer my question. Is this business, or is this something more?"

He remained silent.

"Heath was wrong for what he tried to do, but you're upset because…why? You're threatened? Territorial?" My nails dug into my palms. "I'm not a toy, Dante. You don't get to toss me aside and pick me back up only when someone else wants me."

"I don't think you're a toy," he ground out.

"Then why do you care? Why did you punch Heath when you were the one who told me to leave our feelings out of this?"

More silence. The cords of his neck visibly strained against his skin.

The tension was so thick I could taste it in my throat, but I pushed forward, unwilling to let him off the hook so easily.

"We're only together because of a deal *you* made with my father. What's it to you if my ex shows back up in my life? You know the wedding would move forward either way," I said. "Are you afraid I'll break the engagement? Run off with Heath and leave you looking like a fool in front of your friends? *Why do you care?*"

"I don't know!"

The force of his reply stunned me into silence. Dante's granite mask cracked, revealing the torment underneath.

"I don't know why I care. I just know I *do*, and I hate it." Self-loathing coated his voice. "I hate the idea of you touching anyone else or anyone else touching you. I hate that other people can make you laugh in a way I can't. I hate how I feel around you, like you're the only person who can make me lose control when I. *Don't. Lose. Control.*"

Every word, every step brought him closer until my back pressed against the wall and the heat of his body enveloped mine.

"But I do." His voice dropped, turning ragged. "With you."

My blood thundered in my ears, muffling his words until I was underwater and drowning in a sea of emotions. Shock, hope, fear, elation, uncertainty...they all mingled until they were indistinguishable from each other.

"*I don't know* isn't good enough," I whispered.

Once upon a time, it would've been. But we'd passed that marker long ago.

Dante's jaw tightened. This close, I could see the hints of gold in his eyes, like flecks of light in a sea of darkness.

"Heath said he still loves you. Enough to go against your parents, and me, to be with you. But you broke up two years ago and he didn't do a damn thing about it until he found out you were engaged." The darkness edged out the light. "You want to know the truth, Vivian? If I loved you as much as he claims to love you, nothing would've stopped me from keeping you."

I didn't realize until that moment how easy it was for one simple sentence to dissolve the threads holding my world together.

If I loved you as much as he claims to love you, nothing would've stopped me from keeping you.

"*If*," I breathed, my throat unbearably tight. "Hypothetical."

The gold disappeared completely, leaving pools of midnight in its wake.

A sardonic smile. "Yes, *mia cara*." Warmth brushed my lips. "Hypothetical."

My heartbeat slowed. Time suspended for a brief, agonizing moment, just long enough for our breaths to intermingle.

Then a groan shattered the spell, followed by a low curse.

That was the only warning I got before Dante yanked me to him and crashed his mouth down on mine.

CHAPTER 24

Vivian

I SHOULD PUSH HIM OFF.

We hadn't resolved the heart of our issues yet, and kissing—or more—would only complicate things further.

I should push him off.

But I didn't. Instead, I threaded my fingers through his hair and succumbed to the skillful assault on my senses. The firm grip on the back of my neck. The expert pressure of his lips. The way Dante's body molded to mine, all hard muscle and heat.

His mouth moved over mine, hot and demanding. Pleasure fogged my senses as the rich, bold taste of him invaded my mouth.

Our kiss in Bali had been passionate but impulsive. This? This was hard. Primal. *Addicting.*

My worries from earlier that day melted into nothing, and I instinctively curved my body into his, seeking more contact, more warmth, *more.*

I'd kissed my fair share of men over the years, but none had ever kissed me like this.

Like they were a conqueror hell-bent on breaching my defenses.

Like they were trapped in the desert and I was their last hope for salvation.

A soft gasp escaped when Dante hooked my legs around his waist and carried me out of the room without breaking our kiss. Blurry glimpses of gilt-framed paintings and golden wall sconces passed through my peripheral vision as he navigated us through the maze of hallways.

When we reached his room, he kicked the door shut behind us and set me down, his breath as ragged as my own. Under any other circumstances, I would've savored my first time in his private sanctuary, but I caught only the faintest impression of expensive oak and charcoal before his mouth was on mine again.

I pushed his jacket off his shoulders while he unzipped my dress. Our movements were frantic, almost desperate, as we tore our clothes off. His shirt. My bra. His pants. They fell away with tugs and pulls, leaving only heat and bare skin behind.

We broke apart so Dante could roll on a condom, and my mouth dried at the sight before me. I'd seen him shirtless in Bali, but this was different somehow. His body was sculpted with such perfection I half expected to find Michelangelo's signature lurking on one of his chiseled abs.

Broad shoulders. Muscled chest. Bronzed skin and a faint dusting of black hair that tapered down to...

Oh God.

His cock jutted out, huge and hard, and the mere idea of it inside me sent twin frissons of apprehension and anticipation spiraling through my stomach. There was no way he'd fit. It was impossible.

When I finally dragged my gaze back up to his, his eyes were already focused on me, dark and smoldering with banked heat. A molten flame dripped down my spine when he spun me around so his erection dug into my lower back.

A full-length mirror hung on the wall opposite us, reflecting my bright eyes and flushed cheeks as Dante palmed my breasts, gently squeezing them and rolling my nipples between his fingers until they stiffened.

Lust, anticipation, and a hint of embarrassment pooled in my stomach. Watching him explore my body, his touch almost arrogant in its lazy assuredness, was somehow more intimate than actual sex.

"You shouldn't have let him touch you, *mia cara*." Dante's soft voice sent shivers over my skin a second before he pinched the sensitive peaks, hard.

I instinctively jerked at the jolt of pain and pleasure.

"I didn't..." My reply melted into a breathy sigh when he dipped a hand between my legs.

"Do you want to know why?" he continued as if I hadn't tried to respond.

My teeth dug into my bottom lip. I shook my head, my hips bucking as he pressed his thumb against my clit.

"Because you're *mine*." His teeth scored my neck. "You wear *my* ring. You've come on *my* face and hand. You live in *my* head all the fucking time, even if I don't want you to." His palm slid to my hip, where his fingers dug grooves into my skin. "And God, I want to punish you for driving me so damn crazy. Every. Single. Day."

I didn't get a chance to fully register his last sentence before he slammed into me and tore a cry from my throat. I was so wet he slid in without much resistance, but the sensation was so sudden and intense I clenched without thinking.

He hissed out a breath, but he didn't move until my body acclimated to his size and my whimpers of discomfort faded. Only then did he pull out and push back in. Slowly at first, then faster and deeper until he set a rhythm that made my knees buckle.

All thoughts vanished from my mind as he hammered into

me so deep he hit spots I didn't know existed. My eyes fluttered closed, only to fly open again when a hand closed around my neck.

"Open your eyes," Dante growled. "Look in the mirror when I'm fucking you."

I did. The sight that greeted me was almost enough to tip me over the edge. My breasts bounced with each thrust, and my eyes were glassy with lust and unshed tears as he wrung every ounce of pleasure from me. An endless stream of moans and whimpers poured from my half-open mouth.

I didn't look like the good, respectable girl I'd been raised to be.

I looked wanton and needy and ravished beyond comprehension.

My gaze locked with Dante's in the mirror.

"You like this?" he taunted. "Watching me wreck your pussy while you make a mess all over my cock?"

My lungs couldn't get enough oxygen for me to respond with anything other than a strangled noise. The fucking was too intense, and all I wanted was for him to keep going. To push me further and further until I crashed over the cliff looming ahead.

"I'm the only one who gets to see you like this." His voice turned harsh. "You"—thrust—"are"—thrust—"*my*"—thrust—"wife."

The force of his fucking increased with each word until the last plunge pitched me forward. If not for his hold, I would've collapsed on the floor.

"I'm not...your wife yet," I managed over the thundering of my heart.

Dante's grip tightened around my throat. "Maybe not," he said darkly. "But you *are* mine. You asked if it was still just business." He dragged his cock out slowly, letting me feel every inch of him, before slamming it back in. Electric sensations shot through me, turning my body into a live wire. "Does this feel like business?"

No, it didn't.

It felt like hope.

It felt like desire.

It felt like ruin and salvation all in one.

Dante's pace slowed, but the power in each thrust remained vicious. Still, his next words contained a shadow of vulnerability that took what was left of my breath away.

"You don't know what you do to me." The rawness of his voice matched the desire in his eyes—dark and fathomless and so visceral I felt it in my bones.

It was that look and those words, spoken in that voice, that finally tipped me over the edge.

I came with a sharp cry, my body shuddering around his. He followed soon after, his cock pulsing inside me until we were both spent and gasping for air. We held on to each other, our breaths gradually evening in unison as we came down from our highs.

"Look at us, *mia cara*." Dante's soft command brushed against my skin.

I did.

Our reflections stared back at us, dazed and slick with sweat. His arms wrapped around me from behind, and his cheek pressed against mine as our gazes connected in the mirror.

Something that was both ache and fullness tugged at my heart. What we'd had wasn't soft, emotional sex, at least not on the surface. But beneath the rough hands and filthy words, a storm of emotions had blown through and upended our entire relationship.

Six months of pent-up frustration, lust, anger, and everything in between, all unleashed in one night.

I wouldn't know the aftermath until morning. But I knew there was no going back to the way things used to be.

CHAPTER 25

Vivian

THE EARLY MORNING LIGHT CAST SOFT SHADOWS ON the floor. Stillness weighed heavy in the air, and every movement sounded too loud as I inched my way off the mattress.

It was five after seven, the earliest I'd woken up on a weekend since my crack-of-dawn flight to Eldorra for Agnes's wedding years ago, but I needed to leave before Dante woke up.

My feet grazed the rug.

"Where are you going?" The rough, sleepy rumble of Dante's voice touched my back.

I froze, my toes curling into the plush triple ply while my heart took off on a gallop.

Stay calm. Stay cool.

Even if his voice sparked a host of X-rated memories.

Look in the mirror when I'm fucking you.

You like this? Watching me wreck your pussy while you make a mess all over my cock?

Heat crawled over my cheeks, but I attempted a neutral expression when I turned.

Dante sat up against the headboard, charcoal silk sheets

rumpled around his waist. A smooth expanse of olive skin stretched over the naked, sculpted planes of his shoulders and tapered down to a lean waist. His V cut arrowed beneath the sheets like an invitation to pick up where we left off last night.

I forced my gaze up only to find his eyes waiting for mine. A knowing smirk tugged on his lips as he leaned back, oozing casual arrogance and pure male satisfaction.

Smug bastard.

Yet it didn't stop butterflies from erupting in my stomach.

"I'm going to work," I said breathlessly, remembering his question. "Legacy Ball crisis. It's urgent."

"It's Saturday."

"Crises don't operate on a workweek schedule." I discreetly tugged on the hem of my top.

I wore one of Dante's old college T-shirts, and it fell somewhere between scandalous and midthigh.

His eyes flicked down and darkened. The heat spread from my face to somewhere south of my stomach.

"Perhaps not, but that's not why you're sneaking out of my bed at seven in the morning, *mia cara.*" Some of the sleep evaporated from his voice, leaving satin and smoke behind.

"No?" My voice squeaked like a door hinge in need of oil.

"No." His gaze met mine again. Challenge glinted in its depths.

Who's the one running now?

The unspoken words sank into my bones.

"You wanted to talk," he said. "Let's talk."

I swallowed the nerves lodged in my throat. *Okay then.*

I'd pictured our conversation happening a little differently. I would be fired up and full of indignation—and dressed in my best outfit, of course—not sitting on the edge of his bed, smelling like him and wearing his T-shirt while the memory of his touch was imprinted on my skin.

But he was right. We needed to talk, and there was no point in delaying the inevitable.

I addressed the elephant in the room first.

"Heath came over last night because he said I texted him about wanting to get back together."

A shadow crossed Dante's face at the mention of Heath, but he didn't interrupt.

"I didn't. Well..." I amended my statement. "He showed me his phone, and there *is* a text that looks like it was from me, but I never sent it. Maybe it was a prank or a hack. I don't know, but it doesn't matter. My answer to his...proposal hasn't changed since the last time we spoke. He refused to accept that, and we went back and forth for hours until you showed up."

I should've kicked Heath out long before Dante came home. However, I'd never quite gotten over my guilt for how my parents treated him when they found out about our relationship.

Vivian is a Lau. She's meant to marry someone great, not a so-called entrepreneur with a company no one's heard of. You are not good enough for her, and you never will be.

Two years later, the memory of my father's harsh words still made me wince.

"Did you say no because you no longer have feelings for him or because you feel obligated to keep our arrangement?" Dante's face was unreadable.

"Does it matter? We're getting married either way." I threw his words from last night back at him.

His mouth tightened. "I wouldn't ask if it didn't."

"Yet you haven't answered my question about whether this is still business."

Dante had indirectly admitted it wasn't last night, but I took anything anyone said during sex with a grain of salt.

His lips parted on a sardonic breath. "How many times are you going to make me say it?"

"Just once," I said softly.

He regarded me with dark, hooded eyes.

The clock ticked with deafening precision, and my soft cotton T-shirt suddenly felt too heavy.

"*Business* would be staying in California and celebrating a deal I'd worked a year on instead of rushing back to see you," he finally said, his voice low and loaded with gravel. "*Business* would be completing my DC trip instead of waking my pilot up for a last-minute flight home. In all my years as CEO, I've only cut a work trip short twice, Vivian, and both those instances were because of you." A wry twist of his lips. "So no, it's not just fucking business anymore."

The butterflies took flight again, soaring so high the velvety tips of their wings brushed my heart.

I grasped for an appropriate response before I settled on the only word that came to mind.

"Oh."

Ironic amusement ghosted through his gaze. "Yes, *oh*," he said dryly. "Your turn, *mia cara*. Why did you say no to Heath?"

His tone was lazy, but there was nothing lazy about the way he watched me, like a predator locked on its prey, his muscles coiled with tension.

"Because I don't have romantic feelings for him anymore," I said, my voice soft. "And because I might have them for someone else."

Now that the emotional shock from last night had cleared, I realized my conversation with Heath had provided some much-needed clarity. Once upon a time, I'd loved him, and I felt guilty for the way things had ended between us. But it'd been two years. I wasn't the same person I'd been when we dated, and I hadn't felt anything except surprise, sadness, and a bit of annoyance when we talked.

All this time, I thought I'd missed Heath, but I missed the *idea* of him. I missed having a partner. I missed being loved and being *in* love.

Unfortunately, I could no longer find those things with him.

The morning sunlight filtered through the curtains and gilded Dante's face, casting soft shadows beneath his brow and cheekbones. He was so still he resembled a golden sculpture in repose, but the air sparked like dry kindling.

"It's not just business for you." I forced back the uprising of nerves in my stomach. "And it's not just duty for me."

The air turned dense, heavy with meaning. A faint car horn sounded dozens of stories below, but we didn't look away.

"Good." The rough sound brushed my skin with startling intimacy.

My pulse drummed in my ears. I smoothed a clammy hand over my thigh, unsure what to do or say next.

Do we kiss? Continue the conversation? Go our separate ways?

I stuck with the safest option.

"Well, I'm glad we had that talk. I really do have a work crisis, so I'll get back to my room—"

"This is your room."

I gave Dante a dubious stare. Maybe the lack of caffeine had affected his memory.

"I hate to tell you this, but this is not, in fact, where I've been sleeping the past five months," I said patiently. "My room is at the other end of the hall. You made a big show of distinguishing it when I moved in. Remember?"

"Yes, but I think it's clear the boundaries we set that day are no longer applicable." Dante notched a dark brow. "Don't you agree?"

My pulse tripped into overdrive. "What are you suggesting?"

"That we set new boundaries. No more separate bedrooms, no more sneaking out in the morning..." His expression darkened. "And no more contact with Heath."

Normally, I would've chafed at Dante's attempt to control who I could talk to, but after last night's debacle, I understood where he was coming from. If he had an ex who was hell-bent on breaking us up, I wouldn't want him talking to her either.

"What a shame," I said. "I'd planned to invite him over for dinner."

Dante didn't look amused.

"It was a joke."

Nothing.

I sighed. "On that note, if we're setting new boundaries, I have a few of my own. One..." I ticked them off on my fingers. "No more scowling as your default expression. Your face is close to freezing that way, and I'd rather not wake up to the Grinch for the rest of my life."

"I'm much better looking than the Grinch," he grumbled. "And if people stopped pissing me off, I wouldn't scowl so much."

"Other people aren't the problem. Remember when we passed by a dog park around Christmas and saw those adorable huskies? You glared at them so hard they started howling."

"I wasn't glaring at *them*," he said impatiently. "I was glaring at their outfits. Who dresses their dogs up as reindeer? It's ridiculous."

"It was Christmas. At least they weren't dressed as elves."

Dante's frown deepened. *We'll work on that later.*

"Anyway." I moved on before we veered too deep into an argument about canine fashion. "Back to the boundaries. No more disappearing for weeks at a time with less than forty-eight hours' notice unless it's truly an emergency. No more shutting down when you're upset and things don't go your way. And..." My teeth tugged on my bottom lip. "We should commit to at least one date every week."

Most people dated *before* their engagement, but we were doing everything backward.

Late was better than never, I supposed.

"If you wanted to spend more time with me, *mia cara*, you only have to say so." Dante's drawl slipped back into a velvety cadence.

My cheeks warmed. "That's not the point." Not the whole point anyway. "We're getting married in a few months, and we haven't gone on a single real date."

"We've been on dates. We went to the Valhalla gala."

"That was a social obligation."

"We went to Bali."

"That was a family obligation."

He fell silent.

"Those are my terms. Do you accept?"

His answer came less than two seconds later. "Yes."

"Great." I hid my surprise at his ready agreement. "Well..." God, this was awkward. Why was peace so much harder than war? "We can sort out the bedroom logistics later. For now, I need to fix my work problem before I'm blacklisted."

Trying to find a last-minute venue in Manhattan was like trying to find an earring at the bottom of the Hudson River. Impossible. But if I wanted to save the Legacy Ball and my career, I needed to find a way to make the impossible possible, fast.

"Is it something that requires you to be in the office?"

"No..." I said cautiously. "Not really."

I mostly needed to brainstorm alternatives so I could call them on Monday.

"Perfect. Fix it over breakfast." A smile flickered over Dante's mouth. "We're going on our first date."

CHAPTER 26

Dante

I'D ALWAYS BEEN IN CONTROL OF MY REACTIONS, AT least publicly. My grandfather had driven any impulsive displays of emotion out of me since I was a child.

In the words of Enzo Russo, emotion was weakness, and there was no room for weakness in the cutthroat corporate world.

But Vivian. *Fuck.*

There'd been a moment yesterday when I thought I might lose her. The prospect had unlocked a level of fear I hadn't experienced since I was five, when I'd watched my parents walk away, thinking I'd never see them again. That they'd vanish into the ether, leaving me with my terrifyingly stern-faced grandfather and a mansion too large to fill.

I'd been right.

I'd eventually lose Vivian too, someway, somehow, but I'd deal with that day when it came.

A strange tightness gripped my chest. I didn't know how things would play out after the truth came out, but after last night—after tasting how sweet she was and feeling how perfectly we fit—I knew I wasn't ready to let her go just yet.

"Is this what I think it is?" Vivian's voice dragged me out of my thoughts.

She stared at the retro diner sign above our heads, her expression equal parts intrigued and mystified.

"Moondust Diner." I shook off my uncharacteristic melancholy and held open the door. "Welcome to the home of the best milkshakes in New York and my twelve-year-old self's favorite place in the city."

I hadn't visited the diner in years, but the minute I stepped inside the well-worn interior, I was transported back to my preteen days. The cracked linoleum tiles, the orange pleather seats, the old jukebox in the corner...it was like the place had been preserved in a time capsule.

A twinge of nostalgia hit me as the hostess guided us to an empty booth.

"*Best* is a lofty title," Vivian teased. "You're setting my expectations sky-high."

"They'll be met." Unless the diner changed its recipe, which it had no reason to do. "Trust me."

"I admit, this isn't what I expected from our first date." Vivian's lips curved into a small smile. "It's casual. Low-key. I'm pleasantly surprised."

"Hmm." I flipped through the menu out of habit more than anything else. I already knew what I was going to order. "Should I not mention the private helicopter tour I booked for later then?"

Her laugh faded when I raised an eyebrow.

"*Dante.* You didn't."

"You're engaged to a Russo. It's how we do things. The diner is..." I paused, searching for the right sentiment. "A walk down memory lane. That's all."

I was supposed to play tennis with Dominic today, but when Vivian tried to leave that morning, all I'd wanted was for her to stay.

A date at the diner had been the first thing that popped into my head. The helicopter idea came later, and that only took one call to set up.

"I like it. It's charming." Vivian gave me a mischievous smile. "Please tell me you took advantage of the jukebox when you were younger. I would kill for a photo of twelve-year-old you drinking a milkshake and dancing."

"Sorry, sweetheart, but that's not gonna happen. I'm not a jukebox kinda guy. Not even when I was prepubescent."

"I'm not surprised, but you could've let a girl dream a little longer," she said with a sigh.

Our server arrived. I stuck with my trusty black-and-white shake while Vivian wavered between the strawberry and the peanut butter and chocolate.

I sat back, oddly charmed by the little furrow in her brow as she pored over the menu.

Yesterday, I'd been in DC, meeting with Christian and discussing how to take down Francis Lau. Now here I was, taking his daughter for pancakes and milkshakes like we were suburban teenagers on a first date.

Life had a fucked-up sense of humor.

Vivian finally decided on the strawberry, and I waited until our server left before I spoke again.

"What's the work crisis you mentioned earlier?"

This time, Vivian's sigh was heavier. "The original venue for the Legacy Ball got flooded." She gave me a quick rundown of what happened, her shoulders growing increasingly tense the longer she spoke.

It was a shitty situation. Venues of that size and caliber booked out months, if not years, in advance. Finding one at this late date was like trying to find a lake in the desert.

"Did you try the museums?" I asked. Places like the Met and the Whitney regularly hosted charity galas and balls.

"Yes. Their calendars are full."

"I could make a call. Free up a spot."

"No." Vivian shook her head. "I don't want to put anyone else in the same spot I'm in by making the museum cancel on them."

Typical Vivian. I wasn't sure whether to be impressed or exasperated.

"The New York Public Library?" I suggested.

"Also booked."

Apparently, all the usual suspect hotels were also out.

I rubbed a thumb over my bottom lip, thinking. "You could host it at Valhalla."

Vivian's eyebrows winged up. "They don't allow outside events."

"No, but the Legacy Ball is extremely prestigious. Most, if not all, members will be there. They'd consider it if I asked them."

The managing committee would throw a fucking tantrum about it, but I could convince them.

Maybe.

"I can't ask you to do that," she said warily. She wasn't a member of the club, but she lived in our world. She knew payment for things like these came in the form of favors, not money. And sometimes, the favors cost more than anything money could buy.

"It's not a big deal." I could handle the management committee and anything they threw at me.

"It's a *huge* deal."

"Vivian," I said. "I'll handle it."

The committee required a unanimous vote to approve all decisions. I was a yes. Kai would likely say yes. That left six more people to convince. I had my work cut out for me, but I'd always appreciated a good challenge.

Vivian scraped her teeth across her bottom lip. "Fine, but I'm looking into alternatives anyway. Valhalla will be the last resort."

"Don't let anyone else from the club hear you say that, or you really *will* be blacklisted. Even I won't be able to save you from ninety-nine bruised egos."

"Noted." Her laugh settled somewhere deep in my chest before it faded. "Thank you," she said, her face softening. "For offering to help."

I cleared my throat, my face oddly warm. "You're welcome."

Our server returned with our orders, and I watched, muscles tense, as Vivian took her first sip.

"Wow." Surprise flared in her eyes. "You were right. This is amazing."

I relaxed. "I'm always right."

My shake matched her sentiments. I'd worried it wouldn't live up to my childhood memories, but it was every bit as good as I remembered.

Our conversation soon shifted from work and food to an eclectic mix of topics—music, movies, travel—before it tapered into a comfortable silence.

It was hard to believe Vivian and I had been at each other's throats so often. If I set aside my intense dislike for her family, being with her was like breathing.

Easy. Effortless. Essential.

"You know it's not about the money for me," Vivian said after we finished our drinks and readied to leave.

I raised a questioning brow.

"This. Our engagement." She gestured between us. "I know what you must think of my family, and you're not entirely wrong. Money and status mean a lot to them. Me marrying a Russo is… well, it's the ultimate achievement in their eyes. But I'm not my family." She twisted her ring around her finger. "Don't get me wrong. I like nice clothes and fancy vacations as much as the next person, but marrying a billionaire was never my end goal in life. I like you because of *you*, not because of your money. Even if you piss me off sometimes," she added wryly.

The warmth in my veins died a quick death at the mention of her family, but it rekindled with her admission.

I like you because of you, *not because of your money.*

A fist squeezed my chest.

"I know," I said quietly.

That was the most incredible part. I really did believe her.

Once upon a time, she'd been a Lau. Now, she was Vivian. Separate, distinct, and capable of making me question everything I thought I wanted.

Self-preservation told me to keep her at arm's length. We were heading toward an inevitable collision, and our new boundaries wouldn't mean shit once the truth about her father came to light.

But I'd tried distance, and all it'd done was make me want her more. Her laughs, her smiles, the sparkle in her eyes when she teased me, and the fire in her replies when I pissed her off. I wanted all of it even when I knew I shouldn't.

My head and heart waged civil war against each other, and for the first time in my life, my heart was winning.

For the next week, Vivian and I settled into our new dynamic. She moved into my room, I made it home for dinner every night, and we tested the waters the way swimmers would after a storm, with equal parts hope and caution.

The transition wasn't as difficult as I'd expected. I hadn't had the time or inclination to date properly in years, but being with Vivian was as easy and natural as returning home after a long journey.

There was just one more pit stop I needed to make.

I leaned against my car and watched Heath exit his Upper

West Side rental with a duffel bag slung over his shoulder and white gauze swathing his nose. He looked worse for wear, but if I'd had my way, he would've suffered more than a simple broken nose.

You don't want to marry Dante. We both know that. You're only with him because of your parents.

Fury simmered in my veins. I didn't move, but Heath must've felt the heat of my glare. He looked up, and his stride broke when he saw me.

I smiled past the anger snapping at my chest, though it was more a baring of my teeth than a true smile. If I dwelled too much on what he'd said or how he'd cornered Vivian, I'd ruin a perfectly nice Friday afternoon with murder.

"How's the nose? Healing, I hope." My greeting might as well be a knife unsheathed, cold and sharp enough to cut.

Heath glared at me, but he had the good sense to stay several feet away. According to my team, he was in town for business meetings and scheduled to fly back to California that night.

"I can still sue for your assault," he said, his body language nowhere near as brave as his words. His knuckles were white around the strap of his duffel bag, and his feet shifted continuously like he was preparing to flee.

"Yes, you can." I pushed off the car. I rarely drove myself in the city since parking was a bitch, but I wanted to keep today's meeting between me and the asshole in front of me. "But you won't."

Heath stiffened when I walked toward him, my pace slow and leisurely. I stopped close enough to see the quarter-sized pupils darkening his eyes.

"Do you want to know why?" I asked softly.

His throat worked with a swallow.

"Because you're a smart man, Heath. What you did in my penthouse was dumb, but you had enough brains to scale your company to where it is today. You wouldn't want anything to happen to it before the big IPO, would you?"

Heath's knuckles tightened further. "Are you threatening me?"

"No. I'm advising you." I clapped a deceptively friendly hand on his shoulder. "*Threatening* you would be warning you to stay the fuck away from Vivian if you value your life." My voice remained soft, vicious. "I told you last week, and I'll tell you again. She's *my* fiancée. If you step foot near her again, if you so much as breathe in her direction..."

Pain lanced across his face when I squeezed his shoulder.

"I will burn you, your house, and your entire fucking company to the ground. Understand?"

Beads of sweat formed along his hairline despite the wintry chill. The street was quiet, and I could practically hear the fear and resentment thickening his labored breaths.

"Yes," he gritted out.

"Good." I released him and stepped back. "See, that's what I would say if I were threatening you. But we won't get to that point, will we? Because you'll stay in California, have your nice IPO, and lose Vivian's number the way a smart man would."

His jaw tightened.

"Now..." I checked my watch. "I would stay and chat longer, but I have a date with my fiancée. Dinner and a sunset sail. Her favorite."

I walked off, leaving a fuming, speechless Heath on the sidewalk.

I waited until I reached Fifth Avenue before I called Christian. He was the little shit responsible for the Heath mess, and it was time he cleaned it up.

Just wait until my IPO, okay? Postpone the wedding.

My simmering anger reached a full boil. I'd kept a lid on it earlier for Vivian's sake since I didn't want to ruin our new relationship by hospitalizing her ex, but if I let Heath walk away with nothing more than a broken nose, I wasn't Dante fucking Russo.

"The IPO we were talking about," I said when Christian picked up. I didn't bother with a greeting. "Kill it."

CHAPTER 27

Vivian

DATING DANTE WAS LIKE REDISCOVERING A PART OF myself I'd buried when I realized my future was not my own. The part that dreamed of love and roses, that wasn't afraid to open up to someone in case I fell in love with them and they turned out to be an "unsuitable match."

Even when I'd dated Heath, whom I hadn't heard from since the apartment incident, I'd carried an impending sense of doom. I knew my parents wouldn't approve of him, and the knowledge had followed us like an invisible third wheel.

But with Dante, I could *enjoy* his company without worry. Not only was he a family-approved match, he was actually, well, likable once I looked past the scowls and arrogance.

"Give me *one* hint. I promise I won't tell anyone." I plied him with my best puppy dog eyes.

After a month, I'd finally grown into our new relationship dynamic. Lazy mornings, explosive nights, and all the quiet, beautifully mundane moments in between. I'd even convinced Dante to attend a wedding cake tasting (we would fly the baker to Italy for the wedding), though his input had been questionable at best. He'd liked all the cakes, even the "experimental" coconut meringue one that had no business touching anyone's taste buds.

For the first time, I understood what being part of a real engaged couple felt like, and it was strange and beautiful and terrifying all wrapped into one.

Dante's mouth curled into a grin. We were making progress on the *fewer frowns, more smiles* front. Not a lot, but some.

At this point, I took what I could get.

"That would be a convincing argument if the surprise wasn't for *you*, *mia cara*," he drawled.

"All the more reason for you to tell me. It's *my* surprise. Don't I get a say in when and how it's revealed?"

"No."

I released a long-suffering sigh. "You're a tough nut to crack, Mr. Russo."

Laughter rumbled in his chest. "You'll thank me once we get there. This is a surprise that has to be shown, not told."

We were in the limo on the way to some mysterious date he'd planned for us. Judging by the route we were taking, we were staying in upper Manhattan. He'd also told me to wear something nice but comfortable, so it couldn't be anywhere too fancy.

Was it a private museum exhibit? Dinner at that hot new underground restaurant everyone was raving about?

"If you tell me now, I'll stop putting those flowers you hate so much in the guest bathrooms," I said.

"No."

"I'll stop hogging the covers."

"No."

"I'll watch a soccer game with you. I'll even pretend to like it."

"Tempting," he said dryly. "But no."

I narrowed my eyes. It wasn't about the surprise at this point.

I just wanted to see if I could make Dante crack. He was infuriatingly strong-willed.

I glanced at the closed, soundproofed partition separating us from the driver's seat. Thomas, our chauffeur, was focused on the road ahead. Traffic crawled at a snail's pace; at this rate, we'd reach our destination sometime in the year 2050.

"Is there any way I can convince you to change your mind?" I leaned closer and bit back a smile when Dante's eyes flicked down.

My new Lilah Amiri dress was modest in length, but its V-neck exposed a generous amount of cleavage.

"I doubt it." A hint of wariness crept into his voice when I put a hand on his chest and placed a soft kiss on the corner of his mouth.

"Are you sure?" My hand trailed down his stomach toward his groin.

His muscles were taut beneath my touch, and his throat flexed when I grazed his hardening erection.

Nerves and anticipation fluttered in my stomach. We'd had sex almost daily over the past month, but I'd never initiated it in semipublic before. It was something Isabella or even Sloane would do, if she was in the mood. I was much more private, but the possibility of Thomas glancing in the mirror and seeing us sent a strange, unexpected thrill through my stomach.

Plus, I really wanted to know what the surprise was.

"Vivian…" Dante's voice was heavy with warning.

I ignored it.

"I think you're wrong." I kissed my way down his jaw and neck while I worked his zipper down. "I think…" The soft rasp of metal dropped between my legs and pulsed. "There's a way to persuade you."

I pulled back and slid off the bench onto my knees. A warm heaviness settled in my stomach when I freed his erection. It was huge and hard and already dripping precum, and a harsh groan filled the back seat when I swirled my tongue around the head.

I gripped the base of his cock with both hands and slowly slid its length down my throat until I hit the point where my eyes watered. It wasn't my first time giving Dante a blow job, but I'd never fully get used to how big he was. How thick and long. I'd taken him as far as I could, and there was still a good two inches between my mouth and the top of my stacked fists.

I whimpered, tasting the salty sweetness of him before I swirled my tongue around his head. Softly at first, then more confident as I fell into a rhythm, licking and sucking and bobbing until I was drenched.

I shouldn't be this turned on already. My nipples shouldn't be this hard, my skin this sensitive. Every light graze against his pant leg shouldn't send a fresh jolt of electricity.

But I was, and they did, and I was drowning in so much sensation I couldn't remember where we were or how we got here. I just knew I didn't want to leave.

Dante's hands sank into my hair as the car went over a speed bump, inadvertently forcing him deeper down my throat. I spluttered, my chokes and gurgles filling the car as I struggled to accommodate the extra inches, but I didn't pull back.

"*Fuck*, baby." His groan curled low in my stomach. "That feels so good."

I looked up, my eyes blurry with tears from taking him so deep, but pride rushed through me when I saw the pleasure carving stark, sensual lines into his face. His eyes were closed, his head tipped back to expose the strong, tanned column of his throat. His chest rose and fell with shallow breaths, and his muscles flexed every time I swept my tongue over the underside of his cock. His fingers strangled my hair to the point where pain and pleasure blurred into one.

There was something so heady about having someone like Dante at my mercy. I could either bring him over the edge or keep him there forever. His pleasure was entirely in my hands, and the knowledge thrummed between my thighs with heavy insistency.

I increased my pace, my hands working in tandem with my mouth, and just when I thought he would come, he fisted my hair with one hand and pulled my head back.

My noise of protest died when he lifted me onto his lap and crushed his mouth to mine. His arousal pressed against my core, separated only by a thin layer of silk, and I instinctively ground against it, desperate for more friction.

Another harsh groan vibrated down the length of my spine.

"You're going to be the death of me." Dante's stubble scraped across my skin as his mouth trailed a line of fire down my neck.

He closed his teeth around the strap of my dress and gently tugged it down while he raised my hips so he could push my soaked thong to the side.

I didn't have time to do more than gasp before he was inside me, filling me to the hilt with only one thrust.

I only had a few seconds to adjust before he gripped my hips and slammed me down again on his cock, hard, while he drove up inside me. Again and again, harder and faster, until my toes curled and the pressure building inside me neared a breaking point.

I clung to him, my head thrown back, my body nothing more than a mass of sensation as I matched his rhythm. I bounced up and down, grinding my clit against him on every down stroke.

"Just like that," Dante growled. He grazed his teeth across my nipple, his breath raising goose bumps all over my skin. "Ride my cock like a good girl."

An embarrassingly loud moan climbed up my throat when he closed his mouth around the pebbled peak and sucked. Wetness gushed down my thighs, over his leg, and onto the seat.

"You're making a mess, sweetheart." He turned his attention to my other nipple and tugged on it with his teeth. "Should I make you clean it up, hmm? Have you lick your own cum off the seat while I fuck you from behind?"

It was dirty and depraved, but his words triggered something deep inside me.

My orgasm slammed into me a second later with sudden ferocity, causing my back to arch and my mouth to fall open in a silent scream.

I was still trembling from the aftershocks when I felt Dante's chuckle against my skin. "Here I thought you were so prim and proper when I first met you."

I was too dazed to respond properly or notice when he maneuvered me into a different position.

One minute, I was on his lap. The next, I was on all fours, my hands and knees pressing into the rough black carpet covering the floor. I wasn't sure how Dante managed to move us so I faced our seat and he was behind me, but I didn't particularly care.

A shiver of pleasure zipped down my spine at his next words.

"Spread your legs for me. That's it." Dante's approval rumbled over me when I obeyed. "Let me see how wet that pretty little pussy is."

I was just coming off the high of my release, but anticipation built again when the tip of his cock nudged my entrance.

When he didn't make a further move, I pushed back against him and whined with need.

"Clean up your mess first, Vivian," he said calmly.

I opened my mouth, intending to protest. Instead, my tongue tentatively touched the leather seat of its own accord. The tanginess of my arousal flooded my taste buds.

I should've been disgusted, but my core pulsed with need. My clit was so swollen and sensitive I felt like the slightest breeze could set me off again.

"Good girl."

Dante's praise washed over me like a warm aphrodisiac before he gripped my hair and thrust into me again.

My mind blanked. I broke out into a fresh sweat, my fingers digging into the bench as he pounded into me. Every time I caught my breath, another thrust knocked it out of my lungs again. Sensation stretched my skin taut and made me light-headed until the world dissolved into nothing more than a symphony of squeals, moans, and the slap of flesh against flesh.

Minutes. Hours. Days.

Time grew increasingly disjointed until Dante reached around and pinched my clit.

The sudden spike of pleasure yanked me back to the present and made my back bow from the intensity. Only half my resulting scream made it out before a hand clamped over my mouth.

"Shh," Dante murmured. "You don't want people to hear how much you love being fucked like this, do you? On all fours in the back seat of a car, taking every inch of my cock like you're fucking *made* for it." He gave my clit another long, lazy stroke with his other hand. "It's not very becoming of a society heiress."

The gentleness of his voice, contrasted with the filthiness of his words and the brutal slam of his cock inside me, tipped me over the edge.

My second orgasm of the night crashed over me, so powerful and all-consuming it drowned out every other sound, including my cry of release. It was just silence and the hot, electric pleasure lighting up my body as I came apart so thoroughly I didn't know how I would ever be put back together.

Stars burst behind my eyes. I vaguely heard Dante's groan as he came, but I was riding too high to focus on anything else.

Just when I thought it was over, another wave dragged me under, again and again, until I was a limp, trembling mess held together only by Dante's arm beneath my waist and the weight of his body above my own.

He smoothed my hair back from my face and kissed my shoulder as I gradually drifted down from my peak. I slumped forward, trying to catch my breath while Dante cleaned me up with a tissue and pulled my dress down.

He didn't speak, but the tenderness of his actions said more than words could.

When my breathing evened out, he lifted me onto the seat again and handed me my purse.

"We're here." His voice smoothed into its usual velvet, albeit one with a faintly ragged edge.

"What?" I tried to make sense of his words through my post-climax fog.

A smile tugged on his mouth. I didn't know when, but he'd somehow already fixed his clothes. Save for his tousled hair and the color on his cheekbones, he looked like he'd spent the past half hour chatting about the weather instead of fucking me into oblivion.

"We're here," he repeated. He rubbed a gentle thumb over my bottom lip. "Might want to fix your lipstick, *mia cara*. As beautiful as you look freshly fucked, I would hate to ruin our evening by having to kill every other man who sees you like this."

My cheeks flushed, doubly so when I caught my reflection in the car window and saw the distinctive white building outside.

We were at Valhalla, which meant we'd passed through security while we were...

Heat raced from my face down over my neck and chest. My hair was a mess, my mascara and lipstick smudged, and little red marks from Dante's teeth and stubble peppered my skin. Anyone looking at me would know exactly what I'd been up to.

But despite my embarrassment, I couldn't bring myself to

regret what happened. That had been the best sex of my life. Hands down.

"Don't worry." Dante accurately assessed my worry. "The windows are tinted, and Thomas is on the authorized guests list. They couldn't see us from the front."

Thomas. *Oh God.* What if he'd looked in the rearview mirror and...

"The partition is also tinted," Dante added.

"Right." I avoided his gaze as I fixed myself the best I could. Luckily, I always carried a mini makeup kit with me, but there wasn't much I could do about the marks on my skin, so I settled for borrowing Dante's jacket.

My heart thumped when Thomas opened the door for us. He bid us a polite good evening, his face studiously blank.

My skin flamed anew.

He might not have seen or heard us, but he definitely knew what we'd been doing.

"Don't say a word," I warned as Dante and I walked toward Valhalla's entrance.

"I won't." Laughter lurked beneath his voice. "But if it makes you feel better, it's not the first time Thomas has seen...action in his back seat."

I slid a sideways glance at him. "Make a habit of limo sex, do you?"

Amusement pulled at the corners of his mouth. "He used to work for William Haverton. The man is in his sixties but has a fat wallet and the libido of a college frat boy. You do the math." We passed through the club's foyer. "I assure you, I don't make a habit of limo sex."

"Oh." I cleared my throat. "I see."

His smile blossomed in full, dark and wicked. "Jealous?"

"Not in the least."

I held my head high and ignored his knowing chuckle. It was only when we reached the elevator that I realized I'd completely forgotten to ask him about the surprise date before we arrived.

Since Valhalla's top two floors had been closed during the fall gala, Dante gave me a quick tour of the places we'd missed during my last visit, including the spa, an indoor bowling alley, and an arcade lined with rare vintage games.

I would've enjoyed it more had I not been so impatient to find out what the big mystery date was.

"Are you still mad you didn't get the surprise out of me in the car?" Dante asked as we stopped in front of a set of double doors on the fourth floor.

"No." *Yes.*

"At least we both got orgasms out of it," he drawled. "It was a win-win situation."

Laughter crinkled the edges of his eyes when I swatted his arm, my face hot, but his boyish smile was so endearing I couldn't hold on to my annoyance.

"Like I said, it's something that's better seen than told." He tilted his head toward the closed room. "This is the club's multipurpose space. Members can reserve it and turn it into anything they want. It's been a private concert hall, a vintage porcelain doll exhibit..."

My eyebrows shot up.

"One of the members is a collector. Don't ask." He opened the doors. "Hopefully, this makes up for the wait."

Oh my God.

I sucked in a sharp inhale.

When he'd said multipurpose space, I'd pictured whiteboards and industrial gray carpet. Theoretically, I knew Valhalla wouldn't house something so generic, but nothing could've prepared me for the sight before me.

He'd turned the room into a planetarium.

No, not a planetarium. A virtual galaxy.

Brilliant stars splashed across the soaring walls and ceiling and swirled beneath our feet. Constellations dotted the "sky," including Andromeda, Perseus, and a distinctive hourglass shape that made my breath hitch.

Orion. My favorite.

"You can't see the stars in New York," Dante said. "So I brought the stars to you."

A ball of emotion formed in my throat. "How did you..."

He followed my gaze to Orion. It sparkled front and center, shining more brightly than the rest.

"I had a call with your sister. She told me it was your favorite." He guided me into the room. "Apparently, you wouldn't shut up about Orion when you were younger. Her words."

Agnes *would* say that.

Dante's face softened with an uncharacteristic hint of uncertainty. "Do you like it?"

I laced my fingers with his, my chest indescribably tight. "It's perfect."

We'd gone on more than half a dozen dates over the past month. They'd ranged from lavish, like the helicopter tour after our milkshakes and an overnight getaway to Bermuda, to casual, like a stroll through Chelsea Market and a show at the Comedy Cellar.

But none had hit me quite as hard as tonight's.

The fact that Dante had gone to the trouble of setting this up and consulting my sister when he could've easily taken me to the planetarium instead...it touched a part of me I hadn't thought anyone could reach.

His shoulders relaxed and he squeezed my hand in silent reply as we walked to the center of the room, where a pile of blankets, cushions, and a dinner spread awaited us.

I sank onto a pale-blue cushion while Dante picked up a distinctive wine bottle. Was that…

"Domaine de la Romanée-Conti," he confirmed. Dante uncorked the famous red and poured it into two glasses. "Courtesy of the club's sommelier."

Known for its high quality and limited production, Domaine de la Romanée-Conti, or DRC, was one of the most expensive wines in the world. An average bottle cost upward of twenty-six thousand dollars.

"Bringing out the big guns," I teased. "Dante Russo, are you trying to impress me?"

"Depends." He handed me a glass and watched as I took a small sip. "Is it working?"

The rich flavors of berry fruits, violets, and cassis burst onto my tongue, mixed with a fine minerality and complex earthiness. Textural. Potent. Elegant. No wonder people were willing to shell out the big bucks for a bottle. It was the best wine I'd ever tasted.

"Yes," I said, already heady from one sip and a night that'd barely begun. "Quite well."

"Then yes, I am." His eyes danced with amusement as I went back for seconds. "You're turning red, *mia cara*."

I was extremely sensitive to red wine, which was why I usually stuck with whites and rosés. Even those made my face glow crimson after a glass or two, but the DRC was too exquisite to waste.

"It's not my fault," I said, embarrassed. "It's the tannins."

"It's adorable." He brushed a thumb over my flushed cheek.

Warmth curled low in my stomach. Grumpy, brooding Dante had grown on me the past few months. But sweet, playful Dante? He was kryptonite to my heart.

After dinner, I pulled a blanket over us and rested my head on

Dante's shoulder, half-sleepy and half-buzzing from the high of the date. He wrapped an arm around my waist, the weight strong and comforting against my back.

The stars twinkled above us like a display of diamonds on midnight velvet. They were projections, but they looked so real I almost believed we were somewhere in the wilderness, watching the skies and listening to the silence.

"When I was little, our parents would take us camping." I didn't know where the words came from, but they felt right for the moment. "My father would drive, my mother would pack way too many snacks, and my sister and I would try to spot as many states' license plates on the road as we could."

I hated bugs, and I wasn't a big outdoors person, but I'd loved those trips because we'd done them as a family. Since then, we'd upgraded to summers in St. Tropez and Christmases in St. Barts, but I missed the simplicity of our early family vacations.

"At night, when we were supposed to be asleep, Agnes and I would sneak out of our tent and count the stars," I continued. "We'd pretend they were people living in a celestial realm and made up backstories for all of them."

"Any interesting ones?"

I smiled. "Tons. One was plotting to overthrow the ruler of the kingdom. Another was having an affair with her awful husband's most trusted guard. Shooting stars were people who'd been exiled and cast down to earth."

Dante's laugh vibrated through my body. "Sounds like a soap opera."

"We were children. We had active imaginations, okay?" I nudged his leg with mine. "Don't tell me you never made up stories about the things around you."

"Sorry to disappoint, but my imagination isn't as good as yours." He rubbed an absentminded thumb over my hip. "My family never went camping. My grandfather was strictly a resort or private estate type of person. He didn't want Luca and me to lose touch with our culture, so he sent us to Italy with Greta every summer. We had—have—houses all over the country. Rome, Tuscany, Milan...we visited a different place every year."

"What's your favorite place in Italy?"

"Villa Serafina." His family's estate in Lake Como. "The lake, the gardens...twelve-year-old me thought it was magical."

"Where the wedding will take place," I murmured. "I can't wait to see it."

We were scheduled to stay there in the month leading up to the ceremony. I'd only seen pictures, but even through a screen, it was breathtaking.

"Yes." A strange note entered Dante's voice. "Where the wedding will take place."

"It'll be perfect. My mother wouldn't have it any other way," I said dryly. She'd been driving me nuts with endless calls about the flowers, tableware, and a thousand other details she shouldn't be micromanaging, but I hadn't expected anything less. I was her last opportunity to go all out on a big wedding. "At least my father isn't also hounding me about china patterns. He got the date he wanted. That's all he cares about."

"August eighth. Let me guess. It's the date he made his first million."

I laughed. "Close, but not quite. Eight is his favorite number."

Dante's thumb paused before it resumed caressing my skin. "The number eight? Really?"

"Yes." I yawned. Nothing made me sleepier than wine and sex, and I'd had the best of both tonight. "It's a lucky number in Chinese culture because it's associated with wealth. When my parents were house hunting, they specifically looked for places with eight in their address. My father is very superstitious about things like that."

"I never would've guessed." Dante's tone cooled the way it always did when we discussed my father.

I lifted my head. A distracted expression crossed his face, but it disappeared when he saw me looking.

"You don't like my family very much." I'd picked up on it at our introductory dinner, but it had become increasingly evident since. Every time I mentioned my parents, Dante's face shut down, and I could feel him mentally withdraw. When we visited Boston for Christmas, he spent most of his time communicating in glares and one-word answers. It'd been the most awkward four days of my life.

"I don't like a lot of people," he said evasively. "But if we're being honest, Francis and I will never be best friends. We have different...outlooks on life."

Before I could respond, he cupped my face and brushed my lips with his.

"No more talk about family," he said. "We have the room to ourselves for the night, and I can think of a few other things that I would much rather be doing..."

Any resistance I had melted when he deepened the kiss. My lips parted, and my sigh invited him in. He slid his tongue against mine, tasting like wine and heat and sin.

Dante was right. It was a beautiful night, and there was no reason to dampen it with talk of family.

A lingering sense of unease prickled the back of my neck, but I brushed it aside. So what if Dante and my father didn't see eye to eye on everything? Some antagonism was expected among fathers and their sons-in-law. It wasn't like they were going to punch each other at the next holiday gathering.

Plus, my parents lived in a different city. We wouldn't see them much anyway.

I had nothing to worry about.

CHAPTER 28

Dante

VIVIAN AND I HAD ONE MORE BLISSFUL WEEK TO ourselves before her parents blew into town like a tornado. Sudden, unexpected, and carving a path of destruction in their wake.

One minute, I was planning a symphony date with Vivian. The next, I was sitting across from Francis and Cecelia Lau in Le Charles, fighting the urge not to knock the smug smile off Francis's face.

Our conversation about him at Valhalla had summoned him like a demon out of hell.

"I'm glad we could make this work." He unfolded his napkin and placed it on his lap. "I hope we're not disrupting your plans too much."

"Not at all." Vivian placed her hand over mine under the table and gently uncurled my fist. "We're thrilled to see you."

I remained silent.

Her parents had arrived, unannounced, that morning and requested dinner with us sometime during their stay. Considering they were only here for two nights and they had tickets to a Broadway show with friends tomorrow, tonight was the only option.

"We haven't seen you since Christmas, so we figured we'd check in. See how the wedding planning is going." Cecelia toyed with her pearls. "You never answered my question the other day about the flowers. Shall we go ahead with the lilies?"

Vivian shifted in her seat. Instead of her usual dress, heels, and red lipstick, she wore a tweed suit similar to the one from our first meeting. Her necklace was identical to her mother's, and the sparkling vivaciousness I'd fall—I'd come to appreciate had dulled into painful gentility.

It wasn't *her*; it was some Stepford clone version of her that only showed up when Francis and Cecelia were in the room, and I hated it.

"Yes," she said. "The lilies are fine."

"Excellent." Cecelia beamed. "Now, about the cake—"

Thankfully, our server showed up at that moment and interrupted her before she launched into a spiel about icing or whatever the hell she wanted to talk about.

"We'll have the Golden Imperial caviar and tuna tartare on foie gras to start, and the lamb chops for the main," Francis said, ordering for both himself and his wife. He handed the menu dismissively to the server without looking at him.

"I'll have the tagliatelle, please," Vivian said.

Francis's brows beetled. "This isn't an Italian restaurant, Vivian. They're known for their lamb. Why don't you get that instead?"

Because she doesn't like lamb, you fucker.

My back teeth clenched. Even if Francis weren't blackmailing me, I'd despise him.

How could he have gone twenty-eight years without knowing his daughter's aversion to that particular meat? Or maybe he simply didn't care.

"The waitlist for a Le Charles reservation is four months

long," Francis said. "Even the governor has trouble getting a table when he's in town. It's ridiculous to waste a meal here on anything other than their best."

"I..." Vivian faltered. "You're right. Can I change my order to the lamb, please?" She gave the server an apologetic smile. "Thank you."

"Of course." The server's polite expression didn't waver. We might as well be discussing the weather for all the reaction he showed. "And for you, Mr. Russo?"

I closed my menu with deliberate precision and kept my eyes on Vivian's father while I ordered. "I'd like the tagliatelle."

Francis's lips thinned.

If we were at home, I would've called him out directly, but we were sitting smack-dab in the middle of the restaurant. I wouldn't give him the satisfaction of making a scene.

"How's your brother doing?" Francis asked. "I hear he's working a sales job at Lohman & Sons now. Seems...below his pay grade."

"He's doing just fine," I said coolly. "Contribution is contribution, whether it's in a retail or corporate role."

"Hmm." He lifted his wine to his lips. "We'll have to agree to disagree."

I wasn't fooled by the seemingly innocuous change in topic. Francis was trying to remind me what was at stake. He said he was in town for a show, but the sudden visit was a power play designed to throw me off-balance.

We were only a few months out from the wedding. He was many things, but he wasn't stupid. He must've known I was working behind the scenes to destroy the blackmail evidence.

I'd been quiet too long, and he was getting nervous, for good reason.

My Valhalla date with Vivian had triggered an epiphany. She said he was superstitious about dates and numbers, and the digging I had Christian do in the past week backed up her assertion. His home address, his business address, his license plate...all of them centered around the number eight. I'd bet my brother's life he had eight copies of the blackmail photos.

Christian was already tracking down the remaining three sets. Once he found them, it was game over for Francis fucking Lau.

For the first time that night, I smiled.

The rest of dinner passed without incident. Vivian and her mother carried the conversation, though it took all my willpower not to lose my shit when Cecelia chastised her for wearing the "wrong" makeup shade or when her father overruled her dessert choice the way he had her entrée by insisting she try the restaurant's chocolate tart instead of the cheesecake.

I didn't know what was worse—her parents' overbearing attitude or Vivian's willingness to take it. She would've never let me talk to her the way they did.

"Whatever you want to say, say it," she said when we returned home. She took off her earrings and dropped them in the gold dish on the dresser. "You've been silently fuming the entire car ride home."

I took off my jacket and tossed it over the back of a chair. "Not fuming. Simply wondering how you overcame your lifelong disdain for lamb within the past twenty-four hours."

Vivian sighed. "It's one meal. It's not a big deal."

"It's not about the food, Vivian." Aggravation simmered in my veins. "It's about the way your parents treat you like you're a child. It's about how you turn into a cardboard cutout of yourself whenever you're around them." I gestured at her outfit. "This isn't you. You hate lamb. You're not a tweed and pearls person. You wouldn't be caught dead in that outfit on a normal day."

"Well, it's *not* a normal day." A hint of irritation slipped into her voice. I wasn't the only one on edge tonight. "Do you think I enjoy having my parents show up at the last minute? Or that I *like* being criticized for everything I say and wear? Maybe this isn't what I'd choose to wear if they weren't here, and maybe I wouldn't have ordered the lamb if my father hadn't insisted, but sometimes you have to compromise to keep the peace. They're here for two days. It's *not a big deal.*"

"It's two days this time, but what about in the future?" I asked, my voice hard. "Every holiday, every visit, for the rest of your life. Tell me it's not exhausting pretending to be someone you're not with the two people who should accept you as you are."

Vivian tensed. "People do that every day. They go to work and show one side of themselves. They go out with friends and show another side. It's *normal.*"

"Yeah, except they're not your colleagues or your fucking friends. They're your family, and they treat you like shit!" My frustration boiled over into a shout.

"They're my *parents*!" Vivian's voice rose to match mine. "They're not perfect, but they have my best interests at heart. They sacrificed a lot to give me and my sister the type of life they never had growing up. Even before we were rich, they worked their butts off to make sure we could afford the same clothes and field trips as our classmates so we weren't left out. So if I have to give up some things *temporarily* to make them happy, I will."

"Temporarily, huh? Is that why your father basically sold you both off in exchange for a rung up on the social ladder?"

Vivian's face paled, and regret slammed into me, hard and fast.

Fuck.

"Viv—"

"No." She held up a hand. "That was exactly what you meant to say, so don't take it back."

My jaw tightened. "I don't see you as a bargaining chip, but can you honestly tell me your parents feel the same way? I'm not trying to make you feel bad, *amore mio*, but you don't have to put up with their bullshit. You're an adult. You're beautiful, successful, intelligent, and three times the person either of them will ever be. You have your own money and career. You don't need them."

"It's not about needing them. It's about *family*." Frustration etched lines on Vivian's face. "We do things differently, okay? Respect for our elders is important. We don't talk back just because we don't like what they say."

"Yeah, well, sometimes elders are full of horseshit, and you need to call them out on it." I was belaboring the point, but I hated how Vivian turned into a shell of herself around her parents. It was like watching a beautiful, vibrant rose wither before my eyes.

"*You* can," she fired back. "You grew up the heir to the Russo empire. Yes, I know it wasn't all fun and games, but you were still the center of your grandfather's attention. I had to be perfect just to get an ounce of affection. My grades, my image, *everything*."

"That's my fucking point! You shouldn't *have* to be perfect to get your parents' affection!"

"That's *my* point! I do!"

We stared at each other, our chests heaving, our bodies close but our minds light-years apart.

Vivian broke eye contact first. "It's been a long night, and I'm tired," she said. "But I wish you'd at least try to see where I'm coming from. Your view of the world is not universal. I want a partner, Dante, not someone who'll berate me because he doesn't agree with the way I handle my relationship with my own family."

Remorse blunted the edge of my anger. "Sweetheart..."

"I'm going to take a bath and do some work after. Don't wait up for me."

The bathroom door closed with a *click* behind her.

That night, for the first time since we started dating, we went to bed without kissing the other good night.

CHAPTER 29

Vivian

"CONGRATS! YOU HAD YOUR FIRST FIGHT AS A REAL couple. Let's toast to that." Isabella raised her mimosa in the air, her smile totally sincere.

My and Sloane's glasses remained on the table.

"It's not something to celebrate, Isa," I said wryly.

"Of course it is. You wanted the full couple experience. That includes fights, especially over family." She finished her drink, undeterred by our unwillingness to participate in her toast. "Honestly, couples who *don't* fight freak me out. They're like one broken dish away from snapping. The next thing you know, they'll be the subjects of a Netflix documentary series titled *Love and Murder: The Couple Next Door.*"

I couldn't help but laugh. "You listen to *way* too much true crime."

Isabella, Sloane, and I were eating brunch at a hot new spot in the Bowery. It'd been two days since my fight with Dante, and I was still fuming over it. Not because he was wrong but because he was right.

Nothing stung more than the acrid taste of truth.

"It's research," Isabella said. "Therefore, it's work. You can't blame me for working overtime, can you? Look at Sloane. She's on her phone even though the world's best eggs Benedict is sitting untouched in front of her."

"It's not untouched. I ate two bites." Sloane finished whatever she was typing and looked up. "You try enjoying your food when one of your clients posts a social media tirade about their *very* famous ex-wife and proceeds to get into online arguments with..." She checked her phone again. "User59806 about who should drive their car off a cliff first."

"Sounds tame for the internet," Isabella said. "I'm *kidding*. Sort of. Look, there's not much you can do about it now except take away your client's social media access, which I assume you've already done. People will act stupid all day, every day. Enjoy your food, and deal with them later. Two hours of digital detox won't kill you." She pushed Sloane's plate closer to her. "Plus, you need energy for all the fire breathing you'll do later."

Sloane pursed her lips. "I suppose you're right."

"I'm always right. Now..." Isabella shifted her attention back to me. "This fight. I think you should let it go on for another day before you have hot makeup sex. Three days is adequate time for all that tension to build and—"

"*Isa*."

"I'm sorry! I don't have a sex life at the moment, okay? I'm living vicariously through you." She sighed. "And the argument isn't a deal breaker, right? He's kind of..."

Right.

Silence cloaked the table.

I stared at my half-eaten plate, my skin icy despite the warmth from two mimosas.

"Don't get me wrong. I know how you feel." Isabella's voice softened. "But I think it's one of those cultural differences that'll take time to smooth over. Dante cares about you, or he wouldn't have been so upset. He's just…not great at expressing his thoughts tactfully."

"I know." My sigh carried days' worth of agonizing. "It's just hard to remember that when I'm in the moment and he's being so…so *stubborn*."

In Dante's world, his word was law. He was always right, and people bent over backward to accommodate or appease him.

But that was the thing. It wasn't just his world anymore; it was ours, at least when it came to our home life. Arranged marriage or not, I'd signed up for a husband, not a boss. I just wasn't sure *he* knew that.

"He's Dante Russo," Sloane said, as if that explained everything. "Inflexibility is his middle name. Personally, I think you should make him sweat. Shut him out until he comes to his senses."

"Great. So we'll be waiting until the turn of the next century," Isabella said. "Viv, what do *you* want to do?"

"I—"

"Vivian. What a pleasant surprise." A smooth, creamy voice interrupted our conversation.

I straightened when an elegant older woman with a sleek silver bob and the skin of someone thirty years her junior stopped next to our table.

"Buffy, it's nice to see you," I said, hiding my surprise. She and her friends rarely stepped foot outside their uptown bubble. "How are you?"

I pointedly ignored Isabella's quiet splutter when I mentioned the name *Buffy*.

"I'm well, dear. Thank you for asking." The sixty-four-year-old grande dame looked immaculate as always in a cream silk blouse, gray tailored pants, and Mikimoto pearl drop earrings. "I normally don't come all the way down to the Bowery…" Her tone insinuated the twenty-five-minute car ride from her house was as arduous as the trek from Fifth Avenue to Brooklyn. "But I hear the brunch here is *divine*."

"The best lobster eggs Benedict in town." I gestured at an empty chair. "Would you like to join us?"

Neither of us wanted her to stay, but it was the polite thing to ask.

"Oh, what a sweet offer, but no, thank you," Buffy said on cue. "Bunny and I reserved the corner table. She's glaring at me as we speak—she simply hates sitting alone in public..." She shot a reproving look at where a well-groomed blond woman sat with her equally well-groomed toy poodle poking out of the top of her Hermès bag. Dogs weren't allowed in the restaurant, but people like Buffy and her friends operated by different rules. "However, I wanted to stop by and congratulate you in person on securing Valhalla for the Legacy Ball venue. It's generated quite the buzz."

"Thank you," I murmured.

I'd tried my best to find other alternatives, but none of them panned out, so I'd reluctantly gone with Dante's Valhalla Club suggestion. I'd insisted on putting together the pitch, which he presented to the management committee since they didn't allow nonmembers in the meeting. The approval process took almost a month, but I received the final confirmation two weeks ago.

While part of me thrilled at landing such an exclusive venue, another part worried about what it would cost Dante. Not monetarily but in terms of leverage and reciprocation.

"I'm sure Dante put in a good word for you." Buffy smiled. "It pays to marry a Russo, doesn't it?"

My own smile tightened. The dig was subtle, but it was there.

"Since we're on the subject of the ball, I have a suggestion regarding the entertainment," she said. "It's a shame Corelli lost his voice and can no longer perform."

The famous opera singer was on hiatus while his voice recovered. The issue wasn't as severe as the venue flooding, but it was yet another problem in the pile that was mounting daily.

Murphy's law of event planning—something always went wrong, and the more important the event, the *more* went wrong.

"Don't worry. I've already confirmed an alternative," I said. "There's a wonderful jazz singer who agreed to perform for half her regular rate considering the audience that'll be in attendance."

"How lovely," Buffy said. "However, I was thinking we should book Veronica Foster instead."

"Veronica Foster...the sugar heiress?"

"She's transitioned into the music scene," Buffy said smoothly. "I'm sure she would appreciate the opportunity to perform at the ball. As would I."

Her pointed statement pierced my confusion. I suddenly remembered the other reason why Veronica's name sounded familiar. She was Buffy's goddaughter.

"I'm happy to meet with her and review her tape if she has one." I kept my tone measured despite the knots twisting my stomach. "However, I can't guarantee a spot in the lineup. As you know, the schedule is tight, and I've already agreed to book the jazz singer."

Buffy's eyes cooled into blue ice. "I'm sure she'd understand if you had to cancel," she said, her smile intact but sharper. More deadly. "This is an important event, Vivian. There's a lot riding on it."

Including your reputation and place in society.

The unspoken threat hung over the table like a guillotine.

Across from me, Isabella and Sloane watched the scene play out with wide eyes and icy fury, respectively. I could tell Sloane was holding back some choice epithets, but thankfully, she didn't intervene.

She didn't need to.

Between my parents' visit, my argument with Dante, and the headaches I'd encountered with the ball, I'd reached the end of my rope.

"Yes, there is," I said in response to Buffy. Frost layered beneath my otherwise polite tone. "That's why every detail must be flawless, including the performers. As the chair of the Legacy Ball committee, I'm sure you understand anything less than perfection onstage would not be ideal. I have full faith in Veronica's commitment to her craft, which is why an audition shouldn't be a problem. Wouldn't you agree?"

The sounds from the restaurant became white noise as my heartbeat drummed in my ears. I was taking a huge risk, insulting Buffy in front of other people, but I was sick of people trying to manipulate me into doing what they wanted.

She could blacklist me after the ball, but until then, it was *my* name on the invitations and *my* professional reputation on the line. I'd be damned if I let anyone destroy what I'd worked years for in the name of poorly concealed nepotism.

Buffy stared at me.

In reality, the silence lasted less than a minute, but every second stretched for an eon until her initial shock melted into something more inscrutable.

"Yes," she finally said. "I suppose you're right." Her voice was as cold as her eyes, but if I didn't know better, I'd say it contained the tiniest hint of respect. "Enjoy the rest of your meal." She turned to leave, but before she did, she cast a last look at me. "And, Vivian? I expect this to be the *best* Legacy Ball in the event's history."

Buffy departed in a cloud of Chanel No. 5 and icy regality.

Her exit pulled the pent-up air from my lungs. I slumped, no longer held upright by indignation and a need to prove she couldn't walk all over me.

"Telling off Buffy Darlington." Sloane's green eyes glittered with rare admiration. "Impressive."

"I didn't tell her off," I refuted. "I presented an alternative viewpoint."

"You told her off," Isabella said. "There was a moment when I thought she would have a coronary and collapse right into your eggs. Buffy and Benedict, the new brunch combo."

We stared at each other for a moment, stunned by the cheesiness of her joke, before we broke into laughter. Maybe it was the alcohol, or maybe we were all delirious from overworking and lack of sleep, but once we started, we couldn't stop. Tears sprung to my eyes, and Isabella's shoulders shook so hard the table rattled. Even Sloane was laughing.

"Speaking of B names," Isabella said after our mirth finally died down to a manageable level. "Did I hear wrong, or did she say she was here with her friend *Bunny*?"

"Bunny Van Houten," I confirmed with a grin. "Wife of Dutch shipping magnate Dirk Van Houten."

Horror wiped the remaining amusement from Isabella's face.

"Who comes up with these names?" she demanded. "Is there a rule that the richer you are, the uglier your name has to be?"

"They're not *that* bad."

"Buffy and Bunny, Viv! Buffy and Bunny!" Isabella shook her head. "Once I have the power, I'm banning all names beginning with the letters B and U. God forbid they add a Bubby to their group."

I couldn't help it. I burst into laughter again, with Isabella and Sloane joining me soon after.

God, I needed this. Food, drinks, and a fun, silly morning with my friends, the Buffy incident notwithstanding. Sometimes, it was the simple things in life that kept us going.

We lingered for another hour before we left. I insisted on

covering the meal since they'd spent the majority of the time listening to my problems, and I'd just paid the check when my phone buzzed.

My heart flipped when I read the new message, but I kept my expression neutral as we exited the restaurant.

"There's a new romantic comedy coming out next week," Sloane said. "Let's watch it."

Isabella eyed her with suspicion. "Will you actually watch the movie this time, or will you just complain during the entire film?"

Sloane slid on her sunglasses. "I don't complain. I provide real-time criticism of the film's application in the real world."

"It's a rom-com," I said. "They're not *supposed* to be realistic."

Some people liked to unwind by reading or getting a massage. Sloane liked to watch romantic comedies and type up dissertation-length papers detailing every single thing she disliked about the movie. And yet she kept watching them.

"We'll agree to disagree," she said. "Next Thursday after work. Does that work?"

We'd survived years of rom-com evisceration. We'd survive another night.

After we confirmed the movie date and parted ways, I wound my way up Fourth Street toward Washington Square Park.

My pulse thudded louder with each step until it crescendoed at the sight of a familiar tall, dark figure standing by the arch.

The park bustled with street musicians, photographers, and students in NYU sweatshirts, but Dante stood out like a slash of boldness against a faded backdrop. Even in a plain white T-shirt and jeans, his presence was powerful enough to draw not-so-subtle stares from passersby.

Our eyes connected across the street. Electricity crackled down my spine, and it took me an extra beat to start walking after the last car passed.

I stopped two feet from him. The sounds of music, laughter, and car honks fell away, as if he existed within a force field that prevented any outside intrusion.

"Hi," I said, oddly breathless.

"Hi." He tucked his hands in his pockets, the gesture endearingly boyish compared to his rugged features and broad, muscled frame. "How was brunch?"

"Good." I pushed a lock of hair behind my ear. "How was... your day?" I had no clue what he'd been doing that morning.

"I beat Dominic in tennis. He was pissed." A crooked smile formed on Dante's lips. "Good day."

A laugh bubbled up my throat. It'd only been two days, but I *missed* him. His dry humor, his smiles, even his scowls. He was the only person who could make me miss every individual part of him as much as his whole—the good, the bad, *and* the mundane.

His eyes and mouth sobered. "I wanted to apologize," he said. "For Friday night. You were right. I should've tried harder to understand where you were coming from instead of...ambushing you when we went home."

His voice carried the stiffness of someone delivering an apology for the first time, but the underlying sincerity melted any grudge I might've held.

"You were right too," I confessed. "I don't like admitting it out loud, but I *am* different around my parents. I wish I wasn't, but..." I blew out a breath. "There are some things that might be too late to change."

I was twenty-eight. My parents were in their late fifties or early sixties. At what point were our habits and dynamics so ingrained that trying to change them would be akin to trying to bend a concrete pillar?

"It's never too late for change." Dante's eyes softened further.

"You're fucking perfect the way you are, Vivian. If your parents can't see that, then it's their loss."

His words grabbed hold of my heart and squeezed.

To my horror, a familiar prickle sprang up behind my eyes, and I had to blink it away before I spoke again.

"Maybe I'll wear a silk suit instead of tweed at our next dinner," I half joked. "Spice things up a bit."

"Silk suits you better anyway. Next time they drop in for a surprise visit, we can also tell them we've contracted a terrible, highly contagious stomach bug and lock ourselves in our apartment until they leave."

"Hmm, I like it." I tilted my head. "But what would we do, locked all day in the apartment?"

He slid me a wicked grin. "I can think of a few things."

Heat washed over my skin, and I fought back a blossoming smile. "I'm sure you can. So," I said, switching topics. "Do you have any plans for the rest of the day?"

"Yes." He slid his hand into mine, the action as casual and natural as breathing. "I'm spending it with you."

My smile broke free, as did the butterflies in my stomach.

Just like that, we were okay again. It wasn't a long reconciliation, but it didn't need to be. Moving on didn't always involve big gestures or heavy talks. Sometimes, the most meaningful moments were the small ones—a softening glance here, a simple but sincere apology there.

"Perfect," I said. I kept my hand in his as we walked away from the park. "Because there's a new exhibit at the Whitney I've been dying to check out..."

CHAPTER 30

Vivian

"I'M SORRY, YOU WANT US TO GO *WHERE*?" I LOOKED up from my sushi and pinned Dante with a disbelieving stare.

"Paris." He leaned back, the picture of nonchalant ease. Jacket off, tie loosened, expression unruffled like he hadn't just suggested I drop everything to jet off to Europe.

It was Wednesday, five days after our short-lived fight and three days after our reconciliation.

We were eating lunch in my office and having a perfectly pleasant conversation when he dropped the Paris bombshell out of nowhere.

"I found out today I have to meet some of our subsidiary CEOs there ahead of the Cannes Film Festival," he said. "My VP was supposed to do it, but his wife went into early labor. I'm leaving Saturday and staying there for a week."

Normally, I would've jumped at the chance to join him. Paris was one of my favorite cities, and I was long overdue for another visit, but I couldn't drop everything to cavort around France when the Legacy Ball was only weeks away.

"I can't," I said reluctantly. "I have to be here for ball prep."

Dante raised his eyebrows. "I thought everything's pretty much set."

Technically, he was right. The venue was secured, the caterers on track, and the seating charts and entertainment finalized—Veronica Foster turned out to be surprisingly talented, and I'd squeezed her in for a short performance at the end of the night—but with my luck, something would go wrong the minute I stepped foot on French soil.

"Yes, but still. This is the biggest event of my career. I can't fly off at the last minute. My team needs me."

"Your team seems competent enough to hold down the fort for five days." Dante tapped the stack of papers on my desk. "You'll still have over a week when we get back to finalize everything, and you don't need to be physically in New York to do your work in the meantime. I'll be busy in the mornings too, so we work during the day and explore Paris at night. Win-win."

"What about the time difference?" I argued. "My team will still be working when it's evening in Paris."

"So schedule your meetings for the early afternoon. It'll be morning here," Dante said, practical as always. "It's Paris in spring, *mia cara*. Beautiful flowers, fresh croissants, walks along the Seine..."

"I don't know." I wavered, torn between the picture he painted and my paranoia that something would go wrong.

"I already booked a suite at the Ritz." Dante paused before dropping the second bombshell of the day. "And you can pick out a gown from the Yves Dubois showroom for the ball."

My breath stilled in my lungs. "That's cheating."

Yves Dubois was one of the world's top couturiers. He produced only eight gowns a year, each one of them unique and exquisitely handcrafted. He was also notoriously picky about who he allowed to wear one of his creations; rumor had it he once turned away a world-famous movie star who'd wanted to wear his design to the Oscars.

"It's an incentive." Dante grinned. "If you really can't or don't want to come, you don't have to. But you've been working damn hard these past few months. You deserve a little break."

"Nice way to spin it. Are you sure it's not because you have separation anxiety?" I teased.

"I didn't use to." His eyes held mine like a lone flame flickering on a cold winter night. "But I'm beginning to think I might."

Warmth filled my stomach and rushed to the surface of my skin.

I shouldn't, but maybe I was tired of living my life by *should*s.

I made my final decision in a split second.

"Then I guess I'm going to Paris."

Over the next two days, I prepped my team as much as I could. I gave them six different numbers where they could reach me and ran through emergency protocols so many times I thought Shannon would march me onto the plane herself before she strangled me.

Still, I remained apprehensive about the trip until I was in the car on our way to our hotel, watching the city whiz by outside the window.

Like New York, Paris was a love-it-or-hate-it type of city. I happened to love both. The food, the fashion, the culture...there was nothing quite like it, and once I was actually *in* Paris, it was easy to get lost in the magic of it all.

Our first three days consisted of settling in and, in my case, adjusting to my new work schedule. I spent the quiet morning hours knocking out administrative tasks and took meetings in the afternoon when my team and New York-based vendors were online. I thought I'd be distracted by the draw of the city outside my window, but I was surprisingly productive.

That being said, I couldn't resist a quick shopping trip to rue Saint-Honoré and, of course, a visit to Yves Dubois's showroom, where I spent two hours choosing and fitting a gown for the Legacy Ball.

"Not that one." Yves pursed his lips when I ran my fingers over a breathtaking blush and silver beaded piece. "Pink is too soft for you, darling. You need something bolder, more daring. Something that'll make a statement." He tilted his head, his eyes narrowed, before he snapped his fingers. "Frédéric, bring me the Phoenix gown."

His assistant darted out of the room and returned minutes later with the piece in question.

I sucked in an audible breath.

"My latest creation," Yves said with a flourish. "Eight hundred hours to hand-sew, bursts of gold thread embroidered over the entire surface of the gown. My finest work to date, in my humble opinion."

Nothing about Yves was humble, but he was right. It was his finest work to date.

I couldn't tear my eyes away from it.

"Normally, it's one hundred and fifty thousand dollars," he said. "But for you, the future Mrs. Russo, to wear it at the Legacy Ball? One hundred and thirty thousand. Even."

It was a no-brainer. "I'll take it."

That night, Dante returned to a hotel suite littered with shopping bags on the floor, tables, and half the bed.

Yves would send my gown directly to New York, so I didn't need to worry about ruining it on our flight back, but I may have gone a *little* overboard on the shopping.

"Should I have booked a separate room for your purchases?" Dante eyed the pile of Dior hatboxes on the bed.

"You should've, but it's too late for that." I locked my

new Bulgari diamond necklace in the hotel safe before I fished something from one of the smaller bags. "I bought you something too."

I handed him the small black box and waited, heart thudding, while he opened it.

His eyebrows shot up when he popped open the lid.

"They're ice cream cuff links," I said brightly. "I know a jeweler on rue de la Paix who makes customized pieces. The onyx is the soy sauce. The ruby is the cherry, even though you don't eat it with cherry, but I think the red ties the design together."

It was a half-joke gift, half-sincere. Dante owned dozens of luxury cuff links, but I wanted to give him something more personal.

"Do you like them?" I asked.

"I love them." He removed his current cuff links and replaced them with the new ones. "Thank you, *mia cara*."

The warmth of his voice caressed my skin before he cupped my face with one hand and kissed me.

We never made it out to dinner that night.

Our other nights, however, were filled with whatever activities struck our fancy. We wandered through the charming book-lined nooks of Shakespeare and Company, explored the Louvre after hours, and pretended to watch black-and-white French indie films in an art house cinema while secretly making out in the back like teenagers.

I'd visited Paris many times, but exploring it with Dante was like seeing it for the first time. The smells wafting from the bakeries, the texture of cobblestones beneath my feet, the rainbow of flowers blooming all over the city—everything was brighter, more vivid, like someone had sprinkled fairy dust over the city.

On our last night, Dante took me to a private dinner at the Eiffel Tower. The monument had three restaurants; ours was on the second floor and offered spectacular views of the skyline. He'd booked the entire space, so it was just us, the seven-course menu, and the city laid out at our feet in all its glittering nighttime glory.

"Okay, what's one food you can't *stand* that everyone loves?" I swallowed a thin slice of sea bass before adding, "I'll go first. Olives. I hate them. They're a blight to humanity."

"I want to say I'm surprised, but you're the same person who eats pickles with chips and pudding, so..." Dante lifted his wine to his lips. "Enough said."

I narrowed my eyes. "I'm not the one who cleaned out our pickle supply two weeks ago because he couldn't stop stealing *my* snack."

"Don't be dramatic. Greta bought more pickles the next day." He laughed at my frown. "To answer your question, I can't stand popcorn. The texture's weird, and it smells awful even when it's not burnt."

"Seriously? Then what do you eat during movies?"

"Nothing. Movies are for watching, not eating food."

I stared at him. "Sometimes, I'm convinced you're an alien and not an actual human being."

Another laugh rolled over me. "We all have our quirks, *mia cara*. At least I don't sing Mariah Carey in the shower."

My cheeks warmed. "I did that *once*. I heard the song in a commercial and it got stuck in my head, okay?"

"I'm not saying it's a bad quirk." The corner of his mouth tipped up. "It was cute, even if it was off-key."

"I was *not* off-key," I muttered, but my indignation lasted only seconds in the face of his smile. "How's the prep for Cannes?" I asked when our server swapped out our empty plates for the third course. "Did you get everything done in time?"

"Yes, thankfully. If I had to sit in another meeting discussing what champagne we should serve at the after-party, I would've been arrested for murder," he grumbled.

"I'm sure you would've found a way out of it. You're a Russo," I teased.

"Yes, but the paperwork would've been a pain in the ass."

"You love paperwork. That's what you do all day."

"I'm going to pretend you didn't just insult me horribly in the middle of what's *supposed* to be a romantic last night in Paris." He sounded wounded, but mischief glinted in his eyes.

I laughed before asking, "Do you ever think about what you would've been if you hadn't been born a Russo?"

His life had been set from day one. But where would he be if he could've chosen his own path?

"Once or twice." Dante shrugged, seemingly unconcerned. "I never know the answer. Work takes up most of my time, and while I enjoy my hobbies—boxing, tennis, travel—I wouldn't have entertained them as careers."

I frowned, strangely saddened by his answer.

"I'm a businessman, Vivian," he said. "That's what I was born to be. I enjoy my work, even if certain aspects are not always fun. Don't think I'm throwing my life's passion away to toil in a corner office because I feel obligated to."

I supposed he was right. Dante—brash, bold, charming when he wanted to be but aggressive when provoked—was born to rule the boardroom. I couldn't imagine him in any role other than CEO.

"And you?" he asked. "If not event planning, what would you be doing?"

"I want to say I'd be an astronomer, but honestly, I'm terrible at math and science," I admitted. "I don't know. I guess I'm like you. I'm happy doing what I'm doing. Event planning can be stressful, but it's fun, creative...and there's nothing more satisfying than taking an idea and bringing it to life."

A smile touched his lips. "So we're both happy where we are." The velvet weight of his words made my heart flip.

"Yes," I said. "I suppose we are." The air turned thick and humid with meaning. I hesitated, then added softly, "I'm glad I came to Paris."

Dante's eyes were a lit match against my skin, bright and hot enough to burn. "Me too."

We stared at each other, our food forgotten. The weight of a dozen unspoken words sat between us and threatened to spill into the silence.

Before they could, a harsh ring yanked our gazes apart and toward his phone.

He let out a low curse in Italian. "I'm sorry. I have to take this," he said. "Work emergency."

"It's fine," I reassured him. "Do what you have to do."

He pushed back his chair and answered the call on his way toward the exit.

I finished my course, but I was so distracted I barely tasted the langoustine.

I'm glad I came to Paris.

Me too.

Even in Dante's absence, my pulse raced like it was competing for Olympic track and field gold.

Like I said, I'd been to Paris many times. But this was the first time I was actually falling in love in the City of Love.

CHAPTER 31

Dante

"WE FOUND ALL OF THEM."

I stilled. "Are you sure?"

I'd almost let Christian's call roll to voicemail. I wanted to enjoy my last night in Paris with Vivian, but my curiosity had gotten the better of me. He wouldn't call unless he had a major update.

I was right.

"Yes. We have eyes on all eight locations," Christian said. "Just say the word, and you'll be free of the Laus forever."

My hand closed tight around my phone. I waited for the relief to rush in. The joy, the triumph, the fucking *vindication* now that I could take down Francis the way I'd dreamed of for months.

Nothing came.

Instead, my stomach hollowed like Christian's words had sucked all the air out of it.

I glanced through the doorway at Vivian. I stood outside the restaurant's entrance, far enough that she couldn't hear what I was saying but close enough to glimpse her soft, content smile as she gazed out at the city.

A burn radiated in my chest. She looked so fucking happy.

Even with the last-minute trip and the upcoming Legacy Ball, she'd come alive in Paris in a way that made me want to stay here with her forever.

No blackmail, no Francis, no society bullshit. Just us.

Because this was, most likely, our last trip together.

"Dante?" Christian prompted.

I tore my eyes away from Vivian. "I heard you." The onset of a migraine crawled behind my temples. "What about the business side?"

"Also ready to go."

"Good." The sentiment scraped past my tight throat. "And our other project? With the startup?"

I was stalling. I should've given Christian the go-ahead the second he confirmed we found all Francis's backups, but something prevented the words from reaching my tongue.

"Heath's company has run into some trouble." Satisfaction filled Christian's drawl. "The software has been plagued with issues lately. Employees are nervous. Investors are spooked. IPO looks dead in the water. It's deeply unfortunate."

"Very."

I recognized the hypocrisy, considering what Christian and I had planned would push her away forever, but I didn't give a fuck. I'd never been logical when it came to her. She was my one spark of selfishness in a lifetime of reason.

"Honestly, it was so easy it was almost boring." Christian yawned. "Now that that's out of the way, what do you want me to do about Francis?"

I didn't respond. I didn't know how to.

I heard the heaviness of his pause over the line. "Let me remind you this is what you've been working toward for eight months," he said. "The man blackmailed you and threatened your brother's life."

"I'm well aware," I snapped.

I pushed a hand through my hair, trying to think through the pressure squeezing my skull.

The hypothetical sequence of events following my go-ahead played before my mind's eye like a movie on fast forward.

Christian destroys the evidence and torpedoes Lau Jewels. Vivian hears the news about her family's livelihood going up in flames. I tell her the truth about the blackmail. She leaves…

The pressure spread to my chest.

Fuck. If I had a heart attack in the middle of the Eiffel Tower while on a call with Christian, I'd never hear the end of it.

"Your call, Russo." His voice turned impatient. "What's our next move?"

He didn't say it, but I heard the warning in his voice. He knew exactly why I was hesitating, and he was less than impressed.

I closed my eyes. My migraine pounded with increasing ferocity.

I'm not my family.

The man blackmailed you and threatened your brother's life.

Say the word, and you'll be free of the Laus forever.

I had to get rid of the blackmail. No matter my feelings for Vivian, it was my brother's life on the line, and I couldn't risk those photos leaking. Romano would skin him alive if he found out Luca had touched any woman in his family, much less his beloved niece.

If I destroyed the blackmail, there was nothing keeping me from taking vengeance on Francis. I could let bygones be bygones, but he didn't deserve it.

"Next time you see your brother, you should tell him to be more careful." Francis had the smile of a snake who'd just come across trapped prey. "I would hate for these photos to get into Romano's hands."

I didn't touch the folder on my desk. I'd seen enough. I didn't need to go through every fucking picture.

"Anyway, I'm sure you're busy, so I won't take up any more of your time." Francis stood and smoothed a hand over his tie. "Think about what I said. A marriage with my daughter would be quite beneficial, especially for the…longevity of your family." His smile widened, revealing sharp incisors. "Wouldn't you agree?"

The memory dredged up every emotion from that meeting and poured them into the pit of my stomach.

The shock. The disbelief. The fucking *rage* at both my brother and the bastard who'd had the balls to show up uninvited to *my* office and blackmail me.

No, Francis Lau didn't deserve any mercy from me.

I turned my back to the dining room. Cold finality settled in my chest as I made my decision.

"Take him down."

After I hung up, I returned to dinner and tried my best to act normal. Vivian didn't say anything at the restaurant, but when we returned to our hotel, she cast a concerned look at me.

"Is everything okay?" she asked. "You've been quiet since the call."

"Everything's fine." I shrugged off my jacket and avoided her eyes. "Just annoyed it interrupted our dinner."

"It was still a good dinner." She sighed and sat on the bed with a dreamy smile. "I'll dream of that dessert for the rest of my life."

"The dessert and not me? I'm offended."

Vivian rolled her eyes. "Not everything revolves around you, Dante."

"It should." I smiled at the way her nose scrunched even as my heart twisted.

On the surface, our banter was playful as always. But a clock ticked beneath the lightheartedness, audible only to me as it counted down our moments together.

I should tell her the truth. If not now, then when we landed in New York. She'd find out sooner or later, and I wanted her to hear it from me. But the thought of telling her about the blackmail and shattering the last idealistic notions she had of her father, of confessing to what I'd authorized Christian to do…it tore at me like a knife in the chest.

These were our last moments together, and I was selfish enough to hoard them to myself.

Vivian let out a breathless laugh when I pushed her onto her back and straddled her, my movements gentle enough that she landed with a soft thud rather than something more jarring. She stared up at me, her earlier mock annoyance melting into a smile that made my heart ache.

"Last night in France." I lowered my head so my lips grazed hers with each word. "I wonder how we should spend it…"

"Well, I'd originally planned to take a long bath, read, maybe put on that face mask you said makes me look like Jason from *Friday the 13th*…" Vivian mused, her eyes glinting with laughter and banked heat. "But perhaps you have a better idea."

"I might." I placed a soft kiss on her mouth as I slowly unzipped her dress. The silky material slackened, and I gently lifted her so I could ease off the rest of her clothes.

Normally, I would've been too impatient to go this slow, but tonight, I let my touch linger on every curve and dip. I mapped her body with my mouth and hands, caressing her breasts through her bra and tugging her underwear off with my teeth, inch by torturous inch, until she whimpered with frustration.

"Dante, *please*," she breathed, her skin flushed with pleasure even though I'd barely touched her yet.

My groan vibrated against her skin. I wanted to drag this night out as long as possible, but I couldn't deny her anything. Not when she was looking at me with those eyes and pleading with me in that voice.

I tossed her underwear to the side and took in the perfect sight in front of me. "Fuck, baby, you're so wet for me."

She whimpered again when I gently scraped my teeth over her clit. Once, twice, letting her warm up to the sensation before I drew the sensitive bud into my mouth and sucked.

Vivian's escalating cries were music to my ears as I brought her to her first orgasm of the night. I could listen to her forever—the soft moans, the little gasps and whimpers, and the way she called my name when she came on my tongue. It was the sweetest, dirtiest symphony I'd ever heard.

She was still coming down from her high when I slid inside her.

Another groan climbed up my throat at how tight and wet she was. Her body fit mine the way the ocean hugged the shore—naturally, effortlessly, perfectly.

I held still, kissing my way up her neck and capturing her mouth in a kiss before I started moving.

Vivian's sighs of pleasure vibrated through my body as I glided in and out of her in a slow, sensual rhythm. It took all my willpower to maintain an unhurried pace when she felt so fucking perfect, but I wanted to savor every second.

Eventually, however, my control slipped, and I picked up my pace. I bit back a curse when she arched into me, taking me deeper still.

"Faster," she begged, her voice breathy with desire. "*Please.*"

I gritted my teeth, my muscles taut with the strain of holding back my release. Sweat beaded along my forehead.

"*Se sapessi il potere che hai su di me,*" I said, my voice ragged.

I paused for a second before I gripped her hips and gave her what she asked for, fucking into her harder and faster until her nails dug grooves in my back.

Vivian's eyes were half-closed, her cheeks flushed with pleasure, and her lips half-parted as moan after moan poured out. She looked so beautiful I almost couldn't believe she was real.

My gaze lingered on her face, trying to imprint every detail to memory before I kissed her again. I swallowed her cry of release as she clamped around me.

I held on for another minute before my control finally snapped and my own orgasm washed through me in a hot, blinding rush.

"Well," Vivian breathed after I rolled onto my side next to her. "That was definitely more fun than a bath."

I chuckled even as guilt edged back into my consciousness and carved a hole in my chest. "My ego thanks you for the confirmation."

"Tell it you're welcome." She yawned and snuggled closer to me, draping one arm and leg over my body. "This was the perfect last night," she murmured. "We should…" Another yawn. "Come to Paris more often. Next time..." A third yawn. "Let's go to the…"

Her drowsy voice trailed off into silence. I pressed my lips to the top of her head as her breaths slowed into a deep, even rhythm.

I tried to sleep, but the heavy ache in my chest left me restless. Instead, I stared at the ceiling, counting her breaths, wondering how many more we had left before everything fell apart.

It would take Christian one day to destroy the evidence. One or two for Francis to realize what happened, depending on how closely he monitored the backup sites. And a couple more for the effects of the business takedown to be noticeable.

Realistically, I could tell Vivian the truth when we landed in New York. I'd rather her hear it from me than her father, who would undoubtedly try to twist things in a way that made him look like the victim.

But...*fuck*. I couldn't drop a bombshell on her just like that. At the same time, I couldn't pretend everything was okay and allow her in even more than I already had. Not when our break was inevitable.

Other people spent years trying to get close to me. Vivian didn't even have to try. Every minute we spent together was another chip away at my defenses, whether she knew it or not.

If I let her father off the hook, I could maybe salvage what we had. Even if she found he was a piece of shit, she was too loyal to her family to forgive me for destroying them. And if she *was*, by some miracle, okay with me taking down her father, could our relationship survive the aftermath? I damn sure wasn't going to sit across from the Laus at Thanksgiving every year and make nice, and I doubted they'd welcome me anyway.

I couldn't keep her, and I couldn't let her go.

Not yet.

I closed my eyes, trying to find the best way out of this clusterfuck. Logic told me I'd already stolen my moments with her tonight and that I needed to distance myself before I fell any deeper. Emotion told me to fuck logic and tell it to shove its reason up its ass.

My head or my heart. One of them would win.

I just didn't know which one.

CHAPTER 32

Vivian

I LEFT PARIS ON A BLISSFUL HIGH.

Delicious food. Beautiful clothes. Amazing sex. I'd worked during my time there, but it'd felt like more of a vacation than some of my actual vacations.

Plus, the Legacy Ball planning was *finally* running smoothly, wedding prep was on track, and my relationship with Dante was the best it'd ever been.

Life was good.

"It was awful," Sloane said as we exited the movie theater. "What was with the airplane scene? And the *love confession*. I would throw up if anyone compared me to the planet Venus, especially after knowing me for only three weeks. How could anyone possibly fall in love in three weeks?"

Isabella and I traded amused glances. We'd had to postpone our movie night due to my Paris trip, but we'd finally watched the rom-com Sloane had been hounding us about.

As expected, she hated it.

"Time works differently in fiction," I said. "You know you can stop watching these movies any time, right?"

"I hate-watch them, Vivian. It's therapeutic."

"Mm-hmm."

I caught Isabella's eye again, and we both turned away so Sloane couldn't see our smiles.

"Anyway, I have to go home and feed The Fish before he dies on me." Sloane sounded like the task was equivalent to scrubbing the subway tunnels clean with a toothbrush. "I have enough on my plate without having to deal with a dead animal."

She'd kept the goldfish her apartment's previous tenant left behind, but she refused to give him a proper name since its presence in her life was "temporary."

It'd been over a year.

Isabella and I knew better than to mention it though, so we simply bid her good night and parted ways.

I stopped by Dante's favorite Thai place on the way home. Greta was on her annual leave in Italy, so we were on our own, food-wise, for the next few weeks.

"Is Dante home yet?" I asked Edward when I returned to the penthouse.

"Yes, ma'am. He's in his office."

"Great. Thank you." I'd tried to get Edward to call me by my first name when I first moved in, but I gave up after two months.

I knocked on Dante's office door and waited for his "Come in" before I entered.

He sat behind his desk, his brow furrowed as he stared at something on his monitor. He must've just gotten home since he still wore his office suit.

"Hey." I placed the food on the table and kissed him on the cheek. "It's after work hours. You're supposed to be relaxing."

"It's not after work hours in Asia." He pushed back from his desk and rubbed his temple. He eyed the takeout bag on the desk. "What's this?"

"Dinner." I retrieved the assorted plastic containers, napkins, and utensils. "From that Thai place you like so much on East Seventy-Eighth. I wasn't sure what you were in the mood for, so I got curry puffs, basil stir-fry, *and…*" I opened the last container with a flourish. "Their signature duck salad."

Dante loved that duck salad. One time, he pushed back a call with the editor in chief of *Mode de Vie* just so he could eat it while it was still hot.

He stared at it, his expression inscrutable.

"Thank you, but I'm not hungry." He turned back to his computer. "I really have to get this done in the next hour. Can you close the door on your way out?"

My smile melted at his brusque tone.

He'd been acting a little distant since we returned to New York two days ago, but tonight was the first time he'd been so blatantly dismissive.

"Okay." I tried to keep my voice upbeat. "But you still have to eat. I'll leave this here in case you get hungry later." I paused, then added, "How's work going? Overall, I mean."

He was under a lot of stress with various supply chain issues and the upcoming Cannes Film Festival, of which the Russo Group was a sponsor. I couldn't blame him for being a bit short-tempered.

"Fine." He didn't look away from his screen.

Tension lined his stiff shoulders and shadowed his features. He looked like a completely different person from the teasing, playful Dante in Paris.

"If anything's wrong, you can talk to me about it," I said softly. "You know that, right?"

Dante's throat worked with a hard swallow.

When the silence stretched without any sign of a break, I gathered my portion of the dinner and ate it alone in the dining room. The food smelled delicious, but when I swallowed it, it tasted like cardboard.

Dante's broodiness didn't improve over the next week.

Maybe it was work. Maybe it was something else. Whatever it was, it transformed him back into the cold, closed-off version of himself that made me want to tear my hair out.

The change in his attitude before and after Paris was so jarring I felt like we'd stumbled into a time portal and become stranded in the early days of our engagement.

He didn't visit me for lunch, he was always "busy" during dinner, and he didn't come to bed until long after I was asleep. When I woke up, he was already gone. We talked almost less than we had sex, which was never.

I tried to be understanding because everyone had their dark periods, but by the time the following Thursday rolled around, my patience had edged into the red zone. The straw that broke the camel's back came that evening, when I returned home from work to find Dante in the kitchen with Greta. She'd just gotten back from visiting her family in Naples, or Napoli, as she called it in Italian. However, she was already hard at work again—the marble island and counters groaned beneath the weight of various herbs, sauces, fish, and meats.

The smell beckoned me from the foyer, but when I entered the room, both she and Dante fell silent.

"Good evening, Miss Lau," Greta said. When we were alone, she called me Vivian, but around other people, I was always Miss Lau.

"Good evening." I scanned the banquet-worthy prep. "Are we having a party I don't know about? This seems like a lot of food for two people."

"It is," she said after a brief pause. She frowned and flicked a glance at a stone-faced Dante before busying herself with the food.

My heart accelerated. "*Are* we having a party?"

"Of course not," Dante said when Greta remained silent. He didn't give me a chance to relax before he added, "Christian and his girlfriend are coming over for dinner tonight. They're in town for a few days."

"*Tonight?*" I glanced at the clock. "Dinner is in less than three hours!"

"Which is why I came home early."

Breathe. Do not yell. Do not throw the bowl of tomatoes at his head.

"Were you going to tell me we're expecting guests, or was this supposed to be a surprise?" My fingers strangled the strap of my bag. "Or am I not invited to the meal altogether?"

Greta chopped faster, her eyes fixed firmly on the garlic.

"Don't be ridiculous," Dante said.

Ridiculous? *Ridiculous?*

My patience snapped clean in half. I'd tried my best to be sympathetic, but I was sick of him treating me like a stranger he was forced to share a house with. After the magic of Paris and the progress we'd made over the past few months, our relationship had suddenly regressed to where it'd been the summer of last year.

Then, it'd been understandable.

Now, after all we'd shared? It was unacceptable.

"Which part is ridiculous?" I demanded. "The part where I ask my fiancé for the common courtesy of informing me when we have guests over to *our* house? Or the part where we've grown so far apart in the space of one week that I wouldn't be surprised if you *did* exclude me? I'd like to know, because I'm damn well not the one being unreasonable here!"

Greta's knife hovered, suspended, over the cutting board while she gaped at me with wide eyes.

It was the first time I'd raised my voice in front of her since I moved in and only the fourth time I'd raised my voice ever. The first had been when my sister "borrowed" and lost one of my favorite signed books in high school. The second had been when my parents forced me to break up with Heath, and the third had been the night Dante found Heath in the apartment.

Dante's skin stretched taut over his cheekbones. The tension was so stifling it took on a life of its own, crawling into my lungs and sinking into my skin. The air-conditioned room blazed like we were in the middle of the desert at high noon.

"I just remembered I'm expecting a grocery delivery soon," Greta said. "Let me check where they are." She dropped her knife and bolted faster than an Olympian competing for gold.

Normally, I would've been embarrassed about making a scene, but I was too fired up to care.

"It's a dinner," Dante growled. "Christian didn't tell me he'd be in town until yesterday. You're making a big deal out of nothing."

"Then you could've told me he was coming over yesterday!" My voice rose again before I forced more oxygen through my nose. "It's not about the dinner, Dante. It's about your *refusal* to communicate like a normal person. I thought we were past this." Emotion clogged my throat. "We promised we wouldn't do this. Act like strangers. Shut down whenever things got hard. We're supposed to be partners."

Dante rubbed a hand over his face. When it fell away, I glimpsed the conflict in his eyes—remorse and guilt at war with frustration and something else that chilled the breath in my lungs.

"There are some things you're better off not knowing, *mia cara*." The endearment I'd initially despised and grown to love barely touched my skin before it dissolved. Soft yet rough, like the churn of waves in a raging storm.

The wistful notes lingered for an extra beat before his face shut down again.

"I'll see you at dinner."

He walked out, leaving me with a pit in my stomach and the unshakeable sense that our relationship had somehow been fundamentally altered.

CHAPTER 33

Vivian

DANTE AND I BARELY EXCHANGED A WORD DURING dinner. I did, however, push his fish into his vegetables when he wasn't looking and delighted in his look of absolute horror when he saw his food had touched.

Besides that one petty act of retribution for his behavior, I focused my attention on Christian and his girlfriend, Stella. Christian was perfectly charming, as always, but something about him made me uneasy. He reminded me of a wolf dressed in perfectly tailored sheep's clothing.

Stella, on the other hand, was warm and friendly, if a bit shy. We spent the majority of dinner discussing travel, astrology, and her new ambassadorship with the fashion label Delamonte, which was, coincidentally, a Russo Group brand.

As far as last-minute dinner guests went, it could've been much worse.

After dessert, I took Stella on a tour of the penthouse while Dante and Christian discussed business. It was mostly an excuse to catch my breath after hours of underlying tension between me and Dante, but I genuinely enjoyed Stella's company.

"Don't ask," I said when she tilted her head at one of the paintings in the gallery. The hideous piece stood out like a sore thumb among all the Picassos and Rembrandts. "I don't know why Dante bought that. He usually has more discerning taste."

"It must be worth a lot of money," Stella said as we made our way back to the dining room.

"Apparently. Proof price isn't always indicative of quality," I said dryly.

Our footsteps echoed against the marble floors, but my steps slowed when I heard the familiar rumble of Dante's voice trickling through his office door. I hadn't realized they'd moved from the dining room.

"…can't keep Magda forever," he said. "You should be glad I didn't throw it in the trash after the stunt you pulled with Vivian and Heath."

My throat dried at the unexpected mention of my and Heath's names.

What stunt? Save for an awkward phone call during which I'd checked on his nose (less bruised than his ego) and told him we shouldn't be in contact anymore, I hadn't talked to Heath since he showed up at the apartment.

I also couldn't imagine why Christian would take an interest in either of us. How did he even know Heath? He was big in the cyber world, and Heath owned a tech startup, but that connection seemed tenuous at best.

"It's a fucking painting, not a wild animal," Christian said. "As for Vivian, it's been months, and it worked out fine. Let it go. If you're still pissed, you shouldn't have invited me to dinner."

"Be glad things *worked out fine* with Vivian." Dante's tone could've iced the inside of a volcano. I swallowed, trying to moisten the sudden desert in my throat. It didn't work. "If—"

I couldn't contain my cough any longer. The sound spilled out of me and cut his sentence short.

Two seconds later, the door swung open, revealing two surprised and none-too-pleased faces.

A faint hint of red colored Dante's cheekbones when he saw me. "I see you've finished the tour early."

"Sorry." Stella spoke up, looking embarrassed. "We were on our way to the dining room and heard…" She trailed off, obviously not wanting to admit we'd been eavesdropping even though that was clearly what we were doing.

I should jump in and save her, but all I could do was give a forced smile as Christian and Stella thanked us for dinner and quickly excused themselves.

"What Heath stunt was he talking about?" I found my voice in the silence following their departure.

"Nothing you need to worry about." Dante's clipped voice didn't match the darkening red of his cheeks. "He was being an asshole, as always."

"Considering he mentioned me and my ex-boyfriend by name, I think I *do* need to worry about it." I crossed my arms. "I won't stop asking, so you might as well tell me now."

More silence.

"Christian was the one who sent the text to Heath," he finally said. "The one that was supposedly from you."

My stomach hollowed, and icy shock rushed to fill the void. "Why would he do that?"

"I told you. Because he's an asshole." A small pause, then a reluctant, "I may have provoked him, but he's easily provoked."

"That's why you came home early," I realized.

In all my years as CEO, I've only cut a work trip short twice, Vivian, and both those instances were because of you.

I'd glossed over the specifics of what he said at the time because

I'd been too distracted by everything else happening, but his words suddenly made sense.

"Why didn't you tell me earlier?" I regretted eating so much at dinner. I was starting to feel nauseous. "Even when I said I didn't know how he got the text, you didn't say anything."

"It was irrelevant."

"That wasn't for you to decide!" I eased a deep breath into my lungs. "I don't know what you did to Christian, but I *don't* appreciate being used as a pawn in whatever game you two are playing."

I felt like enough of a pawn with my parents. I didn't want or need to feel that way with Dante too.

"It's not a game," Dante gritted out. "Christian got pissed and did something stupid. What would me telling you have accomplished? You would've just gotten upset over something that already happened."

"The fact that you don't know what the problem is *is* the problem." I turned, too tired to argue anymore. "Find me when you're ready to talk like an adult."

Relationships were a give-and-take, and right now, I was tired of giving.

The next morning, I woke up early to clear my head in Central Park. After forty-five minutes of aimless wandering, last night's embers of indignation still flickered in my stomach, so I did what I always did when I needed to vent: I called my sister.

She grew up with our parents too, and she'd gone through the whole arranged marriage process. If anyone understood me, she did.

"Have you ever wanted to murder Gunnar?" The number of times I'd considered murder since I got engaged to Dante was alarming. Maybe it was a quirk of being married or almost married.

Agnes laughed. "On multiple occasions, usually when he refuses to pick up his socks or ask for directions when we're already late. But I don't have the stomach for blood, so he's safe. For now."

I huffed out a laugh. "If only my problems were as simple as socks on the ground."

"Uh-oh. Did you and Dante get in a fight?"

"Yes and no." I briefly summarized what happened, starting with his weird attitude shift after Paris and ending with the revelation about the text last night.

I hadn't realized how long Agnes and I had gone without talking until now. We used to call each other every week, but it was harder now with our schedules and her living in Europe.

"Wow," Agnes said after I finished. "You've had an...interesting few weeks."

"Tell me about it." I ran the toe of my leather Chloé flat along a crack in the ground. My mother would yell at me about scuffing my shoe, but she wasn't here, so I didn't care what she would say. "I feel like we're regressing," I said. "We were doing so well. He was opening up, communicating...and now we're back to square one. He's silent and withdrawn, and I'm *frustrated*. I can't do this for the rest of my life, Aggie. I'll...oh my God. We'll be the couple in the Netflix documentary," I realized, horrified. "*Love and Murder: The Couple Next Door.*"

"What?"

"Never mind."

"Okay, here's what I think. You're *not* back to square one," she said. "Remember when you first got engaged? You couldn't stand each other. You've come a long way since then, even if you've taken a few steps back recently."

I sighed. "I hate how you're always right."

"That's why I'm the older sister," she quipped. "Look, Gunnar and I weren't huge fans of each other when we met either. There was a point during the engagement when I came *this* close to calling the whole thing off."

My foot stopped fidgeting. "Really? But you two are so in love."

"We are now, but it wasn't a love that hit us at first sight. Or second or third. We had to work for it," Agnes said. "Two days before we visited Mom and Dad for Lunar New Year—remember when Mom freaked out about the sticky rice balls not being sticky enough?—we got lost during a hike and had a *huge* fight. I was ready to throw my ring over the side of the mountain and push Gunnar after it. But we survived, as did our relationship." A dog barked in the background, and Agnes waited for it to quiet before continuing, "No one's perfect. Sometimes, our partners will do things that drive us mad. I know I have habits Gunnar can't stand. But the difference between the couples who make it and those who don't is one, understanding what your deal breakers are, and two, being willing to stick it out through the issues that *aren't* deal breakers."

"You should be a relationship counselor," I said. "Your talent is wasted on jewelry marketing."

She laughed. "I'll keep that in mind. Just don't tell Dad, or he'll make *you* take the chief marketing officer role."

I wrinkled my nose at the prospect.

"Would you have really called off the wedding?" Agnes had always been the "better" daughter out of the two of us. More accommodating, less sarcastic. I couldn't resist a subtle dig now and then, but she was unfailingly genteel at home. "Mom and Dad would've..."

"Probably disowned me," she finished. "I know. But as much as I wanted to make them happy, I couldn't have tied myself to someone I didn't like for the rest of my life. That's one thing I've realized now that I'm older, Vivi. You can't live your life trying to please others. You can be courteous and respectful, and you can compromise, but when it comes down to it? It's your life. Don't waste it."

Emotion tangled in my throat. I wasn't sad or upset, but Agnes's words hit me somewhere that made tears prickle the backs of my eyes.

"But it all worked out for you," I said.

My sister and her husband, Gunnar, were the epitome of rustic wedded bliss. When he wasn't in Athenberg for parliamentary proceedings, they spent their time shopping at the local farmers' market and cooking together. Their countryside manor in Eldorra looked like something out of a fairy tale, complete with two horses, three dogs, and, randomly, one sheep. Our mom refused to stay there whenever she visited because she hated how the animals shed everywhere. I think that only encouraged Agnes to get more pets.

"Yes. I'm very lucky." Agnes's voice softened. "Like I said, it took time and effort, but we figured it out. I think you and Dante can too. I may not be entrenched in East Coast society circles anymore, but I'm well aware of his reputation. He wouldn't have opened up the way he had if he didn't have deep feelings for you. The question is, do you have the same feelings toward him?"

I stared across the lake at the buildings gleaming in the distance. I stood at the far end of the Gapstow Bridge, one of my favorite places in Central Park. The crowds were starting to trickle in, but it was early enough that I could still hear the birds chirping in the background.

Dante was out there. Eating, showering, and doing normal everyday things that shouldn't have the impact they had on me. But as mad as I was at him and as withdrawn as he'd been, just knowing he existed made me feel a little less alone.

"Yes," I said quietly. "I do."

"I figured as much." I heard the smile in Agnes's voice. "Do you still need to vent, or do you feel better?"

"I'm okay for now. Thanks for keeping me out of jail," I said with a laugh.

"What are older sisters for?" I heard the dog bark again, followed by the low murmur of Gunnar's voice. "I have to go. We're flying to Athenberg tonight for Queen Bridget's spring ball, and I haven't finished packing. But call me if you need me, okay? And when you get a chance, check on Dad."

Alarm bells clanged in my head. "Why, what's wrong? Is he sick?" He'd sounded fine when we talked two weeks ago, before I left for Paris.

"No, nothing like that," Agnes assured me. "He just sounded off when I called him a few days ago. I'm probably overthinking it, but I live so far away...it would make me feel better if you checked in on him."

"I will. Enjoy the ball."

I stayed in the park for another hour after I hung up. In some ways, my talk with my sister provided much-needed clarity regarding my relationship with Dante. Venting *did* make me feel better, and as aggravating as Dante's attitude had been, it wasn't a deal breaker. Yet.

But what were my actual deal breakers? Cheating and violence were nonnegotiable. But what about lying? Different values? Lack of trust and communication? Where did I draw the line between what I could compromise on, like a little white lie about something small, and what I couldn't?

I wished there was a definitive guidebook out there for this type of thing. I would pay good money for it.

I would've stayed in the park longer, but the previously blue skies suddenly darkened. The wind picked up, and storm clouds gathered overhead, threatening rain.

I quickly joined the other people streaming toward the exit, but I only made it a quarter of the way before rain gushed down, heavy and sudden, like the heavens were dumping buckets of water over the side of a balcony. Jagged lightning slashed across the sky, accompanied by deafening crashes of thunder.

A curse escaped when I stepped into a puddle and almost slipped. Water plastered my clothes to my skin, and I tried not to think about how transparent my white shirt must be right now.

It'd been such a beautiful day minutes ago, but that was the unpredictability of a New York spring. One second, it was blue skies and sunshine. The next, it was storming like the world was ending.

CHAPTER 34

Vivian

ON MONDAY, I PICKED UP TAKEOUT FROM THE Moondust Diner and brought it to Dante's office for lunch. A burger and his favorite black-and-white shake for him, a chicken sandwich and a strawberry shake for me.

It was a throwback to our first date and an olive branch on my part. Dante was the one who needed to extend the branch, but if I shut down whenever he shut down, we'd never get anywhere. I didn't want us to be one of those couples who stewed in passive-aggressive silence.

Plus, there had to be a good reason why Dante was acting so weird, and I was determined to find out what it was.

"Good afternoon, Ms. Lau." Stacey, the receptionist for the Russo Group's executive floor, greeted me with a bright smile.

"Hi, Stacey. I brought some lunch for Dante." I held up the paper bags. "Is he in his office?"

It was my first time showing up unannounced at his workplace. He could've eaten lunch already, but knowing him, he hadn't. If we didn't eat together, he was likely to skip his afternoon meals altogether.

"Yes, but he's in a meeting," she said after a brief moment of hesitation. "I'm not sure when he'll be out."

"That's all right. I can wait for him in the guest lounge."

I could easily answer emails and check in with the wedding vendors on my phone while I waited. The Legacy Ball was my top priority for now, but once it was over, I needed to double down on wedding prep.

"Are you sure?" Stacey sounded doubtful.

When I reassured her I was okay with waiting, she relented.

The floor had emptied for lunch, and my flats fell softly on white marble as I made my way through the office. The Russo Group's corporate headquarters was a study in sleek modernity mixed with old-world elegance. Black lacquer and glass reflected ornate gold accents and gilt-framed paintings; lush flowers blossomed next to sculptural stoneware painted in varying neutral shades.

The guest lounge sat at the far end of the floor, but I only made it halfway when I heard a familiar voice—one that *didn't* belong to Dante.

My stride broke a few feet outside Dante's office. The tinted windows prevented me from seeing inside, but the tense conversation within bled through the door.

"You have no idea what you've done." My father's harsh timbre skated down my spine, leaving trails of ice in its wake.

If the rest of the floor hadn't been so quiet, I wouldn't have been able to hear him. As it stood, his words came through faint but clear.

My heart picked up pace. I'd planned to check on him later as Agnes had suggested, but I never would've guessed he would be *here*. Right now, in Dante's office, without so much as a warning or notice.

My father rarely visited New York during the workweek, and he never dropped in without telling me either before or right after he landed. So what was he doing here on a random Monday afternoon?

"I know precisely what I've done," Dante drawled. Low. Dark. *Deadly*. "The last time you showed up uninvited, you had the upper hand. You used my brother to get to me. I've simply evened the scales."

His brother. *Luca*.

My stomach hollowed. What had my father done?

"No, you haven't. You didn't find all of them." Despite his confident delivery, my father's voice dipped toward the end. It was a nervous tic I'd picked up on when I was a teenager.

"If I didn't, you wouldn't be here," Dante said, sounding at once amused and indifferent. "You would've run to Romano with one of your backups. Yet you took the time out of your *busy* workday to fly to New York and see me. It doesn't scream *upper hand* anymore, Francis. It screams pathetic." A small rustle. "I suggest you return to Boston and deal with your company instead of embarrassing yourself further. I've heard it could use some help."

A long silence followed, punctuated by the rapid thuds of my heart.

"You're responsible for the fake reports." Realization, fury, and a hint of panic rolled beneath my father's accusation, threatening to split it apart at the seams.

"I don't know what you're talking about." Dante's tone maintained its indifference. "But it seems serious. All the more reason for you to leave and get a handle on things before the press catches wind of it. You know how...vicious they can get once they scent blood."

"Fuck the press!" My father's voice escalated into a shout. "What the *fuck* did you do to my company, Russo?"

"Nothing it didn't deserve. Hypothetically speaking, of course."

The paper bags crumpled in my fist. Blood roared in my ears, making their conversation that much harder to hear, but I forced myself to strain and listen.

I had to know what they were talking about. I had to confirm the horrible inkling in my stomach…even if it destroyed me.

"Vivian will never forgive you for this." My father's snarl was that of a wounded tiger. I'd never heard him so angry, not even when Agnes and I broke his favorite Ming vase while playing hide-and-seek as children.

A brief, loaded pause.

"You're assuming I care what she thinks." Dante's voice was so cold it turned my blood to ice. "Might I remind you I was *forced* into this engagement? I never willingly chose her as my fiancée. You blackmailed me into it, Francis, and now, your leverage is gone. So don't come into *my* fucking office and try to use your daughter to save yourself. It won't work."

"If you don't care, then why haven't you broken the engagement yet?" my father taunted. "Like you said, you were forced into it. The first thing you should've done after getting rid of the photos was get rid of *her*."

A painful crack in my chest drowned out Dante's reply. A burn ignited somewhere north of my heart and spread behind my eyes, so intense I feared it would leave nothing except ashes behind.

I was forced *into this engagement…*

I never willingly chose her…

You blackmailed me into it…

The words echoed in my head like a nightmare stuck on a broken loop.

Suddenly, it all made sense. Why Dante agreed to marry me when he didn't need my father's business, money, *or* connections. Why he'd been so cold toward me at the start of our engagement. Why Luca had disliked me, and why my intuition had always questioned the reasoning Dante gave for the engagement. I'd overlooked the flimsiness of the market access excuse because it'd been the only plausible one at the time, but now...

The omelet I ate for breakfast rose in my throat. My skin flushed hot, then cold, while an army of invisible spiders crawled over my arms and chest.

I should leave before they caught me eavesdropping, but I couldn't breathe. Couldn't think. Couldn't do anything except stand there while my world crumbled around me.

I never willingly chose her.

You blackmailed me into it.

The burn liquefied and blurred my vision. The astronomy date, the Paris trip, and all the little moments in between. Had he been pretending this whole time? Trying to make the most out of a bad situation instead of—

A burst of laughter down the hall yanked me out of my spiraling thoughts. My head jerked up in time to see two suited men walking toward me, filled with the type of swagger one only possessed if they sat in the C-suite of a multibillion-dollar company.

Their arrival broke the immobility spell holding me hostage.

The one on the right noticed me first, but by the time his face lit with recognition, I was already rushing past him, my head ducked and my gaze fixed on the floor ahead.

Just get to the exit. Get to the exit and go downstairs. That's all you need to do.

Five more steps.

Four.

Three.

Two.

One.

I burst into the lobby like a swimmer gasping for air.

I shoved the food at an alarmed-looking Stacey and mumbled

something about a work emergency before I jabbed at the elevator button. Thankfully, it came in seconds.

I stepped inside, the car plummeted toward the ground, and I finally, *finally* let my tears fall.

Dante

"If you don't care, then why haven't you broken the engagement yet?" Francis's eyes glinted with challenge. "Like you said, you were forced into it. The first thing you should've done after getting rid of the photos was get rid of her."

Red crept into my vision. He said *getting rid of her* so easily, like he was discussing a piece of furniture instead of his daughter.

How a piece of shit like Francis shared genes with Vivian, I'd never understand.

He looked like shit now too. Sallow complexion. Dark circles. Grooves of exhaustion in his face. Christian's meddling with his company's internal affairs had taken its toll on him.

I would've taken greater pleasure in his suffering had the mention of Vivian not been a stab to the chest. Shutting her out for a week had been painful enough. Hearing her name come out of her dirtbag father's mouth, knowing what it meant for our relationship…

I clenched my jaw and forced my expression to remain neutral.

"Our conversation is done." I sidestepped Francis's question and deliberately checked my watch. "You've already wasted my lunch hour. Leave, or I'll have security escort you out."

"Those reports are *bullshit*." Francis's knuckles popped from the force of his grip on the armrests. "I've worked decades to build my company. You were still a fetus when I started Lau Jewels, and I won't let a silver spoon–fed, nepotistic child like you ruin it."

"You were all too happy to have said silver spoon–fed, nepotistic child marry your daughter," I said silkily. "To the point where *you* fucked up and blackmailed him. I don't like being threatened, Francis. And I always pay it back threefold. Now..." I tapped my desk phone. "Do I need to call my guards, or are you capable of walking yourself out?"

Francis trembled with outrage, but he wasn't stupid enough to test me any further. He'd stormed in half an hour ago, full of fire and bravado. Now, he looked as pathetic and powerless as he really was.

He pushed his chair back and left without another word. The door slammed behind him, rattling the paintings on the wall.

That fucker. He was lucky none of them fell.

I barely had a chance to enjoy the silence before a knock sounded.

For Christ's sake, what did a guy have to do for some actual quiet and work time?

"Come in."

The door opened, revealing a nervous-looking Stacey. "I'm sorry to interrupt, Mr. Russo," she said. "But your fiancée dropped off lunch for you. I wanted to get it to you while it's still hot."

The temperature instantly dropped ten degrees.

A buzz of trepidation crawled over me and snaked into my veins. "My fiancée? When was she here?"

"Maybe ten minutes ago? She said she was going to wait for you in the guest lounge, but she left in a hurry and dropped this at my desk." Stacey raised two takeout bags in the air. They were stamped with the Moondust Diner's distinctive black-and-silver logo.

The buzz turned into a thousand icy needles piercing my skin. Vivian wouldn't have left without saying hi unless...

Fuck. Fuck, fuck, *fuck!*

I stood so abruptly I banged my knee against the underside of my desk. I didn't even register my pain through the rush of blood in my ears.

"Where are you…" Stacey faltered when I yanked my jacket off the back of my desk chair and brushed past her into the hall.

"Have Helena cancel the rest of my in-person meetings today when she gets back." I forced the words past my tight throat. "I'm working from home for the rest of the day."

I was already halfway to the exit when she replied.

"What about your food?" she called after me. Stacey sounded panicked, like my missing lunch would be cause for firing her.

"Keep it." I didn't give a shit if she ate it, fed it to the pigeons, or used it for performance art in the middle of goddamned Fifth Avenue.

Ten interminable minutes later—that damn elevator moved at the speed of a snail on morphine—I exited the building, my skin clammy and my heartbeat spiking with sudden, indescribable panic. I didn't know how, but I knew with bone-deep certainty Vivian was at home instead of her office.

My apartment was only five blocks away. Walking was faster than taking a car, though not necessarily safer. I was so distracted by the dread leaking into my stomach I almost got mowed down twice, once by a foul-mouthed bike messenger and once by a cab taking a corner too fast.

By the time I entered the cool, air-conditioned foyer of my penthouse, my mouth tasted like pennies and a thin sheen of sweat misted my skin.

I shouldn't be this twisted over the fact that Vivian might've overheard me talking with her father. Everything I'd said had been the truth, and she would find out sooner or later. Hell, I'd been bracing myself for this moment since Paris. But there was a difference between theory and reality. And the reality was, when I stopped in the doorway of our room and saw her open suitcase on our bed, I felt like I'd been sucker punched in the gut and dragged over hot coals, all in the space of two minutes.

Vivian walked out of the closet with an armful of clothes. Her steps halted when she saw me, and a painful, breathless silence stretched between us before she moved again. She dumped her clothes on the bed while I watched, my heart pounding hard enough to bruise.

"Were you going to leave without telling me?" Roughness edged my question.

"I'm doing you a favor." Vivian didn't look at me, but her hands shook as she folded and packed her clothes. "I'm saving you from a hard conversation. I heard you, Dante. You don't want me here. You *never* wanted me here. So I'm leaving."

There it was. No ifs, ands, or buts about it. She'd learned the truth, and this was her way of dealing with it.

My hands fisted.

She was right. She *was* doing me a favor. If she left, no questions asked, she'd sever the last tie I had to the Laus with little to no effort on my part. I could wipe my hands clean of her family and move on.

And yet…

"That's it? After eight months, after finding out what your father did…" *And what I did…* "That's all you have to say?"

Vivian finally looked up. Red rimmed her eyes, but fire flashed in the brown depths.

"What do you want me to say?" she demanded. "Do you want me to ask what my father had on you? To ask whether the past two months meant anything or if you were just trying to make the most out of a shitty situation until you could get rid of me? Do you want me to tell you how *devastating* it is to find out your father is…is…" Her voice broke. She turned away, but not before I glimpsed the tear streaking down her cheek.

My chest crushed like ice beneath a speeding truck.

"Do you know how it feels to learn your fiancé was only with you because he was *forced* into it? To think we were actually getting closer when you secretly hated me? Not that I blame you." She let out a bitter laugh. "If I were in your position, I would hate me too."

It took every ounce of effort to swallow past the lump in my throat.

"I don't hate you," I said, my voice low.

I've never hated you.

No matter what Vivian did or who she was related to, I could never hate her. It was the one thing I hated about *myself*.

"Your father had...incriminating photos of my brother." I didn't know why I was explaining. She'd made it clear she didn't care, but I kept talking anyway, the words falling out faster the more she packed. "He would've died if they landed in the wrong hands."

I told her about the backups, her father's ultimatum, and his insistence I keep her in the dark about the blackmail. I told her about the Paris call and even how I figured out there were eight copies of the evidence.

When I finished, her skin was two shades paler than when I'd started. "And my father's company?"

A lengthy silence pervaded the space.

That was the one part I'd left out. An important part, but one that made my heart pinch when I finally said, "I did what I had to do. No one threatens a Russo."

My gaze fixed on Vivian while she processed my reply. The air crackled with a thousand tiny stinging wasps on my skin.

How would she react to my veiled confession? With anger? Shock? Disappointment?

Regardless of her feelings toward her father right now, I

couldn't imagine she'd be okay with me tampering with her family's company. But to my surprise, Vivian didn't betray any visible emotion beyond a tightening of her features.

"I'm sorry for what my father did," she said. "But why are you telling me this now? You were fine with keeping me in the dark until now."

My hands fisted again. "I wanted to clear the air," I said stiffly. "Before..." *You left.* "We parted ways."

If you don't care, then why haven't you broken the engagement yet?

Francis's question haunted me. I could've told her any time over the past week, but I'd stalled. Made excuses. Told myself I was preparing her for our break by pulling away when, in reality, I simply hadn't been ready to let her go.

But time was up. I chose vengeance over Vivian, and these were the consequences.

No more stalling.

"I'm sorry you got caught in the middle of this. You were never at fault. But I had to protect my family, and this is..." The words lodged like a knife in my throat before I forced them out. "This is just business."

The taste of pennies returned, but I kept my expression detached even when every instinct screamed at me to cross the room, hold her, kiss her, and never let her go.

I'd let emotion rule for too long. It was time for logic to rule again.

Even if she forgave me for what I did to her family, we couldn't move forward when her father and I hated each other's guts. And if I stayed with her, her father would still win. He'd know Vivian was a weakness I couldn't afford to have, and he'd use it to exploit the situation any way he could.

For both our sakes, it was better for us to split up.

No matter how much it hurt.

Vivian stared at me. A gallery of emotions flickered through her eyes before a shutter slammed down.

"Right," she said softly. She closed her suitcase and hauled it off the bed. She stopped in front of me, twisted her engagement ring off her finger, and placed it in my hand. "Just business."

She brushed past me, leaving the faint scent of apples and a horrible ache in my chest behind.

I closed my fist around the ring. It was cold and lifeless against my palm.

My throat worked with a hard swallow.

Vivian hadn't packed all her things. Most of her clothes still hung in the closet. Her perfume bottles were on the dresser, a vase of her favorite flowers next to them. Yet the room had never felt emptier.

CHAPTER 35

Vivian

INSTEAD OF SEEKING OUT MY FATHER OR CHECKING into a hotel after leaving Dante's house, I wandered around Central Park with my suitcase like a tourist fresh off the train at Penn Station. I'd hoped the spring air would clear my head, but all it did was remind me of my engagement photo shoot with Dante.

Bow Bridge. Bethesda Terrace. Even the bench where we ate breakfast after the shoot.

I did what I had to do. No one threatens a Russo.

I had to protect my family… This is just business.

I waited for emotion—any emotion—to set in, but other than a brief pinch when I passed one of our photo shoot spots, I only felt numb. I couldn't even summon anger or concern over the possible implosion of my father's company. Too much had happened, and my brain refused to work properly.

I was an actress living someone else's life, untouched by the chaos rolling in overhead. For now at least.

I wandered the park until the sun set. Even in my zombified state, I knew better than to stay in the park alone after dark.

I climbed into the nearest cab, opened my mouth to tell the

driver to take me to the Carlyle, and ended up giving him Sloane's address instead. The thought of spending the night in an impersonal hotel room finally sparked a flicker of panic.

I arrived at Sloane's apartment twenty minutes later. She answered after the second doorbell ring, took one look at my luggage and ringless finger, and ushered me inside without a word. I sank onto the couch while she disappeared into the kitchen.

Now that I wasn't alone anymore, feeling crept back in. The ache in my arms from dragging my suitcase all day. The blisters on my feet from walking in my expensive but impractical shoes. The gaping, *excruciating* hollow in my chest where my heart used to beat, healthy and whole. Now, the organ lurched like a car on its last fumes, struggling to return somewhere it'd never belonged.

I blinked away the pressure mounting behind my eyes when Sloane returned with a mug and a pack of my favorite lemon butter cookies in hand.

We sat in silence for a second before she spoke. "Do I need to sharpen my knives and prepare contingency plans for a homicide charge?"

I mustered a weak laugh. "No. Nothing quite that drastic."

"I'll be the judge of that." Her gaze narrowed. "What happened?"

"I...Dante and I broke up." Another piece of my earlier numbness splintered into a painful throb.

"I gathered as much." Sloane's reply was matter-of-fact, not sarcastic. "What did the fucker do?"

"It wasn't his fault. Not entirely." I managed to summarize the day's events without breaking down, but my voice cracked toward the end.

I'm sorry you got caught in the middle of this... I had to protect my family... This is just business.

Another splinter, this one large enough to knock the breath out of my lungs. The pressure behind my eyes amplified.

To Sloane's credit, she didn't fall into dramatics over the shocking revelations. It wasn't her style, and it was one of the reasons I'd come to her instead of Isabella. As much as I loved Isa, she'd want to know every detail and rehash the situation ad nauseam. I didn't have the energy or emotional bandwidth for that right now.

"Okay, so the engagement is officially off, which means we need a plan," Sloane said crisply. "We'll call the wedding vendors in the morning and cancel. It might be too late for a full refund, but I'm sure I can convince most, if not all, of them to issue partial reimbursements. Actually..." She pursed her lips. "Scratch that. We need to draft language for the breakup announcement first. We don't want any of the vendors leaking to the press. The society papers will be all over this, and—"

"Sloane." My hands strangled my mug. Every word out of her mouth ratcheted my anxiety up another notch. "Can we discuss this later? I appreciate the help, but I can't...I can't think about all that right now."

The enormity of the next few weeks overwhelmed me. I had to move the rest of my belongings out of Dante's house, confront my father, figure out where my relationship with him went from here, cancel the wedding, and deal with the public fallout of my broken engagement. On top of all that, the Legacy Ball was in less than a week, and we were entering another busy season for events.

Cold sweat broke out on my forehead, and I forcibly dragged air through my nose to slow down my frantic heartbeat.

Sloane's face softened.

"Right. Of course." She cleared her throat. "Do you want me to call Isa? She's much better at...this"—she gestured vaguely around us—"than I am."

"Later. I just want to shower and sleep, if you don't mind."

I stared at my tea, feeling stupid and ashamed and embarrassed and a thousand other things in between. "I'm sorry for showing up without warning like this. I just...didn't want to be by myself tonight."

"Vivian." Sloane placed her hand over mine, her voice firm. "You don't need to apologize. Stay as long as you want. My guest room wasn't getting much use anyway. You, Isabella, and the maintenance guy are the only people I allow in my apartment."

"I didn't know you had that kind of a relationship with your maintenance guy," I half-heartedly joked. "Scandalous."

She didn't smile, but concern lined her brow. "Get some rest. We'll figure everything out in the morning."

My attempted smile collapsed. "Thank you," I whispered.

Sloane wasn't a hugger, but the squeeze of her hand conveyed the same sentiment.

Later that night, I lay in bed, unable to sleep despite my exhaustion. I'd lost both my father and my fiancé in some way or another today. Two of the most important people in my life, unrecognizable or gone.

My father lied, manipulated, and used me while Dante...

I never willingly chose her.

This is just business.

The pressure behind my eyes finally exploded. The remaining pieces of numbness disintegrated, replaced with pain so sharp and intense I would've doubled over had I been standing. Instead, I curled into a fetal position and gave in to the sobs racking my body. They crashed over me, one after another, until my throat turned raw and wetness scalded my cheeks.

But no matter how hard I cried or how much I shook, I couldn't make a sound. My sobs remained silent, felt but unheard.

Dante

I took the next three days off work.

I tried to work, I really did, but I couldn't focus. During every call, I heard Vivian's voice. During every meeting, I saw her face.

At this point, I was a liability to the company, so I instructed Helena to cancel my meetings for the week and took the time to get my head straight. That meant cracking open a bottle of whiskey every night, retreated to the living room, and ignoring Greta's questions until she stormed off in a flurry of curses.

Tonight was no exception.

I tipped my head and bottle back. The liquor burned down my throat and filled my stomach, but the aching emptiness remained.

I was simply unused to Vivian's absence after living with her for so long. It'd pass, as would my emotional attachment to her. People broke up and moved on every day. It wasn't anything fucking special.

I tossed back another swig. The fireplace was unlit for spring, but a hazy memory of its flames and the way their light danced across Vivian's features filled my mind.

Are you afraid I'll break the engagement? Run off with Heath and leave you looking like a fool in front of your friends? Why do you care?

They're ice cream cuff links. I know a jeweler on rue de la Paix who makes customized pieces…

It's not just business for you. And it's not just duty for me.

I'm glad I came to Paris.

Pain lashed at my chest, a stinging burn.

"Maybe you can talk some sense into him." Greta's grumble drifted into the room from the hall. "He's been sitting and drinking these past few days like his no-good great-uncle Agostino used to do. *Non mi piace parlare male dei morti, ma grazie al cielo non è più qui con noi.*"

"I'll try." Luca's voice gave me pause before I shrugged it off and lifted the bottle to my lips again.

He probably needed an advance on his allowance. He rarely visited unless he wanted something.

I didn't look at him when he entered and took the seat across from me. He watched me for a moment before speaking.

"What the hell happened?"

"Nothing." My head swam, and I blinked away the fuzziness before correcting myself. "Vivian and I broke up."

The words tasted bitter. Perhaps I should switch from whiskey to something sweeter, like rum.

"*What*?"

Luca's pale face came into my line of vision when I finally turned. The small movement required as much effort as swimming through molasses. Christ, had my head always been this heavy?

It's your ego. It adds at least *ten pounds.* Vivian's hypothetical teasing sounded in my ears.

A vise clamped around my heart. It was bad enough her every word and smile were burned into my memory. Now I was hearing things she *didn't* say?

"Why?" Luca demanded. "What about Francis and the photos?"

Right. I hadn't told him I'd destroyed the photos yet, partly because I'd been distracted and partly because they kept him in check. Hell, he deserved to sweat a little longer after the fucking mess he landed me in.

"I took care of them," I said curtly. "Which was why Francis visited me earlier this week. Vivian overheard. We broke up. The end."

"*Christ*, Dante, you couldn't have told me this earlier? Why'd

I have to get a call from Greta fretting about how aliens took over your body?"

"I don't know, Luca. Maybe because I was busy saving *your* ass," I bit out.

He stared at me for a second before slumping in his chair. "Shit. Well, this is good, right? Blackmail's gone. Francis is gone. Vivian's gone. This is what you wanted."

Another long pull. "Yep."

"You don't look very happy," he observed.

Anger snapped free of its leash. "What do you want me to do, throw a parade? For fuck's sake, I just saved your *life*, and all you can do is comment on whether I look *happy*!"

Luca didn't flinch. "You're my brother," he said calmly. "Your happiness is important to me."

Just like that, my anger fizzled as quickly as it came. "If that were true, you wouldn't have gotten us into this mess in the first place."

He grimaced. "Yes, well, I've done my fair share of...questionable things, as you might know."

I snorted in agreement.

"But you were right to make me get a job. I actually like working at Lohman & Sons, and the structure has been good for me. It's nice not waking up with a hangover every day." A smile flitted over Luca's mouth. "I admit, I was resentful as hell when you first brought it up. The whole blackmail thing didn't seem real at the time, and I hated how you punished me like I was your child instead of your brother. The job, breaking up with Maria. I was...selfish."

I lowered my bottle and narrowed my eyes. "I'm not the one whose body was taken over by aliens. Who are you, and what the hell have you done to my brother?"

Luca laughed. "Like I said, the structure has been good for me.

So has not hanging out with my old crowd as much. Actually…" He cleared his throat. "I met a girl. Leaf. She's really put things into perspective for me."

"You're dating someone named *Leaf*?" I asked, incredulous.

"Her parents were hippies," he said by way of explanation. "She's a yoga instructor in Brooklyn. Very flexible. Anyway, that's not the point. The point is I've been doing a lot of inner work with her."

I bet he had. I should've known. All the big shifts in Luca's life revolved around women, booze, or parties.

"She's helping me heal my inner child," he continued. "That includes fixing our brotherly relationship."

Jesus. I supposed a Brooklyn yoga instructor named Leaf was better than a Mafia princess. Higher chance of turning my brother vegan, lower chance of getting him killed.

"What about Maria? I thought you were in love."

"I haven't talked to her in—er, since we spoke in your office." Luca coughed. "I was talking to Leaf about it. I think I mistook the thrill of the forbidden for *love* love, you know? The two are easily confused."

You don't fucking say.

"But enough about my love life. We were talking about yours. With Vivian."

I tensed again. "We sure as hell weren't."

"You should be celebrating after getting rid of the Laus," he said, ignoring me. "But you're here drinking alone like Great-Uncle Agostino after losing at poker. We both know why."

"Because I'm trying to forget I have an annoying as fuck brother with terrible taste in women."

"No. Because you actually like Vivian," he said pointedly. "You might even love her."

The wrecking ball of his speculation ricocheted through my chest and knocked my heartbeat off-kilter. "That's ridiculous."

"Is it? Be honest." Luca leaned forward and fixed a hard stare on me. It wasn't an expression I was used to seeing on him. It was unsettling. "Putting aside all the bullshit with Francis, do you *want* to be with her?"

I tugged at my tie, only to realize I wasn't wearing one. Then why the hell did my throat feel so tight? "It's not that simple."

"Why the hell not?"

"Because it's *not*," I snapped. "What do you think will happen? We'll have happy family meals at Thanksgiving after I destroy her father's company? Get married in front of all our friends like the way we got together wasn't completely fucked? If I marry her, Francis wins. He'll still have a Russo as an in-law. People will question why the fuck I'm not saving him when his company goes up in flames. It'll be a goddamn mess!"

"Sure," Luca said, seemingly unimpressed by my explanation. "But that doesn't answer my question. Do you want to be with her?"

Forget Romano's wrath. I was seconds away from giving in to mine and strangling Luca with my bare hands. If it weren't for him, Francis wouldn't have blackmailed me. If he hadn't blackmailed me, I wouldn't have gotten engaged to Vivian. If I hadn't gotten engaged to Vivian, I wouldn't have fallen—

Realization punched me in the chest, so hard and sudden I swore I heard a crack. Bruised heart, fractured ribs, stolen breath, all in the space of a minute. It was like my body was punishing me for not recognizing the truth earlier when it'd been so damn obvious.

The way I'd stayed in bed longer every morning just to catch her first smile of the day.

The way our takeout lunch dates became my favorite part of the workweek.

The way I'd opened up to her about my family, my life, *myself*...

And the way watching her walk away on Monday had cost me an irretrievable piece of my soul.

The breath left my lungs. Somehow, somewhere along the way, I'd fallen in love with Vivian Lau.

Not like or lust. *Love*, in all its terrifying, unpredictable, unwanted glory.

Luca watched me process the realization, his expression equal parts amused and concerned. "That's what I thought."

Fuck. Fuckfuckfuckfuck FUCK.

I rubbed a hand over my face, restless and unsettled.

What the hell was I supposed to do now? I'd never been in love. Never planned to be in love. And now I'd gone and fallen for the one woman I shouldn't have like a damn idiot.

"When the hell did you turn into the older brother?" The topic was safer than the unresolved one hanging in the air.

"Trust me, I'm not, and I don't want to be. Too much responsibility. But that's the point." Luca's face sobered. "You've sacrificed a lot for me, Dante. I don't always acknowledge or openly appreciate it, but I..." He swallowed hard. "I know. All the times you showed up for me when others couldn't or wouldn't. Agreeing to marry Vivian, then giving her up. That's what I meant when I said we need to fix our relationship. You've always been a parent figure because I *needed* a parent figure. But now...I'd like us to try and be brothers."

This time, the pinch in my chest had nothing to do with Vivian. "Meaning?"

"Meaning I'll try not to fuck up and have you bail me out." He gave me a lopsided grin. "And I call you out on your bullshit when I need to, like now. You love Vivian. I saw it happening even in Bali. But you let her go because of what? Your pride and vengeance? Those things will only get you so far."

"Did Leaf tell you that?"

"Nah." Another grin. "I read an article about the seven sins in my dentist's waiting room."

I let out a scoff, but his words replayed on a loop in my head.

You let her go because of what? Your pride and vengeance? Those things will only get you so far.

"I should've put you to work sooner. It would've saved me a shit ton of money and headaches." I scrubbed my face again, trying to make sense of this roller coaster of a day. "Why are you so invested in my relationship with Vivian?"

Luca's grin disappeared. "Because you've protected me my whole life," he said quietly. "And it's time I returned the favor."

I blamed the burn in my heart on the alcohol. "That's what my security team is for."

"Not from other people. From yourself." Luca nodded at the half-empty bottle still loosely clasped in my hand. "Don't let your pursuit of wrath ruin the best thing that's ever happened to you. Yeah, figuring things out with Vivian will be hard, but you've always been a fighter. So fucking fight."

CHAPTER 36

Vivian

THE WEDNESDAY AFTER I MOVED OUT OF DANTE'S house, I chartered a flight to Boston. According to my mom, whom I'd called under the guise of discussing wedding arrangements, my father was already back home.

I'd spent the plane ride rehearsing what I would say. But as I sat across from him in his office, listening to the clock tick and the shallow cadence of my breaths, I realized no amount of rehearsal could've prepared me for confronting my father.

Silence stretched between us for another minute before he leaned back and raised a bushy, gray-tipped brow. "What's the emergency, Vivian? I assume you have something important you'd like to discuss if you showed up unannounced like this."

He was the one who had something to apologize for, but his stern voice sent a knee-jerk spiral of shame through me. It was the same voice he'd used whenever I received anything less than a perfect test score. I tried not to let it affect me, but it was hard to overcome decades of conditioning.

"Yes, I do." I lifted my chin and straightened my shoulders, trying to summon the fire from two days ago. All I managed were a few puffs of smoke.

It was much easier to rant at my father in my head than in real life.

Part of the reason was how exhausted he looked. Heavy bags hung beneath his eyes while lines of worry formed deep crags and crevices across his face.

News articles had started popping up about trouble at Lau Jewels. Nothing major yet, just a few whispers here and there, but they were a sign of the storm to come. The office buzzed with nervous energy, and stock values had dipped.

An unreasonable pang of guilt pierced my gut. My father was responsible for this mess. I *shouldn't* feel guilty for calling him out on it, no matter how tired or stressed he was.

"Well?" he said impatiently. "I already pushed back a meeting for this. I'm not going to postpone it again. If you don't have anything to say now, we'll discuss it over din—"

"Did you blackmail Dante into marrying me?" I blurted out the question before I lost my nerve.

My heart slammed against my rib cage as my father's expression hardened into an unreadable mold. The clock continued its deafening march toward the half hour.

"I overheard you. In Dante's office." I clutched the purse in my lap for support. I wasn't wearing tweed or neutrals today. Instead, I'd opted for a custom-tailored silk sheath and an extra coat of red lipstick for confidence. *I should've put on two extra coats.*

"If you overheard, then why waste my time by asking?" My father's tone was as indecipherable as his face.

An ember of anger sparked to life.

"Because I want you to confirm it! Blackmail is *illegal*, Father, not to mention morally wrong. How could you do that?" I forced air past my tight chest. "Am I so undesirable you had to *force* someone into marrying me?"

"Don't be dramatic," he snapped. "It wasn't *anyone*. It was Dante Russo. Do you know the doors marrying a Russo would open? Even with our wealth and your sister's marriage, some people look down on us. They'll invite us to their parties, and they'll take our money for fundraisers, but they whisper behind our backs, Vivian. They think we're not good enough. Marriage to Dante would've shut those whispers down immediately."

"You blackmailed someone because of a few *whispers*?" I asked disbelievingly.

My father had always been conscious of his appearance and reputation. Even before we were rich, he'd stretch our budget and insist on paying for the table during get-togethers with his friends so he didn't lose face. But I never could've guessed his need for social validation ran this deep.

"The opportunity arose, and I took it," he said coolly. "His brother was foolish and reckless. What were the chances I'd catch him with Gabriele Romano's niece during a visit to New York?" An unrepentant shrug. "Fate put him in my path, and I took advantage of it for *our* family. I won't apologize for that."

"You could've chosen anyone else." It was hard to hear over the buzz in my ears, but I pushed forward. "Someone who would've *willingly* agreed to an arranged marriage."

"Someone who would've willingly agreed wouldn't have been good enough."

"Do you hear yourself?" The embers fanned into flames. My fury came roaring back, so hot and bright it blurred my father's face. "These are people's *lives*, not toys you can bend and manipulate. What if the photos leaked and Dante's brother got killed? What if *you* got killed for holding on to the evidence? How could you be so..." *Cruel. Callous. Morally corrupt.* "Short-sighted? It's not—"

"Don't raise your voice at me!" My father slammed his hands on the desk so hard the items on it rattled. "I am your father. You do *not* speak to me this way."

My heart threatened to explode from my chest. "The father I knew would've never done this."

The silence was so acute you could hear a moth flap its wings.

My father straightened and leaned back again. His gaze bore into me.

"You only have the luxury of caring about morals because of *me*. I do what I have to do to make sure our family is protected and the *best* it can be. You and your sister grew up sheltered, Vivian. You have no idea what it took for me to get to where I am today because I shielded you from the ugly truth. The number of people who laughed in my face and stabbed me in the back... it would make you sick. You think the world is rose-colored when it's gray at best."

"Protecting our family doesn't mean destroying someone else's. We don't stoop that low, Father. It's not who we are."

The briefest shadow of remorse passed through his eyes before disappearing. "I'm the head of the family," he said, his tone final. "We are who I say we are."

The words touched my skin, cold and unfeeling. A shiver skated down my spine.

"And my relationship with Dante?" The clasp of my purse dug into my palm. "Did you not think how your actions would affect me? There's a difference between an arranged marriage and a forced one. I would've had to spend my life with someone who resented me simply because you want his name in our family tree."

"Don't act like a martyr," my father said. "It's unbecoming. Your sister never complained about being married to Gunnar, and *she* had to move to another country."

"She doesn't complain because *they actually love each other*."

He continued like I hadn't spoken. "There are worse things than being a billionaire's wife. You're young and charming. You would've worn Dante down eventually. In fact, he already seemed quite smitten with you over the holidays."

"Well, you're wrong," I said flatly. "It's over, Father. I moved out of Dante's house. We're not getting married. And…" I glanced out the window onto the main office floor. "The company isn't doing well."

Because you provoked someone you shouldn't have.

The words sat unspoken between us.

My father's jaw tightened. He hated being reminded things were less than perfect under his watch.

"The company will be fine. We're merely experiencing a hiccup."

"It sounds like more than a hiccup."

He stared at me, his ire melting into something more calculating. "Perhaps you're right," he said. "It might be more than a hiccup, in which case we could use Dante's help. He's upset now, but he has a soft spot for you. Convince him to…assist."

Cold sank into my bones. "I told you, we *broke up*. He hates us. He doesn't have a soft spot for me or anyone else in the family."

"That's not true. I saw the way he looked at you when your mother and I visited. Even if you broke up, I'm sure you could make him see reason if you tried hard enough."

The cold spread to the pit of my stomach. I stared at my father, taking in his perfectly gelled hair, expensive suit, and flashy watch. It was like facing an actor pretending to be Francis Lau instead of the man himself.

How had he morphed from the slightly corny but well-meaning parent of my childhood into the person before me? Cold. Devious. Obsessed with money and status and determined to gain—and keep—both at any cost.

He looked the same, but I barely recognized him.

"I won't." My voice wavered, but my words were firm. "This is *your* mess, Father. I can't help you."

I hated how my mother and sister would be affected should Lau Jewels capsize, but I couldn't play pawn and possession for my father anymore. Plus, they each had their own nest eggs; they would be fine, financially speaking.

I'd turned the other cheek for too long. Been too willing to go along with whatever my parents told me to do because it was easier than rocking the boat and disappointing them. For all his faults, I loved my father and my family. I didn't want to hurt them.

But I didn't realize until now that not speaking up when they crossed the line would hurt us more in the long run than anything else.

Disbelief filled the grooves of my father's face.

"You're choosing your *ex*-fiancé over your family? Is this how we raised you?" he demanded. "To be so disrespectful and *disobedient*?" He spat the word out like a curse.

"Disobedient?" Indignation blew through me like a sudden gale, sweeping aside any remnants of guilt. "I've done *everything* you've asked of me! I went to the 'right' college, broke up with Heath, and played the role of perfect society daughter. I even agreed to marry a man I barely knew because it would make *you* happy. But I'm done living my life for you." Emotion thickened my voice. "It's *my* life, Father. Not yours. And the same way you can't make decisions for me any longer...I can't make excuses for you. Not anymore."

This time, the silence was so heavy it pressed down on me like a lead blanket.

"Of course, you are free to make your own decisions," my father finally said, his voice terrifyingly calm. "But I want you to know this, Vivian. If you walk out of this office today without making amends for your *insolence*, you are no longer my daughter. Or a Lau."

His ultimatum barreled into me with the force of a runaway train, skewering my chest with a bayonet and filling my ears with the roar of blood.

The temperature dropped into subzero territory as we stared at each other, his cold fury waging silent battle with my pained determination.

There it was. The invisible monster I'd feared since childhood, laid out like a gruesome corpse of the relationship we used to have. I could cover it with a blanket and look away, or I could stand my ground and face it head-on.

I rose, my blood electric with fear and adrenaline as my father's composure slipped the tiniest fraction. He'd expected me to back down.

I'm sorry. The apology almost fell off my tongue through force of habit before I remembered I didn't have anything to apologize for.

I wanted to stay a minute longer, to memorize his face and mourn something that'd died a long time ago.

Instead, I turned and walked out.

Don't cry. Don't cry. Don't cry.

My father had disowned me.

My father had disowned me, and I hadn't tried to stop him because the price was too high.

Tears crowded my throat, but I forced them back even as a crushing sense of loneliness invaded me. In the space of a week, I'd lost my family and I'd lost Dante.

The only thing I had left was myself. And for now, that would have to be enough.

CHAPTER 37

Vivian

THE LEGACY BALL'S PROXIMITY TO THE CHAOS UPENDing my life turned out to be a blessing in disguise. In the two days between my confrontation with my father and the gala, I threw myself into work with such fervor even Sloane, the consummate workaholic, expressed alarm.

Five a.m. wake-up calls. Dinner at the office. Lunch spent reviewing every detail and ensuring I had contingency plan upon contingency plan for everything from a citywide blackout to a brawl between guests.

By the time the actual ball rolled around, I was delirious from lack of sleep.

I didn't mind. Busy was good. Busy meant less time agonizing over the shambles of my personal life.

However, despite all my planning, there was one thing I hadn't prepared for: the effect walking into Valhalla Club would have on me.

Tightness crawled into my chest as I smiled and made small talk with the guests. Tonight, I was the hostess, which meant no running around checking on the food or music. That was my team's job. My job was to mingle, look good, pose for photographs...and not spend every second subconsciously searching for Dante.

I'd only visited Valhalla twice, both times with him. I hadn't seen him yet. He might not show at all. But his presence—dark, magnetic, and omnipresent—permeated the room.

His laughter in the corners. His scent in the air. His touch on my skin. Hot kisses and stolen moments and memories so vivid they were painted all over the walls.

Dante *was* Valhalla, at least to me. And being here tonight, without him, was like a ship leaving port without an anchor.

"Vivian." Buffy's voice pulled me from the edge of a breakdown I couldn't afford. I'd cried more this past week than I'd cried my entire life, and frankly, I was sick of it. "What a *stunning* dress."

She came up beside me, elegant as always in a green brocade gown that paid tasteful homage to the ball's secret garden theme. Magnificent diamonds draped across her neck and dripped from her wrists.

I blinked back a suspicious prickle and pasted on a smile. "Thank you. Your outfit is lovely as well."

Buffy swept a discerning gaze over my dress.

The Yves Dubois piece had turned many heads tonight, and for good reason. It cascaded to the ground in an exquisite sweep of red silk and gold-dipped feathers, so tightly packed they looked like a pile of fallen, gilded leaves. Shimmering gold thread formed an intricate phoenix pattern across the silk, so subtle it was almost invisible unless the embroidery hit the light at a certain angle.

It was clothing, art, and armor all rolled into one. A statement piece bold enough to declare power but so dazzling few people looked past it to the sadness underneath.

"Yves Dubois couture," Buffy said. "Dante is a generous fiancé."

Her gaze coasted to my empty ring finger.

Tingles of unease crystallized beneath my skin. Dante and I hadn't announced our breakup yet, but my lack of an engagement ring had drawn every person's notice tonight.

Whispers were already circulating, not only about our relationship status but about Lau Jewels' stock market free fall. The negative press coverage had exploded in the past forty-eight hours. Although everyone had been perfectly nice to me so far—I was still the hostess, regardless of my family troubles—their murmurs hadn't gone unnoticed.

"I bought the gown myself," I said in response to Buffy's observation. I smiled at her flicker of surprise. "I'm a Lau." *Even if my father disowned me.* "I can afford my own clothes."

I wasn't a billionaire, but between my trust fund, investments, and event planning income, I held my own money-wise.

Buffy recovered quickly. "Of course," she said. "How... modern of you. Speaking of Dante, will he be joining us tonight? It's your big night. I'm surprised he isn't here already."

My smile tightened. She was too refined to ask outright about the ring, but she was clearly fishing.

"He had an emergency at work." I hoped she couldn't hear the thumps of my heart over the music piping through the speakers. "He'll make it if he wraps up the call in time."

"I certainly hope so. It wouldn't be a proper Legacy Ball without a Russo in attendance, would it?"

I forced a laugh alongside hers.

Thankfully, Buffy soon excused herself, and I was free to breathe again.

I circulated the room, more aware than ever of the guests' subtle digs and glances at my hand. I ignored them the best I could. I'd worry about the gossip mill tomorrow.

Tonight was my big night, and I refused to let anyone ruin it.

Dante's conspicuous absence aside, the ballroom was packed with a who's who of Manhattan high society. Dominic and

Alessandra Davenport held court with a group of Wall Street titans; a crop of the season's "it girls" flirted with floppy-haired trust fund scions near the bar.

The room itself was a masterpiece. Three dozen trees imported from Europe ringed the space, twined with ethereal strings of light that glittered like jewels against a leafy backdrop. Seventy thousand dollars' worth of hanging flowers and shrubbery adorned the tables, where vintage key tags hand-calligraphed with each guest's name delineated their seating assignment.

Everything was perfect—the four-tier cake with textural buttercream, floral garnishes, and edible twenty-four-karat gold leaf keyhole; the pink-and-white strawberry and rose towers; the mossy wooden arches and oversized Edison bulbs adorning the bar.

And yet the stares and whispers continued.

I eased a deep breath into my lungs.

It's fine. No one is going to make a scene in the middle of the Legacy Ball.

I whisked a glass of champagne off a tray in an attempt to drown the self-consciousness pricking my skin.

"The hostess drinking by herself on her big night? That won't do."

I smiled at the familiar voice before turning. "I needed a break from..." I gestured around the room. "You know."

"Oh, I do," Kai said dryly, handsome as always in a bespoke tuxedo and his signature glasses. "May I have this dance?"

He held out his hand. I took it and let him guide me to the dance floor.

Dozens of pairs of eyes homed in on us like laser-guided missiles seeking their targets.

"Is it just me," he said, "or do you also feel like you're in a giant fishbowl?"

"A nice, expensive one," I agreed.

Amusement touched his lips before it melted into concern. "How are you doing, Vivian?"

I assumed he was talking about my breakup with Dante. They were friends, but how much did he know about what happened?

I chose a safe, neutral answer. "I've been better."

"I haven't seen Dante in the ring this week. It's unlike him. He usually goes straight for violence when he's upset."

The joke failed to pull a smile from me. I was too hung up on the mention of Dante. "Maybe he's not upset."

We hadn't spoken to each other since I moved out. I should be upset with him. Most of the blame lay with my father, but Dante wasn't completely innocent either.

Still, it was hard to summon anything except sadness when I thought about him. There'd been a time when I really thought…

"Maybe." Kai glanced over my shoulder. His gaze turned speculative. "You know, I didn't want to say anything while you were engaged, but you're one of the most beautiful women I know."

I blinked, startled by the sudden shift in tone and topic. "Thank you."

"This might be too soon, but since you're no longer with Dante…" Kai's hand slid down my back and rested above the curve of my ass. Low enough to be suggestive but high enough to skirt the line of inappropriate. I stiffened. "Perhaps we can go out sometime."

Shock and alarm bubbled in my chest. Was he drunk? He didn't sound like the Kai I knew at all.

"Um…" I let out an uncomfortable laugh and tried to twist out of his hold, but it was hard in my dress. "You're right. It *is* too soon. And, while I really like you as a *friend*…" I emphasized the last word. "I'm not sure I want to date right now."

He wasn't listening. He was too busy looking over my head with a wicked smile.

"Here he comes," he murmured.

Before I could ask who he was talking about, a warm, *familiar* hand landed on my shoulder.

"Take your hands off my fiancée." Dark and turbulent, the order was packed with so much tightly leashed danger it was a spark away from combustion.

"Apologies." Kai released me, his expression strangely self-satisfied. "I didn't realize..."

"I don't give a fuck what you did or didn't realize." The lethally quiet statement poured ice down my spine. "Touch Vivian again, and I'll kill you."

Simple. Brutal. *Honest.*

Kai's eyes flickered along with a ghost of a smile. "Noted." He inclined his head at us. "Enjoy."

I watched him walk away, too stunned to speak.

It was only when Dante whirled me around and clasped my hand in his that I found my voice.

"What are you doing here?" My feet followed his lead out of instinct, but the rest of my body tingled with alarm.

His presence was too powerful, his scent too all-consuming. It crowded my lungs, filling them with clean earthiness and rich spices. When I was around him, it was easy to lose myself, no matter how upset or heartbroken I was.

My ability to breathe ceased when his eyes connected with mine.

Dark hair. Sculpted cheekbones. Firm, sensual lips.

It'd been less than a week since we last saw each other, yet he was somehow more beautiful than I remembered.

"I was invited. By you, I believe." The cold brutality vanished, replaced with warm amusement. It was like Kai's departure had flipped a switch.

I thought I detected a hint of nerves as well, but I must've heard wrong. Dante was never nervous.

"You know what I mean. What are you doing *here*, dancing with me?"

His palm practically burned mine. I desperately wanted to pull away, but I couldn't with everyone watching. It seemed like every set of eyes was trained on us.

"Because you're my fiancée, and this is your big night. You've worked months on the Legacy Ball, Vivian. Did you think I was going to miss it?"

The words were needles to my heart, injecting it with a rush of electricity and adrenaline before I forced it to calm. If the past week had taught me anything, it was that every high came with a devastating crash.

"I'm not your fiancée anymore."

Dante fell silent.

At first glance, he looked every inch the enigmatic CEO out for a night on the town. His custom-made tuxedo molded to his body, emphasizing broad shoulders and sleek, powerful muscles. The soft lights threw his bold features into sharp relief, and his chin held its usual proud, arrogant tilt.

But a closer look revealed the faint purple smudges beneath his eyes. Lines of tension bracketed his mouth, and his grip was tight, almost desperate when he replied.

"We had a fight," he said, his voice low. "We didn't officially break up."

Disbelief roused from its slumber, joining its cousins shock and frustration.

"Yes, we did. I *gave you back my ring*. You took it. I moved out." *Sort of.* I needed to get the rest of my belongings once I had a chance to breathe. "In my world, that means we broke up. And that's not even touching all the...the complications between you and my father."

The difference between this Dante and the one who'd watched

me walk away four days ago was so stark, I was convinced an alien imposter had hijacked his body.

"Yes, well, that's what I wanted to talk to you about." A swallow worked its way down his throat. All remnants of his playful mask disappeared, revealing nerves I never thought he possessed. "I fucked up, Vivian. I said a lot of things I shouldn't have, and I'm trying to make it right."

The words vibrated through the air and somehow reached my chest before they did my ears. By the time my brain processed them, my heart was already twisted and in shambles.

He couldn't do this. Not now, not here, when I'd *just* started functioning properly after the havoc earlier this week.

"It doesn't matter." I willed the words past my tongue. "Like you said, it was just business."

Anguish darkened the edges of Dante's eyes. "*Mia cara…*"

My throat constricted.

The rest of the ball fell away, disintegrating like crumpled pieces of paper thrown into the fire of Dante's presence.

Mia cara.

He was the only person who could utter that phrase so softly and achingly, like it was a beautiful substitute for another set of words we were too afraid to say.

I blinked away the emotion in my eyes. "I left four days ago, Dante. You were happy to let me walk away then. Do you expect me to believe you did a one-eighty in such a short period of time?"

"No. I don't expect you to believe anything I say, but I hope you do," he said quietly. "I'm sorry you found out the truth the way you did. I should've told you earlier, but the truth is…" His throat flexed with another hard swallow. "I wasn't ready to let you go. I pulled back after Paris and told myself I was easing you into the truth when in reality, I wanted the best of both worlds. To keep you and to fool myself into thinking I wouldn't.

"I *hated* your father, Vivian. I still do. And I hated the idea of him winning in any way, including..." Dante's grip tightened around mine. "Including if I stayed with you the way I wanted. It wasn't my finest reasoning or proudest moment, but it's the truth. Yes, I was forced into the engagement, but everything that happened afterward? Our dates, our talks, our trip to Paris...no one forced me to do those things. They were real. And I was stupid enough to think I could get over them or you when..." His voice dropped, turning raw. "You've been gone less than a week and I already feel like I've spent an eternity in hell."

The breath fled my lungs. Oxygen solidified into something sweet and honeyed that dripped into my stomach, filling it with warmth. A choked sob entered the mix before I swallowed it.

There was no one near us. Everyone gave Dante a wide berth, and the majority of guests had returned to their conversations instead of staring at us.

Still, I couldn't afford any break in composure. One crack was all it would take for me to shatter completely.

"But nothing's changed," I said, my voice thick. "You still hate my father, and he still wins if we marry."

I didn't mention the disowning or company troubles yet. Those were whole other cans of worms.

"You're wrong," Dante said. "Something *has* changed. I thought I could live without you. That my vengeance meant more than my feelings for you. It took only a few days—hell, a few hours—to realize I can't, and it doesn't. I didn't want to distract you while you were preparing for the ball, which is why I haven't reached out earlier. But..." His throat worked with another swallow. "I love you, Vivian. More than I could ever hate your father. And more than I ever thought I was capable of."

My heart soared; my stomach plunged into a wild free fall. The contradiction defied the laws of physics, but nothing about our relationship had ever adhered to rules.

I love you, Vivian.

The words echoed in my head and spilled into my chest, where they met their counterparts for the first time.

I love you too. Even after what you did. Even if I shouldn't. I love you more than I could ever hate you.

The only difference was I couldn't bring myself to voice them yet.

"You and me," Dante said. His eyes held mine. "For real this time. We can make it work. That is...if you want to."

If you can forgive me.

The real meaning brimmed between us.

Could we really move past what happened this easily and quickly? He seemed sincere, but...

I never willingly chose her.

I did what I had to do.

This is just business.

I plummeted back to earth.

I loved Dante. I'd known since Paris, and there was no point pretending my feelings had magically changed overnight despite what happened.

I loved the way his smiles peeked through his scowls.

I loved how he kissed my shoulder every morning when I woke up.

I loved his humor and intelligence, his strength and vulnerability, his thoughtfulness and ambition.

But just because I loved him didn't mean I trusted him *or* myself.

We can make it work. That is...if you want to.

The week's emotional roller coaster had taken its toll on me, and I had no clue what I wanted. I hadn't even worked out how I felt about my father's company's troubles. Obviously, Dante had a hand in it. But how upset was I *really* when a tiny, secret part of me blamed Lau Jewels for what my family had become?

"Go on a date with me," he said when I didn't answer. "We'll do anything you want. Even eat popcorn."

I didn't smile at his joke. Another flicker of nerves surfaced in his eyes.

"We've been on dates before."

"That was before. This is now." His face softened. "Just one date. Please."

My heart wrenched, but I shook my head. "I don't think that's a good idea."

Frustration and a splash of panic tightened his features. "Why not?"

"There're a thousand different reasons. You hate my family. You never wanted to get married, and you never wanted *me*. You were forced into it, and if we get together again, my father still wins. And..." Dryness coated my throat. "We're not good together, Dante. Our relationship was so hot and cold, but we made it work because we *had* to make it work. Now that we don't..." I searched for the right way to phrase my thoughts. "Things have been difficult since day one. Maybe it's a sign."

The last part came out quietly, like a pin dropping into the ocean.

Our relationship had been tainted from the start. Even if I loved him, I couldn't see how we could overcome the mistakes of our past.

My heart twisted again, this time with pain so sharp I wasn't sure how I'd survive it.

But I would. I had to.

"That's six reasons," Dante said. "I can work with six. I can even work with a thousand."

My chest ached. "Dante..."

"You don't think we're a good idea, but I'll prove we are." Determination lined his jaw, but his voice and lips were soft as they brushed my forehead. "Give me time, *mia cara*. That's all I need, besides you."

CHAPTER 38

Vivian

"HEY, VIVIAN. THE USUAL?"

"Yes, please. Make it four," I said as the barista rang me up. I frequented the coffee shop near my office so often they'd memorized my order. "Thanks, Jen."

"No problem." She smiled. "See you tomorrow."

I paid and moved to the pickup area, only half looking at where I was going. I was too distracted by the flood of new messages scrolling across my screen.

My phone had been blowing up all weekend. Friends, acquaintances, society reporters, everyone wanted to congratulate or talk to me after the smashing success of the Legacy Ball.

Mode de Vie had deemed it "one of the most exquisite balls in the institution's history" in their Sunday style roundup, which meant I woke up that morning with even more messages crowding my inbox. It was only Monday, and I already had twenty-two new client inquiries, five interview requests, and countless invitations to balls, screenings, and private parties.

The whispers about Lau Jewels' troubles were still circulating, but they weren't enough to override the prestige of hosting the Legacy Ball. It was equal parts thrilling and exhausting.

I opened a new email from a prospective client right as I bumped into another patron. Coffee splashed over the side of their open cup and onto their shoes.

Horror streaked through me. "I'm so sorry!" I looked up, the email forgotten. "I didn't mean..." My apology died a quick death when my eyes landed on a familiar head of dark hair and bronzed skin.

My lips remained parted, but my words had fled to some far-off island for an unplanned vacation.

"That's all right," Dante said easily. "We've all been there. It was my fault for leaving my cup open when it's so crowded."

I watched, stunned, as he plucked a lid from the counter and fitted it over his coffee.

It was the middle of the workday, but instead of a suit, he wore black dress pants and a white button-down with the sleeves rolled up. No tie.

"What are you doing here?" I found my voice somewhere between the rapid thumps of my heart and the dryness in my throat. It was the second time I'd asked him the question in twice as many days.

His office was a few blocks away, but there were at least half a dozen coffee shops between here and there.

A small, playful hitch of his brow. "Getting coffee, like you."

He placed a hand on my arm and gently moved me to the side before a harried twentysomething blond blitzed past us with a full tray of coffee.

If I hadn't moved, I'd be wearing Americano and cold brew with my Diane von Furstenberg.

Dante's hand lingered a beat on my arm before he removed it and held it out. "I'm Dante, by the way."

The imprint of his touch burned into my skin.

I stared at his outstretched hand, wondering if he'd bumped his head and developed a sudden case of amnesia over the weekend.

I couldn't work out how else to respond, so I slid my hand into his with a wary, "I'm Vivian."

"Nice to meet you, Vivian." His palm was warm, *rough*.

My stomach fluttered at hazy memories of that roughness mapping my body before I shoved them aside. They belonged in the past, not here in my favorite coffee shop, where I was having the world's most bizarre conversation with my (amnesia-ridden?) ex-fiancé.

"So do you come here often?" he asked casually.

The cheesiness of the pickup line pulled me out of my shock. "Seriously?" I said, my tone dubious.

His eyes crinkled at the corners. I hated how endearing it was. "It's an honest question."

"Yes, I do. You *know* I do." I pulled my hand away and glanced at the counter. The barista hadn't called my order yet. "What are you doing, Dante? And I don't mean the coffee."

His good humor slipped. "You said our relationship had a rocky start, and you were right," he said quietly. "So here I am, trying for a fresh start. No business, no bullshit. Just us, meeting normally like any two people would."

The admission reached into my chest and squeezed.

If only.

The tense beat passed, and Dante's smile returned, slow and devastating. I regretted all the times I told him to scowl less. A scowling Dante was much easier to resist than a smiling one.

"I don't want to come off as too forward, since we just met," he said. "But would you like to go out sometime?"

I squashed a reluctant bloom of amusement at the absurd situation and shook my head. "Sorry. I'm not interested in dating right now."

"So it won't be a date," he said without missing a beat. "It'll be dinner between two people getting to know each other better."

My gaze narrowed. He stared back at me, his expression innocent but his eyes alive with mischief.

The barista finally called my name.

I broke eye contact and picked up my coffee. "It was nice to meet you, *Dante*," I said pointedly. "But I have to get back to work."

He followed me to the door and held it open. "If not a date, then your number. I promise I won't prank call you or send you inappropriate photos." A wicked slant of his lips. "Unless you want them, of course."

I suppressed another smile and arched a skeptical brow instead. "Are you always this persistent with women you meet in a coffee shop?"

"Only those I can't stop thinking about," he said, his eyes steady on mine.

The air turned humid. A breeze swept past, doing nothing to alleviate the sudden heaviness of my dress or the warmth unspooling in my stomach.

We were tangled in such a complicated web, but for a moment, I let myself get swept away by the fantasy of us as a normal couple. Normal first meet, normal dates, normal relationship. Just a woman wanting a man who wanted her back.

"If I give you my number, will you stop following me?"

A faint curve of his mouth. "We were both leaving, so I don't know if that counts as *following*, but yes."

I gave him my number. He already had it, of course, but he typed it into his phone like he didn't.

"Dante." I stopped him when he was halfway down the sidewalk.

He looked back at me.

"How did you know I would be here at this time?"

"I didn't. But I know it's your favorite coffee shop, and you always come here around lunchtime." His parting words drifted toward me on the breeze. "It was nice meeting you, Vivian."

Dante

One ring. Two. Three.

I paced my room, my stomach twisted with nerves as I waited for her to answer.

It was ten thirty, which meant she was getting ready for bed. She usually took an hour to wind down with a shower or a bath, depending on how stressed she was, a bafflingly intricate ten-step skin-care routine, and some reading, if she wasn't too tired.

I'd timed my call so I'd catch her after she got out of the shower.

Four rings. Five.

Assuming, of course, she picked up my call.

My nerves pulled tighter.

Vivian gave me her number that afternoon, which meant she wanted me to call, right? If she didn't, she would've simply left. Hell, a part of me had *expected* her to.

I'd lingered in that damn coffee shop for almost two hours on the off chance I'd see her. She went there every day, but her timing varied depending on her workload. It wasn't the world's greatest plan, but it'd worked, even if it'd meant skipping a lunch meeting.

Six rings. Sev—

"Hello?" Her voice flowed over the line. Clear and sweet, like the first gasp of air after surfacing from a frigid lake.

The breath released from my lungs. "Hi. This is Dante."

"Dante..." she mused, like she was trying to remember who I was.

At least she was playing along. *Progress.*

"We met at the coffee shop this afternoon," I reminded her with a touch of amusement.

"Ah, right. You're supposed to wait three days," Vivian said. "Calling a woman the same day you get her number could be considered desperate."

I paused in front of the window and stared out at the dark sprawl of Central Park below. The image blended with the room reflected behind me—the half-empty perfume bottles lining the dresser, the perfectly made bed where her scent still lingered, the armchair where she liked to curl up and read at night.

She hadn't picked up the rest of her belongings yet, and I didn't know whether it was a blessing or a curse. A blessing, because it gave me hope she would return. A curse, because everywhere I turned, there she was. A beautiful, haunting presence I felt but couldn't touch.

A familiar ache worked its way into my chest.

"Not could, *mia cara*," I said, my voice low. My reflection stared back at me, taut with exhaustion and self-loathing. I hadn't slept properly in a week, and my appearance suffered for it. "I *am* desperate."

Silence followed, so deep and profound it swallowed everything except the painful thuds of my heart.

Admitting weakness, much less desperation, was unheard of for a Russo. Hell, I didn't even admit when I had a cold. But denying my feelings had landed me in my current hell, and I wasn't going to make the same mistake twice.

Not when it came to Vivian.

My hand strangled my phone while I waited for her answer. None came.

She was quiet for so long I double-checked whether she'd hung up. She hadn't.

"I've never..." I cleared my throat, wishing I was more eloquent at expressing my emotions. It was one of the few skills my grandfather hadn't drilled into me since I was young. "I've never had to...pursue someone before, so perhaps I'm not doing this right. But I wanted to hear your voice." Without pretty words, all I had was the truth.

More silence.

The ache bled from my chest into my voice. "The apartment isn't the same without you, *mia cara*."

Despite the bustle of staff and deliveries, the smell of Greta's cooking, and the millions of dollars' worth of art and furniture, it'd turned into a shell of itself in her absence.

A sky without stars, a home without heart.

"Don't," Vivian whispered.

The air shifted, our earlier playfulness vanishing beneath the weight of our emotions.

"It's the truth," I said. "Your clothes are here. Your memories are here. But *you're* not here, and I..." I dragged in a shaky breath and pushed my hand through my hair. "Fuck, Vivian, I didn't think I was capable of missing someone so much. But I am, and I do."

I had all the money in the world, but it couldn't buy me the only thing I wanted.

Her, back by my side.

It was what I'd wanted since I came home and found her packing. Hell, it was what I'd wanted since we returned from Paris and I pulled away like an idiot, but my head had been so far up my ass about Francis and revenge I couldn't see anything except my own bullshit. It took my brother, of all people, to make me see the light.

I loved Vivian. I'd been falling in love with her, bit by bit, since she crashed my exhibition and stared me down with defiance in her eyes.

"Say something, sweetheart," I said softly when she went quiet again.

"You say you miss me now, but the feeling will pass. You're Dante Russo. You can have anyone." A waver rippled beneath her voice. "You don't need me."

The tiny crack on the word *me* hit me like a punch in the gut.

You never wanted to get married, and you never wanted me.

One of her six reasons, and one I took a fair share of the blame for. But I wasn't the only one. Her parents had a hand in making her feel like she was dispensable other than what she could do for them, and I'd never forgive them for it.

It was hypocritical, but I didn't care.

"I don't want *anyone*," I said fiercely. "I want *you*. Your wit and intelligence, your kindness and charm. The way your eyes crinkle when you laugh and how your smile makes the world tilt just a little bit. I even want the disgusting food combinations you put together and somehow make taste good."

A half laugh, half sob bled over the line.

"But that's the thing about you, Vivian." My voice softened into something rawer. "You take the most ordinary or unexpected things and make them extraordinary. You see the silver lining in every situation and the good in everyone, even if they don't deserve it. And I'm selfish enough to hope you'll see how much I don't just want but *need* you. Today, tomorrow, and all the days that come after that."

Another sob, this one quieter but no less powerful.

Fuck, I wished I could see her. Hold her. Comfort her. And look into her eyes so she knew I meant every damn word I said.

"I know it took me a while to get here, sweetheart, and I'm not the best with expressing my emotions, but..." A ragged breath. "Give me a chance to prove it to you. Go on a date with me. Just one."

The first silence had been long. This one was torturous.

My heart slammed, fast and hard enough to bruise, then stopped altogether when Vivian finally replied. Soft and hesitant, yet thick with emotion.

"Okay. Just one."

CHAPTER 39

Dante

"*MICETTA*, IT'S SO NICE TO SEE YOU!" GRETA BRUSHED past me and swept Vivian up in a hug. She only used the *little kitten* endearment for her grandchildren, but apparently, she'd extended it to Vivian. "The house isn't the same without you."

I scowled at her pointed tone. She'd given me the cold treatment all week. I was pretty sure she'd burned my pork chops on purpose the other night. I'd forced down two bites before I gave up and ordered takeout. It wasn't just her either; even Edward had cast disapproving glances my way when he thought I wasn't looking.

My staff didn't know what happened with Vivian. They only knew she was gone, and they blamed me for it.

Hell, I blamed myself too, which was why I was trying to make amends.

I'd spent the past two days since my call with Vivian planning the date, and my nerves were a humiliating wreck. I hadn't been this nervous since I was a high school freshman asking out the most popular girl in school.

I pushed my hands into my pockets while Vivian returned Greta's hug. An irrational plume of green smoke curled through me. Hell must be frigid if I was jealous of my damn seventy-four-year-old housekeeper.

"It's good to see you too," Vivian said, her voice warm. "Not working too hard, I hope."

"No, just making sure my *boss*"—Greta raised her voice even though I stood less than five feet away—"doesn't mess up any more than he has. It's a full-time job, *micetta*. Not for the faint of heart."

Fucking Greta. Every day, I questioned why I hadn't fired her yet.

An awkward silence bloomed. Vivian glanced in my direction and quickly looked away. My already raw nerves shredded into ribbons.

"Well," Greta said, obviously realizing she'd made things more uncomfortable than intended. "I'll let you two get to it. I'll be in the kitchen." She patted Vivian's hand and glared at me as she passed.

Don't fuck up, her eyes said.

My scowl deepened. Like I needed her to tell me that.

"Should I be wary of the fact that the date is at your house?" Vivian asked.

I'd told her to dress comfortably, but even in a simple cotton sundress and sandals, she was so fucking beautiful it took my breath away.

Our house. "Not unless you're scared of food and a good time."

"You have a high opinion of your date planning skills."

"You've never complained."

She rolled her eyes, but my mouth curved at her faint smile. It was progress, no matter how small.

"So." I cleared my throat as we walked toward the den, where I'd set everything up. "The Legacy Ball was a hit. The whole city's buzzing about it."

"They're buzzing about Veronica Foster's appearance more than anything," she said. "Who could've guessed she has such good vocals?"

Most socialites who dabbled in the arts "succeeded" due to nepotism, not talent. Veronica was a surprising exception.

"You did," I said. "You gave her a slot after watching her tape. I'm sure Buffy's happy."

"Yes. My reputation lives to see another day."

Another awkward silence thudded between us.

Lau Jewels' stock had plummeted to record low levels after a deluge of bad press. Vivian wasn't too affected yet—I'd made sure of that—but she wasn't immune to the whispers and speculation.

Things I had a hand in fomenting.

Guilt pierced my gut.

I'd played a Hail Mary at the ball Friday night. Part of me had expected her to slap me and storm off, but another, uncharacteristically idealistic part had hoped she would hear me out.

And she had.

I didn't know what I did to deserve it, but I was fucking taking it.

We arrived at the den. I hesitated for a beat before opening the doors.

Get your shit together, Russo. I was in my late thirties. I was too old to be acting like a damn teenager on his first date. But that was exactly what this was, minus the teenager part. Our first real date.

No lies, no secrets, no deceptions.

Just us.

A rush of anxiety spiked through me when Vivian surveyed the room with wide eyes. I'd agonized over the date for hours before settling on something simple yet personal. Today wasn't about the glitz and glamour. It was about spending time together and fixing our relationship.

She liked romance and astronomy, so I'd cued up some romantic fantasy about a fallen star who was actually a woman (or some shit like that) on the flat-screen TV. I'd never heard of the movie, but according to Greta's granddaughter—yes, I'd resorted to asking a high schooler for help—it was "super cute."

Over two dozen takeout containers sat on top of the coffee table next to Pringles, pickles, and pudding. I'd bought a vintage popcorn machine and rushed to install it yesterday for the full movie experience. The snack was disgusting, but Vivian and most of the world liked it for some godforsaken reason.

"You said you haven't found a new favorite dumpling place after the shop in Boston closed, so I figured I'd help you," I said when her eyes lingered on the takeout boxes. "Samples from thirty-four of the best dumpling places in the five boroughs, as determined by Sebastian Laurent himself."

The CEO of the Laurent Restaurant Group was a renowned gastronome. If he said something was good, it was good.

"Are you sure this isn't a ploy to stuff me with so much food I won't be able to leave?" Vivian teased. Her shoulders relaxed for the first time since she arrived.

I grinned. "Can't confirm or deny, but if you want to stay, I won't stop you."

She hadn't moved the rest of her belongings yet. I knew it was because she'd been busy with the Legacy Ball, but I took it as a sign they were already where they—and she—belonged. With me.

Vivian's cheeks pinked, but she didn't reply.

"How did you know this was one of my favorite movies growing up?" she asked when the film got underway.

She plucked a dumpling from one of the containers and took a delicate bite. I wasn't sure she could fit all thirty-four in one day, but we could always try the ones she missed later.

"I didn't," I admitted. "I was looking for a movie about

stars that *wasn't* a documentary or sci-fi. Greta's granddaughter helped me out."

I should buy the girl a thank-you present. Maybe a car or a vacation of her choice.

"Taking advice from a teenager? Very un-Dante Russo-like."

"Yeah, well, being Dante Russo-like hasn't been the best decision lately."

Our gazes touched. Her smile faded, leaving soft wariness behind.

"Luca came over Monday night," I said. "I told him what happened. For the first time, he gave me advice instead of taking it. It was damn good advice too."

"What did he say?"

"That I needed to fight for you. And he was right."

Vivian's breaths shallowed. Something exploded on-screen, but we didn't look away from each other.

My heart slammed against my rib cage. The air thickened and sparked like kindling doused with gasoline, and just when the silence stretched to its breaking point, she spoke again.

"I confronted my father on Wednesday," she said quietly, shocking the hell out of me. "I flew to Boston and showed up at his office. I didn't tell him I was coming. I might've lost my nerve if I had."

I waited for her to continue. When she didn't, I gave her a gentle nudge. "What happened?"

She toyed with her food. "Long story short, we got into a huge fight over what he did. He asked me to ask *you* to...help with the company's troubles. I said no. And he disowned me."

The words were matter-of-fact, but her voice was sad enough to make my heart ache.

Shit.

"I'm sorry, sweetheart." I loathed Francis with the fire of a thousand suns, but he was her family. She loved him, and the split must've devastated her.

"It's okay. I mean, it's not, but it is." Vivian shook her head. "It was my choice. I could've gone along with what he wanted, but it wasn't right. I was still a pawn to him, and I refused to let him use me to manipulate you."

It would've worked.

Francis Lau had deduced my weakness. There was nothing I wouldn't give Vivian if she asked.

"It's your family's company," I said, watching her carefully. Honestly, I was surprised she wasn't more upset about what I did. I'd pushed the button knowing it would hurt her family and, by extension, her. And I had no excuse other than my pride and thirst for vengeance. "What do you want to happen?"

"I don't want it to crash, obviously. If I could help in any other way, I would. But…" She blew out a breath. "This is going to sound bad, but my father has never faced many consequences for his actions. He's the boss in the office and at home. He does what he wants, and other people have to go with it. This is the first time he's had to deal with repercussions. And the thing about him is he only understands strength and power. Subtlety doesn't work on him, not when it comes to things like this. I don't agree with what you did, but I understand it. So even though I should hate you…" Her voice lowered until it was barely audible. "I don't."

My knuckles turned white from gripping my knee. "Even if the company goes bankrupt?"

A frown tugged at her lips. "Do you think it will?"

"It's very possible." I didn't take my eyes off her. "Tell me the truth, Vivian. Do you want me to step in and end it?"

We hadn't reached a critical juncture yet. What'd been done to Lau Jewels was reversible, but there was a ticking clock on the operation. Soon, it would be out of even my hands.

"I will," I said. "No manipulation from your father. No questions asked. Just say the word."

I meant what I said the other night. I loved her more than I ever hated Francis, and if being with her meant I had to save him, I'd do it without hesitation.

Vivian's eyes shone in the light pouring from the TV. "Why do that when you went to all this trouble to punish him?"

"Because I don't care about punishment or revenge anymore. I care about you."

The shine brightened. A tiny tremble rolled through her when I brushed my thumb over her cheek, the food and movie forgotten.

I had no frame of reference for the indescribable ache in the pit of my stomach. It was endless and starved, satiated only by the softness of her skin beneath mine.

Vivian didn't touch me back. But she also didn't pull away.

"What are we doing, Dante?" she whispered.

My thumb traveled south and skimmed the curve of her bottom lip. "We're working things out the way any couple would."

"Most couples aren't as dysfunctional as we are."

"There's nothing wrong with a little dysfunction. It keeps things interesting." I smiled at her soft huff before turning serious again. "Move back in, *mia cara*. You can have your old room if you don't feel comfortable sleeping in ours yet." I swallowed. "Greta misses you. Edward misses you. *I* miss you. So damn much."

Vivian dragged in a shaky breath. "You really think it's that simple? I move back in and everything's fixed?"

"No." We were in a hell of a mess, and I wasn't that naive. "But it's a first step." I removed my hand and brushed my lips over hers, just light enough to steal a hint of a taste. "You and me, sweetheart. That's the destination. And I'm willing to take as many steps as I need to get there."

CHAPTER 40

Vivian

I DIDN'T MOVE BACK IN WITH DANTE.

Part of me wanted to, but I wasn't ready to jump in with both feet again so soon.

I did, however, agree to another date with him.

Three days after our movie night, we arrived at a quiet corner of the Brooklyn Botanic Garden. It was a gorgeous afternoon, all clear skies and golden sunshine, and the picnic setup looked like something out of a fairy tale.

A low wooden table stretched across a thick ivory blanket, surrounded by huge cushions, gold and glass floor lanterns, and an oversize wicker hamper. The table itself was set with porcelain plates and a feast of foods, including baguettes, charcuterie, and desserts.

"Dante," I breathed, stunned by the sheer intricacy of the setup. "What..."

"I remembered how much you like picnics." His palm slid from my hip to the small of my back. Fire licked over my skin, chasing away my goose bumps from the sight before us.

"Please don't tell me you shut down the garden for this."

Most visitors picnicked on one of the grassy lawns, but we were smack-dab in the middle of an actual garden.

"Of course not," Dante said. "I only reserved part of it."

His amusement following my groan was a cool glass of water on a hot day, and the atmosphere was comfortable enough to sink into as we settled around the table.

It was easy and effortless, a far cry from the poignant but charged air the other night. Here, I could almost forget the troubles waiting for us outside the lush confines of the garden.

"This might be the longest date I've been on," I said. It'd started with a special exhibition at the Whitney Museum, followed by mimosas at an exclusive brunch party, and now this.

On the surface, it seemed like any other lavish date, but I suspected Dante had an ulterior motive. The rumors regarding our relationship and my father's company were escalating. By taking me out so publicly, he was making a statement: our relationship was rock solid (even though it wasn't), and any slander about me personally wouldn't be tolerated. My tie to him was the best form of protection against vicious society gossip.

No one wanted to piss Dante off.

"We can make it longer." His grin worked its way into my chest. If he was upset about me rejecting his proposal to move back in, he didn't show it. He hadn't brought up the issue since his initial disappointment. "Overnight trip to upstate New York? I have a cabin in the Adirondacks."

"Don't push it. I'm docking the extra hours off our next date."

"So there *is* going to be a next date."

"Maybe. Depends if you keep annoying me or not."

His deep-rumbled laugh scattered tingles down my spine.

"I don't come to Brooklyn often, but I've been visiting more since my brother's girlfriend lives here." A grimace touched his mouth. "Guess what her name is."

"I have no idea."

"Leaf," he said flatly. "Her name is Leaf Greene."

I almost choked on my water. "Her parents have a, uh, unique sense of humor."

Leaf Greene? Her middle school years must've been horrific.

"She's been helping Luca do 'inner work,' whatever the hell that means. But he's not doing cocaine or drinking himself into unconsciousness at a nightclub, so it's progress." Dante's tone was dry.

"How are things between you and Luca?" He'd mentioned they were talking more, but I didn't know where things stood with them.

Dante poured a glass of mint iced tea and slid it across the table toward me. "Different. Not bad, but…different. He's matured over the past year, and I don't worry as much about getting a call to bail him out of jail in the middle of the night. We agreed to bimonthly meals together." Another grimace. "Last one was at Leaf's house, and she cooked fucking tofu chicken."

A laugh spilled out. "Tofu can be good if prepared properly."

"Tofu as tofu, not as chicken. *Chicken* should be chicken," Dante growled. "And in case you were wondering, no, she *didn't* prepare it properly. It tasted like chewy cardboard."

I couldn't help laughing again.

The public thought we were still engaged, but it was private moments like these that I'd missed—the little jokes and asides, the personal details, the conversations about mundane topics that, taken as a whole, meant as much as more meaningful talks.

Love wasn't always about the big moments. More often, it was tucked in the small moments connecting the major ones. This date felt like one of those. A stepping stone on our path toward potential reconciliation.

I wasn't ready to fully trust Dante again, but I might one day.

"For someone who hasn't had a serious relationship in years, you're pretty good at putting together these dates," I said after we finished eating. We walked through the garden to stretch our legs and soak in our surroundings before we left.

All around us, spring flowers bloomed—lilacs, peonies, azaleas, dogwoods, wild geraniums, and Spanish bluebells. The air was alive with the sweet scents of nature, but I barely noticed. I was too distracted by Dante's scent and the heat emanating from his body. It touched my side, warm and heavy even though we walked a respectable distance from each other.

"It's easy when you know the other person." His reply was both casual and intimate.

My heart wavered for a beat. "And you think you know me?"

"I like to think I do."

We stopped in the shade of a nearby tree, its trunk against my back, its branches arching overhead in a canopy of leaves. Sunlight dappled through the foliage, turning Dante's eyes into the color of rich, molten amber. A five-o'clock shadow stubbled his strong jaw and cheeks, and my entire body tingled when I remembered the scratch of that stubble on my inner thighs.

The air sparked, a lit match in a pool of gasoline. All the banked heat we'd suppressed during lunch surged toward the surface in an unabashed wave. My skin was suddenly too hot, my clothes too heavy. An electric link snaked around us, slow and sinuous.

"For example..." Had my voice always been that high and breathy?

"For example, I know you're still scared," Dante said softly. "I know you're not ready to fully trust me again, but you want to. Otherwise, you wouldn't be here."

His observation pierced my mask like it was made of nothing more than breaths and whispers.

Another wavering heartbeat. "That's quite an assumption."

"Perhaps." A step brought him closer. My pulse sped up. "Then tell me. What do you want?"

"I..." His fingertips grazed my wrist, and my pulse broke into a flat-out sprint.

"Whatever it is, I'll give it to you." Dante threaded his fingers with mine, his gaze steady. *Hot.*

Words eluded me, lost in the haze clouding my brain.

We stared at each other, the air heavy with things we wanted to but couldn't say.

Amber darkened into midnight. Dante's body was a study in tension, his jaw hard and his shoulders so taut his muscles were almost vibrating.

His next words pitched low and rough. "Tell me what you want, Vivian. Do you want me on my knees?"

Oh God.

Oxygen disappeared when he slowly lowered himself to the ground, the movement both proud and subservient.

His breath fanned across my skin. "Do you want this?" His fingers trailed from my hand down over the back of my leg, leaving fire in their wake.

My thoughts were muddled, but I had the remaining sense to know this wasn't about sex. It was about vulnerability. Atonement. *Absolution.*

It was a pivotal moment disguised as an inconsequential one and condensed into one word.

"*Yes.*" It was both command and capitulation, moan and sigh.

Dante's breath released.

If I were with anyone else, I'd worry about someone walking by and seeing us. But Dante's presence was like an invisible shield protecting me from the rest of the world. If he didn't want anyone to see us, they wouldn't.

His palms burned as they parted my thighs. He'd barely touched me, and I was already on fire.

I tipped my head back, drowning in arousal, in heat and lust and the reverence of his touch as he kissed his way up my thigh. His stubble rasped against my skin and sent tiny shocks of pleasure down my spine.

"I'm sorry." The aching whisper ghosted over me, seeping into my veins and settling into my bones. Another shiver ran through me. "I'm sorry for hurting you…" A soft kiss at the delicate crease between my thigh and insistent heat. "For pushing you away…" He slid my underwear to the side and gently touched his tongue to my clit. "For ever making you feel unwanted when you're the only person I've ever loved."

His raw words blended with my cry when he drew my clit into his mouth and sucked. My body arched away from the tree. My hands sank into his hair, and I could only hold on as he worshipped me with his lips and hands and tongue.

Rough yet smooth. Firm yet pleading. Carnal yet tender. Every movement sent another jolt of pure sensation through me.

Pressure built simultaneously in my chest and at the base of my spine. I was breathless with it, flying high on nothing but emotion and adrenaline.

He drew back and grazed his teeth against my sensitive clit. He pushed two fingers inside me, thrusting and curling while I writhed with abandon.

Dante knew my body. He knew exactly which buttons to push and which spots to hit, and he played it like a finely tuned instrument. A maestro conducting an orchestra of sighs and moans.

He pressed his thumb against my clit at the same time as he hit my G-spot.

The pressure exploded.

My orgasm rocked through me, and my cries still echoed in the air when Dante rose to his feet, his chest heaving.

He braced his hands on either side of my head and tenderly kissed away the tears sliding down my cheeks. I hadn't realized I'd been crying.

He paused when he reached my lips. Silence thickened between us as his mouth hovered a hair's breadth from mine, waiting. Hoping. Seeking permission.

I almost gave in. Almost tilted my chin up and closed the breath between us while my body buzzed from the aftershocks of my climax.

Instead, I turned my head. Just a fraction, but enough for Dante to step back with a ragged breath.

We took a big step forward, but I wasn't ready for another one yet. I was too physically and emotionally drained.

"I'm sorry," I whispered.

"You don't have to apologize, *mia cara*." His fingers twined with mine again, strong and reassuring. His eyes were soft. "As many steps as it takes, remember? We'll get there."

CHAPTER 41

Vivian

DANTE AND I DIDN'T SPEAK OF OUR GARDEN DATE again, but it hovered in the back of my mind for days after.

Not because of the sex but because of the vulnerability. The patience. The glimpse at *how* our relationship would be different this time around.

For the first time, I truly believed reconciliation was possible. Maybe not now, but one day. Like Dante said, we'd get there.

We were walking off dinner at the top of the Empire State Building on our third date when my phone buzzed.

I paused in the middle of telling him about Buffy Darlington's offer to plan her sixty-fifth birthday. She was becoming a loyal client, which was both a blessing and a curse. Her expectations were higher than the building we were currently standing on.

I checked my phone, and my pulse jumped when I saw the caller's name. "I'm sorry, I have to take this. It's my sister."

It was the middle of the night in Eldorra, and I hadn't talked to Agnes since I told her about my showdown with our father. Did something happen to her or Gunnar?

"Of course." Dante tucked his hands into his pockets and

nodded at the other end of the observation deck. "Take your time. I'll be there."

It was hard to reconcile this Dante with the rude, arrogant CEO I'd met last summer, but we weren't the same people we were nine months ago.

Old him wouldn't have been this patient or understanding. Old me wouldn't have held out this long against his charm offensive. And old us wouldn't be here, trying to rebuild from the rubble of our relationship when it would be so much easier to abandon the project and move on.

"Thank you," I said, my heart strangely warm.

I waited until he was out of earshot before I picked up.

"You have to save me," Agnes said without preamble. "Mother is driving me *up the wall.*"

Relief loosened the knot of anxiety in my chest. "It's four a.m. your time. Did you really call to complain about Mother?"

"I couldn't sleep, and yes, I did. She tried to redecorate our house, Vivi. *Twice.* And she's been here for less than a week."

According to Agnes, my mother had gotten into a massive fight with my father when she found out he disowned me. She was currently staying at my sister's place in Eldorra, which was how I knew things were bad. She hated Agnes's animal menagerie because they shed so much.

"What do you want me to do? I'm in New York." I glanced at Dante, his tall frame cutting a striking figure against the city lights. "You shouldn't be talking to me anyway. Father will be upset."

"Please. I'm upset with *him*, and this fight is between you two, not us." She hesitated, then added, "That's another reason I called. He's here. In Eldorra."

My stomach plummeted.

"He's trying to make amends with Mother and says he needs

some time away from the office while the board 'discusses how to move forward.'"

Translation: they were thinking of firing him.

Lau Jewels' stock value had stabilized since Sunday, but it was lower than it should've been. The negative press coverage had done a number on the company.

"You should visit," Agnes said.

I couldn't contain a scoff. "Come on, Aggie."

"I'm serious. We need to stand together as a family now more than ever, not fight. What he did was awful, but he's still our father, Vivi."

"At what point is that not enough?"

If I was confused about my feelings toward Dante, I was twice as confused about my feelings toward my father. Did I want to reconcile with him, or was our relationship irreparable?

Agnes fell silent. "Just give it a chance," she finally said. "Please. For me, Mother, *and* you. Talk it out now that everyone's had a chance to calm down. Even if you don't make up, you'll get closure. Plus, I miss you. I haven't seen you since last fall."

"This is emotional manipulation."

"I learned from the best."

"Mother," we said in unison. When it came to guilt trips, Cecelia Lau was a diamond status frequent flyer.

"When's he leaving?" I stared at the city below. If only I could stay here forever, removed from the worries and uncertainties plaguing life on the ground.

"Monday. I know it's short notice, but if you can make it, I'd love to see you." Agnes's voice softened. "I really do miss you."

My teeth scraped my bottom lip. I could breathe now that the Legacy Ball was over, and I hadn't visited Eldorra in over a year. But was I ready to see my father again so soon?

Indecision twisted my insides.

"I miss you too," I finally said. "I'll see what I can do. Say hi to Mother for me, and get some sleep. I'll call you tomorrow."

I hung up and rejoined Dante by the edge of the deck.

"Sorry. Family stuff." I sighed and pulled my jacket tighter around me. The wind had died down, but a chill remained. "My parents are in Eldorra, and Agnes wants me to visit. Talk things out with them."

Dante was an odd person for me to discuss this with, considering his history with my father, but I didn't know who else to talk to. He was the only one besides my father and me who had a full understanding of the situation. Even Agnes and my mother didn't know the role he'd played in Lau Jewels' troubles, though they were aware of everything else.

His expression was one of studied neutrality. "Do you want to go?"

"Maybe." Another sigh. "I do want to see my sister, and I need to talk to my mother in person. But I don't know if I'm ready to face my father alone again. He's leaving Monday though, so I have to make a decision. Fast."

"You should go."

My head jerked up in surprise.

"If you don't, you'll always wonder *what if*." The moon cast Dante's face in light and shadow—sharp lines and bold features, but with a softness in his eyes that slayed me. "Do I want you to be near your father? No. I don't think he deserves to have anything to do with you. But I have a feeling you need more closure than what you got in Boston. So for that reason, you should go. See your sister. Find some clarity."

"Right." I released a long, controlled breath. "I guess I should look up flights soon." It was Thursday night. Realistically, I wouldn't fly out until Saturday, which left me with a day and change in Eldorra.

"You could." Dante paused. "Or you could take my jet."

My eyes widened.

"You said you might not be ready to face your father alone again. If you want, I can go with you." His voice grew soft. "Given my...complications with your family, I understand if you don't want me to, but the offer's on the table. You can take my jet either way. It's easier than finding a flight at this late notice."

My heart fluttered without my permission. "If you go, it means you'll have to stay in the same house as my father." There were no hotels or inns near my sister's estate. It was too remote.

A shadow crossed Dante's face. "I know."

"You'd be okay with that?"

"I'll survive. It's not about me, *mia cara*."

Warmth curled low in my stomach. "And work?"

He gave me a crooked smile. "I think I can convince the boss to give me a day off."

The warmth spread into my veins.

Going on a long-distance trip with Dante was a bad idea...but going to see my father without backup was worse.

"Can we leave tomorrow?"

CHAPTER 42

Vivian

MY SISTER AND BROTHER-IN-LAW LIVED IN HELLEJE, AN idyllic county of beautiful villages, centuries-old manors, and state-preserved heritage sites located three hours north of Eldorra's capital, Athenberg.

Dante and I landed at Helleje's tiny airport on Friday afternoon. It took us another forty minutes by car to reach Agnes and Gunnar's thirty-acre countryside estate.

"Vivian!" My sister answered the door, the picture of country chic in her loose white blouse and riding boots. "It's so good to see you. You too, Dante," she said graciously.

I assumed my father hadn't told her what Dante did either. She wouldn't have been so calm otherwise.

I wasn't surprised. My father would never willingly admit someone got the better of him.

Dante and I dropped our luggage in our rooms upstairs before rejoining Agnes in the living room. Gunnar was in session in Parliament, so it really was a Lau family weekend.

I paused when I saw my mother sitting on the couch next to my sister. At first glance, she looked as put together as ever, but a closer examination revealed the lines of tension bracketing her mouth and the faint purple smudges beneath her eyes.

A pang hit my chest.

Her eyes brightened, and she rose halfway at my entrance before sitting back down. It was an unusually awkward move for Cecelia Lau, one that made my heart squeeze.

Agnes's gaze ping-ponged between us.

"Dante, why don't I give you a tour of the house?" she said. "The layout can be confusing..."

He glanced at me. I gave him a small nod.

"I'd love a tour," he said.

My mother stood fully when they left the room. "Vivian. It's good to see you."

"You too, Mother."

And then I was engulfed in her arms, my eyes stinging when I breathed in the familiar scent of her perfume.

We weren't big on physical affection in our household. The last time we'd hugged had been when I was nine, but this felt like a much-needed embrace for both of us.

"I wasn't sure you would show," she said when she released me. We took our seats on the couch. "Have you lost weight? You look skinnier. You need to eat more."

I was either eating too much or too little. There was no in between.

"I haven't had much of an appetite," I said. "Stress. Things have been...chaotic."

"Yes." She took a deep breath and ran a hand over her pearls. "What a huge mess this is. I've never been so angry with your father. *Imagine*, doing *that* to Dante Russo, of all people—"

I cut her off with the question that'd been plaguing me since I overheard Dante's conversation with my father. "Did you know about the blackmail?"

Her mouth parted. "Of *course* not." She sounded appalled. "How could you think that? Blackmail is beneath us, Vivian."

"You've always gone along with what Father does. I just assumed..."

"Not always." My mother's face darkened. "I don't agree with him trying to disown you. You're *our* daughter. He doesn't get to decide whether I can see you or single-handedly kick you out of the family. I told him as much."

A ball of emotion tangled in my throat at the unexpected development. My mother had never stood up for me before.

"Is he here?"

"He's upstairs, sulking." A frown pinched her brow. "Speaking of which, you should go to your room and change before dinner. A T-shirt and yoga pants? In public? I hope no one important saw you at the airport."

Just like that, the warmth from her earlier words disappeared. "You always do that."

"Do what?" She looked bewildered.

"Criticize everything I do or wear."

"I wasn't criticizing, Vivian, merely making a suggestion. Do you think it's appropriate to wear yoga pants to dinner?"

It was amazing how fast she switched from indignant and concerned to critical.

My father was responsible for most of my family problems, but a different type of frustration had simmered toward my mother for years.

"Even if I wasn't wearing yoga pants, you'd criticize my hair, skin, or makeup. Or the way I sit or eat. It makes me feel like..." I swallowed. "It makes me feel like I'm never good enough. Like you're always disappointed in me."

If we were discussing our issues, I might as well lay it all out there. The blackmail issue was the straw that broke the camel's back, but trouble in the Lau household had been brewing for years, if not decades.

"Don't be ridiculous," my mother said. "I say those things because I *care*. If you were a stranger on the street, I wouldn't bother trying to help you improve. You're my child, Vivian. I want you to be the best you can be."

"Maybe," I said, my throat tight. "But it doesn't feel that way. It feels like you're stuck with me as your daughter and you're making do."

My mother stared at me, genuine surprise shining in her eyes.

I knew she meant well. She wasn't deliberately malicious, but the tiny cuts and barbs added up over time.

"Do you want to know why I'm so hard on you?" she finally said. "It's because we are Laus, not Logans or Lauders." She emphasized those names. "We're not the only new money family in Boston, but we're the ones who are looked down on the most by the blue-blood snobs. Why do you think that is?"

It was a rhetorical question. We both knew why.

Money bought a lot of things, but it couldn't buy off inherent biases.

"We have to work twice as hard to get an iota of the same respect as our peers. We are criticized for every misstep and examined for every flaw when others get away with much worse. We *have* to be perfect." My mother sighed. With her flawless skin and immaculate grooming, she usually passed for someone in her late thirties or early forties, but today, she looked her full age. "You're a good daughter, and I'm sorry if I ever made you feel like you're not. I criticize you to protect you, but..." She cleared her throat. "Perhaps that's not always the right approach."

I managed a laugh through the tears crowding my throat. "Perhaps not."

"I can't change entirely. I'm old, Vivian, no matter how

good my skin looks." She gave a small smile at my second laugh. "Certain things have become habit. But I can try and tone down my…observations."

It was the best I could ask for. If she'd offered anything else, it would've been unrealistic at best and inauthentic at worst. People couldn't change entirely, but effort mattered.

"Thank you," I said softly. "For listening to me, and for standing up to Father."

"You're welcome."

An awkward silence descended. Heartfelt conversations weren't common in the Lau household, and neither of us knew where to go from here.

"Well." My mother rose first and smoothed a hand over her elegant silk dress. "I have to check on the soup for dinner. I don't trust Agnes's chef. They put too much salt in everything."

"I'll shower and change." I paused. "Is Father…will he be at dinner?"

The trip would be a waste if he locked himself in his room and avoided me the entire time.

"He'll be there," my mother said. "I'll make sure of it."

Two hours later, my father and I sat across from each other at the dining table, him next to my mother, me in between Agnes and Dante.

Tension suffocated the air as we ate in silence.

He hadn't looked at me or Dante once since he entered. He was furious with us. It was obvious in the set of his jaw and the darkness of his scowl. But whatever he had to say, he didn't say it at the table with my mother and sister present.

Dante ate languorously, seemingly unaffected by my father's silent rage, while my poor sister tried to make conversation.

"You should've seen the interior minister's face when the royal cat ran across the stage," she said, recounting a story from the palace's spring ball. "I don't know how it got into the room. Queen Bridget was a good sport about it, but I thought her communications secretary would have a stroke."

No one responded.

Meadows, Eldorra's royal feline, was adorable, but none of us particularly cared about her daily adventures.

Someone coughed. Silverware clinked loudly against china. Deep in the house, one of the dogs barked.

I cut into my chicken so hard the knife scraped the plate with a soft screech.

My mother glanced at me. Normally, she would've berated me for it, but tonight, she didn't say a word.

More silence.

Finally, I couldn't take it anymore.

"We were better as a family before we were rich."

Three forks froze midair. Dante was the only one who continued eating, though his eyes were sharp and dark as he watched the others' reactions.

"We had family dinners every night. We went camping and didn't care whether our clothes were last season or what type of car we drove. And we would've never forced someone into doing something they didn't want to." The insinuation hung heavy over the frozen table. "We were happier, and we were better people."

I kept my eyes on my father.

I was being more confrontational than I'd planned, but it had to be said. I was tired of holding back what I thought simply because it was *unbecoming* or *inappropriate*. We were family. We were *supposed* to tell each the truth, no matter how hard it may be to hear.

"Were we?" My father appeared unmoved. "I didn't hear

you complaining when I paid your full college tuition so you could graduate without debt. You weren't concerned about being *happier* or *better people* when I bankrolled your shopping sprees and year abroad."

Viciousness coated his words.

The metal handle of my fork dug into my palm. "I'm not saying I didn't benefit from the money. But benefiting from and even enjoying something doesn't mean I can't criticize it. You've changed, Dad." I deliberately used my old address for him. It sounded distant and strange, like the echoes of a long-forgotten song. "You've strayed so far from—"

"Enough!" Cutlery and china rattled in an eerie déjà vu from my father's office.

Beside me, Dante finally set down his fork, his muscles tensing and coiling like a panther ready to pounce.

"I won't sit here and have you insult me in front of my own family." My father glared at me. "It's bad enough you chose *him*"—he didn't look at Dante, but everyone knew which *him* he was talking about—"over us. We raised you, fed you, and made sure you wanted for nothing, and you thank us by walking away when the family needs you most. You do *not* get to sit here and lecture me. I am your *father*."

That was always his excuse. *I am your father.* As if that absolved him from any wrongdoing and gave him the right to manipulate me like a chess piece in a game I never consented to.

My mouth tasted like copper. "No, you're not. You disowned me, remember?"

The silence was loud enough to make my ears ring.

My mother's lips parted in a silent inhale; my sister's eyes turned the size of half quarters.

Dante didn't move an inch, but his warm reassurance touched my side.

"You didn't treat me like a daughter," I said. "You treated me like a pawn. Your willingness to cut me off the minute I refused to do your bidding is proof of that. I'll always be grateful for the opportunities you provided me growing up, but the past doesn't excuse the present. And the truth is, present you is not someone I would be proud to call a parent."

I fixed my stare on my father, whose face had turned a lovely shade of crimson.

"Are you at all sorry about what you did?" I asked quietly. "Knowing how it would affect the people around you?" *How it would affect us?*

I wished, *prayed* for a single spark of remorse. Something that told me my old father was still buried under there somewhere. If he was, I didn't see him.

My father's eyes remained stony and unyielding. "I did what I had to do for my family."

Unlike you.

The unspoken words bounced off me, unable to find purchase.

I didn't bother replying. I'd heard all I needed to hear.

Dante

I found Francis in the living room after dinner, staring at the fireplace. It was spring, but nights in Helleje were cold enough to warrant extra heat.

"It doesn't feel good, does it?"

He startled at the sound of my voice. A scowl pinched between his brows when he looked up and saw me enter. "What are you talking about?"

"Vivian." I stopped in front of him, half-empty scotch in hand, blocking his view of the fire. "Losing her."

My shadow spilled onto the couch, looming large and dark enough to swallow him whole.

Francis glared up at me.

He looked smaller without the bluster backing him up. Older too, with craggy lines crisscrossing his face and bags beneath his eyes.

A month ago, I'd hated him with a burning passion, so much so the mere thought of him hazed my vision with red. Now, looking at him, I just felt scorn and yes, a bit of remaining hatred too. But for the most part, my anger had cooled from molten lava into hard, unfeeling rock.

I was ready to put Francis Lau behind me and move the hell on...*after* we had a little chat.

"She'll come to her senses." He sank deeper into the couch. "She'll never turn her back on family."

"That's the thing," I said. "You're not her family anymore."

It'd taken every ounce of willpower to hold my tongue at dinner. This was Vivian's trip and her time to confront her family; she didn't need my help. But now that dinner was over and it was just me and her father, I didn't have to hold back.

"You use your family as an excuse," I said. "You say you want what's best for them, but you did what you did for yourself. *You* wanted the status and influence. *You* pawned your daughters off to men they barely knew for your own ego. If you truly cared about your family, you would've put their happiness over your selfish desires. You didn't."

Things had worked out well with the Lau daughters' arranged matches—though a question mark still hung over my relationship with Vivian—but Francis had no way of knowing how they'd turn out when he made the deals.

Crimson darkened his skin. "You know *nothing* about us or what I had to do to get to where I am."

"No, I don't, because I don't care," I said coldly. "I don't give a shit about you, Francis, but I *do* love Vivian, so I'll keep this short and simple for her sake."

He opened his mouth, but I continued before he could speak.

"You say she walked away from her family when she's the *only* reason you're sitting here right now. If you weren't her father and she didn't still care about you despite the shit you put her through, you'd be buried beneath the fucking rubble of your company. But I'm not as nice as Vivian."

The soft menace of my words curled through the air and settled on the surface of my scotch.

"If she wants to reconcile with you in the future, that's up to her. But if you talk to her again the way you did at the dinner table tonight—if you hurt her in any way, if you make her shed a single tear or cause her a single fucking second of sadness, I will take *everything* from you. Your business, your house, your reputation. I will blacklist you so thoroughly you won't even be able to get past the bouncer at your shitty local bar." My gaze burned into Francis's as his face lost color. "Do you understand?"

My anger may have cooled, but it was still there, one wrong word away from erupting again. I was ready to put Francis in the rearview mirror where he belonged, but if he upset Vivian...

Heat scorched my gut, warmer than the fire at my back.

Francis gripped his knee. He vibrated with resentment, but without Vivian as a buffer or leverage over me, there wasn't a damn thing he could do.

"Yes," he finally ground out.

"Good." My smile was devoid of warmth. "Remember, this time, I showed you mercy for her. Next time, I won't be so forgiving."

I finished my drink in one easy pull and tucked the empty glass in his hand like he was one of the servers he sneered at before walking away.

Six months ago, I would've burned the fucking room down with Francis in it. But tonight, I wasn't interested in a showdown or argument.

My hatred of him had almost cost me the person I loved, and I refused to waste a single second more on him. Not when there was someone else I'd much rather spend my time with.

CHAPTER 43

Vivian

THE KNOCK CAME WHILE I WAS GETTING READY FOR BED.

I knew who it was before I answered the door, but that didn't stop my stomach from doing a strange flip when I saw Dante standing in the hall.

He wore the same cashmere sweater and jeans as he had at dinner.

I didn't know where he went after the meal, but he was here now, and the sight of him made my chest twist with unexpected emotion.

I hadn't realized how much I'd needed to see him, *just* him, until now. He was the only person who could ground me after such a roller coaster of a day.

We stared at each other, the silence brimming with unspoken words until I opened the door wider in invitation. The small movement broke the spell, and both of us visibly relaxed as he walked in and I took a seat on the bed.

"You did good back there." Dante leaned against the wall, one hand tucked in his pocket while his eyes found mine. "Standing up to your father."

"Thanks." I offered a rueful smile as I sat on the bed across from him. "But I wish the conversation had gone better."

"It went the way it was supposed to." Silver shards of moonlight glinted in Dante's eyes. "Now you know the type of man he is. He's too far gone, *mia cara*. I'm not just saying this because I'm biased against him. If I could choose, I would rather you mend your relationship with him and be happy, but who he is right now?" His voice softened. "He doesn't deserve your time or energy."

An ache settled in my throat. "I know."

I didn't have the closure I wanted, but I had the one I needed.

"I'm impressed you held back at dinner," I added, trying to lighten the mood. "I'd prepared myself for the verbal insults. Maybe a few threats and punches to keep things interesting."

Dante hadn't said a word during the confrontation. I'd never seen him so quiet for so long, but I appreciated it. I had to fight my own battles instead of relying on others to fight them for me.

"I've been practicing my restraint." The faintest tip of his mouth. "Like I said, this trip isn't about me."

Awareness tingled as our eyes held.

My room was large enough to accommodate four, but Dante's presence filled every corner, making the edges of my mind hazy and the hollow in my chest a little less empty.

"Thank you for coming with me." I tried to ignore the way his stare bathed me with warmth. "I know how busy you are, and it can't be fun staying under the same roof as someone you hate."

"I don't know. It was pretty fun seeing him almost burst a blood vessel at the table."

An involuntary laugh spilled past my lips. "You're horrible."

"Only to those who deserve it." Another smile tugged at his lips. "It's nice to hear you laugh again, *mia cara*."

My smile faded at the soft, heavy meaning tucked between his words.

Another silence fell between us, thick and charged with tension. Lit fireflies danced over my skin, leaving trails of electricity in their wake. My dress felt heavy, and I shifted on the bed, trying to ease the new ache blooming in my stomach.

Dante's eyes darkened at the corners. His jaw ticked for a moment before he pushed himself off the wall.

"It's late." Roughness edged his voice. "We should both get some rest."

He made it halfway to the door before I stopped him. "Wait."

He paused, his shoulders stiff. He didn't turn to look at me.

The air stretched taut around my chest as I worked through my next move.

I'd made amends with my mother, sort of. I'd found closure with my father. The only relationship I had left to untangle was Dante's.

It'd shifted and rearranged into multiple forms over the past year. We'd gone from strangers to roommates to adversaries to friends to lovers to exes…the list went on. Eventually, it would have to end, and it was up to me to decide where the cutoff was.

I stood, my pulse beating faster with each step as I slid between Dante and the door.

He stared down at me, his expression indifferent but his eyes hot enough to make every inch of me burn.

What was my deal breaker?

Keeping my father's manipulation a secret from me? Pushing me away? Trying to destroy my family's company? All things worthy of my anger, but also all things backed with a reason.

It took time and effort, but we figured it out. I think you and Dante can too.

"You didn't have to be here." His time was the most valuable thing he owned.

Those coal-black eyes burned hotter. "No."

My pulse became a roar. "This afternoon, several major newspapers retracted their stories about fraud at Lau Jewels." I'd gotten the alerts before dinner. "Interesting timing."

"Interesting or coincidental."

"Maybe. But I don't believe in coincidence anymore." The words drifted between us on air and hope. "Why did you do it?"

Indifference melted into something softer. "Because they're still your family, *mia cara*. Because if I could go back in time and stop your father from blackmailing me, I wouldn't. Otherwise…" His voice dipped, just the tiniest fraction. "I wouldn't have met you."

The words throbbed in my ears and hummed in my blood. Emotion blocked any words from leaving my throat, so I did the only thing I could.

I stood on tiptoes and gently pressed my lips to his.

A breath passed between us. A motionless beat stretched.

And then his palm was on my cheek, and his mouth was moving over mine. Softly and desperately, as if he wanted to take his time reacquainting himself with my taste but was afraid I would disappear any second.

Lazy tendrils of desire curled through me as I slid my tongue against his and savored the taste of our kiss. Bold and rich, like hunger spiced with longing and sweetened with forgiveness.

I panted into his mouth, licking and exploring, as I edged us toward the bed. Dante was usually in control, but this time, he let me take the lead. He watched me, his eyes heavy-lidded and chest heaving, as I removed our clothes.

Our hands roamed, our hearts pounding in sync and our kisses growing in intensity until the heat became too much to bear.

I sank onto him, slowly accepting him inch by inch until he was buried fully inside me.

We groaned in unison. Dante's hands gripped my hips while I rocked against him. Sweat misted my skin, soft pants and moans filled the air, and a delicious pressure built inside me, climbing higher and higher until my mind was hazy with lust.

His muscles visibly strained from the effort of holding back, but he didn't attempt to take over as I rode us into a simultaneous, toe-curling orgasm. It was the first time we'd ever come together.

The overwhelming intimacy of the moment set off a second, smaller climax, and the aftershocks were still rippling through me when Dante pulled me down for a kiss.

"You look good in control, *mia cara.*" His velvety rumble caressed my skin as surely as his hand on my neck.

"I think so too." I brushed my lips against his before growing serious. "I'm not ready to move in with you again just yet. I still need time to breathe. But…we'll get there eventually."

"Take all the time you need. I'll be here." Dante rubbed his thumb over my nape. "*Per te aspetterei per sempre, amore mio.*"

"*Spero non ci vorrà così tanto.*" I smiled at his shock. "I speak six languages, Dante. Italian is one of them."

His surprise dissolved into a laugh. "You're full of surprises." He kissed me again, his face softening. "*Ti amo.*" *I love you.*

Maybe it was my closure with my family. Maybe it was the thrill of finally taking control of my life. Whatever it was, it'd demolished the walls in my chest, and my reply finally made its way out in a whisper.

"I love you too."

CHAPTER 44

Dante

"THAT'S SCORPIO." VIVIAN POINTED TO A SPOT IN THE sky. "Do you see it?"

I followed her gaze toward the constellation. It looked like any other cluster of stars.

"Mm-hmm. Looks great."

She turned her head and narrowed her eyes. "Do you really see it, or are you lying?"

"I see stars. Lots of them."

Vivian huffed out a half groan, half laugh. "You're hopeless."

"I told you, I'm not and never will be an astronomy expert. I'm just here for the view and the company." I kissed the top of her head.

We lay on a pile of blankets and cushions outside our glamping resort in Chile's Atacama Desert, one of the world's top stargazing destinations. After all the shit that'd gone down last month, this was the perfect place to reset before our wedding, which we'd pushed back to September due to renovations taking longer than expected.

We'd spent the past four days hiking volcanoes, luxuriating

in hot springs, and exploring sand dunes. My assistant had nearly keeled over with shock when I told her I was taking ten days off from work, but she'd put together the perfect itinerary for my first real vacation since I became CEO.

I'd even left my work phone at home. My team had the resort's number in case of emergencies, but they knew not to bother me unless the building was literally burning down.

"True. I guess you can stick to looking pretty." Vivian patted my arm. "We all have our talents—"

She broke off into a squeal when I rolled her over and pinned her beneath me.

"Watch your mouth," I growled, giving her a playful nip. "Or I'll punish you right here where anyone can see."

The stars reflected in her eyes and glittered with mischief. "Is that a warning or a promise?"

My groan traveled between us, dark and filled with heat. "You're a fucking tease."

"You're the one who started it." Vivian wrapped her arms around my neck and kissed me. "Don't start something you can't finish, Russo."

"When have I ever?" I skimmed my lips over the delicate line of her jaw. "But before we shock the other guests with an X-rated show…" Her laughter vibrated down my spine. "I have a confession."

My heart picked up speed. I'd spent a month preparing for this moment, yet I felt like I was teetering on the edge of a cliff without a parachute.

Vivian tilted her head. "Confession as in you forgot to book our horseback rides tomorrow, or confession as in you murdered someone and need my help burying the body?"

"Why do you always default to the morbid?"

"Because I'm friends with Isabella, and you're scary."

"I thought you said my talent was looking pretty," I teased.

"Pretty *and* scary." An impish smile curved her mouth. "They're not mutually exclusive."

"Good to know, but no, I didn't murder anyone," I said dryly. I pushed off her and sat up straight.

The desert night was cool and crisp, but heat clung to my skin like a tight-fitting suit.

"Thank God. I'm not great with shovels." Vivian sat up as well and eyed me with curiosity. "So this confession. Is it good or bad? Do I need to mentally prepare myself?"

"It's good. I hope." I cleared my throat, my heart now throttling full speed ahead. "Do you remember my trip to Malaysia a few weeks ago?"

"The seventy-two-hour one? Yes." She shook her head. "I can't believe you flew all the way there just to stay for one day. It must've been an important meeting."

"It was. I went to see my mother."

My parents had moved on from Bali and were now in Langkawi.

Confusion pinched a frown between her brows. "Why?"

She knew my mother and I didn't have the type of relationship where I'd drop everything to see her. My parents still exasperated the hell out of me, but I'd made peace with their shortcomings. They were who they were, and compared to people like Francis Lau, they were fucking saints.

"I needed to get something." I bit the bullet and retrieved a small box from my pocket.

Vivian stared at it, her expression stunned. "Dante..."

"When I first proposed to you, it was hardly a proposal," I said. My blood drummed in my ears. "Our engagement was a merger, the ring a signature. I chose that"—I nodded at the diamond on her finger—"specifically because it was cold and impersonal. But now that we're doing this for real..." I snapped open the box, revealing a dazzling red stone set in gold. One of less than three dozen in existence. "I wanted to give you something more meaningful."

Vivian released a sharp, audible exhale. Emotion sketched a vivid picture across her features, painting it with a thousand shades of shock, delight, and everything in between.

"Red diamonds are the rarest colored diamonds in existence. Only thirty or so have ever been mined. My grandfather bought one of the first red diamonds in the 1950s and proposed to my grandmother with it. She passed it to my father, who gave it to my mother..." I swallowed the lump in my throat. "Who gave it to me."

The ring blazed like a fallen star against midnight black.

My mother rarely wore it. She was too afraid of losing it during her travels, but she'd kept it safe for the day I needed it. It was one of the few sentimental things she'd done since I was born.

"A family heirloom," Vivian murmured, her voice thick.

"Yes. One that reminds me very much of you. Beautiful, rare, and difficult as hell to find...but worth every minute it took to get there." My face softened. "I spent thirty-seven years thinking my perfect match didn't exist. You proved me wrong in less than one. And even though we didn't do it right the first time, I'm hoping you'll give me a chance to prove myself a second time." My pulse thumped with nerves as the most important question of my life left my mouth. "Vivian Lau, will you marry me?"

Her eyes brimmed with unshed tears. A lone drop escaped and streaked down her cheek as she nodded.

"Yes. *Yes*, of course I'll marry you."

Tension dissolved into laughter and sobs and cool, aching relief. I slid the old ring off her finger and replaced it with the new one before kissing her.

Fiercely, passionately, and wholeheartedly.

Sometimes, we needed words to communicate. Other times, we didn't need words at all.

EPILOGUE

Dante

OUR WEDDING DAY DAWNED CLEAR AND SUNNY OVER the waters of Lake Como.

Two hundred and fifty guests flew in from around the world to attend the festivities at Villa Serafina, where renovations had wrapped up just in time for an army of wedding staff to swoop in and transform it into a paradise of lights, flowers, and hanging greens.

The ceremony itself took place outside, on the villa's highest terrace overlooking the lake. The sun beat hot and heavy as I stood beneath the arbor, waiting for Vivian to appear.

"I can't believe you're getting married." The whisper slid from the corner of Luca's mouth. "I didn't think it'd actually happen. I know I told you to fight for her, but I was certain she'd kick you to—"

"Shut up," I said through my smile. The cameras were watching, and I wanted today's photos to be perfect. "Unsolicited commentary isn't the best man's job."

I swept my eyes over the crowd, restless. Almost every guest had RSVP'd yes. I spotted Dominic and Alessandra between the Laurents and the Singhs, and Christian's girlfriend, Stella, seated next to Queen Bridget and Prince Rhys of Eldorra. Surprisingly, my parents had made it as well, and they'd ditched their usual beach clothes for the appropriate wedding attire.

My gaze skimmed over the Laus. Francis was here as Cecelia's plus one, but he'd been stripped of all father-of-the-bride duties. Cecelia would be walking her down the aisle instead. It was a humiliating public snub for someone so obsessed with his reputation, but he must've thought *not* attending was worse than attending as the guest of a guest.

He sat next to his son-in-law, dour but silent. Vivian had agonized for weeks over whether to invite him before we settled on the current compromise. She was worried I'd be upset, but I'd pushed Francis so far in the back of my mind he was a speck in the rearview mirror.

As long as Vivian was happy, I was happy.

"It should be. You wouldn't be here without me," Luca said, bringing my attention back to him. He reeked of self-satisfaction. "Who pulled your head out of your ass when you were busy wallowing?"

"I'm about to put my foot up your ass if *you* don't shut up."

Whoever invented younger siblings deserved a special place in hell.

"*Both* of you shut up," Christian said from Luca's other side. "Christ, brothers are annoying. Thank fuck I don't have one."

A-fucking-men.

Kai was the only groomsman with the good sense to keep his mouth shut.

He'd fixed his gaze across the archway, where Agnes, Sloane, and Isabella stood in blush-pink bridesmaid dresses.

Isabella cocked an eyebrow at him; his gaze narrowed a fraction before the rich, majestic tones of the wedding march filled the air and he flicked his eyes toward the aisle.

The guests rose as one. All thoughts of annoying brothers and equally annoying groomsmen ceased when Vivian appeared at the end of the aisle. Hell, all thoughts ceased, period.

The only thing that existed was her.

My breath stilled as she walked down the aisle with her mother, her face glowing and her smile soft as she met my eyes.

Vivian once told me about a Chinese proverb that said an invisible thread connected those destined to meet, regardless of time, place, and circumstance. I felt the phantom tug of that thread now, stretching between us and vibrating with the promise of something only fate could deliver.

I used to think we wouldn't be together if her father hadn't forced us together. I was wrong.

A part of me would always find my way to her. She was my North Star, the brightest jewel in my sky.

A suspicious haze blurred my vision when Vivian reached me. I blinked it back. If I didn't, I'd never hear the end of it from Luca, Christian, or Kai.

Her mother handed her off to me. Cecelia had been upset when Vivian refused to let her bulldoze her way into wedding preparations. Now, she looked suspiciously misty-eyed.

It seemed she possessed emotions other than disapproval after all.

"You clean up nice, Mr. Russo," Vivian murmured. Her hand was small and soft in mine.

"I could say the same for you, Mrs. Russo." She wore a custom-made gown and the best hair and makeup money could buy, but even in a burlap sack, she'd be the most beautiful woman I'd ever seen.

"I'm not Mrs. Russo yet. There's still time for me to live out my runaway bride fantasy," she quipped.

A wicked smile spread across my lips. "I do love a good chase."

Vivian's cheeks pinked at the double meaning.

The priest cleared his throat, interrupting our whispered conversation. We exchanged a last secret smile before we turned our full attention to the ceremony.

Priest's remarks, vows, ring exchange. The pounding of my heart muffled sound and motion until we reached the end of the ceremony.

"I now pronounce you husband and wife. You may—"

I swept Vivian into my arms and kissed her before the priest finished his sentence.

The crowd erupted into cheers and whistles. I barely heard them. I was too busy with my wife.

Wife. The word sent an electric thrill down my spine.

"Impatient as always," Vivian teased when we broke apart. Her face was flushed with pleasure and laughter. "We'll have to work on that. Patience is a virtue."

"I never claimed to be virtuous, sweetheart. Sinning is more fun." Another wicked grin. "As you'll find out tonight."

Pink blossomed anew across her face and chest.

My grin widened.

I'd never get tired of making her smile and blush.

She was my wife, my partner, my guiding star.

And I wouldn't have it any other way.

Vivian

"My baby is married. They grow up *so fast.*" Isabella let out a dramatic sniffle. "I still remember when you were an innocent twenty-two-year-old, navigating the jungle of New—"

"Stop being dramatic. Vivian is a year older than you." Sloane took a delicate sip of champagne. "Several years, if we're talking about maturity."

I swallowed a laugh at Isabella's offended gasp.

Day had bled into night as the wedding festivities continued. The reception took place in the villa's massive walled courtyard, beneath a canopy of flowers and twinkling lights.

The guests were still going strong after hours of drinks and dancing, but I'd needed a breather. Being the bride at a wedding reception was a full-time job. *Everyone* wanted to talk.

"*Maturity slander aside*," Isabella said with a pointed stare at Sloane, "I'm glad you and Dante made it work. Now I can cross *bridesmaid in Italy* off my bucket list."

"I'm glad I can make your dreams come true," I said dryly.

"Me too. All that's left is finding a hot Italian one-night stand to—" Isabella's sentence broke off at the light cough behind me.

I turned and stifled another laugh when I saw Kai. He had the worst, or best, timing when it came to my talks with Isabella, depending on how you looked at it.

"I'm sorry to interrupt yet another...fascinating conversation." His mouth twitched. "But Dante is getting restless without his bride. Vivian, you may want to check in on him. He's had to tell the story of how he proposed ten times, and I think he's ready to deck someone."

I glanced at where Dante stood with a small group of guests, looking bored and irritated. He caught my eye and mouthed, *help*.

I bit back a smile. "I'll be right back," I said. "I need to save my husband."

Sloane waved me off. "We'll be fine. Enjoy your wedding night."

"Congratulations again!" Isabella chirped, studiously avoiding Kai's eye.

I left them to their conversation and wound my way through the courtyard. I only made it halfway before my mother stopped me.

"Vivian! Have you seen your sister?" she fretted. "She went to the restroom an hour ago but isn't back yet."

"No. Maybe she's in there with Gunnar," I joked.

"*Vivian.* Honestly." Her hands flew to her necklace. "That's not a joke to make in public."

"I'm sure she's fine, Mother. It's a party. So party." I handed her a glass of champagne from a nearby tray. "Louis Roederer. Your favorite."

Our relationship had been getting better since our talk in Eldorra. It wasn't perfect; like she said, she couldn't change completely. Her micromanaging had driven me up the wall in the weeks leading up to the wedding, but she *was* trying. She hadn't even argued when I asked the makeup artist for red lipstick instead of neutral, though my mother considered red lips and nails "unbecoming" for a society heiress.

My father, on the other hand, was as distant as ever. He'd left immediately after the ceremony; according to Agnes, he couldn't stand all the whispers about why he wasn't the one who gave me away.

No one outside our circle knew the reason behind our estrangement, and they never would. Some things were meant to be private.

I'd made peace with our strained relationship, and I barely gave him any thought as my mother accepted the champagne bribe.

"Fine," she said. "I have to speak to Buffy Darlington anyway. But if you find your sister, tell her I have her phone. Honestly, I don't know *what* she's doing…"

I disengaged from my mother and made it to Dante just in time.

"So tell me how you proposed," the poor guest said, seemingly oblivious to the groom's twitching eye. "I want to hear *every* detail."

"Many apologies for interrupting." I placed my hand on

Dante's chest before he could respond. "But can I steal him away? Wedding duties."

"Oh, of course," the woman said, flustered. "Congratulations again. You look beautiful."

I smiled and steered Dante toward a quiet corner of the courtyard. "Thank you. Enjoy the rest of your evening."

"Thank fuck," Dante said when the woman was out of earshot. The ice cream cuff links I bought for him in Paris glinted as he wiped a hand over his face, and the sight made me embarrassingly happy. "Now I know why people elope. The small talk at these things is insufferable."

"Yes, but I'm sure you can find *one* thing you like about it." I looped my arms around his neck.

The tension eased from his shoulders, and his frown loosened in a faint smile. "Maybe one." His hand rested on my waist. The heat seared through my dress and into the pit of my stomach. "The lobster canapés are pretty good."

"And?"

"And..." He pretended to think about it. "The flowers are impressive. Though for one hundred and twenty thousand dollars, they better well be."

"What about the people?" I tilted my chin up. "Anyone tolerable?"

"Hmm. There is this woman I've been eyeing all night..." Dante dipped his head so his lips brushed mine. "She's beautiful, charming, has the best smile I've ever seen...but I think she's married."

"How...unfortunate." My breath snagged when his palm slid up my waist, lighting tiny fires along the way.

"Very." Another brush of his lips. "I hear her husband is quite protective of her. If he sees me talking to her, he might do something rash."

"Like?" My mind went hazy when his hand made it over the curve of my shoulder and to the back of my neck.

"Like kiss the hell out of her in front of two hundred and fifty people, propriety be damned."

Dante captured my mouth in a proper kiss, and the party, the music, the guests…they were all gone, obliterated by the heat of his touch.

It seeped into my chest and my veins, filling me with warmth from the inside out. The type that existed only when you reached the end of a long journey…and found home.

Thank you for reading *King of Wrath*! If you enjoyed this book, I would be grateful if you could leave a review on the platform(s) of your choice. Reviews are like tips for author, and every one helps!

Much love,

Ana

She's his opposite in every way…

…and the greatest temptation

he's ever known.

Preorder *King of Pride* now for Kai and Isabella's story.

For bonus Dante and Vivian content,
type this link into your browser:
https://BookHip.com/HCVAKRD

Read on for a look at the first book in Ana Huang's Twisted series

Ava

THERE WERE WORSE THINGS THAN BEING STRANDED IN the middle of nowhere during a rainstorm.

For example, I could be running from a rabid bear intent on mauling me into the next century. Or I could be tied to a chair in a dark basement and forced to listen to Aqua's "Barbie Girl" on repeat until I'd rather gnaw off my arm than hear the song's eponymous phrase again.

But just because things could be worse didn't mean they didn't suck.

Stop. Think positive thoughts.

"A car will show up...*now*." I stared at my phone, biting back my frustration when the app reassured me it was "finding my ride," the way it had been for the past half hour.

Normally, I'd be less stressed about the situation because hey, at least I had a working phone and a bus shelter to keep me mostly dry from the pounding rain. But Josh's farewell party was starting in an hour, I had yet to pick up his surprise cake from the bakery, and it would be dark soon. I may be a glass half-full kinda gal, but I wasn't an idiot. No one—especially not a college girl with zero fighting skills to speak of—wants to find herself alone in the middle of nowhere after dark.

I should've taken those self-defense classes with Jules like she wanted.

I mentally scrolled through my limited options. The bus that stopped at this location didn't run on the weekends, and most of my friends didn't own a car. Bridget had car service, but she was at an embassy event until seven. My rideshare app wasn't working, and I hadn't seen a single car pass by since the rain started. Not that I would hitchhike anyway—I've watched horror movies, thank you very much.

I only had one option left—one I *really* didn't want to take—but beggars couldn't be choosers.

I pulled up the contact in my phone, said a silent prayer, and pressed the Call button.

One ring. Two rings. Three.

Come on, pick up. Or not. I wasn't sure which would be worse—getting murdered or dealing with my brother. Of course, there was always the chance said brother would murder me himself for putting myself in such a situation, but I'd deal with that later.

"What's wrong?"

I scrunched my nose at his greeting. "Hello to you too, Brother Dearest. What makes you think something is wrong?"

Josh snorted. "Uh, you called me. You never call unless you're in trouble."

True. We preferred texting, and we lived next door to each other—not my idea, by the way—so we rarely had to message at all.

"I wouldn't say I'm in *trouble*," I hedged. "More like… stranded. I'm not near public transport, and I can't find a rideshare."

"Christ, Ava. Where are you?"

I told him.

"What the hell are you doing there? That's an hour from campus!"

"Don't be dramatic. I had an engagement shoot, and it's a thirty-minute drive. Forty-five if there's traffic." Thunder boomed, shaking the branches of nearby trees. I winced and shrank farther back into the shelter, not that it did me much good. The rain slanted sideways, splattering me with water droplets so heavy and hard they stung when they hit my skin.

A rustling noise came from Josh's end, followed by a soft moan.

I paused, sure I'd heard wrong, but nope, there it was again. Another moan.

My eyes widened in horror. "Are you having *sex* right now?" I whisper-shouted, even though no one else was around.

The sandwich I'd scarfed down before I left for my shoot threatened to make a reappearance. There was nothing—I repeat nothing—grosser than listening to a relative while they're mid coitus. Just the thought made me gag.

"Technically, no." Josh sounded unrepentant.

The word *technically* did a lot of heavy lifting there.

It didn't take a genius to decipher Josh's vague reply. He may not be having intercourse, but something was going on, and I had zero desire to find out what that "something" was.

"Josh Chen."

"Hey, you're the one who called me." He must've covered his phone with his hand, because his next words came through muffled. I heard a soft, feminine laugh followed by a squeal, and I wanted to bleach my ears, my eyes, my *mind*. "One of the guys took my car to buy more ice," Josh said, his voice clear again. "But don't worry, I got you. Drop a pin on your exact location, and keep your phone close. Do you still have the pepper spray I bought for your birthday last year?"

"Yes. Thanks for that, by the way." I'd wanted a new camera bag, but Josh had bought me an eight-pack of pepper spray instead. I'd never used any of it, which meant all eight bottles—minus the one tucked in my purse—were sitting snug in the back of my closet.

My sarcasm went over my brother's head. For a straight-A med student, he could be quite dense. "You're welcome. Stay put, and he'll be there soon. We'll talk about your complete lack of self-preservation later."

"I'm self-preserved," I protested. *Was that the right word?* "It's not my fault there are no—wait, what do you mean 'he'? Josh!"

Too late. He'd already hung up.

Figured the one time I wanted him to elaborate, he'd ditch me for one of his bed buddies. I was surprised he hadn't freaked out more, considering Josh put the *over* in overprotective. Ever since The Incident, he'd taken it upon himself to look after me like he was my brother and bodyguard rolled into one. I didn't blame him—our childhood had been a hundred shades of messed up, or so I'd been told—and I loved him to pieces, but his constant worrying could be a bit much.

I sat sideways on the bench and hugged my bag to my side, letting the cracked leather warm my skin while I waited for the mysterious "he" to show up. It could be anyone. Josh had no shortage of friends. He'd always been Mr. Popular—basketball player, student body president, and homecoming king in high school; Sigma fraternity brother and big man on campus in college.

I was his opposite. Not *un*popular per se, but I shied away from the limelight and would rather have a small group of close friends than a large group of friendly acquaintances. Where Josh was the life of the party, I sat in the corner and daydreamed about all the places I would love to visit but would probably never get to. Not if my phobia had anything to do with it.

My damn phobia. I knew it was all mental, but it *felt* physical. The nausea, the racing heart, the paralyzing fear that turned my limbs into useless, frozen things…

On the bright side, at least I wasn't afraid of rain. Oceans and lakes and pools, I could avoid, but rain…yeah, that would've been bad.

I wasn't sure how long I huddled in the tiny bus shelter, cursing my lack of foresight when I turned down the Graysons' offer to drive me back to town after our shoot. I hadn't wanted to inconvenience them and thought I could call a car and be back at Thayer's campus in half an hour, but the skies opened up right after the couple left and, well, here I was.

It was getting dark. Muted grays mingled with the cool blues of twilight, and part of me worried the mysterious "he" wouldn't show up, but Josh had never let me down. If one of his friends failed to pick me up like he'd asked, they wouldn't have working legs tomorrow. Josh was a med student, but he had zero compunction about using violence when the situation called for it—especially when the situation involved me.

The bright beam of headlights slashed through the rain. I squinted, my heart tripping in both anticipation and wariness as I weighed the odds of whether the car belonged to my ride or a potential psycho. This part of Maryland was pretty safe, but you never knew.

When my eyes adjusted to the light, I slumped with relief, only to stiffen again two seconds later.

Good news? I recognized the sleek, black Aston Martin pulling up toward me. It belonged to one of Josh's friends, which meant I wouldn't end up a local news item tonight.

Bad news? The person driving said Aston Martin was the *last* person I wanted—or expected—to pick me up. He wasn't an *I'll do my buddy a favor and rescue his stranded little sister* kinda guy.

He was a *look at me wrong and I'll destroy you and everyone you care about* kinda guy, and he'd do it looking so calm and gorgeous you wouldn't notice your world burning down around you until you were already a heap of ashes at his Tom Ford–clad feet.

I swiped the tip of my tongue over my dry lips as the car stopped in front of me and the passenger window rolled down.

"Get in."

He didn't raise his voice—he never raised his voice—but I still heard him loud and clear over the rain.

Alex Volkov was a force of nature unto himself, and I imagined even the weather bowed to him.

"I hope you're not waiting for me to open the door for you," he said when I didn't move. He sounded as happy as I was about the situation.

What a gentleman.

I pressed my lips together and bit back a sarcastic reply as I roused myself from the bench and ducked into the car. It smelled cool and expensive, like spicy cologne and fine Italian leather. I didn't have a towel or anything to place on the seat beneath me, so all I could do was pray I didn't damage the expensive interior.

"Thanks for picking me up. I appreciate it," I said in an attempt to break the icy silence.

I failed. Miserably.

Alex didn't respond or even look at me as he navigated the twists and curves of the slick roads leading back to campus. He drove the same way he walked, talked, and breathed—steady and controlled, with an undercurrent of danger warning those foolish enough to contemplate crossing him that doing so would be their death sentence.

He was the exact opposite of Josh, and I still marveled at the fact that they were best friends. Personally, I thought Alex was an asshole. I was sure he had his reasons, some kind of psychological trauma that shaped him into the unfeeling robot he was today. Based on the snippets I'd gleaned from Josh, Alex's childhood had been even worse than ours, though I'd never managed to pull the details out of my brother. All I knew was Alex's parents had died when he was young and left him a pile of money he'd quadrupled the value of when he came into his inheritance at age eighteen. Not that he'd needed it, because he'd invented a new financial modeling software in high school that made him a multimillionaire before he could vote.

With an IQ of 160, Alex Volkov was a genius, or close to it. He was the only person in Thayer's history to complete its five-year joint undergrad/MBA program in three years, and at age twenty-six, he was the COO of one of the most successful real estate development companies in the country. He was a legend, and he knew it.

Meanwhile, I thought I was doing well if I remembered to eat while juggling my classes, extracurriculars, and two jobs—front desk duty at the McCann Gallery and my side hustle as a photographer for anyone who would hire me. Graduations, engagements, dogs' birthday parties, I did them all.

"Are you going to Josh's party?" I tried again to make small talk. The silence was killing me.

Alex and Josh had been best friends since they roomed together at Thayer eight years ago, and Alex had joined my family for Thanksgiving and assorted holidays every year since, but I still didn't *know* him. Alex and I didn't talk unless it had to do with Josh or passing the potatoes at dinner or something.

"Yes."

Okay then. Guess small talk was out.

My mind wandered toward the million things I had to do that weekend. Edit the photos from the Graysons' shoot, work on my application for the World Youth Photography fellowship, help Josh finish packing after—

Crap! I'd forgotten all about Josh's cake.

I'd ordered it two weeks ago because that was the max lead time for something from Crumble & Bake. It was Josh's favorite dessert, a three-layer dark chocolate frosted with fudge and filled with chocolate pudding. He only indulged on his birthday, but since he was leaving the country for a year, I figured he could break his once-a-year rule.

"So..." I pasted the biggest, brightest smile on my face. "Don't kill me, but we need to make a detour to Crumble & Bake."

"No. We're already late." Alex stopped at a red light. We'd made it back to civilization, and I spotted the blurred outlines of a Starbucks and a Panera through the rain-splattered glass.

My smile didn't budge. "It's a *small* detour. It'll take fifteen minutes, max. I just need to run in and pick up Josh's cake. You know, the Death by Chocolate he likes so much? He'll be in Central America for a year, they don't have C&B down there, and he leaves in two days so—"

"Stop." Alex's fingers curled around the steering wheel, and my wild, hormonal mind latched on to how beautiful they were. That might sound crazy, because who has beautiful *fingers*? But he did. Physically, *everything* about him was beautiful. The jade-green eyes that glared out from beneath dark brows like chips hewn from a glacier; the sharp jawline and elegant, sculpted cheekbones; the lean frame and thick, light brown hair that somehow looked both tousled and perfectly coiffed. He resembled a statue in an Italian museum come to life.

The urge to ruffle his hair like I would a kid's gripped me, just so he'd stop looking so perfect—which was quite irritating to the rest of us mere mortals—but I didn't have a death wish, so I kept my hands planted in my lap.

"If I take you to Crumble & Bake, will you stop talking?"

No doubt he regretted picking me up.

Acknowledgments

To my readers—Thank you for coming along on this new journey with me! Writing can be a lonely profession, but your messages, comments, and general love and support are the best company I can ask for as an author.

To Becca—Thank you for being my sounding board and putting up with my million and one DMs about covers, scenes, and basically everything that crosses my mind. I am beyond grateful for you!

To Brittney, Sarah, Rebecca, Salma, Aishah, and Mia—Your detailed feedback, reactions, and comments always brighten up my inbox (even if you sometimes tell me things I don't want to hear for the good of the story). Thank you for helping me make Dante and Vivian shine.

To Viola and Aliya—Thank you for your story notes, translation wizardry, and making sure I don't butcher the Italian language (Google Translate isn't always a writer's best friend). Dante, Greta, and I are eternally grateful.

To Amy and Britt—You are absolute gems. One day, we will NOT have a tight deadline. I promise!

To Cat—After so many messages, iterations, and brainstorming sessions...we did it! Your patience and talent are truly admirable, and I'm lucky to have you on my team.

To my PAs Amber and Michelle and my agent Kimberly—You are rock stars, and I appreciate you so much!

Finally, to Christa Désir and the entire Bloom team—Thank you for all your hard work and support. We've achieved so much together, and I'm beyond excited to enter a new Kings of Sin era with you!

xo,
Ana

Keep in Touch with Ana Huang

Reader Group: facebook.com/groups/anastwistedsquad
Website: anahuang.com
BookBub: bookbub.com/profile/ana-huang
Instagram: instagram.com/authoranahuang
TikTok: tiktok.com/@authoranahuang
Goodreads: goodreads.com/anahuang

About the Author

Ana Huang is a #1 *New York Times*, *Sunday Times*, *Wall Street Journal*, *USA Today*, and #1 Amazon bestselling author. Best known for her Twisted series, she writes New Adult and contemporary romance with deliciously alpha heroes, strong heroines, and plenty of steam, angst, and swoon.

Her books have been translated in over two dozen languages and featured in outlets such as NPR, *Cosmopolitan*, *Financial Times*, and *Glamour UK*.

A self-professed travel enthusiast, she loves incorporating beautiful destinations into her stories and will never say no to a good chai latte.

Also by Ana Huang

KINGS OF SIN SERIES

A series of interconnected standalones

King of Wrath

King of Pride

King of Greed

King of Sloth

TWISTED SERIES

A series of interconnected standalones

Twisted Love

Twisted Games

Twisted Hate

Twisted Lies

IF LOVE SERIES

If We Ever Meet Again (Duet Book 1)

If the Sun Never Sets (Duet Book 2)

If Love Had a Price (Standalone)

If We Were Perfect (Standalone)